"I need you, Prescott."

"And yes, you are perfect for the job because you are the only man I can imagine even *pretending* to be engaged to."

"I suppose I should feel flattered," he scoffed.

"As far as your touch, well..." She looked away. "I wasn't lying. I'm not like the other ladies of your acquaintance. I'm not built for... passion."

His brow furrowed. "Not built for passion? I've never heard of such a thing."

"Well, it's true. And frankly, I'm a bit embarrassed by it."

His mouth opened and closed as if he was going to say something. Then, instead, he reached for her, gripping her waist and pulling her up against his hard, virile form.

Her heart leapt. "Ah...what are you doing?"

"Consider it an experiment."

Then his head lowered and his lips pressed down to hers.

Other **AVON ROMANCES**

SARI ROBINS

What to Wear to a Seduction

AVON BOOKS
An Imprint of HarperCollinsPublishers

AVON BOOKS
An Imprint of HarperCollins*Publishers*
10 East 53rd Street
New York, New York 10022-5299

Copyright © 2006 by Sari Earl
ISBN-13: 978-0-06-078247-4
ISBN-10: 0-06-078247-1
www.avonromance.com

First Avon Books paperback printing: May 2006

Avon Trademark Reg. U.S. Pat. Off. and in Other Countries, Marca Registrada, Hecho en U.S.A.
HarperCollins® is a registered trademark of HarperCollins Publishers Inc.

Printed in the U.S.A.

10 9 8 7 6 5 4 3 2 1

For Dorothy,
I cherish our friendship.

Acknowledgments

Special thanks go to my family and friends, who continue to enthusiastically champion my efforts, especially my sister, Nanci (I don't want to ever write a book without you!) and my mother, who is the best promoter a daughter could have.

I want to acknowledge specifically the following people for their wonderful support: Nancy Yost, Susan Grimshaw, Jan Epstein, Martha Jo Katz, Barbara Kaufman, Esther Levine, Liz Hayes and Carol Nagel, Laurie Ann Goldman, Paloma Llorens, Willa Cline, Barb and everyone at Romance and Friends, Frances Drouin, The Paradies Shops, Becky Rose, Joahnna Barron, Tonda Fuller, and the lovely ladies at A Nose for Clothes.

My heartfelt thanks to the incomparable Avon Books team, including but not limited to: Darlene; the two Brians; Donna, Judy, and the entire Merch Sales Team; Mike, Carla, and the whole Field Sales Team; International Sales; Adrienne and Nicole in Marketing; Pam and Joan in Publicity; Lara and Laurie for Foreign Rights/Sub Rights; Tom, Gayle, and Patricia for my gorgeous covers; Managing Editorial; Carrie, May and most especially, Lyssa!

Finally, I sincerely thank my husband and children for giving me the opportunity to follow my passions and meet my deadlines.

Your support means the world to me.

Chapter 1

Andersen Hall, London
Summer 1811

Barely taking in the birds chirping in the trees, the squirrels darting about, or the sun riding on the pine-scented breeze, Prescott Devane strode down the path to the orphanage's guesthouse, his irritation at full boil.

He growled under his breath as his eyes fixed on the liveried footman standing on the small wooden porch. He didn't recognize the uniform, but suspected that Mrs. Nagel, Andersen Hall's crusty matron, was right about his visitor being female; only a woman would choose to dress her servant in purple with marigold lapels.

Ever since he'd saved little orphan Evie from the fire, he'd practically had to fend off the ladies. Despite

1

his every effort to avoid Society, the ladies came to him at his childhood home, the only haven he'd ever known, making a nuisance of themselves. He'd had enough doe-eyed, overeager females fawning over him as if he'd trounced Napoleon himself! And the offers! He couldn't quite believe their...generosity. If one could use that word.

And, blast him, he wanted none of them.

The wretched truth was, he'd changed. He traced the start of this alteration to a very small incident only eleven months before. It was at a birthday fete for his then paramour, Lillith, Lady Willis, held in Hyde Park. Upon returning with her requested glass of lemonade, Prescott had overheard her speaking with one of her friends.

"It's his very commonness that drew me to Devane," Lillith had drawled. "Anticipating that his beastliness would reveal itself between the sheets, *if you know what I mean.*" The friend had giggled. "The problem is, his hearty appetites aren't limited to the bedroom. Who would have thought he would be such a *bon vivant*? For a lowly orphan, the man certainly enjoys his champagne and caviar. He eats enough for three men and consumes every morsel as if it's to be his last crumb. But I suppose such loutishness is to be expected from an—"

It was at that moment that she'd become aware of his presence. Her cheeks had flushed pink and her gaze had skirted away, but other than that, she'd acted as if she'd done nothing wrong. And blast him, so had he.

To his ultimate shame, he'd remained at the fete, his mask of charming escort firmly in place. But underneath the mask, he'd seethed. It was one thing to know on an intellectual level that he would never be a member of the club. But it was entirely another to feel the humiliating slash of the ladies' scorn as it staked his heart. Especially since he'd thought that Lillith cared about him.

Throughout the rest of the picnic he'd reflected on his experiences in Polite Society. The small slights he'd ignored, the references to his birth hidden behind a thin veneer of contempt, the absolute conviction that Prescott was there to *serve* and was around *by their leave*.

He'd ended it with Lillith later that day, and she hadn't had one word of apology. Things hadn't been the same for him since. Yet he'd continued his charade as the charming escort to ladies in Society. Oh, he'd been more selective about whom he'd chosen to escort, and from among them, with whom he might share a bed. Habits were hard to break, it seemed.

Then Headmaster Dunn had been murdered and Prescott's transformation had been complete. The head of the orphanage had been the only real father Prescott had ever known. Prescott had felt more than a little lost, alone in a way he hadn't been in ages, except of course for Cat...

Then she'd upped and married another man.

Prescott could no longer be the rakish *cicisbeo* looking for the next grand ball to grace, or sumptuous feast to relish or stunning lady to charm. Boisterous crowds raked his nerves. Fine food held no flavor. Boldly sensual ladies held no appeal. It was the life he'd once loved, and yet now, it all seemed so...superfluous. The farce that had become his life left him feeling hollow and suddenly very old for his seven-and-twenty years.

Annoyed with his pitiful musings, Prescott pushed away the heartache, instead stoking the fires of his anger against his unwelcome visitor. Better to be cross with an inconsiderate Society dame than act like the miserable sod he'd been the last few weeks.

Not bothering to pretend nonchalance, Prescott marched up the short staircase and nodded to the apple-cheeked, soot-haired footman, saving his animosity for the employer inside.

He stormed through the door. A lady he did not know sat on the sofa, rifling through the account ledger detailing Prescott's new business venture that would make his life as a *cicisbeo* ancient history.

A small snarl escaped from his lips.

"Oh!" The unknown lady jumped up from her seat and the book dropped from her lap to the floor with a thud. Shoving her plum-colored bonnet back from her face, she gushed, "Beg pardon! I didn't mean to pry! I sat on the sofa to wait for you, and well, it was so lumpy, and I looked underneath, and well, I didn't mean to be so appallingly rude...I just...I just...I'm sorry!"

Judging by the lack of lines on her pale skin and absence of gray in her ebony hair, she seemed to be recently past twenty. Her oval face might have been pretty, except her hair was constricted more tightly than even Mrs. Nagel's. The decidedly unflattering chignon did nothing to detract from her pointy chin or generous nose that, albeit straight, overwhelmed her thin face.

Her best feature was her eyes, so dark as to appear almost black, and shining with the gleam of intelligence. His heart skipped a beat.

How long had she been reading? How much did she deduce? Did it matter? Members of Polite Society disdained trade, treating it as if it was akin to the plague. She certainly wouldn't try to undercut his new business. So why did he care?

Because his dream was so fresh, so fragile, and every last pence of his funds was sunk into it. If something caused his venture to fold even before it had begun...

Leaning over, the lady brushed aside her brown woolen skirts, retrieved the book and held it out with outstretched arms. "I apologize, Mr. Devane. I had no business looking at this. I am so sorry for my inexcusable rudeness. I barely had opened it when you arrived."

Her voice sounded sincere, if a bit breathless. Her moon-pale cheeks bloomed rosy with color, ostensibly from embarrassment. And those velvet black eyes *appeared* contrite. But he, of all people, knew that appearances could be deceiving. Moreover, she could've simply been upset that she'd been *caught*.

Not giving any indication of his anxiety, he feigned nonchalance, jerking his chin and motioning for her to set the ledger on the table. He'd learned long ago not to give away any indication of vulnerability; it only drew the sharks to the scent of blood.

"Oh, dear, yes, your hands...I'd heard about the burns you'd sustained while saving that little girl's life." In a flutter, she spun and set down the volume. Turning to face him, she raised a brow. "I assume that you're still wearing bandages beneath your gloves?"

He glowered, not bothering a reply.

She frowned. "I see that I've made an absolute mess

of things. And I was so hoping for a pleasant start to our acquaintance."

"We have no acquaintance." His words were clipped and he didn't bother to keep the anger from his tone.

"Of course not. We haven't been properly intro—"

"Which makes it unseemly for you to be alone in my company." Stepping aside, he motioned to the open door. "If you will."

She blinked. "But you haven't even heard—"

"I'm not receiving visitors."

"But Lady Pomfry's been to see you. And Mrs. Bright. Mrs. Haymarket . . ."

What? Had she been spying on him? No matter. Once more, he motioned to the door. "I am not receiving visitors *any longer.* Now go."

Her mouth opened and then closed as if she couldn't sort out what he was saying. After an annoyingly long moment, her head tilted. "Is it because I'm not pretty enough?"

"Yes, that's it. Whatever you say. Now, if you'll please just go."

She stilled, immobilized like one of Lady Pomfry's porcelain dolls. The only sign of life in her was the suspiciously bright gleam in her gaze.

Suddenly he realized what he'd just said. He bit back a groan. *Oh, dear Lord.* Even *he* was not so callous as to intentionally harm a woman's self-esteem; he'd simply wanted her to go. Now he was probably going to have to deal with a blubbering damsel in need of cheer. Could this day get any worse?

"I must confess," she whispered, "you're nothing like I'd imagined."

"You don't even know the half of it," he muttered,

trying to figure a smooth way out of this wretched fix. He raised his hand to run it though his hair and was arrested by a now-familiar searing pain. That was one nervous habit that he had to adjust for his burn injuries.

"Look, I didn't mean that the way it sounded," he ventured.

She smiled sadly. "There is no need to apologize, Mr. Devane. I know I'm no beauty."

He wondered if it was worth arguing the point with her. Granted, with her unfashionable ebony hair and dark eyes, she would never be considered a fine English rose. And she was far too thin for conventional fashion. Moreover, she'd do better with a coiffure of elaborate curls to balance out her strong features. No, she was not an exceptional beauty.

And yet...

"Would you believe me if I told you that I disagree?" he asked gently, knowing that any woman who would suggest her looks as a reason for rejection had to be sensitive on that very point.

The lady studied him a long moment, her black-jeweled gaze considering. "No. And I would prefer that you be honest with me in all of our future dealings together."

Prescott gritted his teeth. Although he was glad that she hadn't wilted like a sodden handkerchief, that didn't mean that he was willing to put up with her designs. "Look, I may not have been particularly politic about it, but—"

"Oh, really?" Crossing her arms, she raised a brow. "For a moment there I thought you were Solicitor General Dagwood."

Comparing him to one of the most ambitiously

political men in government was obviously sardonic. He almost smiled at her wit, but forced a frown. "Regardless, I still want you to leave."

Slowly, her small shoulders squared and her pointy chin lifted. Her pink lips firmed into a mulish line and her gaze became decidedly determined. Turning, she stepped over to the sofa and sat, hands folded in her lap. "I'm not quite ready to leave yet, Mr. Devane. My business with you is not yet concluded."

Prescott blinked, astounded by her cheek. "This is my house." *At least until Cat and her new husband return from their honeymoon....*

"Then perhaps you would be so kind to at least *pretend* to be hospitable."

Careful of his injuries, he crossed his arms, wondering if she were daft or simply an overindulged shrew.

As if to match him, she crossed her arms. "The only way I'm going is if you carry me out kicking and screaming."

Glaring at the stubborn woman, he tried to decide how difficult it would be to do exactly that. She was small, but she moved with a healthy vitality indicating that she was familiar with exercise. More importantly, from the mulish set to her shoulders and the determined look in her eye, he recognized that she'd kick up a riot if he tried.

"Pray don't glare down at me as if you're sizing me up for market," she admonished, with a frown. "We both know that you'd never do anything so crass or ungentlemanly."

"Why the blazes not? I'm no gentleman."

"No, but you have principles."

She said it with such certainty he blinked. Who was

this perplexing woman? And what the dickens did she want with him?

Her demeanor was very different from the usual sensual display or demanding entreaty that most of the ladies interested in him exhibited. There was no suggestive cadence to her tone. She came across as businesslike, plain-speaking.

In fact, now that he thought about it, *everything* about her seemed a far cry from most of the ladies he knew. The first indicator was her attire. Although fine in line and fabric, her clothes were staid, undistinguished, and more akin to a Quaker than an *élégante*.

The majority of the females he associated with exhibited their skin in an artful display of ruffles, bows and silky fabrics. Through the open front of her demure plum coat, he could see that there was not a bow or ruffle in evidence on this lady's sober brown gown.

Likewise, her mien was...*contained*. As if any natural inclination for exuberance had been extinguished long ago. She reminded him of a schoolmarm, one who oversaw children but could not comprehend their liveliness.

And yet, her actions bespoke a deep-seated strength of purpose and her self-assurance seemingly indicated a depth of character.

Prescott felt something inside of him stir, something he hadn't felt in a very long time: *curiosity*. Irritably, he pushed it aside, knowing that despite her dissimilar mien, in the end she would behave like every other lady he'd ever known, wanting to use him for her ends, then discarding him when she was through. There was one way to know for certain.

"What do you want with me?" he asked.

"For the moment, your ear."

"Just an ear?"

Her porcelain cheeks splotched cherry. "I wish you wouldn't speak like that."

"I'm trying to give you the opportunity to state the very business for which you claim you must remain in my presence." His tone reflected his limited patience. "Are you here in the hopes of engaging me as an escort?"

Her eyes blazed like black coals as she was obviously discomfited at being pigeonholed. Well, that made two of them.

Her chin lifted another notch. "Yes. But it's much more complicated than you can imagine."

He was surprised at the disappointment shafting through him. Well, what else did he expect? He was a *cicisbeo,* for heaven's sake, no one was going to treat him any better. *Had been* a *cicisbeo,* he reminded himself. That chapter of his life was now closed.

"I'm not interested." Before she could argue, he held up his hand. "And it has nothing to do with your looks. Venus herself could ask me at this moment and my answer would be the same."

"But this is about more than a simple arrangement. My needs are distinctive. As is what I am offering you."

He laughed, knowing it was cruel but not caring. "Every woman thinks she's so special. That her offer is a treasure worthy of kings." Folding his arms, he looked away. "Besides, I don't bed women for recompense. No matter how 'unique' the arrangement you think you're proposing."

She rose from the sofa with her fists curled at her

sides. "I require your services, Mr. Devane. That much is true. But I don't want you in my bed, near my bed or even *thinking* about bedding me."

"So what is it, then? A ruse to get your husband jealous?" Unfolding his arms, he waved a dismissive hand. "Nay. Don't even tell me. Regardless, I'm no organ-grinder's monkey."

"I wouldn't be here if you were," she bit out. "Look, how would you feel if I decided to use the information in that book"—she pointed to the ledger on the table—"to my own ends?"

His body stilled, and his fury was so white-hot his body thrummed.

Her eyes widened and she rushed on, "Not that I would ever do such a thing! I don't even know what the blazes it is!"

"Then why even mention it?" he ground out, barely keeping control on his mounting temper.

"Well, because you seemed so sensitive about it and well"—she bit her lip—"I'm being blackmailed and need your help to stop the knave."

Chapter 2

~~~~~~~~~~⚬~~~~~~~~~~

Edwina felt as if her confession had sucked the very air from the room so that she was finding it hard to breathe. Realizing that her hands were shaking, she curled them into fists so Mr. Devane wouldn't notice. Her heart was hammering, her cheeks in constant flame and her belly twisted with anxiety. Facing the man in the flesh was much different than she'd imagined.

She hadn't realized that he would be so...volatile. And so *affecting*. He had a vigor that seemed to charge the air with energy, like during a lightning storm, making her nerves quiver with awareness of his every move.

Each time his blazing emerald eyes met hers, an unsettling spark flashed in her belly. When he spoke in that low rumbling burr, her skin prickled as if caressed. Despite his underpinning of annoyance, she hadn't

12

expected him to sound so... well, cultured. When she'd considered conversing with him, she'd assumed that his voice would be coarse and colored with the roughness of his humble beginnings. However, his diction was perfect, his low voice a rich melodious reverberation that stirred the very hairs on her flesh.

With each whiff of his musk cologne, she couldn't help thinking *male,* as if his scent was some sort of animal mark. And when he moved, she truly appreciated why so many women sought out his company. He had a lithe vigor that reminded her of a male lion in his prime: languid, powerful, and dangerous. The picture was completed by his golden-hued skin and chocolaty copper mane.

And just like the king of beasts defending his territory, he was proud, prickly and protective.

This is a man to be reckoned with, she thought. Which was why she knew deep in her heart that he was exactly the man she needed.

She also knew that she'd better keep talking before he recovered and really did toss her out the door. Unlike most of the men she knew, Prescott Devane was a man of action. Part of her secretly wondered what it would feel like to be hauled into his arms....

She shook off the strangely titillating thought, and continued, "I'm being blackmailed, Mr. Devane, by a terrible man whom I cannot seem to identify, but I'm certain with your help I can do so, recover the materials he's holding against me and stop the knave."

Scratching his chin, Prescott nodded, pretending to consider her plight. He had no doubt this woman had escaped from Bedlam and he would do well to treat her with kid gloves until she was out of his hair. *Placate* was the word that his mentor, Headmaster Dunn, had always used when dealing with people of a delicate mind.

"From the look on your face I can see that you don't believe me, Mr. Devane. That you think I've gone 'round the bend. But I assure you my mental capacities are fully in order and I am perfectly sane. Moreover, I am most serious in my declarations and fully committed to stopping this blackmailer. I need an escort who will forestall distractions and guard my back while I work to identify the villain."

A trickle of doubt seeped into Prescott's brain. She sounded sensible. She sounded sincere. Moreover, she seemed well, damned confident. She wasn't weeping woefully or bemoaning her plight. It was very simply a situation she needed to overcome. Despite himself, he was intrigued.

What could a blackmailer have on such a contained, bright woman? Was there more to her than met the eye? Despite her dowdy appearance, his eyes weren't so displeased. Let down the ebony hair, loosen up that tightly knit brow and give those luscious lips something to latch on to and this woman could be a wildcat just waiting for a tussle.

"Why me?" he found himself asking.

"I came to you, Mr. Devane, because of Headmaster Dunn."

Prescott started, as the pain of his loss speared through him with renewed anguish. "What the blazes are you talking about?"

"Headmaster Dunn never turned out anyone in need. I need you."

Not mad. Not appealing. She was simply a manipulative bitch.

"Ballocks." His voice was a harsh whisper. "Headmaster Dunn never approved of what you're asking." Grief and shame surged through him. Prescott had always wanted Dunn to be as proud of him as he'd been of some of the other charges, like Nick Redford or Cat. It tormented Prescott to know that Dunn had died still disappointed in him and how he lived his life. That he hadn't had the chance to prove to Dunn that he was worthy of the efforts Dunn and Andersen Hall had invested in him.

Prescott turned away. "Don't dare try to use Headmaster Dunn's memory for your ends."

"The Headmaster Dunn that I knew believed that one did what was necessary to ensure justice. It was one of his most cherished values."

"What the hell does that have to do with anything?"

She moved to stand beside him and he caught a whiff of lily of the valley, an unusually delicate scent for such a mulish woman. "This blackguard hides behind a mask of darkness, cloaking himself in anonymity to do his dirty deeds." Her voice was impassioned, persuasive. "With your help, we can identify him, and stop him. Take away his power."

His eyes lifted to meet hers. Zeal burned within that onyx gaze. Prescott knew that look well, as he'd seen it countless times before but contained within familiar azure eyes. Headmaster Dunn had always driven his charges to pursue justice with fervor. But zealots tended to plow down as many innocents as they saved.

"You're trying to stop this man alone?" He raised a brow.

"I have friends. You..."

Thinking of Nick Redford, he shook his head. "Why

not simply hire a Bow Street Runner to unearth the man?" He couldn't quite believe that he was debating with this woman and could only attribute it to her enthusiasm for the scheme. Her eyes were bright, her cheeks a lovely shade of cherry and her chest heaved in a wholly chaste yet affecting way.

She waved a dismissive hand. "I certainly can't move about in Society followed by a hulking brute with a tipstaff. I'm sorry to say it, but every Bow Street Runner I've ever met was about as subtle as a herd of cattle nearing water."

She moved closer, her voice low and persuasive. "You move about in Society with an ease that I can't help but admire. This matter calls for a delicate hand. We need to blend in with the very Society we are investigating."

"You said that you didn't know his identity."

"Yes, but the first two exchanges with the blackmailer took place at a musicale and then at a picnic. Only the *haut ton* was invited to each, giving me the sense that this man is no stranger to High Society."

"You paid him?"

She rolled her eyes. "I was trying to catch the bastard—" She suddenly pressed her hand to her mouth. "Oh, I ah, I didn't mean to offend, ah..."

Prescott gritted his teeth, knowing that she was a creature of Society and couldn't quite help herself. Even though her comment rankled, he remarked, "I live in an orphanage; I can hardly waste my time taking umbrage at such a customary slur."

She pressed her hand to her chest. "Thank you for being so understanding. I get very angry when I think about that terrible blackmailer and try very hard not to blaspheme, but this wasn't much better, I'm afraid. I am truly sorry."

She really did talk like a schoolmarm, and again he wondered what a blackmailer could possibly hold over her so threateningly. He forced a smile. "Think nothing of it."

"Yes, well, the blackmailer is wily. Despite my trying to be on the matter as keenly as a foxhound, he's managed to do the exchanges and make away with my catching barely a glimpse of him."

He could just imagine her peeking out from a draped alcove. "You saw him?"

"Only his back as he raced away and I'm quite certain he was wearing a wig." She motioned to her hair. "You know, the old-fashioned powdered kind? But what was most telling were his shoes."

"His shoes."

"Yes, they were quite unique." Lifting her leg, she pointed to the bottom of her shoe. "On the sole was a remarkable red shape. Like a club in a deck of cards. I've never seen such a thing before. Have you?"

"Hmm." He had, but only once. The shoes were quite rare, indeed, having been made in Paris by François Millicent, and might actually be a decent way of identifying someone. *If* he was to become involved, which he was not.

Grimacing, she sighed. "So now I'm in search of a man with a special red mark on the bottom of his shoes. And it wouldn't be such a daunting task except my efforts are being stymied."

He couldn't quite help himself from asking, "Stymied?"

Squaring her shoulders, she exhaled as if pained.

"You see, my father has told every available gentleman from here to kingdom come that I am moneyed and intent on remarrying."

"Ah." He nodded. "You must be receiving quite a bit of attention."

"Decidedly unwanted attention. I have no desire to remarry."

Again, she spoke plainly, without emotional charge, as if this was something quite customary.

She shot him a tight smile. "But with you by my side, I can discourage unwanted attentions and focus on identifying this blackmailer."

"Pardon my obtuseness, but nary a gentleman would see me as enough of a threat to dissuade him from pursuing you." Prescott stalked over to the window, staring out at the army of trees surrounding the guesthouse. "I cannot see how my being your escort helps you in any tangible way. This whole scheme sounds like madness."

"You would be enough of a damper on unwanted attention if you were..." She coughed into her hand. "More than simply my escort."

His mouth dropped open. "You are not proposing...?"

"I am going to pretend to be head over heels in love with you. And, as such, have accepted your offer of marriage."

Prescott blinked, then shook his head. Was it his imagination or with every new revelation about this little scheme did the web seem even more tangled? It didn't matter, though; he wasn't about to get snarled in her madness. Still, he was curious. "Why me?"

"Because of Headmaster Dunn, as I said before. His influence regarding justice. Matters of honor..." Her moon-pale cheeks reddened. "And, your background certainly helps…"

"Ah…there's the rub." He nodded. "You want me because I am *not* a gentleman. I can get my hands dirty."

Opening her palms wide, she shrugged a shoulder, looking away. "There are certain advantages to your situation…"

"You mean, other than being willing to dirty my hands…"

Her gaze met his, unapologetic. "You're tougher than many of the gentlemen of my acquaintance. You've faced hardship and know how to deal with adversity. You're quick on your feet and can handle difficulty."

"You want someone willing to steal, lie…essentially not be bound by any code of honor."

"That's not true. You are honorable in the ways that count. Everything I've learned about you indicates that you do not turn on those who need you. That you honor your word like law, once given. That you protect those incapable of protecting themselves."

Unable to believe what he was hearing he crossed his arms. "Everything you've learned about me?"

Her cheeks bloomed to full cherry. "I've studied you. To know everything I could about your character." Her dark eyes skated away to stare at the corner of the small parlor. "You are the perfect man for the job. I know it in my heart."

"There's where you're patently mistaken in your studies. Had you been complete in your research, you would have easily ascertained that I don't put my neck on the line for others. It goes against the very code that you claim binds me."

"What about little Evie?"

Silence charged the room and he turned away to stare blindly out the window. He could not deny that seeing the little girl with her gown blazing on fire had brought out something in him. He hadn't given one whit for his own safety as he'd stamped out the flames with his hands. If there was a way to remove the pain she'd suffered then and suffered still, he would give his right arm, possibly more. The incident had made him aware of a side of himself that he hadn't known existed. But that didn't mean he would allow himself to be wheedled into assisting this crazy woman's plan.

"Evie is no stranger to me," he bit out. "You are." Slowly he shook his head, amazed that he'd even considered listening to her proposal. "I'm not getting involved with you or this insanity. Nothing you say can convince me otherwise."

Edwina turned and paced to the far corner of the salon as her mind scrambled for another line of reasoning. Coming up empty-handed, she spun on her heel and studied him once more, hoping for a flash of insight.

The man certainly had a flare for color. He wore an amethyst coat over a decidedly bright waistcoat with narrow willow green, purple and white stripes. He wore white breeches snug to the skin, as was the fashion, but never before had she noticed the harmony of curves, slopes and muscles that made up a man's leg. His thighs bulged in the most stimulating manner and tapered down into black Hessians that managed to give a hint of the muscled calves inside. With her cheeks flaming, she veered her gaze from that unsettling view. The man's clothes were...bold. Evocative. Daring.

"It will be exciting," she ventured, grasping for straws.

He raised a brow in derisive enquiry.

Self-consciously, she raised a hand to the high neck of her dowdy brown dress. She'd chosen it with care, trying to project a serious image. But her drab clothing countered the very message she was trying to convey.

Attempting to ignore the pit of disappointment deep in her belly, she argued, "What I am talking about is the challenge of stopping a coldhearted fiend. The excitement of unmasking a—"

"You can stop right now." He exhaled noisily. "Sorry, you have the wrong man." The lout didn't sound regretful in the least.

"But—"

"I've heard enough of your tales. I have given you my answer, now please leave."

"But I haven't even—"

A knock tapped at the door. The wooden entry swung slowly open and a shiny bald spotted head ringed with brown hair poked inside. "Ah, there you are, Prescott. I'm here to check on your hands—"

Dr. Michael Winner's eyes lighted upon the young lady and his thin lips that usually slipped easily into a smile dipped into a disapproving frown. His brown brows furrowed. "If I may be so bold, what the blazes are you doing here, alone in Mr. Devane's quarters, Lady Ross?"

Lady Ross? Prescott started. "The Earl of Wootton-Barrett's daughter?"

Her cheeks heated as she tilted her head in acknowledgment. "The very same."

Prescott felt his brows lift. "The man who's such

a stickler about pedigree that he had his own nephew removed from the line of succession because he suspected that the baby might be the result of his sister-in-law's having had an extramarital affair? An affair that many suspect never occurred?"

Her jaw worked. "The very same."

Prescott laughed for the first time in weeks. "I had my doubts before, but now I know you must be mad."

"But as I explained—"

Shaking his head, he interrupted, "You, my lady, made your own bed, now you must lie in it."

"You're going to simply feed me to the wolves?" she cried.

"With salt and pepper, my lady. Salt and pepper."

Chapter 3

"**H**ow dare you, Prescott?" Shaking his head, Dr. Winner looked over at Edwina and she gave him a weak smile, trying to recover from Prescott Devane's scathing rejection. "Calling her mad? Lady Ross is a levelheaded lady of fine sensibilities—"

"Who just asked for my hand in marriage." Mr. Devane's voice held an infuriatingly smooth cadence.

When he said it like that, Edwina felt as if she'd swallowed a sardine whole, and the fishy aftertaste lingered on her tongue.

The good doctor shot Mr. Devane a censorious glance. "Don't jest about such things, Prescott." Turning to her, Dr. Winner held open his hands. "Pray pardon Prescott, my lady. He's had a rough time of it, of late."

Mr. Devane's eyes widened. "Doctor, please!"

Dr. Winner lifted his hands. "What? I'm talking

about Headmaster Dunn." Turning back to Edwina, he explained, "We feel his loss enormously, but especially the children—"

"I'm not a child," Mr. Devane ground out.

"He was their savior, their guide," Dr. Winner continued, oblivious to Mr. Devane's irritation. "Our compass through the most trying of times...The accident with Evie, and Prescott's injuries, and well, it makes the loss all the more...difficult..." He swallowed, suddenly overcome. "It's...difficult to explain...It's just so dreadfully...difficult." His eyes glistened and he looked away.

Mr. Devane's face softened. Reaching inside his pocket and pulling out a handkerchief, he handed the doctor the linen. The men did not touch, but it was as if a communion of sorts passed between them. Dr. Winner dried the corner of his eye and shot Mr. Devane an appreciative glance. It was a simple exchange but one that spoke volumes.

As he turned, Mr. Devane's emerald gaze met Edwina's and that stirring jolt shafted through her middle once more. *How does he manage to do that?*

With a nod, Mr. Devane offered, "My jest was in poor taste, my lady, and I apologize if I offended."

Edwina swallowed, knowing that he'd just given her a graceful way out of the encounter. Part of her knew she should take it, but Mr. Devane's actions today had convinced her more than ever that he was her man. Well not exactly *her* man, but the one she needed. But how to convince him?

Noting how the men stood side by side, Edwina suddenly knew what she had to do. "Mr. Devane wasn't jesting about my proposing marriage, Dr. Winner."

Dr. Winner's eyes bulged. "But that's...that's..."

"Preposterous, ridiculous, absurd," Edwina supplied. "Especially since I've only just met the man. But it's true, nonetheless."

Mr. Devane's gaze was sharp and assessing, as if trying to figure out what she was going to do next. Well, that made two of them.

Edwina bit her bottom lip, then realized what she was doing and stopped. "You spoke so highly of Mr. Devane, and how he saved that little girl's life, that I came to meet the man for myself."

"So I have you to thank for this unsolicited visit, Dr. Winner," Mr. Devane murmured.

She sent him a somewhat quelling glance. "Actually it was your actions that gave me the idea to seek you out, Mr. Devane." Turning back to the doctor, she clutched her hands to her chest. "You see, Dr. Winner, I want Mr. Devane to act as my betrothed, for a time at least, while I hunt a blackmailer who is plaguing me."

Dr. Winner's mouth dropped open. "W-what?" Blinking rapidly, his gaze shot to Mr. Devane and then her and then Devane again. "Is she? Is she...?"

Mr. Devane shrugged. "You're the one insisting she's sane."

The man's face whitened. "A blackmailer?"

Stepping over to Dr. Winner, Edwina grasped his arm. "Would you like to sit down, Doctor?"

He swallowed, then shook his head "no."

Edwina sighed. "I need Mr. Devane's help to stop the knave and had assumed that Headmaster Dunn's influence would sway him to endorse my efforts. And certainly the incident with Evie convinced me that he would help another in need."

"You're not on fire," Mr. Devane interjected. "You gave the blackmailer whatever ammunition he's using. Whatever's going on is your own fault."

Edwina rounded on him. "So what am I to do? Pay the bastard until I'm bone dry? And in the meantime live with the devil's scythe over my head trusting that the blackguard is going to honor his word and not destroy me? He's malicious. He needs to be stopped."

Dr. Winner scowled, seemingly recovered. "Why won't you help the lady, Prescott? Where's your honor, man?"

Mr. Devane's eye narrowed, obviously not pleased to be forced on the defensive. "For one thing, I'm convalescing—"

"Your burns are just about healed. I can't see that as any reason not to help a woman in distress."

"You're assuming she's telling the truth—"

"Why would she lie when it's so damaging to her reputation? Besides, I've known Lady Ross for years and have always found her to be quite truthful."

Mr. Devane locked eyes with Dr. Winner for a long moment, and it appeared as if he was going to argue. Then he looked away. "How do you two know each other, anyway?"

"I treated Lady Ross's husband, Sir Geoffrey, may he rest in peace," Dr. Winner supplied. "And I know her family well." A new light entered his gaze. "What does your father think of this matter, anyway, my lady?"

Edwina's belly flipped. She swallowed. "My father doesn't know about the blackmail. And if I can help it, he'll never know."

Mr. Devane raised a brow. "And how is he going to

feel about your getting engaged to a grasping fortune hunter mongrel of dubious parentage?"

As sarcastic as he was being, Edwina still flinched at his harsh assessment. Her father would certainly see him as such, as would most in Polite Society. As if Mr. Devane could have helped the situation into which he was born. As if his feelings couldn't be inspired by anything but material gain. Not that he would ever have any feelings for her in truth...But that wasn't the point; the inequity of the judgments was.

But her father would never change his ways, any more than Society would. With its often unfair conventions, stratified tiers, and inequitable branding, lineage ruled, much more so than anything else, including money, although that often lent a shine to a lesser pedigree.

Having always been part of a family that was fixated on its ancestry, Edwina suddenly wondered how it felt for Mr. Devane to be so unaffiliated. For all of her family's idiosyncrasies, they gave her a sense of belonging. Had Prescott Devane ever felt that?

"I have to agree with Prescott there," Dr. Winner interrupted her thoughts. "Your father would no doubt disapprove of the association, and there'd be hell to pay."

Bracing herself with a deep breath, Edwina nodded. "No doubt about it."

"Then why hatch this plan?" Dr. Winner asked. "I don't understand."

"I need someone to discourage my suitors. Someone trustworthy to guard my back and help me unmask the blackmailer. I also, well..." Turning away, she nodded. "I must impress upon my father once and for all that he cannot rule my life. I will not abide by his dictates and will not marry the present suitor my father's been pressing on me, Viscount Bellwood. This seems the most direct, and"—she shrugged—"effective means of showing that I will not remarry at all."

Dr. Winner looked appalled.

"Of course." Mr. Devane scratched his chin. "To your father, your being unmarried is preferable to soiling the bloodlines."

Prescott Devane was far sharper than even his admirers gave him credit for, and Edwina couldn't rightly blame them; it was hard to see past that handsome exterior to the astute mind within.

She tilted her head. "Just so you know, I don't share my father's opinions on such matters, but yes, that is exactly how he will see it."

"And under your plan, once the blackmailer is stopped the engagement is over."

"Yes. We end the engagement after a row or some such."

Dr. Winner looked horrified. "But your reputation will be blemished by the entire affair so that you won't be able to marry a decent sort."

"And as a consequence, my father will finally stop trying to press me to remarry and leave me be. That's the very end I am hoping for, Dr. Winner."

Shaking his head, Mr. Devane smiled and Edwina felt his charm like a cloud of perfume that envelops you, heady, yet not so potent as to be offensive. "It's an interesting plan, Lady Ross. I'll grant you that."

Dr. Winner scratched his receding hairline. "I am most unsettled by this entire situation. A blackmailer, well, that's dreadful. But manipulating your father...

Although the Earl of Wootton-Barrett can be quite, ah..." His cheeks reddened.

"You needn't say it, Dr. Winner. I love him dearly, but he can be quite...a bull."

Dr. Winner looked relieved but still troubled. "Yet, to put a father through the agony of watching his daughter in an unfavorable alliance..."

"Thanks, Doctor," Mr. Devane interjected, yet his tone was teasing.

Dr. Winner shot him a glare. "You know what I mean, Prescott. I love you like a son, but on the surface, you're not exactly a father-in-law's dream catch."

"It's all right, Doctor. Besides, from what I've heard the Earl of Wootton-Barrett is not the man I would want for a father-in-law." Mr. Devane's smile was amused. "Not that I'm in the market for one."

Edwina stepped forward, facing the doctor. "I came up with the idea primarily to stop the blackmailer. The situation with my father was merely...well, inspiration to address another issue. Two birds with one stone, so to speak." She grimaced. "There has to be a positive aspect to this mess. But ultimately, I need Mr. Devane's help to go up against the blackmailer. I've tried to go it alone and he's outwitted me every time, taking my money at Society affairs and leaving me with barely a glimpse of him."

"The blackmailer's in High Society?" Dr. Winner's brows lowered. "The devil!"

Edwina nodded. "And he likes to make his exchanges at musicales and the like. But I've been stymied in my efforts by suitors pressing for my attentions. Suitors, I might add, who hold more affection for my purse and my father's connections than they do for me. There's no harm in discouraging them as they have no chance for success. Moreover, with them no longer hampering my efforts I can discover the identity of the blackmailer and free myself of his evil tyranny." Her gaze traveled to Mr. Devane. "But I am smart enough to recognize when I need help."

"Of course you are. You can't face this knave alone!" Dr. Winner cried, shooting the younger man a telling glance.

"Ask her why she chose me," Mr. Devane urged. "Why she thinks I have the skills for such a task."

Dr. Winner's expectant gaze swung to face her as if a tennis ball had landed on her side of the net.

She opened her mouth and then closed it, realizing that she needed to choose her words with care.

"The only reason she picked me is for my *lack* of honor," Mr. Devane remarked.

"That's not true," Edwina countered. "It is your principles that make you perfect. You will aid me in stopping this evil man, and then when all is said and done you will keep your word and leave me be. You're perfect because you're not one to actually hold me to..." Her voice trailed off as she suddenly realized how terrible that sounded.

"To the betrothal," Mr. Devane finished for her, his tone derisive. "Nay, an orphaned commoner like me wouldn't dream of rising to such heights."

"Prescott, please." Dr. Winner's face looked troubled. "It's not as if you aspire to be her husband."

"Not in a million years," he ground out, irking Edwina, but she pushed away the irritation; it was vanity, nothing more.

"Then you must help her. Honor demands it." Dr. Winner waved a hand. "She can change her hair, get some new gowns..."

"What do new gowns have to do with anything?" Mr. Devane frowned.

Edwina's hand involuntarily lifted to her chignon.

Dr. Winner's cheeks shaded pink. "Isn't that what ladies in love do? And you're quite the dresser. I'm certain Fanny could take her on as a client in her presentation business—"

"If you somehow managed to identify the blackmailer"—Mr. Devane turned to Edwina—"what then?"

Edwina blinked at the sudden change in topic. "I have connections at the dock, and this man will find himself penniless, sailing for distant shores."

"The dock?" Mr. Devane licked his lips and Edwina had the oddest sense that what she'd just said had more of an impact on him than anything else.

"The London dock. My husband was a principal. I know it's not very fashionable for the aristocracy, and a lady no less, to associate with trade of any kind." Her cheeks heated thinking of Dr. Winner's suggestion that she improve her hair and wardrobe. "Obviously, I don't worry overmuch about appearances." *To my father's constant horror.* "And, well, over the years I've had the opportunity to make some acquaintances in my husband's business. They will do as I ask."

"Let me escort you to your carriage," Mr. Devane suddenly offered, stepping closer and extending his arm.

Edwina blinked, wondering if admitting she engaged in trade had invited such immediate rejection. "But..."

"We can finish our conversation on the way."

Shooting her an encouraging glance, Dr. Winner bowed. "Good day, my lady. And fare thee well with your..." He seemed to struggle. "...efforts."

As she placed her hand on Mr. Devane's elbow, Edwina suddenly shivered. Between the scent of musk, the well-muscled arm, and Mr. Devane's obvious charm, she was feeling suddenly in over her head.

But that was nonsense. He was simply escorting her outside. She shook off the feeling and walked beside him toward the door.

As they descended the narrow stairs out of the guesthouse, Edwina's skirts brushed against Mr. Devane's thighs in an exceedingly disturbing manner. It didn't help that it seemed overwarm outside with a marked lack of wind, as if Mother Earth was holding her breath.

Walking in the direction of the stables, Edwina hoped that Mr. Devane's participation in her plan wasn't more than she'd bargained for. Oddly, when she was with him, she didn't quite feel like the efficient, confident Edwina Ross that she usually was. In fact, she felt a bit breathless, a bit giddy and more than a bit uncertain. She felt like...a lady in need of rescue.

Edwina started, appalled by the thought. Then she shook her head, deciding that it must simply be the fact that she hadn't been around a good-looking man with a brain in his head for so long.

Or more to the point, that she'd actually *noticed* that the man was attractive. And had perceived his appeal on a very primal level. Edwina swallowed, thankful that the contemplative Mr. Devane couldn't hear her thoughts.

Her reaction to Mr. Devane didn't change anything, not really. She supposed spending time with him would effectively eradicate the sense of excitement he stirred. Make her immune so to speak, like to an odor. Stay around it long enough and you didn't smell it anymore.

The sounds of children's voices rising up in hymn emanated from the chapel nearby and Edwina suddenly realized that they were almost at the stables where her carriage awaited. They hadn't yet decided upon anything! Was this Mr. Devane's way of shrugging her off, like a pesky tradesman?

"We've much to discuss yet, Mr. Devane." Her voice was tinged with anger.

He started, as if surprised. "Ah, yes." Upon looking up and seeing the stables with the servants mingling nearby, his steps slowed. "But not here. Too many ears. Walk with me, if you will, my lady?"

A sudden tingle crept up her spine as Edwina allowed Mr. Devane to lead her into the darkening wood.

Chapter 4

Their steps were muted by the mossy ground as Edwina and Mr. Devane traversed the path through the wood behind the orphanage's stables.

At a gap in the trees, Mr. Devane released Edwina and moved to lean on a large oak tree. She couldn't tell if she was more relieved or disconcerted by the sudden distance between them.

Lounging against the oak, Mr. Devane rested the backs of his hands on his muscled thighs. In that position, Edwina could hardly help but notice his sculpted form as his white breeches were tighter than cream on milk.

Edwina pulled her eyes away from the sight of Mr. Devane's bulging thighs and looked up. His gaze was so frankly assessing as to border on rude. Lord, the very hairs on her skin rose in unison, as if she were naked to his unwavering eye. Self-consciously, she raised a hand to her shoulder and was gratified to feel the wool of her coat. She was being a ninny and forced herself to at least pretend to be her practical self.

Clearing her throat, she wished that her mouth wasn't quite so dry and her heartbeat would calm a bit. It was the brisk walking, of course.

"I'll get right to the point, Mr. Devane. I need your help and you are in a wonderful bargaining position. You seem to be interested in the dock. Is there something I can help you with in that regard?"

Prescott hid his surprise that she would speak so bluntly. Yet he did not immediately answer, understanding with great clarity that he was at a pivotal juncture. He didn't believe in destiny any more than he believed in luck; he distrusted good fortune, knowing it usually hid an underlying scourge. Yet here stood Lady Ross, offering him the very access he'd been struggling for weeks to acquire.

He had been banging his head against the proverbial brick wall trying to secure warehousing for his shipments in London's congested, delay-ridden and thievery-infested facilities. He desperately needed the warehousing at the dock, but was space for his goods worth the risks her madcap scheme entailed?

He'd be dragged back into the existence he had already sworn to forsake. He was ready for a new chapter in his life and feared that if he was sucked back now his resolve would weaken, his choices would wane. Headmaster Dunn would have considered it a test of sorts. One that would strengthen his character, the good headmaster would have claimed. Were he here. The grief sliced through Prescott once more, ever the more potent since Prescott knew that Headmaster Dunn would have wanted him to help this woman.

An unsettling feeling twisted in Prescott's gut as he considered this young lady's going up against a blackmailer alone. The disquiet was wholly his own and not dependent on Dunn's approval. No doubt this blackmailer's scheme was a dangerous hornet's nest of trouble.

Yet, his instincts were telling him that Lady Ross wasn't telling the whole truth, no matter what Dr. Winner said. Then there was the fact that the blackmailer was targeting her because of something that she'd done. Again, he couldn't help but wonder at her secret. He knew his curiosity shouldn't cloud his judgment, yet it did.

Staring off into the trees, he surmised, "Even if I ask for your assistance with some business at the docks, there are still more holes in your plan than in a beggar's shoes."

Her brow knitted and he could tell that she was affronted but trying not to be. "Once I explain it all more fully to you, perhaps you will have a different opinion." Her shoulder lifted in a faint shrug. "And I suppose that, as you are involved..."

He liked how she said it as if it was settled; she had a knack for business, this one.

"I welcome your suggestions on how to deal with this terrible man."

Silence descended once more, interrupted by the leaves rustling on an agitated wind.

The breeze smelled moist as it pressed Edwina's cheeks and she realized that she was holding her breath and forced herself to relax.

"I'd intended to make a change." Mr. Devane's deep

voice was rough with emotion. "Alter the course of my life in a new...more respectable direction. No longer be at another's beck and call. No longer pretend I have a place in a Society where I have none..." He cleared his throat. "I had wanted to be someone Headmaster Dunn would be proud of. Hell, I wanted to be someone I would be proud of...A man of my own making."

A stab of guilt speared Edwina's middle as she suddenly realized the source of Mr. Devane's obstinacy. She'd heard that he had not been with a lady since Headmaster Dunn's death, had been living here at Andersen Hall, but she'd had no idea that he was hoping to change his life. Now she was trying to force him back into the very Society that he'd come to spurn and be at a lady's beck and call once more. Moreover, she was putting him at risk, albeit a limited one, and he really had no vested interest in her cause.

But if Mr. Devane didn't help her, then she couldn't bear to consider the consequences that had kept her awake so many nights.

Edwina forced her resolve to harden. "Perhaps a time limit might do? If we don't have the blackmailer by then...Well, after that, we part ways. Would that make a difference?"

His lips pursed. "How long?"

"Ah, six weeks..." At the look on his face, she adjusted, "Or three." His face seemed to relax. "Three weeks should do it rightly enough, I'd say. Then you are no worse off for your efforts than you are today, but better off in whatever your business undertaking." Again, she wondered at his need for assistance at the dock but supposed she'd find out soon enough. Agreement was starting to feel so close she could almost taste it.

"Better off in terms of my venture possibly." Mr. Devane's eyes were hard as jade. "But lower in terms of disrepute, my lady. You're asking me to lie, pretend to be someone I'm not, and Lord only knows what else is involved in your scheme."

He was a good negotiator; she'd grant him that.

She opened her hands. "For a good cause. Also, as far as your reputation goes, Mr. Devane, all will believe that I loved you and yet you chose to leave me. I can only imagine that your reputation might be enhanced from this little ruse. You will be known as a man who can't be chained by the mighty coin."

"And what of your reputation, my lady? I know what it's like having a soiled name. Do you?" The anguish she glimpsed in his gaze shocked her. Then his eyes hooded, hiding any trace of emotion on his handsome countenance. Yet by the working of his jaw and the tight set to his broad shoulders, she could tell that he was incensed.

With her heartbeat clamoring, Edwina swallowed. "I'm a widow, not some young lady searching for a husband. It should not warrant. Besides, my true friends...those who love me...will know me to be the same person that I was before..."

Mr. Devane shook his head. "You have no idea what you're signing yourself up for. When we're done, you will have been known as the foolish woman who lost her heart to a nobody and lost her reputation for nothing."

She straightened. "It's not *nothing* to me, so pray don't belittle my comprehension of the situation."

"This man must hold some pretty terrible secrets over your head."

Biting her inner cheek, her traitorous skin flamed, but she refused to look away and lifted her chin instead.

He shrugged a broad shoulder. "I think I have a right to know—"

She bristled, rearing up. "You have no right whatsoever! It's indecent of you even to ask!"

He pushed himself away from the tree. "It's my neck on the line—"

"And my reputation!" Anger made her voice shrill. "As you noted, I'll be aligning myself with you, one in a long succession of ladies, I might add!" Lord how it irked her, but she didn't know why.

His eyes blazed with indignation as he stepped nearer. "Popularity with the ladies is not exactly a crime."

She moved forward, showing him she wasn't afraid. "A little discretion would go a long way in repairing your good name, Mr. Devane."

"Repairing!" he ground out, the muscle in his jaw working. "I don't have a good name, if you recall. Which is exactly why you wanted me in the first instance!"

"I don't want you!"

His eyes flashing, he stepped closer, moving barely inches away. "Don't you?" His voice was such a low rumbling caress, it unsettled her nerves. "Are you sure?"

"Absolutely!" Stepping forward, she stood toe-to-toe with the man and glared up at him. "I don't want you in the least!"

"Liar."

"How dare you insinuate that I—"

Her words were swallowed up as his lips pressed down to hers.

Shocks rocketed through Edwina like a lighting bolt sears the earth, scorching her every thought to ash. The birds stopped chirping, the wind died, the sun eclipsed. All was black behind Edwina's closed lids. There was only the heat of Prescott Devane's smooth lips pressed against hers and the heady flavor of him, a hint of cinnamon, of all things, in her partially opened mouth. Never had anything tasted so shockingly divine.

All semblance of her astonishment was almost immediately replaced by an exhilarating warmth that cascaded down her body from her hairline to her toes, making her feel so good she was light-headed.

She did want him. Badly. The knowledge was like a moth fluttering about in her mind, there but not truly acknowledged.

Somehow her hands crept up to rest against his broad chest, her palm feeling a hint of the bold heart beating within.

His kiss was a powerful combination of daring offensive tempered with delicate tease as he sucked gently on her lower lip. Her lips clung unashamedly to his, seeking more of his delicious spice.

His arms wrapped around her, pulling her even more tightly against him. The force of his chest against hers gave a heady thrill, but nothing compared to the rush of pleasure that surged through her as his knee pressed into the juncture between her thighs.

Through her skirts, his well-muscled thigh pressed deeply, causing a wild conflagration of liquid heat inside of her. Brazenly, she leaned forward, pushing him deeper, driving him against her, yearning for something she didn't quite understand.

Her ears roared and the earth seemed to shake beneath her. Her body was a chorus of sensation harmonizing in a melody she hadn't known existed before.

Before. Sir Geoffery. Her deceased husband. Edwina blinked her eyes open, appalled to find that she was clinging to Mr. Devane more closely than moss to a rock. Her stomach clenched. She stiffened. She ripped herself away from him, horror-struck.

Mr. Devane released her without a word.

Edwina stepped aside and stood under the cover of a nearby tree. Her heart was pounding, her chest heaving. It took a few moments for the world to come back into focus. Only then did she realize that the sky had darkened and that the earth that had been shaking beneath her before had been a boom of thunder as a storm threatened in the gray sky overhead. But there was another kind of tempest raging within her as Edwina struggled to regain her composure.

"I'm not like the other ladies of your acquaintance." The quiver in her voice betrayed how shaken she truly was.

"That's for damned sure," Mr. Devane muttered, looking troubled.

Tears burned the backs of her eyes and she wished that the mossy ground would cleave open and swallow her whole. The only thing keeping her on her feet was the idea of embarrassing herself further before Prescott Devane.

Pride had its uses and the Earl of Wootton-Barrett's daughter had been infused with it from birth. Enough so to declare, "This was a mistake." A foolhardy, idiotic mistake that Edwina knew she was going to regret for as long as she lived.

"What?"

"I'm sorry to have bothered you." More sorry than he would ever know.

"You don't want my help?"

"No."

"What about the blackmailer?"

She looked away. "I don't know what I was thinking."

"You were trying to protect yourself and stop a villain."

"The plan was idiocy."

"And what about my business at the dock?"

She swallowed. "Send a note to my man of affairs. Now I must go." Lifting her skirts, she stepped through the trees, her only thought moving away from him as quickly as possible.

"My lady!" Mr. Devane grabbed her arm.

"Let me go!" Large drops of rain splattered down on them, blurring her gaze.

"But you're going the wrong way." He motioned in the opposite direction. "Your coach is at the stables, that way."

"Oh." She felt even more the fool.

"Are you crying?"

"Certainly not!" She brushed her hand over her face. "It's raining."

She moved to go, but his hand was like an iron vise on her arm, not hurting but not releasing her either.

"You can't just walk away, my lady. You pulled me into your troubles; you can't close the door on me now."

"This was a mistake, Mr. Devane. Can't you see

that?" Her voice had risen with a hint of panic; couldn't he just let her go? "I'll leave and you'll never have to see me again."

"It's too late; I'm already involved."

"Not really—"

"I know about the blackmail, I know about your scheme. I can't just forget it all—"

"It'd be for the best."

"For whom? The blackmailer?"

For me, she thought, knowing that she was lying to herself but couldn't face the alternatives. She was still so certain he was the man to help her, but she'd mucked it up beyond repair.

"I'll give you four weeks," he declared. "But that's it. No more pressing for a better deal."

Edwina blinked, the rain making her lashes heavy with wet. "What . . . what are you saying?"

"I'm saying that you're a tough negotiator, but four is all I'm willing to give. In exchange, I want your help in acquiring some warehousing at the docks, and obviously, a say in how we proceed."

Edwina shook her head, feeling woolly-headed. "You'll do it?"

"You get four weeks, not a day more."

The awful feeling in Edwina's chest was still there, but she straightened, experiencing a hint of hope.

"I suggest we return to the guesthouse and get out of the rain, my lady." The broad shoulders of Mr. Devane's coat glistened with moisture, and the scent of moss and damp filled the air. It had begun to pour in earnest and Edwina suddenly realized that the rain was beginning to soak through her coat.

Releasing her, Mr. Devane extended his arm as if

they were at a ball or soiree, and not in a deluge in the wood. "If you will allow me?"

Edwina did not miss the symbolism that the arm he offered was not only assistance out of the copse but a means of saving face.

She accepted his arm.

"Very well, it's settled then." He nodded. His wet coppery mane was a spiky mess, making him look so dashingly adorable she had to force herself to stop gaping up at him like a puppyish fool. "For four weeks, Lady Ross, I am at your disposal and will do my best to see you through this."

"At my disposal," she repeated quietly, still feeling less than sure of herself. "That's very ... good."

"And you're right about those shoes, my lady. They are unique."

She looked up. "You know of them?"

"They're from Paris, designed by a famous shoe-maker named François Millicent. Given the embargo and the war with Napoleon, there won't be many in Polite Society with such shoes. It's a distinctive mark to search for."

A small swell of excitement bubbled inside of her. "I'd thought so ... But it's so good to know for certain."

Edwina's spirits began to rise as they trudged through the trees, the pitter-patter of the rain the only conversation. She pushed away all thoughts of that kiss and instead focused on the success of today's encounter. She'd convinced Mr. Devane to help her! She had a soldier on her side, one with the mettle to trump the vile blackmailer! And already he was being helpful. The shoes *were* a distinctive clue. François Millicent.

Paris. She was gaining ground on this blackmailer, she just knew it!

For the first time in weeks Edwina felt hopeful. For the first time in ages, she felt...not so very much alone.

Chapter 5

Puffing from the thin cigar, Sir Lee stepped into the card room of his club and scanned the half-empty tables. His nose twitched, and he blinked his eyes from the smoke, disappointed by the lack of opportunity for play at Brooks's that afternoon.

As usual, Lord Wilmington and his crony Mr. Foreman engaged in a quiet game of *vingt-et-un* in the far left corner while Mr. Oglethorpe and Mr. Harris were in heated play of cribbage in the center of the room, egging each other on with one feigned insult or another. As if cribbage could ever be that exciting.

A few younger gents were halfheartedly playing spades at a table near the wall. It was early yet, Sir Lee understood, sighing, wondering if the day could get any longer. Yet having passed his seventieth birthday, he supposed he ought to be thankful for the early hour; he seemed barely able to stay awake past nine o'clock these days and was usually up before the crack of dawn.

Sir Lee was about to turn and depart, when from the doorway across the room he spied a familiar figure. With his stout belly, white hair, and shiny pink cheeks, the tall man could easily be mistaken for Father Christmas. Ironically, that fatherly exterior cloaked one of the most calculating, coldhearted men Sir Lee had ever met. And he should know, for he'd taught Tristram Wheaton everything he'd known about being a master of spies.

Unbidden, a smile leaped to Sir Lee's lips and his heart warmed as he remembered his glory days at the Foreign Office, the thrill of the hunt, the mental challenge of outwitting his opponents and struggling to think one step ahead of, well, everyone. Being the man in charge of intelligence on every suspicious foreigner in England had been Sir Lee's greatest pleasure. It had, actually, been the focus of his entire existence after his daughter's death. His work had been his only refuge from the grief, effective as much as anything could have been, because he'd been bloody good at it and had loved every Machiavellian moment.

Wheaton's bushy white brows lifted as he acknowledged Sir Lee across the room. As if by signal, Lord Wilmington and Mr. Foreman quietly rose from their seats and departed, leaving the corner free from any who might overhear.

Wheaton ambled over to the corner table and claimed the now-empty chair, adjusting his coattails and sleeves as he sat.

Hiding his smile, Sir Lee strolled between the tables and joined his former pupil.

A servant quietly placed two snifters of port before them and departed as unobtrusively as he'd come.

"Haven't seen you here in a while, Wheaton." Sir Lee leaned back in his chair, the wooden slats feeling good on his achy back.

"Some of us actually have a useful occupation." Wheaton sniffed, holding the port up to the flame of the candle on the table, as if appraising its quality.

Sir Lee licked his lips, concealing how keen his interest really was. "Oh? Anything exciting?"

"Gnats is what they are. Minor irritations."

"But in a swarm they can be bloody inconvenient." Sir Lee had an inkling that Wheaton was fishing for help. The man never made a move without an ulterior motive, even coming to his club at an hour when he'd know he would see his former superior.

"You're damn right about that." Wheaton's lips drooped into a frown as he leaned back in his chair. "It certainly doesn't help when one inherits someone else's mistakes."

Sir Lee shook his head. "Par for the course, I'm afraid, no matter how astonishingly talented your predecessor."

"Astonishingly talented?" Wheaton scoffed. "Your memory is fading in your old age."

"My memory fades the day Hades freezes over, old friend, and you well know it."

Silence stretched long between them, as each man took the other's measure.

Wheaton broke first. As he sipped his port, his eyes skated away. "Well, if your memory is so good, perhaps you'd recall the man you placed in Gérardin Valmont's service."

"I didn't place him. Hendricks did. And his name was..." Scratching his head, Sir Lee stared up at the carved ceiling. "Quinn or Quick, no, it was Quince. Yes, Quince."

"You're sure?"

"Of course, I'm certain. Alexander Quince."

"Have you ever met him?"

Sir Lee frowned, irritated that Wheaton felt the need to ask questions he already knew the answer to. "You know very well that I did."

"But he didn't know who you were or even that you were assessing him at that meeting?"

"Of course not. Standard procedure. Stop all the shim shamming and tell me what this is all about."

Wheaton lifted a shoulder in a faint shrug. "Well, I suppose given that this mess was started under your watch, you might be able to scratch up something of use to me."

Sir Lee suddenly wondered how Wheaton's callous manner was taken by his underlings. Intelligence officers were a hard-hearted lot for the most part, yet they had to be handled deftly. They lived excruciatingly complicated lives in service to King and Country and a good master spy needed to respect each and every agent's particular sensitivities. How did Wheaton fare in that regard?

Sir Lee forced himself to dismiss the critical thought, realizing that he was probably just being envious. He'd give his right arm for a chance to change places with the man sitting across from him.

"I'd heard Gérardin Valmont was dead. His heart gave out in a Paris bordello."

Wheaton's blue eyes twinkled. "I knew you still kept your oar in the water."

"I'm old, Wheaton, not dead." Glancing about the room Sir Lee lowered his voice. "So why the sudden interest in Quince, an intelligence officer who's hardly been worth his salt these last few years?"

Wheaton sipped his port, stringing him along.

Sir Lee sighed. "You know if you ever want my help you're welcome to it, Wheaton." He knew that his former pupil was always loath to ask for a favor. "It doesn't mean you will owe me anything." He smiled. "Well, not necessarily."

"Gérardin Valmont was the king of secrets. Hell, his forte for holding nasty tidbits over the heads of those in influence was the only thing that kept the firebrand in England for as long as it did."

"Nothing could save him after he published that idiotic pamphlet mocking the King, though," Sir Lee shook his head. "I don't know what the fool was thinking."

"Who knows, and at this point who cares? It was one less problem to deal with, was what you'd said at the time. Now that problem seems to be making a nuisance of itself once more, but in the form of our very own Alexander Quince."

"What'd he do?"

"A certain man of influence who assists me now and again suddenly took off for the country and refused my messages requesting his return. When I went to see him, a bloody two days' ride in the middle of nowhere, I was shocked to find him a complete wreck. After much coaxing, he finally confessed that he was hiding out in the country, hoping that his troubles might not chase him down. Those troubles, it seems, are in the form of a blackmailer. One with some very nasty secrets he's ready to exploit."

"You suspect Quince is picking up where his former employer left off?"

"Yes. Valmont is dead and suddenly a few of the older set in Society are fielding blackmail demands."

"A few?"

"I know of at least one more and suspect there are others. These blackmailing buggers dig until they find as many worms as possible and make them squirm. Until the field dries up, of course, or someone stops them."

"So arrange a payment and nab him. There's not much to it."

"Actually, it's not that simple. The man's crafty. He has the payments exchanged for bits of damaging evidence, at fashionable affairs, if you can believe it. Balls, soirees and the like. He doesn't set the terms of the delivery until the affair is in full swing. Usually by slipping a note to the target when he's least expecting it. It's a damned nuisance, I tell you."

Wheaton sniffed. "Then there's the damaging stuff he leaves behind. He tends to leave little tidbits of the secrets, as if to tease his victims. Letters and the like, exposing some very sensitive surprises." Exhaling noisily, he looked up. "All in all, this isn't exactly a major threat to King and Country." His lip curled. "And the victims are, well, Society."

"You were never particularly good at dealing with the aristocracy."

"Not my forte," Wheaton agreed.

"And you always tended to blame the victims of blackmail if I recall correctly."

"Who else is there to blame?"

Sir Lee frowned. "Everyone has skeletons in the

cupboard, Wheaton. A little compassion wouldn't kill you, you know."

"In my line of work, I must hasten to disagree. Skeletons are enormously helpful ... if properly aired." Lifting his port he sipped and watched Sir Lee over the rim of his snifter. "But back to the matter at hand, the more vexing thing is that no one knows what Quince looks like." His gaze sharpened. "Except you."

"I met him eighteen years ago, Wheaton. Once, and only for a moment at that. He couldn't have been more than twenty. It's not like he'd look the same in his late thirties. Moreover, what makes you think that it's not someone else? Another servant perhaps or a friend of Valmont's?"

"Poppet's gone missing. And Wiggins, too."

Sir Lee's heart skipped a beat, a very frightening thing for a man over seventy. "Neither one of them has worked for us in years."

Wheaton smiled, clearly not missing Sir Lee's reference indicating that he still considered himself part of the Foreign Office. Wheaton tossed some grease into the fire. "Poppet and Wiggins were the only two of our men yet alive who'd met Quince in his time in London. Except you." He raised a snowy brow. "Do you think you ought to be worried?"

"Nay. Quince didn't know I was observing him." Sir Lee shook his head, disturbed. His heart was heavy as he recalled Fred Poppet, a father of two with a flair for passing messages in crowded places. And Timothy Wiggins, a man with enough jokes in his repertoire to keep even the most skittish informants at ease. Sir

Lee's hopes for them were slim. Pushing away the grief and homing in only on the strategy, he asked, "What are you proposing, Wheaton?"

"Track him down and bring him in."

Sir Lee sat quietly a long moment. He'd been wishing for something very much like this for a long time now. Ever since his retirement years earlier. He'd imagined being called upon once again, as a hero, the only man to handle a dangerous situation that required his very special talents. But not at the cost of two men who'd served under him faithfully for years. Never would he have wanted it at his men's expense.

"How many men can you give me?" Sir Lee asked.

"None. We can't have any connection to this matter, I'm afraid. Too messy with the *haut ton* involved. But I have asked a couple of Bow Street Runners I know to back you."

"That's pathetic," Sir Lee growled. "Bow Street Runners are not professional intelligence officers. If two of your men had gone missing, you'd certainly find a way to supply more resources."

"Of course I would. But they're not my men." The ice in his gaze was only matched by the coolness of his tone. "I'm giving you all I have to give. But more to the point, this situation requires a delicate touch. We're dealing with Society. Muckety-mucks with nasty secrets. Less is more."

Reaching into his pocket, Wheaton pulled out two folded sheets of foolscap. "Here's the name of my informant who's being blackmailed. I want him back in town and free from this nuisance. You must protect his reputation at all costs." He held out the paper. "Are you in?"

Sir Lee inhaled a deep breath and then reached for the foolscap. Unfolding it, he noticed that Wheaton had been thoughtful enough to print clearly and in bold letters for a change. He didn't even need his spectacles. Noting the name listed, Sir Lee raised his brow, impressed.

Wheaton shrugged. "He has his uses. May I?"

Sir Lee nodded and handed over the foolscap.

Holding it over the candle's flame, Wheaton watched it burn to ash. Then he held out the second piece of foolscap. "Here's a list of those I believe or suspect are being blackmailed. For all I know some may be accomplices helping Quince get back into Society. I don't give a rat's ass if they burn for their sins, especially if they're in league with the bugger." Wheaton sniffed. "Investigate them and their associates. Use them to lead you to Quince. Do whatever you have to do. Just free up my man. As soon as I can get him back in town, he'll be useful to me once more."

Sir Lee's eyes scanned the list.

"You can keep that one," Wheaton offered.

Sir Lee pocketed it for later perusal. "And once I have Quince?"

"Use your imagination. Just ensure he doesn't bother me again." Wheaton lifted his glass. "To serving just deserts."

Nodding, Sir Lee joined in the familiar toast. "To just deserts."

The men sipped in silence, then Wheaton lifted his bulky form from the chair and stood. "I want it done,

Sir Lee. The mess cleaned up and my man back in business." Wheaton sniffed. "Whatever it takes, I want it done."

Knowing that tone, Sir Lee nodded. "It will be. Whatever it takes."

Chapter 6

◦◦◦◦◦

"He's agreed to help!" Edwina declared as she rushed into the library of The Society for the Enrichment and Learning of Females and joined her three friends.

Lady Janelle Blankett peered up from the tome lying open on the well-used brown desk and, with her usual dour expression, stared at Edwina through her quizzing glass. "Who's agreed to what?"

Aware of the open door behind her, Edwina whispered, "Him! You know, the perfect man for the job..." Closing the heavy wooden doors behind her, Edwina turned and caught sight of her reflection in the small gilded mirror above the pedestal cupboard. She was appalled to see that her tight chignon had come loose and her mousy hair was fairly plastered to her head, making her nose appear even larger. A swell of mortification blossomed inside her chest, knowing that

Mr. Devane, Prescott, she had to remind herself to use his Christian name, had seen her like this.

But the humiliation couldn't quite overshadow her triumph at securing his help for her scheme. So despite hearing the echo of her mother chiding her to run a brush through her hair before anyone else saw her, Edwina decided that she was amongst friends and could set such trivialities aside.

"You look like a drowned blackbird." Janelle sniffed as she patted one of her graying blond curls. "And a half-starved one at that."

Well, perhaps not all friends. "I'll be sure to consume a worm or two before dinner." Edwina waved a hand, feeling so glorious not even Janelle could pull her down. *"Une délicatesse crue."*

"A raw delicacy, you say?" Janelle's blue-green eyes narrowed, creasing the lines around the fifty-year-old matron's face. "The French don't actually eat worms, do they? Although I wouldn't be surprised with their aberrant tastes."

"I told you not to bother, Edwina." Lady Genevieve Ensley, known to her friends as Ginny, dropped her needlepoint on her lap and moved to stand. Poor Ginny; her arthritic hip caused her to have to lean on the arm of the chair for support.

Although she was still a handsome woman with sparkling blue eyes and rosy cheeks, her slate gray hair and awkward shuffle made her appear much older than her forty-five years. "My problem is my own and I will not drag you into it, Edwina. Besides, I thought you'd given up."

Edwina snorted. "And let that knave win? Never!" She moved to stand before the flaming hearth and held her hands to the fire. The warmth reminded her of another heat she'd experienced that afternoon.

Lord, oh, Lord, what a kiss that had been! Prescott Devane was a master, she marveled, as she recalled how hungrily she'd kissed him back and how desperately she'd clung to him.

But did he know? Did he realize? A ball of ire welled in her belly; he was practiced in the art of passion and would undoubtedly know her mortifying secret. Swallowing, Edwina was glad her face was to the hearth and prayed her friends assumed the redness in her cheeks was from the flames.

Pushing aside all upsetting thoughts, Edwina focused only on the moments after the kiss. The walk back to the guesthouse. The lively discussion, and the earnest way Prescott threw himself into her plan. The man was sharp, insightful, and more than a little brave. The perfect man for the job. Oh how she loved being right.

"I appreciate your trying to help me, Edwina." Ginny had moved to stand beside her. "But you've already done enough and I don't want that wretched man hurting you."

Edwina grasped Ginny's hands. "I'm not about to stand aside like a worthless Thatch-gallows while everything you cherish is at risk." She smiled. "Besides, you know I'm only doing it for the sport. I hate losing." At least on that account, Edwina and her father were alike, which is why they butted heads so acutely.

"Just so you don't do anything that you're not comfortable with, Edwina." Despite her arguments, Ginny's face looked relieved. Edwina could hardly blame her; Ginny wasn't the sort to go up against a scoundrel alone. She was simply too sweet.

"I consider it our *obligation* to stop this villain." Edwina didn't mention that not since establishing the society three years earlier had she felt this passion to set forth boldly on a mission of principle.

Recently, she'd felt adrift, as if her life was moving forward yet going nowhere. Like something was waiting for her, but she didn't know which way to go to find it. All she knew was that it was decidedly *not* in the direction the Earl of Wootton-Barrett wished her to go: to the Viscount Bellwood's side in marriage. But her frustration with her father and sense of being directionless could all be conveniently brushed aside now that her dear friend was in need. And if all went as planned, then her problems with her father would disappear, at least when it came to remarrying.

Dropping her quizzing glass on its chain, Janelle scowled. "I still have my reservations about your little scheme, Edwina. It seems fraught with peril. Primarily for you and your reputation." Resistance from the gangly matron was no surprise, as Janelle used every opportunity to try to spike Edwina's wheels, so to speak.

Janelle resented the fact that Edwina was the president of the society while she was only a vice chair. Typically, she used Edwina's younger age of three-and-twenty as her excuse for needing a more senior leader. To Janelle's utter frustration, the rest of the members usually ignored her.

"I appreciate your concern, Janelle," Edwina replied, forcing herself to recall that Janelle did not have it easy. Her husband, Lord Blankett, showed more affection for his mounts than he did his wife and spent the majority of his time in search of the next Derby winner. Janelle's daughter had moved far away and rarely deigned reply to her mother's letters. And then there was Janelle's son who all of London knew had a weakness for cards and spirituous liquors. "But my reputation is my own and I think I can protect it well enough."

Janelle waved her quizzing glass. "But what of your family's reputation? Particularly your father's. You're quite free with that."

Dropping Ginny's hand, Edwina turned to the fire, trying to ignore the twist of guilt in her belly. She forced herself to remember how disdainfully her father often treated her. He persistently raked her over the coals for having the cheek to create a club for females and satirized their good works with marked contempt.

Then, after she'd begun contesting his attempts to marry her off to Viscount Bellwood, he'd called her "a rogue specimen in need of a man to rein in her 'outlandish' propensities." In need of a man! What utter rot!

Sir Geoffrey was the only husband she would ever have; no one would ever fill his place.

Squaring her shoulders, Edwina turned. "My father is out of town and not expected back this season. By the time he hears of anything, it will all be over." And so will any attempted betrothal to Viscount Bellwood.

Mrs. Lucy Thomas scribbled out a note on a bit of foolscap. The dark-haired, doe-eyed beauty had lost her husband to a terrible wasting disease less than a year earlier and when her dying husband had lost his ability to speak, inexplicably, so had she. Lucy would sit quietly and listen, read, and only now and again scratch a note. One might have assumed that anything she wrote was worth reading, but often as not her notes were as trite and self-absorbed as anyone else's verbal commentary, like asking if you admired her new hair comb.

Stepping over, Edwina read the message aloud, "Which one is he?" She smiled. "Getting right to the point, Lucy. It's Mr. Prescott Devane."

"Mr. Devane?" Janelle scowled. "The man's a *cicisbeo,* for heaven's sake!"

"Some might argue that being a charming companion at balls, soirees, picnics and the like, provides a service in our society," Ginny disputed. The rosy-cheeked matron loved to argue a point, whether she believed it or not. She warmed to the subject as evidenced by the twinkle in her pale blue eyes. "In fact, in this instance, at least, the lady retains complete control of the funds and the terms of the relationship. She has an engaging escort, nothing more."

Janelle shook her head. "Any arrangement where one person uses another is invariably opportunistic and immoral. The man's a parasite."

"He's an escort," Edwina scoffed. "Don't make it sound as if he's a gallant or a fancy man. He doesn't sleep with women in exchange for material gain." Yet, the list of his lovers was long. A strange twinge flared in her middle once more, but she disregarded it.

"He does have a rakish reputation with the ladies..."

Ignoring the burning in her cheeks, Edwina crossed her arms. "From what I hear, it's the ladies who chase after him, not the other way around. And when was the last time you saw a man censured for earthly appetites? Or a woman castigated for accepting a gift?"

Pursing her lips, Ginny's eyes took on a dreamy cast. "I knew a *cicisbeo* once. He was quite charming and had the largest hands..."

"Yes, we know all about your obsession with hands." Janelle snorted. "Which is why you find yourself in such a fix."

"Janelle!" Edwina cried, alarmed by the hurt look on Ginny's face.

Lucy brandished her note in the air and Edwina was thankful for the change in subject. "Lucy's right. I must tell you why Mr. Devane is the man to help us out of this mess."

"Us." Ginny looked up, a suspiciously bright gleam in her eyes. "When I read that first letter from the blackmailer I thought my life was over. I couldn't have Judith discover the truth. And if anyone else learned about me and Gérardin...Well, Judith's fiancé would end it for sure, and Judy and I...we would become outcasts. My daughter would never have forgiven me, and I wouldn't have been able to forgive myself!"

Ginny's smile was pained. "But you've given me hope, Edwina. Real hope that we can get through this mess. But am I being naïve? Dare I trust your plan will succeed? Dare I?" Pressing her hand to her mouth, she cried, "Oh, what a wretched fix I'm in!"

Edwina grasped her hand. "We have a solid plan, Ginny. Mr. Devane will help us identify the man, search for and then recover your letters to Gérardin Valmont—"

"So now you're a common house thief?" Janelle scoffed.

Edwina shot Janelle a frosty glance. "It's only burglary if the item in question belongs to that person—"

"Stealing applies to the act, not the property taken."

"The act doesn't exist if the property—"

Waving a note, Lucy hammered her fist on the table.

The willowy widow might be mute, but she knew how to make herself heard when she wished to.

Edwina had to admit that at the society a certain amount of discussion was engaged simply for oratorical exercise, but it did tend to slow matters down. She read Lucy's latest note aloud, "Tell me about Devane's hands."

"I'm being serious, Lucy." Edwina set the foolscap aside.

Lucy motioned that so was she.

Sniffing into a handkerchief, Ginny straightened, collected once more. "Hand size notwithstanding, I want to know Edwina's reasoning for drafting Mr. Devane." She stepped before the window, her peach silken skirts swooshing as she limped, a hand on her arthritic hip. "Especially since Edwina was the one to eliminate Devane from consideration in the first instance."

"You deemed his character questionable, if I recall." Janelle stood, squaring her broad shoulders so that her mint green gown lifted and then settled on her ample bosom. Janelle paced, the long white feathers of her lavender turban flopping to and fro with each gliding step. "How, you had asked, could we trust that he wouldn't turn on us? Would he use Ginny's secret against her?"

Ginny crumpled the handkerchief and slipped it into a hidden fold of her gown. "Although you also said that his limited means and connections would cause him to benefit from an association with you, Edwina. And I might add he should be grateful for the attention by such a beautiful, fine—"

Edwina raised a hand, knowing that her friend saw

her through rose-tinted lenses. "Prescott Devane has had the benefit of associations with ladies far more attractive than I." Why did that thought rankle?

"How can we be certain he won't try to use the faux engagement to his advantage?" Janelle demanded. "We cannot rely on his honor. He's *not* a gentleman."

Having experienced Prescott's decency firsthand, Edwina shook her head. "Being born to privilege does not necessarily assure noble character. And the opposite is true as well—"

"But being born a gentleman does give a certain indication of"—Janelle waved a hand—"expectation, deportment, education, and so on. The man was raised in an orphanage, for heaven's sake."

"He grew up at Andersen Hall," Ginny pointed out, a great supporter of the institution. "And if Headmaster Dunn held any influence over him, Mr. Devane may be a creditable person indeed."

"Headmaster Dunn may have made it his mission in life to save London's orphaned children and make them productive members of society," Janelle countered, hands on hips, "but anyone who makes his way by being a leech is hardly productive. And hardly a person suitable for Edwina to be engaged to. But let us get to the real issue." Janelle's face was smug. "Edwina wants her father's attention, and this is her only way of securing it."

Ginny gasped.

Edwina's fists curled and her eyes narrowed.

"One would think you were still in the nursery, the way you behave." Janelle sighed as if the notion pained her. "Honestly, Edwina, you're so transparent. We all see it. You crave attention, always must be the center of everything."

"That's it," Edwina growled. "I'm done with your—"

"Edwina, please!" Ginny stepped forward, her gaze pleading. If it weren't for Ginny, Edwina might have tossed Janelle out of the society long ago, but for some unknown reason Ginny loved Janelle like a sister, and time and again begged Edwina to be forbearing.

Edwina wondered why Ginny never asked Janelle for a bit of restraint. But she pushed aside the twinge of anger. Ginny was suffering enough with this blackmailer and her daughter's impending nuptials, Edwina was not about to carp at her now.

So Edwina bit her inner cheek, squared her shoulders and did the one thing that would infuriate Janelle the most: she turned to Ginny and Lucy and acted as if Janelle didn't exist. "The reason why I changed my mind about Mr. Devane—"

"Do tell," Ginny urged, shooting Edwina a grateful glance.

Lucy nodded, lifting both of her dark brows in entreaty.

"Is because I learned that he saved a young girl's life. At peril to his own."

"My, oh, my, that is character telling indeed." Ginny bit her thumbnail, a habit she engaged in whenever excited.

Shaking her head, Edwina could hardly imagine the terrible accident. "The poor child's gown had caught on fire and she would have burned to death if Mr. Devane hadn't used his hands to extinguish the flames."

"How horrible!"

Janelle's green-blue eyes narrowed. "Was she connected? Was there a reward for his heroics?"

"She's an orphan, for heaven's sake!" Edwina raised

her hands in exasperation. "Could you be any more calculating?"

"How did you come upon this intelligence?" Janelle demanded.

"I was speaking with Dr. Winner—"

"A man of fine character and a good doctor." Ginny nodded.

"But can his opinion be trusted?" Janelle crossed her arms. "Being Andersen Hall's doctor may color his viewpoint."

Pressing her hand to her chest, Edwina prayed for forbearance. "I spoke with Mr. Devane myself. *I* interviewed him, and must declare, in no uncertain terms, that I was most impressed by his character."

Janelle lifted a haughty shoulder. "Oh, so it was his *character* that impressed you?"

"Janelle, please!" Ginny cried.

"This plan is idiocy! And its architect just as—"

"If you don't have anything productive to add then remain quiet!" Ginny blinked, as if shocked that she'd actually spoken.

But no more stunned than anyone else in the room.

Shaking her head, Ginny's shoulders drooped. "I'm sorry. This is all just so upsetting..."

Edwina's eyes met Janelle's. A truce of sorts flashed between them. Ginny was about the only thing upon which they could agree.

Edwina squeezed Ginny's shoulder. "Mr. Devane has agreed to help us, Ginny. And from all I've learned of him and my own impressions, he's just the sort of man to get the job done."

Janelle rolled her eyes but blessedly held her tongue.

"In fact," Edwina added, "he shed some light on our

mysterious shoe marking. As I suspected, the shoes are rare, made in Paris by François Millicent. Not many men in London will have such shoes. So we have something to go on." She bit her lip. "The only thing is, Mr. Devane thinks I'm the one being blackmailed, Ginny, not you."

Ginny gasped, raising her hand to her mouth.

Lucy's black brows knitted in concentration.

Throwing her head back, Janelle cackled so shrilly it was a wonder the paper didn't peel right off the walls.

Later, Edwina came to decide that it was the most disturbing comment that Janelle had made all day.

Chapter 7

⟨◦○○◦⟩

The next morning, Dr. Winner unwound the yellow-tinged bandages from Prescott's proffered hands. The scents of the calendula flowers and olive oil of Dr. Winner's special ointment filled the air.

"You really don't even need these anymore, Prescott," Dr. Winner remarked. "Not even at night. You're a quick healer."

"I've had good medical care." Prescott curled his fingers. His skin felt oddly stretched and yet ticklish, as if ants crawled on it.

"I still thank the heavens that you found Evie when you did. Otherwise..." The good doctor shook his head.

"Evie seems to be doing fine." Rising, Prescott crossed the guesthouse bedroom and opened the dresser. He scanned the gloves inside and, skipping over the fancy French kid in favor of the more sturdy English leather, selected a brown pair. "In fact, I know she's getting better because she's been begging me to sneak her sweets."

"Children do rebound very quickly..." Sighing, Dr. Winner gathered the bandages from the bed and set them inside his black medical bag. "Yesterday she asked me how old she needed to be to get married." He smiled. "I think little Evie may be smitten."

"She's in a romantic phase, I'll grant you that. But it's only because we're reading *Beauty and the Enchanted Prince*." Tugging on the gloves, Prescott felt better for the coverings. "Which, by the way, means that I'm the beast, thank you very much."

"You have been a bit of a grumpy bones of late," Dr. Winner teased.

Prescott couldn't disagree. He'd been hiding out, holing up at the orphanage to avoid the Society he'd come to dread. But at Andersen Hall he could not escape the one thing that pained him far more than any meager burns. Prescott could almost smell Catherine's lemon-scented soap hanging in the air like a bouquet of sunshine, making him feel like the black cloud of doom.

All the more reason for Prescott to help Lady Ross...Edwina, as he'd insisted he call her for the ruse. He had four weeks until his shipment arrived. Four more weeks of lagging about trying *not* to think about Cat. Edwina would provide the perfect diversion.

That kiss had been a surprise. A very agreeable surprise.

Oh, he'd concealed his reaction well enough from Edwina, but once he was alone, he'd gone over the kiss again and again in his mind, trying to unravel its mystery.

He'd had no intention of kissing her. But he'd been so roused and there'd been something about her too tempting to ignore. It was like coming upon a fresh pond on a sweltering day. Jumping in was a wholly natural impulse that just *had* to be acted on.

And oh, her taste had been quite *reviving.* More than anything had been in the last long, dark weeks. She'd felt good in his arms. Warm, supple, and soft in all the right places, just like a woman was supposed to feel. But there'd been something different about her. Something that had made him wonder about her: She'd responded like no woman he'd ever kissed before.

Thinking back on that embrace, he realized that she was a woman who knew the touch of a man and hadn't reacted like an innocent.

And yet...

And yet, her response had been so artlessly passionate as to make him sweat just thinking about it. He could always tell when a woman controlled her kisses, molded her lips just so, groaned at a timely moment, ground her hips with purpose. There had been none of that.

Edwina had felt...swept away. Completely and utterly carried away by his kiss, and in response, he'd been overcome. He, the worldly, jaded *cicisbeo,* had felt that kiss down to his boot tips. At first it had been as if the world had fallen away, leaving only him and the lovely woman in his arms. Then the kiss had metamorphosed into something significantly more. Making him feel as if he'd been crawling through a desert and yet hadn't known how truly parched he'd been. Until he'd taken a sip from clear blue waters. Edwina had been that taste, the perfect antidote to the thirst he hadn't known he'd had. For that moment at least.

But the kiss and how it had made him feel were likely an anomaly. Somehow the combination of the storm, her story of peril, the lush woods, and the fact that he'd been without female company for so long had converged into his startling reaction. The circumstances caused him to feel something that he *thought* was unique to Edwina, but in truth, was simply a union of things going on around him. Still, he wondered.

There was only one way to know for certain. And, he had to admit, he was eager to explore the issue further to find out. Even if it turned out to be a disappointment, the distraction from losing Cat would, by itself, be worth it.

"Ah, Prescott..." Dr. Winner scratched his ear, obviously trying to broach a topic that bothered him.

Prescott hid his smile; he'd been waiting for the good doctor to ask what had happened with Edwina yesterday and if Prescott was going to help her. The man was as curious as a cat, Headmaster Dunn used to say. Lord how Prescott missed the bossy old gent.

"I still can't quite believe that our sweet Catherine is a nobleman's daughter," Dr. Winner began. "And Jared...well, he's a baron, for heaven's sake!"

Wishing that Dr. Winner had asked about Edwina instead, Prescott turned and moved to stare blindly out the window. The subject of Cat was too raw, too painful and too damn private to discuss with anyone, even Dr. Winner.

Dr. Winner continued mercilessly on, "I'd always known there was more to our Catherine than met the eye."

Many of the staff at Andersen Hall had been speaking along those very same lines. That they'd suspected the truth. But only Headmaster Dunn had known. And he'd kept the secret from everyone. As had Catherine. If it hadn't all come to light with the recent Caddyhorn theft, would she ever have told him? Scowling, he wondered when she'd told her new husband.

Prescott's shoulders were corded with tension as the anger boiled inside of him. Staring at the green leaves shimmering on the wind, Prescott schooled his heart to calm, his breath to even. He needed to rein in his temper; it seemed to flare up these days as if it had a will of its own. He'd wrestled with his anger when he was young and had believed that he'd had it conquered. Now it seemed to be on the advance once more, and a more powerful adversary than ever.

Shouts and squeals could be heard through the glass. They were happy sounds, sounds of childhood, where impulse and glee reigned. Stepping closer to the window, he looked left toward the garden. The children were playing "wage-war" in the green grass. It had been his favorite pastime when he'd first come to Andersen Hall. The battles were a great avenue for screaming, running about and thumping the other lads. A perfect pastime for an angry little monster like him. He'd won a lot and had relished every victory.

Cat hadn't played much, he recalled. She'd been so timid, so afraid of letting the troops down. She'd always assumed responsibility for everyone else. It was one of the reasons Prescott had always loved her.

Well, not always. It was near his fourteenth year, he recalled, that he'd started to notice how she'd leave an extra seat for him if he was late to the dining hall. She wouldn't say a thing, yet the space would be there, and he the only one missing. He was usually taking one punishment or another. Lord, what a monstrous scamp he'd been.

It was Cat who would look the other way when he was up to his mischievous tricks. It was almost as if she somehow forgave him in advance for his misdeeds. So he'd tested her. Again and again subjecting her to his most devilish pranks. She would be furious, but there was a softness to her mien, a wounded sigh, as if he was simply being himself and couldn't help it.

Headmaster Dunn had seen it all and had finally pulled Prescott aside, and asked, "Do you want Catherine to hate you?"

"N-no," he'd sputtered. "O' course not."

"Then do you wish her to be your friend?"

"Yah…"

"Yes is the appropriate response," Headmaster Dunn had chided. "What is one of the things you admire most about Catherine?"

Put on the spot, Prescott had blurted out the first thing to come into his head. "She speaks fancy."

So Headmaster Dunn had asked Cat to help Prescott with his elocution. Quickly Prescott had realized the benefit to such assistance, since an expensive coat could cover many things but how one spoke belied all origins. And since Prescott had always felt destined to "get ahead" in the world, he'd felt that Cat's polish was part of his ticket out.

Catherine had been skeptical at first, but when

Prescott had shown her how much he wished to improve his speech, she'd relented and given everything to helping him better himself.

Yet all the while that he was working to move into higher circles, that was where his dearest friend belonged. She truly fit in where he was the interloper. The great pretender.

"I should have known she was hiding secrets," Prescott muttered. She'd always been one to ignore his lures or change the subject when he veered into more serious topics. Or was it that he hadn't pressed her to share? Perhaps he'd even done it on purpose, decrying anything unpleasant. And secrets tended to be bloody awkward. Still, she should have told him.

"Don't feel bad about it." Dr. Winner snapped his black leather medical case closed. "Headmaster Dunn found out by accident. She hadn't told anyone, not even him."

That fact did make him fell *a little* better.

"She blames herself for his murder," Dr. Winner added, sadly.

"What utter rot!" Prescott turned to face Dr. Winner. "Her bloody relations had no idea she and Jared were even alive."

Scratching the tuft of brown hair fringing his crown, the doctor sighed. "She says it wouldn't have happened if it weren't for her. You can't argue with that."

Fury lashed though him so powerfully Prescott had to stop his hands from curling into fists. "No one can blame her for those murderous bastards' misdeeds! She did everything in her power to escape them! Hell, she even gave up her fortune! No one can convince me that there was anything Cat could have done to stop the blackguards!"

"I suppose she can't help what family she was born into," Dr. Winner agreed with a nod.

"Of course not! She hid from them to save herself and her brother. Obviously with just cause—"

"So keeping the secret was critical..." Dr. Winner interrupted.

Prescott started, suddenly seeing the doctor's point.

"And what would you have done had you known the truth?" Dr. Winner pressed. "Would you have been able to stand aside and do nothing as she wanted?"

Prescott shook his head, the anger still simmering so close to the surface he didn't trust himself to speak. Cat had done the best that she could. It wasn't for him to judge her actions. But he'd kill her villainous uncle, Dickey Caddyhorn, if he ever got his hands on the bloody bastard. For the man to have tried to lock up young Cat and her baby brother in Bethlehem Lunatic Asylum to steal their fortune...Prescott's fingers curled hard and an ache seared across his healing skin. "If Solicitor-General Dagwood can't get the job done..."

"Oh, Caddyhorn will hang. Along with all of his nasty accomplices. But enough of that." The doctor opened his hands wide. "What of your future, Prescott? Catherine and Marcus return in ten days time and will, undoubtedly, want to reside here. Do you have any plans of what you'll do? Anything...on the horizon?"

Ah, getting to the doctor's real inquiry. The man was cunning, but he could dangle in the wind a bit longer.

Prescott shrugged, all innocent. "Mayhap I'll enlist."

Dr. Winner straightened. "Don't try competing with Marcus Dunn. You're two entirely different men."

Prescott withheld a groan. "Of course I'm not competing with Marcus." Even if Prescott did envy the man within an inch of his life. "I was only jesting. I'm starting my own business venture. One that should prove to be quite fruitful." It had better be or Prescott would be without a pence to pinch.

"But what of Lady Ross?" Dr. Winner demanded. "What of her terrible plight?"

Crossing his arms, Prescott harrumphed. "I should be insulted, Doctor, that you even entertained the thought that I might turn down a lady in need."

Dr. Winner's smile was wide as he rushed over to Prescott and grabbed his arm. "Never did I doubt you, my dear boy! Not for one moment! Oh, I can't wait to tell Fanny!"

"You can't tell Miss Figbottom about Lady Ross!"

Dr. Winner waved a hand. "Not about the blackmail, but simply as a potential client to help her select a few new gowns and such. It's her new business." The man's brown eyes glistened and his face took on a pining glow. "Fanny's got...*savoir-faire*. She's so fascinating, stimulating, enthralling..." He sighed. "Every moment I'm with her feels like a grand adventure."

"Sounds like you're in love." Prescott stepped away and motioned for Dr. Winner to proceed out of the bed chamber and to the salon. "Shall we?"

"I suppose it must be catching these days." Collecting his satchel, Dr. Winner followed Prescott into the next room. "Catherine and Marcus, now me. Love is a curious thing; when you least expect it, it finds you."

A snort Prescott would know anywhere resounded near the guesthouse door. He smiled. "Hello, Mrs. Nagel."

"You know that I'm not one to comment on such things," the matron huffed as she adjusted the gray chignon in her white bonnet. "But I feel that it is my duty to caution you, Dr. Winner. That woman is not of your...caliber."

Dr. Winner's cheeks reddened. "Now see here, Mrs. Nagel. Miss Figbottom is as fine a female as I have encountered. If you have heard otherwise, then I must declare that she is the victim of hearsay and slander."

"She's an *actress*." Mrs. Nagel said it as if it was akin to leprosy.

"Retired actress, to be completely accurate," Prescott corrected. "And I wish that I'd have had the opportunity to see her tread the boards. I've heard it said that she was a rare talent, indeed."

"You, of all people, Mrs. Nagel, cannot blame a person for trying to make a living," Dr. Winner defended. "And now she has a new vocation."

"Oh, really?" Mrs. Nagel raised a haughty brow. "I can't imagine how she'd apply her 'talents.'" The slander hung in the air like a foul odor.

"Yes, tell me of her new vocation, Dr. Winner," Prescott rushed in. "I am most intrigued."

The doctor shot him a grateful glance. "She is helping people with their..." He waved a hand, seemingly at a loss. "Presentation. You know, deportment, fashion and the like."

"How frivolous." The matron sniffed. "It's the inside of a person that matters, not the outside."

"Very true, Mrs. Nagel." Prescott nodded. "And in that spirit, Headmaster Dunn would no doubt have invited Miss Figbottom to Andersen Hall by now and learned more of her character."

Dr. Winner tried to hide his pleased grin by coughing into his fist.

"Aren't the children studying Shakespeare's *Hamlet* right now?" Prescott enquired, knowing Mrs. Nagel's soft spot for the children. "Wouldn't it be grand to have Miss Figbottom give a performance for the children?"

"Miss Figbottom would make a wonderful Ophelia!" Dr. Winner declared. "And I'll bet she'd love to do it!" Upon seeing the censorious look on Mrs. Nagel's face, he added, "The children could certainly use a diversion..."

Crossing her arms, Mrs. Nagel lifted a shoulder. "I suppose it's something to consider. We can talk about it with Catherine once she returns. Just so long as we keep certain *influences* from tainting Andersen Hall." Turning her glacial gaze on Prescott, she added, "Speaking of which, I was thinking, Prescott...We're in need of a new Latin tutor. Would you consider...?"

Prescott choked on his own spit.

Dr. Winner stepped over and patted him on the back. "You all right, my boy?"

Nodding to the doctor, Prescott tried to catch his breath. "You're jesting, right?"

Mrs. Nagel scowled. "Well, we have to find something productive for you to do!"

"I thank you for your concern. But I'm going to be quite occupied as it is." Stepping over to the closet,

Prescott removed his hat and set it upon his head. "Why don't you tell her the good news, Doctor? I'm off to visit my fiancée."

Smiling, Prescott escaped outside and trotted down the stairs. He could almost hear Mrs. Nagel's jaw as it hit the floor.

Chapter 8

~~~~~~~~~~~~~~~

Prescott strolled up the lane heading toward 183 Girard Street, the address Edwina had given him. As he neared the crimson-painted door denoted "183," he wondered at the second doorway just a few feet away, also painted red and numbered 183A in gold. The two doors were situated along the same building. Interesting. Did Edwina lease out part of her home? Based upon their conversation yesterday, he doubted that she'd have any issue with capitalizing on such a valuable asset as her property.

It was impressive that Edwina didn't feel compelled to pretend to disdain trade. In fact, when she spoke of her husband's business a light lit her dark eyes and excitement infused her voice. Passion. The lady definitely had it, albeit well contained.

Again, Prescott's mind reeled back to that startling kiss. Anticipation swirled in his middle as he considered the next opportunity to discover more about Edwina's passion and his own response to it.

Quickly, he trotted up the stairs to the residence and neared the first crimson door. Before he could knock, horses' hooves clattered and a carriage rolled to a halt behind him.

Thinking it might be Edwina, Prescott turned. Unfortunately, it wasn't her coach; there wasn't a hint of marigold or purple in sight.

Instead, a first-rate, black-and-wood carriage populated by two brown-liveried footmen and a driver sat at the curb. One of the footmen set the steps and opened the door as another held out his hand to assist the passenger from inside.

An ivory-gloved hand grasped the man's offering and a stout matron with graying brown hair and sharp brown eyes descended from the carriage. She wore a dove gray promenade dress, matching cottage mantle and an extravagant gray bonnet with lacy blond ribbons that bobbed with every step to the street. Her ensemble was completed by the sour expression on her face that could have curdled the milk inside a cow's udder.

"You there!" The matron's upper lip twisted. "I know who you are and what you are about! You'll not get away with your evil designs! Of that, I assure you!"

Upstairs in the society's library, Edwina tried not to be conspicuous when, for the tenth time in an hour, she stepped over to peer out the open window in the hopes of spotting Prescott.

"Oh, no!" she gasped, pressing her hands to her mouth.

"What is it?" Ginny rushed over, with Janelle and Lucy following close at her hem.

"The dowager...Penelope, Lady Ross...*my mother-in-law*!" Panic and dread rushed through her. She hadn't seen her mother-in-law in over a year and she chose now of all times, when Prescott Devane was at her door, to call! "I'd best get down there!" Turning, she lifted her skirts and raced from the room.

"I never liked that woman," Ginny commented, watching as Devane bowed to the dowager and the lady wagged a cane at him as if she were having an epileptic fit. None of the woman's rant could be heard above the street noise, but there was no doubt that she was on a tirade. "She's never been particularly kind to Edwina."

"My sense is that Edwina isn't necessarily so fond of her mother-in-law, either," Janelle muttered, stepping to stand beside Ginny and peer down at the street four stories below. "Perhaps she's the one who started it? A mother being disregarded when a child marries isn't unheard of."

Leaning forward for a better view, Ginny shook her head. "Edwina wanted to embrace her mother-in-law, but that woman was...well, I hate to say it but she seemed very small-minded to me."

"I'm sure having Edwina as a daughter-in-law was no picnic in the park," Janelle countered, tilting her head and leaning so that her ear was out the window. "She can be such a crosspatch. And that habit of always wanting attention can be quite trying." She scowled. "I wish I could hear what they're saying, but those wretched carriages traveling down the street are making too much noise."

Janelle looked over Ginny's head and met Lucy's gaze. "I read somewhere that people who lose the use of one of their senses may have another sense enhanced. Can you hear what's being said?"

Lucy rolled her eyes, and then stuck her face out the window for a better view.

Glaring at Janelle, Ginny scolded, "If Lucy could have heard, she would have told us."

"How?" Janelle retorted. "By writing a note?"

Ginny straightened. "You can be so infuriating sometimes."

Shrugging, Janelle peered down at the street.

"Lord. I didn't think you could see spittle flying from so high up," Janelle commented. "And the dowager's screeching reminds me of a cat whose tail got slammed in a door."

"This is bad, isn't it?" Ginny bit her lip. "What do you think is troubling her?"

"Oh, probably the fact that Devane is a gold-digging, covetous snake. Although she should save the scolding for her unruly daughter-in-law, who started this whole mess."

"But how could she know about the engagement? No one knows..." Ginny's eyes widened. "Janelle, you didn't!"

"She was bound to learn of it sooner or later. At least this way she heard it before anyone else."

"That note you sent! It was to the dowager, Edwina's mother-in-law, telling her about the engagement! Edwina's going to kill you."

Grasping Ginny's sleeve, Lucy pointed out the window.

Ginny turned.

Edwina raced down the stairs of the society, bonnet-less, gloveless and without even so much as a shawl.

Janelle smirked. "Edwina can hardly kill me if she's slaughtered first."

Boldly, Edwina stepped between the dowager and Devane.

"As if to protect him," Janelle commented. "How droll."

Ginny wrung her hands, uncertain of what to do. She'd heard stories about the dowager that were enough to make one set sail for France. Still, it was Edwina. "Should we go lend our support?"

"Nay," Janelle squinted down at the scene. "It's a family squabble, and I think Edwina's doing well enough handling it on her...Ouch!" Janelle winced. "That had to hurt."

Ginny gasped. "I can't believe she struck Edwina! The dragon! I'm going down there!" Turning, Ginny hurried from the room as fast as her arthritic hip would take her.

Tapping Janelle's arm, Lucy pointed out a footman's carrot-topped head poking out from an under-stair entry, and farther down the street an elderly couple who stood blatantly staring at the scene.

Janelle made a face. "Leave it to Edwina to cause a scene."

Lucy motioned that they should go down to the street.

"Fine. Fine. She makes a mess and we're left to clean it up. Very well, if we must."

Prescott wrapped his arm around Edwina's shoulders and stepped between her and the dowager. Turning to the dowager's footmen, he ordered, "Gather your mistress and leave. Now!"

"I'm not finished with you!" the dowager hissed, brandishing her cane.

"But we're finished with you." Ignoring the ranting harpy, Prescott herded Edwina up the stairs to the red door marked 183 just as the butler opened the entry and stepped aside.

Edwina was shaking, her body clenched tightly. She hadn't said a word since the slap, reasonable since she was probably shocked that her mother-in-law could do such a thing. Prescott, on the other hand, wasn't surprised. The dowager was one of those people who would do anything under the rationalization that she was the one who'd been wronged first.

"Close and lock the door," Prescott ordered the grim-faced butler dressed in a purple uniform with marigold lapels. The man immediately complied, slipping the bolt with a firm hand. The butler quickly stepped through an inner door into an adjacent vestibule and locked that door as well.

Two vestibules side by side with a connecting door in between? Distantly Prescott wondered at it, but he had more pressing matters to attend to.

"How ... ?" Edwina bit out. "How can you manage to remain so calm when someone is so ... *vile* to you?"

"I use my mask."

"Mask?"

"The world only sees the façade that I choose to show them."

"And behind it?"

"Is my own business."

A gray-haired, rosy-cheeked matron limped into the

foyer. "Are you all right, dear? I saw the whole thing! I hate that wretched woman, Edwina! I swear I hate her!"

Edwina blinked, and her face softened. "Ginny."

Ginny's pale blue eyes were filled with anxiety and her face lined with worry. She rushed to Edwina's side. "I'll set the dogs on her," she jested, her voice pitched with anxiety. "Have her tarred and feathered."

Edwina clenched the other woman's hand. "She's going to write to my father. Insist that he make haste to London."

"You're the one always telling me that we'll figure out a way to deal with obstacles," Ginny urged. "We'll get through this."

A storklike matron with graying blond curls and greenish blue eyes glided into the room. "What are you complaining about now?"

Edwina stiffened and her lips pinched.

From behind the tall lady came a sable-haired, ivory-faced young woman. If the black bombazine wasn't indicator enough of her widowhood, there was an aged sadness in her doelike eyes, reminiscent of a Renaissance Madonna.

"You're the one who wanted the Earl of Wootton-Barrett to find out." The storklike matron's tone was smug. "Only you were foolish to believe that he would simply learn of your engagement after the fact."

"Let us save this discussion for upstairs, Janelle," Edwina bit out.

"Why?" Smiling, the lady named Janelle opened her hands wide. "You usually love making an exhibit of yourself."

Edwina's hands curled into fists.

Hoping to lower the heat on this boiling confrontation, Prescott bowed to the ladies. "I don't know that we've had the pleasure of an introduction—"

Lifting her chin in the air, Janelle turned aside. "I do not condescend to recognize your acquaintance."

"Janelle!" Ginny's eyes widened.

The sable-haired widow silently rested a gloved hand on Janelle's arm but the matron shook her off. "I will have my say and do what's right, Lucy. Edwina has no sense of reason about this matter, but I, thank the heavens, do."

"You promised, Janelle!" Ginny exclaimed.

"And I had grave reservations about doing so. I'm sorry, but I cannot keep my word and sit by while Edwina brings wrack and ruin upon us all."

"She's doing nothing of the sort!" Ginny wrung her hands. "Just the opposite in fact—"

"You're too generous when it comes to Edwina and can't see that she's too immature to make sensible decisions."

"Watch what you say, Janelle," Edwina warned, her tone almost as taut as the muscles in her back. "I may be younger than you but that doesn't mean I am any less rational. Nor does it mean that you can treat me with disregard."

"Please don't argue, you two," Ginny cried, clasping her hands before her in entreaty. "Why don't we all go upstairs to the library and have a nice cup of tea?"

"I'll not have that man inside our society!" Janelle shook her fist. "It's unacceptable! And if Edwina was any kind of president, she would feel the same!"

President? Society? So the dowager's rant outside wasn't completely senseless.

Edwina eyed her meaningfully. "You are aware of Mr. Devane's role and why his presence here is—"

"Simply unacceptable!" Janelle raised a finger. "Your entire plan is a debacle! It was only my benevolent nature that kept me from challenging you more stridently."

"Benevolent nature!" Edwina sputtered.

"But haven't you learned anything from your little tête-à-tête with your mother-in-law outside?"

"All I learned was that someone blabbed the news," Edwina bit out, her dark eyes flashing. "And not in the way we'd planned for or intended."

Stepping forward, Janelle loomed over Edwina and glared down with a self-satisfied glint in her catlike greenish blue eyes. "Your oh-so-marvelous plan called for people to know. Now they do. Don't grouse about it now."

Slowly, Edwina lifted her chin. "That aside, you cannot stop me from welcoming Mr. Devane into my home."

Janelle's eyes narrowed. "I always considered it ill conceived to house the society in your residence. Now I know why."

Ignoring the woman, Edwina turned to Prescott and quickly grasped his arm. "If you would please join me upstairs, Mr. Devane?"

For a moment, Prescott wondered how to proceed. The sable-haired doe named Lucy bit her lip and unhappiness filled her gaze. Ginny was wringing her hands before her as anxiety lined her brow. The poor lady seemed to be on the brink of tears.

Janelle looked ready to spit sixpence and Edwina was wound tighter than whipcord. Yet, somehow, despite the acrimony, or perhaps because of it and the great familiarity it evidenced, Prescott had no doubt that these ladies cared deeply for each other.

Still, he didn't know them and this was not his problem.

Accepting Edwina's hand on his arm, he nodded.

"I will have you removed as the society's president!" Janelle shrieked. "I will see the society itself moved from this residence! Your little scheme will bring ruin down upon us." Squaring her shoulders, the matron blocked their way. "And I will die before letting that happen!"

Chapter 9

❧◦❧

Never in her life had Edwina felt the urge to strike someone, yet at that moment she hated Janelle with a force that made her fisted hand quiver with urgency.

The very notion shook her to the core. She wasn't like the dowager. Just thinking of how she'd felt when her mother-in-law had slapped her caused a wave of shame to wash over Edwina and a nasty tang to coat her tongue.

Inhaling an unsteady breath, Edwina unfurled her fingers. She felt as if she were hurling from one terrible encounter to the next but unable to stop it. Well, someone had to. Edwina was resolved and yet saddened; this parting was long overdue.

Turning toward Ginny, Edwina shook her head. "I know it pains you to see us at odds, but I will not suffer her barbed tongue any longer, even for you." Facing

Janelle once more, Edwina was glad her voice was steady as she declared, "I hereby invoke my right, as president of The Society for the Enrichment and Learning of Females, to eject Lady Janelle Blankett from our membership."

Janelle reared back, her face aghast. "You wouldn't dare!"

"You leave me little choice." Glancing at Ginny and Lucy, Edwina asked, "Do you second the motion?"

Awkward silence encased the small vestibule.

Prescott moved to stand before Edwina, leaned down, and whispered, "Actions taken in anger often make for later regrets. Trust me, I know."

She looked away. "You don't understand."

"All I'm saying is that this is obviously a significant decision and one that should be made after clear reflection, not after you've been attacked by that pretentious hag outside."

"This isn't the only incident..." Unable to explain, she shook her head.

Turning to face the other women, Prescott declared, "I hate to see Edwina's mother-in-law's most ardent wish come true."

"What wish?" Ginny asked, stepping forward.

Edwina looked up.

Prescott exhaled noisily. "You should have heard the atrocious things she said about your society. She said that you were 'bombastic, bluestocking, dowdy women whose mediocrity compelled them to create a club from which to foment vulgar behavior.'"

"She didn't!" Ginny gasped.

Edwina raised her hands over her ears. "Please don't repeat those horrible things!"

" 'Fools,' the dowager said," Prescott went on, " 'with misplaced notions of charity that have them socializing with the lowest dregs of society.' "

Janelle's face reddened. "She slandered my prison reform program? Has she any idea how many women we've helped train for productive positions after they've served their time?"

Edwina looked up, whispering, "It was poison aimed at me. Not at any of you..."

"She also said that the founders of the society, and she used that designation in the plural sense, were 'uncultured, underbred, presumptuous.' "

"Uncultured! Underbred!" Setting her hands to hips, Janelle glowered. "Why, that bacon-faced, hog-buttocked frump!"

Shaking his head, Prescott remarked, "No doubt, Lady Ross would relish any damage to your society. Celebrate any injury she'd be able to inflict to the fundamental principles you ladies have embraced." He sighed. "Nothing would please her more than to see you at odds. It's a shame to let her win."

"We can't allow it," Ginny declared. "It would be a tragedy."

Lucy shook her fist, indicating the need to fight this affront.

Pursing her lips, Janelle murmured, "It would certainly be a betrayal of all we've worked for..."

"You know," Prescott addressed Janelle, "you remind me of one of the women that I admire most in this world."

Turning to peer over his shoulder at Edwina, Prescott calmly motioned to Janelle. "Doesn't she remind you of Mrs. Nagel? I know you only met Mrs. Nagel for a moment this morning, but can't you see the similarities?"

Edwina's eyes widened. She appreciated his efforts to bring the ladies together and cool the confrontation. But the last thing in the world that would help was to compare Janelle to a school matron. It wouldn't matter to Janelle that Mrs. Nagel was a woman who cared so much about her former charge that she insisted upon meeting Prescott's fiancée posthaste, Janelle would still be insulted beyond salvage.

Prescott turned to Janelle once more. "Mrs. Nagel always told me that she felt as if she was the voice of reason crying out in the darkness. But that all of her words of wisdom fell upon deaf ears."

Janelle's eyes narrowed. "What are you about, Mr. Devane?"

Certain that Janelle was about to haul poor Prescott over the coals, Edwina placed her hand on his arm. "Uh, Prescott—" But he shot her a look to wait. The confidence shimmering in those emerald eyes stopped her short.

"I know that she found it terribly frustrating that her advice was so easily discarded," he continued. "When she *knew* what was best for those she was simply trying to help."

"Sounds like a creditable woman, this Mrs. Nagel," Janelle muttered.

Edwina started. Was Janelle actually *listening* to Prescott instead of ripping him to shreds?

Janelle was looking down at the floor, not meeting anyone's eyes. "I can certainly understand how the woman might feel."

"I know she suffered great aggravation with us

wretched unfortunates." Prescott shook his head. "We never truly appreciated her or her attempts to aid us."

Janelle nodded. "I often feel that my own attempts are similarly unacknowledged." Her tone lacked its usual potency and instead was interlaced with a hint of grief.

Shocked, Edwina held her breath.

"My children, in particular..." Janelle's voice trailed off. She shook her head. "I try to speak with them, I write to my daughter, but it's as if my every word is"—she swallowed—"abhorrent to them. All I want... all I want to do is to be a help to them. To be a part of their lives..."

Immediately the memory came into Edwina's mind of the first time she'd been introduced to the dowager. Edwina had been so hopeful of embracing her new family, but the stout, sour-faced matron had glowered at Edwina and coolly informed her that she was a source of income, of enhanced connections, nothing more. At first, Edwina had been shocked speechless, unable to comprehend. But she soon learned that the dowager had meant every word. Edwina had tried convincing herself that it was better to know the lay of the land than be under illusions, but the rejection had always hurt. Always.

Edwina's heart pinched and her anger dissolved faster than vapor from a boiling kettle. Prescott could see what she'd been blind to: Janelle didn't feel included or needed. Her children had rejected her efforts. Her husband was fairly lost to his horses. And at the Society, her one haven, Edwina had always taken the tack of ignoring her. Janelle was always claiming that Edwina hungered for attention, but maybe she had really been speaking of herself.

Prescott nodded. "Like the other orphaned children at Andersen Hall, I never truly valued Mrs. Nagel until she was lost to me."

Janelle looked up. "She's gone?"

"No, thank the heavens. I was speaking of the time when Mrs. Nagel took sick one winter. She had a cough that was so terrible it hurt your chest just to hear it. She took to bed and suddenly we were free from the woman we'd all considered the bane of our existence."

He shook his head and Edwina could see the cloud of memory in his gaze. "We certainly couldn't celebrate her illness, but a few of us fools thought that life might improve without Mrs. Nagel to dress us down for our mischief. What we realized, to our surprise, was that Mrs. Nagel was the binding that kept our pitiful lives together. We'd never grasped all that she'd done in a day to keep us safe, fed, clothed, and reasonably upstanding."

He chuckled, a low, warm sound from deep in his throat. "We almost threw a party on her first day out of bed. Lord, I can't tell you how I welcomed the next time she smacked me over the head with her straw broom. I was so glad she was there to do it I almost wanted to kiss her." His lips quirked. "Not quite, but almost."

Listening to his story, Edwina could almost picture the scamp of a lad he'd been. Adorable, playful and with a mischievous gleam in his emerald eyes.

"Headmaster Dunn always taught us to endeavor to learn from our mistakes." Prescott set his hand over his heart and bowed toward Janelle. "If you would grant me the privilege, I would very much like to hear your concerns about all that is taking place. I can only hope that it will help to avoid unnecessary complications."

A silence so profound filled the vestibule that one could almost hear Janelle's brain grinding through the options.

After a moment, Janelle cleared her throat. "I do believe I may have underestimated Headmaster Dunn's influence on you, Mr. Devane." Turning to the butler, she ordered, "We'll take our tea in the society library."

Edwina released the breath she'd been holding.

Stepping forward, Prescott offered his arm. "I am at your disposal..."

"Lady Blankett," Janelle supplied, accepting his arm. Staring up at his handsome face, she added, "I had no idea you were such an astute man, Mr. Devane. Perhaps this plan of Edwina's is not so foolhardy after all."

Edwina felt her eyes widen and her jaw drop open.

Prescott nodded. "I try, Lady Blankett. But often I suffer under the ignorance of my upbringing."

"Nonsense, Mr. Devane," Janelle chided with a wave of her hand. "Good judgment is innate if the mind is sharp and the vision clear."

Ginny and Lucy quickly stepped aside and the mismatched pair walked through the doorway leading to the society's part of the house.

Ginny grabbed Edwina's arm and pulled her close. "That has to be the most disarming man in the entire kingdom. I had no idea he was so perceptive."

Edwina shook her head. "Much more so than I, I'm afraid."

"Don't be too hard on yourself." Ginny hugged her shoulders. "Janelle's been pretty terrible to you. It takes the patience of Job to see past that tough armor she wears."

Which was all the more reason that Edwina had to help save Ginny; the woman was a saint. Edwina couldn't endure watching her life torn asunder by a blackmailer.

"I need to withdraw that motion to expel Janelle," Edwina resolved.

"Don't even bother. Let it all simply be forgotten."

"You believe it will?"

"Janelle doesn't wish to fight, any more than you do. You two are just like...a cat and a dog. Natural enemies who've yet to figure out a way to live together." Ginny smiled. "But that doesn't mean you both don't mean well."

"Do I get to be the cat or the dog?"

"Whichever you wish." Ginny drew Edwina toward the doorway leading to the society's rooms. "Now let us proceed upstairs. I want to hear what Janelle has to say."

As she allowed herself to be propelled forward, strangely, Edwina found herself feeling the same way.

Chapter 10

"Oh, you'll need much more than a few new gowns, Lady Ross," Miss Figbottom intoned the next afternoon. Her voice reminded Edwina of a melodious songbird with a very powerful call.

She had the look of an exotic bird as well, with her shocking red hair, crimson-painted lips and powdery white skin. Her olive green ensemble and the bright green feathers in her hair comb only added to the effect.

"Certainly a new coiffure." Miss Figbottom glided across the red carpet of the ornately furnished red-and-gold boudoir, her generous hips swaying to and fro. The woman's olive green gown was etched with purple swirls that drew the eye in the most astonishing manner. Edwina felt as if she was in the presence of an artist, one who's very self was the work of art. "Then there are the gloves, shoes, oh, there's much to be done."

Edwina bit her lip. "Ah, I'm not a great fan of shopping expeditions, Miss Figbottom."

"My dressmaker arrives in an hour and always comes with a few gowns almost done."

"Almost done?" Again, Edwina wondered at the wisdom of working with someone whose tastes were so divergent from her own.

"There are only so many basic sizes, I've learned," Fanny continued. "And Michael, Dr. Winner, already told me about your shape. So you should have some new things straight away."

Dr. Winner had talked about her "shape"? Edwina was appalled. But then again, he was a medical doctor, and he'd surely never looked at her with scandalous intentions. Now, if another man had looked at her with scandalous intentions...

"Are you feeling ill?" Fanny enquired. "Your face is flushed."

"Ah, no, I'm fine." Edwina had to stop thinking about Mr. Devane... *Prescott.* Just saying his Christian name sent a thrill chasing up her spine.

After their walk through the rain, he'd remarked, "I suppose if we are to be engaged, you should call me Prescott."

"That's not necessary, you know," she'd blurted. "There are many couples engaged, married even, who don't use each other's Christian names."

"Yes. But *I* wouldn't use my wife's family name any more than I would have her use mine. You want this engagement to be believable, don't you?"

"Of course... Prescott." She'd swallowed. "And you should call me Edwina."

"*Edwina.* I like that."

She shivered now as she'd done then, her name sounding so . . . stimulating on his lips.

"Michael also told me about your coloring," Fanny commented, tearing Edwina from the memory. "So I've selected some fabrics that I think will suit you just perfectly."

Edwina blinked. "Don't I get to pick . . . ?"

"This is what I do, Lady Ross, and my taste is *infallible*."

Eyeing Miss Figbottom's red-and-gold boudoir, Edwina reminded herself that she'd promised Dr. Winner that she'd maintain an open mind. Nodding, she swallowed.

"As far as the rest of the ensemble," Miss Figbottom drove relentlessly onward, "my vendors always know what I like, and I only work with the best. So we'll have you set up in a trice. Oh, and call me Fanny. All my clients do."

Edwina felt as if she were inside a runaway carriage without a driver up top. Yet she didn't quite know how to stop it without insulting Miss Figbottom. Inwardly she shrugged; at the worst, she'd wind up with a few gowns she might never wear. At the best, she might learn something useful; she'd never been particularly fashion-minded.

"Now, let us see about your hair." With narrowed eyes and pursed red lips, Fanny studied her, giving Edwina the feeling that she was a bug under glass and Fanny the curious scientist trying to decide whether to dissect her.

Fanny turned to the footman standing in the corner and motioned for him to set a chair before the gilded mirror. "If you would, Kilpatrick?"

After he'd performed this function, Fanny tapped a finger to her chin. "Please send for Mojgan, Kilpatrick, and then have Cook prepare some tea for us. It looks as if it's going to be a long afternoon."

Edwina's stomach sank.

After the servant had departed, Fanny waved a hand toward the seat. "Please, Edwina. If I may call you Edwina?"

At that point, Edwina felt she could hardly say no. "Yes, of course." She sat.

Fanny moved to stand behind her and began removing the pins from Edwina's hair. The scent of Fanny's rose perfume wafted around them like a pungent cloud, making Edwina's nose itch.

"You really have lovely hair," Fanny commented.

"There's no need for false flattery, Miss...Fanny. I know I'm no beauty."

Fanny straightened, the pins still raised in her hands. "Who ever told you that?"

"Well, everyone. My sister got the looks in our family."

"You speak as if all the beauty to which your family is entitled ended up with your sister." Anger shimmered in Fanny's hazel eyes. "The very notion is ludicrous."

"But Adrienne is lovely. She has long, golden hair, bright blue eyes, a perky nose." Self-consciously, Edwina raised her hand to her protruding appendage. "She's a perfect English rose."

"There's no such thing. England is a land of mongrels." Fanny waved a hand in a graceful arc. "Between all of the invasions, the wars, the uprisings, I can't imagine there's family that has not intermarried or otherwise intermixed with a foreigner at least ten times over."

Edwina couldn't help the grin from stretching her lips. "Don't say that within earshot of my father. He lives and breathes for our pristine bloodlines."

Fanny snorted. "I'm sorry for saying so, but his pedigree is only distinguished by the fact that he keeps track of the damn thing." She didn't sound sorry at all. "Look a little higher in your family tree and at all the branches and you'll see more than a few so-called 'contaminating influences.'"

"I agree, my father can be very...shortsighted when it comes to the purity of our pedigree. But he's certainly not alone in valuing the sanctity of English bloodlines."

Fanny harrumphed. "Pure blood, perfect English rose, indeed! It's all an illusion crafted by those who wish to keep Society exclusive and thus themselves the 'haves' and not the 'have-nots.'" She smiled. "But illusion is my forte as well, which you shall soon see."

Setting aside the pins, Fanny shoved her fingers into Edwina's hair and loosened the tresses from the tight chignon. Edwina felt the weight of her hair fall to her shoulders. "Hmm." Fanny pursed her crimson lips. "Now, tell me what you see in your reflection."

Inhaling deeply, Edwina studied the dark-haired woman staring back at her. "Black eyes, like coals. Skin like farmer's cheese—"

"I have my work cut out for me, indeed." Fanny t'sked. "Half the trick to being beautiful is *believing* that you are beautiful."

"But what if it's not true?"

"Shhh! Of course it is. And you must have the

absolute uncompromising knowledge that you *are* beautiful. Now," Fanny clucked, "close your eyes, relax and tell me about the man."

Edwina's heart skipped a beat. *Did Dr. Winner tell Fanny about the blackmailer?*

"I've heard he's quite the blade," Fanny remarked. "I've not yet had the good fortune to meet him for myself."

"Oh, Prescott..." Edwina murmured.

Fanny's hands stilled. "Who else would I be asking about?"

Edwina swallowed. "No one else, of course." *You're in love, you ninny, remember?* "Well, he's quite handsome."

"That's so bland. Details, darling, details. And close your eyes."

Obediently, Edwina allowed her lids to drop and she pictured Prescott as he was yesterday at the society. He'd been so daringly insightful, and had the tact of a practiced diplomat. Sitting in the library having tea, he'd been so at ease one would have thought he'd been part of the group for years and not hours. And he was so good with questions, guiding the conversation so that no more conflicts erupted. *He's really quite masterful...*

"Masterful, eh?" Fanny intoned.

Edwina blinked her eyes open. *Did I just say that aloud?*

Fanny's smile was amused. "Tell me what he looks like. Face. Hands...Close your eyes, I want my efforts to be a surprise."

Lowering her eyelids, Edwina licked her lips. "Well, ah, his hair is the loveliest shade of brown. Not plain like mine, but with copper running through it. It's wavy, and moves when he does, almost like a river of auburn."

The fingers massaging her scalp and manipulating her hair felt divine. Edwina's limbs felt heavy as she sank a bit in the chair and sighed. "His eyes flash like emeralds in sunlight." *And cause the most delicious flutter in my middle.* "Especially when he's angry."

The hands stilled. "Michael, Dr. Winner, told me that he has a temper. Has he ever raised a hand to you?"

"Oh, no. And I highly doubt he ever would. He's not the type."

"Good. I have no use for such men." Fanny's fingers began their ministrations once more. "Is he strapping? I heard something about his father being a laborer. Manual workers have the most marvelous brawn..."

With her eyes still closed, Edwina frowned. "No one seems to know his true story. Some say his mother was a laundress and his father a lord who died, leaving everything to his legitimate sons. Another story has him as the bastard son of a duke. And yet another has him as the son of a tradesman and his wife who fell on hard times and then died of a lung disease."

"Hmmm. Michael tells me that Headmaster Dunn did not press children for information; it was his policy to allow the children to leave the past behind. So mayhap Mr. Devane is the only one who knows the true tale?"

Edwina had to admit that she was eager to learn more about Prescott's origins. Even though she knew it didn't matter, she had an insatiable curiosity where he was concerned. She supposed that she'd be fascinated with anyone who had had such a different life from hers.

"He's certainly unlike any male I've ever known," she murmured.

"They always are, honey, when you're in love."

Edwina bit her lip wondering if she had the courage to ask about the concern that had been keeping her awake at night ever since meeting Prescott. "May I...may I ask you a question...it's a bit...risqué."

"Oh, good, the more risqué the better."

"Ah, actresses have the reputation...although I don't want to paint you with such a broad brush—"

"Just ask the question, Edwina."

"Yes, of course. Well, actresses are known to be very...*experienced* when it comes to men..."

"That we are." Fanny's hands continued working without pause. "I suppose it's the flair for drama within us."

"Well, you didn't always...I mean...how did you come to know how to...well, please a man?"

"I thought you were a widow. Weren't you married?"

"I am. I was." Edwina felt her cheeks burn. "Never mind."

"Oh, I grasp what's bothering you! You've only been with one man and Prescott Devane's had more than his share of women. Don't you worry about it, honey. I've heard him called 'London's Perfect Lover' so you're in good hands. Besides, don't ever forget that he may have dallied with them, but he's marrying you."

"Ah, thanks." Forcing a smile, Edwina lied, "That makes me feel much better."

Fanny removed her hands. "There. Have a look."

Obediently Edwina opened her eyes. "Oh, my heavens!" she cried, raising both hands to her mouth.

"Now let us get ready for your fiancé's visit."

Later that afternoon in Fanny's drawing room, Edwina couldn't help but admire the graceful way the former actress moved, as if her entire body was an artful accessory.

Fanny sank onto the bottle green chintz chaise, adjusted her aquamarine skirts and popped open a lacy black fan. "Stop fidgeting. And don't touch your brows. They look flawless."

Edwina lowered her hand and stood behind one of the two wide-backed olive chairs facing the grate. Sighing, she studied the dancing flames as she tried to ignore the nervous flutter in her belly.

Although she knew that rationally it didn't matter what Prescott thought of her or her appearance, she had to admit she wanted him to like her, if only a little. So they could get along during the ruse, of course.

"That woman, Mojgan, really has a talent," Edwina stated, for lack of anything else to say. Her hands strayed back to her thinned brow. "I confess, I had never imagined that ladies did such a thing."

"Any woman worth her salt knows she can't rely on nature." Fanny sniffed with a wave of her lacy fan. "It's all about enhancement."

Edwina didn't know if she truly believed Fanny's assessment, but had to admit her appearance was drastically altered. She'd hardly recognized the lady staring back at her in the mirror this afternoon.

A hint of musk filled the air and even though she

couldn't see him, Edwina felt Prescott's gaze on her back like a hot wind on a sultry evening.

Bracing herself, she turned.

Prescott's gaze widened. "Oh...my."

Chapter 11

Prescott tried to quell the sudden skip of his heart-beat. Whereas before, Edwina's face had merely been one that drew a second glance, now he was finding it hard to tear his gaze from her.

Edwina raised a hand to her hair. "Don't you like it?"

Chiding himself for not being more subtle about his reaction to her altered appearance, Prescott bowed. "I do like it. The style is becoming on you, Edwina."

Instead of the tight chignon, piles of ebony curls carefully adorned her head, giving her oval face a sense of proportion, which, in balance with her nose and chin, added appealing character to her features. Her dark brows had been shaped to accentuate her luminous eyes.

All in all, the effect was...striking, like a rare bird that catches your gaze with a flash of color and then mesmerizes with its natural splendor.

But all was not natural with Edwina's appearance. Prescott did not like the white powder covering her face, neck and shoulders. Nor did he favor the smudges of crimson delicately applied to her cheeks and mouth. To his eye, those changes were unnecessary and overdone, despite the artful application.

Edwina adjusted her sleeve. "The gown is very different from my usual attire. It takes some getting used to."

"It's perfect." He meant it. The dress was alluring, giving a hint of the bounty beneath, without being bawdy. The elegant cut accentuated the graceful curve of her swanlike neck, the width of her moon-pale shoulders, the ripe swell of her breasts and the small waist that a man could hold between his hands. Moreover, the royal blue shade was the ideal accent to her lovely skin and the unadorned silk just begged for a man to skim his hands over it. In all innocence, of course.

"Mr. Prescott Devane, I presume," came a singsong voice.

Tearing his gaze from Edwina, Prescott turned, noticing for the first time a lady in acquamarine. The woman had the studied grace of the great actresses who'd trod the boards, and with her flaming hair and crimson lips, there was only one person she could possibly be.

"Miss Figbottom, I presume." He bowed. "Prescott Devane at your service."

"My, oh, my, the stories haven't told the whole tale about you, darling." She was obviously a veteran in the art of flirtation. Gliding over to the bottle green chintz chaise, she sank down with a flourish of aquamarine ruffles, popped open her lacy black fan and languidly swayed it before lush crimson lips. "If my attentions weren't already engaged, I might just consider breaking my 'no redhead' rule."

"His hair is not red," Edwina murmured, fingering the lace of her sleeve. "It's auburn."

"Close enough," Miss Figbottom clucked.

Prescott raised a hand to his heart. "I feel honored that you would even consider the possibility, Miss Figbottom."

"Fanny, darling," she corrected with a wide smile. "You must call me, Fanny. I've heard so much about you, I feel as if I already know you."

Dr. Winner stepped into the parlor. "So good to see you again, Fanny, my dear." Moving over to the chaise, he accepted the actress's proffered hand and leaned over to plant a kiss. Straightening, he explained, "Sorry for the delay. Your man, Stanley, had sliced his hand in the kitchen and I wanted to check the dressing."

The woman's veil of coquetry fell away as she straightened and asked with obvious concern, "Is Stanley all right?"

"Oh, he's fine," Winner reassured, with a squeeze to her fingers. "It's a nasty cut, but it should heal soon enough."

Prescott noticed that the good doctor did not release Fanny's hand straightaway.

Sighing, the former actress leaned back. "Thank you, Michael. I appreciate you seeing to him. And I insist that you allow me to pay for your services."

"Very well," Dr. Winner readily agreed, surprising Prescott. Then the doctor's lips lifted into a smile. "Later I'll have some of that fancy cognac you were telling me about."

Fanny trailed her white-gloved hand across her powdered shoulder, leaving no doubt as to her intentions. "Oh that as well, darling."

Prescott had to give the woman credit; Fanny Figbottom certainly knew how to work with the hand she'd been dealt. Moreover, her environment was set to display her attributes to greatest advantage. Everything in the room, the walls, the furnishings, down to the rug of emerald waters, was a variant of the color green almost as if an accessory to the actress's attire.

Poor Dr. Winner didn't stand a chance. And by the puppy-dog look on the doctor's face, he didn't seem to mind in the least.

All in all, the room, the aquamarine ruffles, the crimson lips... left Prescott feeling as if he were being worked upon, a sensation he did not favor. He preferred his women less... contrived.

Turning, he noticed that, in contrast to Fanny's flamboyant display, Edwina seemed ill at ease. Her shoulders were set stiffly, her chin lifted as if preparing to receive a blow, her bare hands clenched before her so tightly her knuckles showed white. The rigid line of her lips did nothing to lessen the uncomfortable impression.

Tearing his attention from Fanny, Dr. Winner declared, "Why, I hardly recognized you, Lady Ross. You look beautiful!" Facing the actress once more, he added, "You're a genius, Fanny!"

Fanny preened. "I'm merely the sculptor..."

"It's unbelievable the difference!" Dr. Winner marveled. "Don't you think, Prescott?"

"It's an improvement." Tilting his head as if considering, Prescott couldn't help but tease, "Much needed, of course."

Edwina glared and Prescott was glad to see some of the fire back in her eyes.

Just then, Stanley appeared in the doorway, leading two servants into the room.

"How are you, Stanley?" Fanny leaned forward, concerned.

The stout carrot-headed butler smiled at his mistress, giving one the sense that he and his employer had a less formal relationship than most. "I am well, thank you." He nodded to the doctor. "Again, Dr. Winner, I'm much obliged to you."

"It was nothing," Dr. Winner dismissed. "Just keep it clean."

"I will be sure that he does," Fanny declared, with a henlike cluck.

Turning, Stanley directed as the servants set up the tea service.

Prescott strolled over to the hearth. A hearty fire flamed therein, adding a smoky aroma to the rose perfume scenting the air. Prescott assumed that it was Fanny's fragrance as, for some inexplicable reason, he doubted that Edwina would wear such a heavy scent. Wondering if she still wore lily of the valley, he stepped closer and was gratified to know he was right.

"How do you fare, my lady?" Prescott murmured, seeing that Dr. Winner and Fanny were engrossed in conversation.

"Well, thank you." She exhaled.

"You seem...ill at ease."

Looking up at him, she gave him a wobbly smile. "I'm just, well, unused to"—her hand motioned to her hair—"all of this. It seems a bit much, don't you think?"

Prescott had a rule when dealing with ladies; never say anything negative about a woman's appearance, no matter how true. But for some reason, he found himself yearning to tell Edwina exactly what he thought. Still, that little rule had served him well. "The truth?"

Biting her lip, she nodded. "Please."

"The gown is perfect, the hair quite becoming. But you don't need the powder or face paints. And your brows are nice, albeit a bit thin for my tastes."

She blinked. "You're certainly quite forthcoming."

Shrugging, he tilted his head. "You asked."

"I suppose I did." Edwina frowned. "Are you always this honest? For, if so, I would certainly do well to brace myself the next time I ask for your opinion."

Prescott felt his lips lift, but before he could reply, Fanny intoned, "Let us enjoy the tea before it grows cold."

The apple tarts were delicious, as was the tea. Top-rate; no reused tea leaves for Fanny Figbottom's guests. Prescott wondered how successful her "presentation" business was, given that there did not seem to be a well-heeled sponsor in the wings. Prescott knew that Dr. Winner didn't have the kind of blunt that a woman like Miss Figbottom usually required. Seeing how the two of them looked at each other, though, it was unlikely that finances entered into the equation.

Fanny, Dr. Winner and Prescott exchanged pleasantries, discussed the weather, gossip and the like, yet, all the while, Edwina remained silent. At most she gave a monosyllabic reply now and again. Had he insulted her with his frank assessment of her appearance? She hadn't seemed as concerned with her appearance as most of his acquaintances. Had he misjudged her?

Fanny rose with a fanfare of aquamarine ruffles. "If you will excuse us a moment? I would like a word with Edwina, if you please."

Quickly, the men jumped to stand. "Certainly."

Edwina set her teacup on the table and rose.

Fanny's gliding sway gripped Dr. Winner's attention, while Edwina moved like an automaton, all gears and levers within a royal blue gown.

Once the ladies were gone, Dr. Winner seemed to recover. Walking over to the doorway, he peered outside. "I can't see them. They must have turned the corner." Dr. Winner paced to the hearth and back again. "You must do something about Lady Ross, Prescott."

Prescott reclined into the green sofa. "What do you mean?"

"Something to make her less ill at ease. She can hardly project the image of lady in love if she can't relax around you."

Prescott scratched his forehead. "The lady obviously has no experience as an actress. Perhaps your Fanny can give her some tips?"

Winner's cheeks reddened. "She's not *my* Fanny..." He spun on his heel and paced back again.

"But she will be."

Stopping midstep, Dr. Winner turned, his russet eyes bright. "You think?"

"Undoubtedly."

A worried look entered Dr. Winner's brown gaze. "But I'm not a rich man, Prescott..."

"The woman doesn't seem to be in need of that kind of support. Moreover, she seems terribly interested in your attributes."

Dr. Winner beamed like a school lad who's just been told he has the summer to play. "I'll confess, I've been hoping…"

"Fanny is obviously enamored." Prescott tilted his head. "Unlike Edwina…"

Winner's lips sank into a frown. "You must fix this, Prescott. Even though it was an arranged marriage, Lady Ross came to feel quite deeply for her husband. During those last dark days for Sir Geoffrey, she refused to leave his bedside. She would not eat, she would not sleep. She was devoted to him and still evidences an ardent attachment seldom exhibited in young women these days." Dr. Winner exhaled. "She's a deep-feeling lady who clearly loved her husband so profoundly she refuses to even consider the possibility of remarrying. This ruse must be very difficult for her."

"But not for me, the shallow *cicisbeo* that I am…"

Winner scowled. "Don't be melodramatic, Prescott."

Exhaling loudly, Prescott nodded. "I suppose something must be done…" A sweet idea flashed in his mind. "I will speak with her, see if there's not something I can do." He smiled. "No doubt inspiration will come to me."

In the dormer down the hallway, Fanny rounded on her client. "I told you to remain cool with your fiancé, not act as if he has the plague!"

Edwina stared over Fanny's head, out the window behind. Green leaves jostled against the yellow stained glass as if vying for a better view of the discussion. "Our relationship is just fine…"

"Do you want to keep your fiancé or not?"

"Of course."

"For no man wants a lady wound tighter than a clock, one who's stiffer than a light post, as charming as a chill—"

"All right, I grasp your point." Edwina stared down at her gown, trying to explain, "I suppose I don't feel like...me in this attire. It all feels so...artificial."

Fanny's irritation was palpable. "It's a façade, but you don't change. That's the beauty of it; you control how you're perceived."

"I would like to be judged on what's here." She pressed her hand over her heart, then to her temple. "Or here. Not by the shape of my brows. To be frank, I am the kind of woman who values those things more than appearances."

Planting hands on hips, Fanny raised a brow. "And what 'kind of woman' do you think I am?"

Edwina blanched. "Wait, no...you can't think that I meant..."

"Well, what did you mean then, Edwina? Because it all sounds like Holy Willy nonsense from where I'm standing."

"I don't know," she moaned. "I don't understand it myself, Fanny..."

Biting her crimson lip, Fanny's eyes narrowed. Suddenly her eyes widened as if an idea burst upon her. "When was the last time the earth shook for you?"

Edwina blinked, uncomprehending.

"Oh, dear Lord in heaven." Fanny raised her arms skyward in supplication. "You need Prescott Devane more than I thought."

"What...what are you talking about?"

Lowering her arms, she grasped Edwina's hand. "Let us hope that his reputation is more fact than tales."

At that moment, Edwina felt as if Fanny was speaking in tongues. Her bewilderment must have shown on her face because Fanny explained, "What you need is a hot, salacious roll in the bedsheets until you and your fiancé have to peel your bodies apart."

Edwina felt her cheeks heat as she peered around the hall hoping that no servants overheard. "Uh, Prescott and I agreed...uh, not to engage in such...activity until after we're married."

"Oh fiddle!" Fanny waved a hand. "You're a widow, for heaven sakes!" She winked. "Where's the harm in a bit of play before the bells chime?"

"Uh, I...well, we agreed."

"But you need to loosen up if that's going to happen," Fanny went on as if Edwina hadn't spoken. "Else he won't believe you're interested enough to be his betrothed."

And neither would the rest of the world. Edwina started. "Oh, dear..." Her voice trailed off as she realized the importance of Fanny's expertise to make this ruse believable. She leaned forward. "What should I do?"

As Fanny scratched her chin, Edwina could almost see the wheels turning in her head. "Follow his lead. Sit near him whenever possible. Let him touch you. Be charming."

Edwina gnawed her bottom lip. "I'm not very good at charming..."

Tapping her chin, Fanny murmured, "What you really need is a tall helping of cognac."

"I don't imbibe..."

"Well, you'd better start."

Straightening, Fanny's eyes narrowed, and she

reminded Edwina of a general on a mission. "The Vaughns' ball will be your first outing in Society. That gives us two days to work on easing your nerves and helping you to embrace the 'new' you. Then, the night of the ball, I will come to your house and help you dress. Prescott Devane and the rest of Society are going to be turned on their heads. Or my name isn't Fanny Figbottom."

"I thought you said it was a stage name..."

Rolling her eyes, Fanny groaned, "Oh, do I have my work cut out for me."

Chapter 12

❧◦○◦❧

"She's late," Prescott muttered to the empty chamber as he helped himself to his second glass of brandy that evening. "I hate when a lady keeps me waiting."

Fanny sauntered into Edwina's salon in a splash of olive ruffles on black lace. The heavy scent of rose perfume floated around her like a bouquet. "Oh she's worth the delay, I assure you. She'll be the belle of the ball tonight."

"Not if we don't ever get there," Prescott replied, wondering at the nervous edge to his voice. He rarely suffered a bout of the nerves, since usually he didn't care one whit what anyone thought of him. But tonight felt different. To the world he would be an engaged man. And betrothed to the Earl of Wootton-Barrett's daughter.

He tossed back another swallow. What the hell had

he gotten himself into? Although he'd been out and about in Society, this was a whole new level of play. And if Edwina couldn't discover the actress within her, well, it might well become a farce.

Edwina.

The lady was turning out to be more multifaceted than he'd originally assumed, like a diamond that's held up in different lights exhibits new colors. No doubt she was as refined a lady as they came, but to also be hunting a blackmailer? A lady who was enamored of trade? President and founding member of a society which promoted the edification of females? Architect of charitable projects where the ladies actually met the beneficiaries of their work?

Janelle had waxed effusive on the society's latest endeavor, a prisoner reform program where she and the members of the society provided clothing and financial assistance to women just out of debtors' prison and helped them train for productive employ. The ladies of the society used their servants to conduct the training and oversaw the efforts themselves. Her success stories included seamstresses, dairymaids, scullery maids and the like. It was impressive, and reminded Prescott more than a bit of dear old Headmaster Dunn.

No doubt Dunn would have applauded Prescott for assisting Edwina in any way possible. For the first time in weeks, some of Prescott's grief was tinged with a hint of gladness.

Fanny sashayed over to stand beside him, her rose perfume wafting around them. "Tonight might be a bit...challenging for you and Edwina."

Setting his empty glass on the sideboard, he turned. "Just tonight?"

"We're outsiders, you and I, so I will speak plainly." Fanny tilted her head. "They'll never embrace you." She needn't explain the "they" that made up English Society.

"Of course they won't. But it won't matter, since they'll have to put up with me."

"In that regard you're wrong; it will matter. For all of Edwina's distinctiveness, she is but a creature of Society, and more importantly, the daughter of the Earl of Wooten-Barrett. Although she pretends to be independent, the girl yearns for her father's love and approval."

"Doesn't every child?" Prescott shrugged. "In my experience, respect and acceptance give love its legs."

"So you understand."

"Yes." But Edwina's relationship with her father wasn't his problem; stopping the blackmailer was. And if Edwina's scheme went as planned, he would never encounter the Earl of Wooten-Barrett. "I'm sure I can handle anything we come across tonight."

"Of course you will. Michael tells me that your skin's tougher than bear hide and you've a few sharp teeth of your own."

"I *think* there's a compliment in there..."

"Just remember that arrows that you can shrug off can pierce Edwina deeply."

"Arrows piercing me?" Edwina's voice floated across the room.

Prescott turned to the door. His heart skipped a beat.

Edwina stood in the entry, looking like an angel stepped out from a fresco to frolic with mere mortals. And like any angel's, her attire was audacious in its simplicity.

She wore a gown of diaphanous virgin white with shiny white silk bands gathering at just the right points to draw the eye to her willowy hourglass figure. The first band showed off her swanlike neck as it dipped over her moon-pale shoulders. The next gathered just beneath her breasts, accentuating the bounty any man would beg to explore. The remaining bands accentuated the graceful curve of her small waist and the arcing slope of her luscious derriere.

A matching glossy white band wove throughout her ebony curls, and her gloves each had a long strip of white silk traveling from wrist up her arm. She wore simple diamond cluster earrings, each arranged in the shape of a flower. She had no necklace or other adornment except a lacy white fan hanging closed at her wrist. All she needed were wings on her back and she'd be ready to fly to the heavens, or possibly carry a man there with her divine charms.

Notwithstanding Edwina's innocent attire, there was knowledge gleaming in those onyx eyes. Not worldliness, but a flash of intelligence that belied the angelic air. That, along with her lovely arched brows, aristocratic nose, smooth lips and pointy chin, made for a less than oh-so-sweet air. Her face had character, so much so that one could not doubt that she was a flesh-and-blood woman.

It was the juxtaposition that fascinated, he realized. One that would be heightened by the fact that the angelically dressed widow would have a fiancé on her arm tonight, a fiancé who was less than saintly.

Shaking his head, he let out a long breath, not realizing that he'd been holding it. Prescott bowed. "You look lovely, my lady."

"Thank you, Prescott." Edwina's voice was tight with tension.

He turned to Fanny and tilted his head. "My hat is off to you, Fanny Figbottom. You are a master."

The actress's smile was satisfied, like that of the cat who'd eaten the canary. "I was *inspired*."

"No young lady at her coming-out ball could look so enticingly chaste." Prescott grinned, suddenly looking forward to the rest of the evening; he was always up for a bit of a prank, especially when it was on the *ton*. "Eyes will bulge, tongues will wag. We'll be the scandal of the moment, my lady."

"What you will be," Fanny corrected, "is the *envy* of the moment. At the change in Edwina, the ladies will wonder at your charms, and the men will all wish that they'd pursued Edwina more vigorously." Her smile was wicked. "It will be glorious good fun."

"Fun." Edwina licked her pink-tinged lips. "That's an interesting perspective."

"It's the only one that will get you through. That and some very strong tipple." Fanny stepped over to the sideboard. "Now where did your servants put my...? Ah, here it is." She opened the cabinet and removed a crystal decanter filled with burgundy liquid and placed it upon a tray beside the three cut-crystal glasses.

Looking up at Prescott, Edwina silently mouthed, "It seems a bit over the top."

"Honestly?" he mouthed back.

Mutely, she nodded.

"It's perfect," Prescott spoke aloud. "You'll be the loveliest lady at the Vaughns' ball."

Edwina's brow seemed to lighten and her shoulders lifted. Timidly her gaze trailed from his low-heeled black shoes, to his black pantaloons, iron gray waist-coat, ivory neckcloth and black coat. Her eyes met his with a gratifying glint of approval. "You look very nice as well."

"Very nice?" Fanny rolled her eyes. "You're about as flirtatious as a nun."

"Edwina knows I prefer sincerity to disingenuous flattery," Prescott reassured, pleased just the same. He'd chosen his ensemble with care, opting for a more conservative mien than his usual bright colors. He and Edwina would be attracting enough attention as it was. Seeing her costume made him all the more satisfied with his choice.

Walking over to the mahogany table, Fanny set down the tray, lifted the carafe and poured. "You can't leave before we have a toast with my very special cognac."

"Cognac..." Prescott murmured, intrigued. He'd never tasted the libation; its importation was banned because of the war with Napoleon.

"Isn't this illegal?" Edwina asked. "I mean, this had to have been smuggled into the country, right?"

"The nun speaks again," Fanny teased. She handed out the glasses. "You need this more than the rest of us, so please simply keep your opinions to yourself and enjoy."

Poor Edwina, everyone was carping at her about being nervous.

Edwina stuck her nose into the glass and sniffed. "It smells smoky. Like burned oak."

Prescott inhaled. "It smells *rich*. And not in the moneyed sense."

Fanny raised her glass and Prescott and Edwina fol-lowed suit. "To your engagement." Fanny's hazel eyes twinkled. "May you enjoy the bountiful rewards of procreation."

Prescott's eyes met Edwina's and he couldn't help but smile. "Hear, hear."

She shot him a look of long-suffering.

He drank. Rich, yes, velvety fire.

Sipping the amber liquid, Edwina's eyes widened with pleasure. "Hmmm."

Prescott shifted, feeling that little hum a bit more than he should.

"Isn't there an interesting legend about cognac?" Edwina enquired, licking her lips. Prescott couldn't help but recall their soft feel and could just imagine the taste of the rich cognac on that sweet ripe mouth...

Edwina tilted her head. "It had something to do with infidelity, if I recall?"

Fanny's face became serious as if she recalled something unhappy. "Yes. There is." Seemingly collecting herself, Fanny's features lightened and she was all smiles and effusive charm once more. "Of infidelity or murder, which would you choose?"

"Oh, I would choose murder," Prescott sipped, tearing his mind from thoughts of Edwina's lips. "It's a more straightforward business."

"Must we select one at all?" Edwina inquired, moving over to stand by the hearth. The delicate scent of lily of the valley perfume filled the air.

"Well, the myth surrounding cognac has both," Fanny began in a singsong voice that accompanied all the best tales. "Legend has it a knight in the sixteenth century thought he would burn in hell once for murdering his unfaithful wife, and a second time for killing her lover."

"So he 'burned his wine' twice." Prescott nodded, trying to keep his mind on the story. "I'd heard that one."

"Yes, and put it in the far corner of the cellar. Whereupon he promptly forgot about it."

"Did he repent?" Edwina turned, her cheeks glowing with a pink flush. Somehow, the nose that had seemed too prominent and the chin that had seemed too pointy "fit" her face now and gave character to her countenance. But it was more than a change of hairstyle; it was likely knowing her as a person that made the difference.

In Prescott's experience, a visage rarely corresponded with the disposition of its wearer, but in this instance, it did. Edwina Ross had character and was unlike anyone he'd ever encountered before. With her do-good society, her zeal for justice, her passion for business and, he hoped, for other things...She was certainly more interesting than any ladies of his recent acquaintance. Yes, she was turning out to be a fine distraction, indeed.

"No, just the opposite." Fanny grinned wickedly. "Years later, upon finding the burned wine, he partook. And enjoyed."

Tearing his gaze from Edwina's features, Prescott shrugged. "I suppose the idea of a good nip overcame any fear of burning in hell."

"Yes." Fanny gestured to the glass in her hand. "And supposedly, that's how acidic poor wine was reborn as cognac."

Edwina smiled. "The story is completely untrue, of course. As all myths tend to be."

"As false as Lady Horton's pedigree," Fanny declared,

referring to the former opera singer who'd landed herself an aristocratic husband and thus a title for herself.

"And the truth?" Edwina tilted her head as interest gleamed in those striking onyx eyes.

"The wine was burned to gain cargo space for transport." Fanny sniffed. "And someone had the good sense to figure out that the longer it ages, the better it tastes."

Raising the glass to the candelabra on the table, Edwina stared at the amber liquid as it shimmered in the light. "How old is this cognac?"

"Aged twenty-five years."

Prescott let out a low whistle. "This is some *very* fine tipple."

"Yes," Fanny cooed. "Only the best to celebrate such a fortuitous match."

Edwina's eyes met his and he saw a twinkle of mischief within. She raised her glass. "To my betrothed, Prescott Devane. May he sire many sons."

Shaking his head, Prescott withheld his smile. It was an old toast, one that no doubt irked the president of The Society for the Enrichment and Learning of Females.

He lifted his glass in salute. "I look forward to siring those many sons, my dear. Was it nine or ten that you mentioned wanting?"

Edwina choked on her cognac. Two high spots of color infused her cheeks as her eyes widened with horror. "Uh...ten?"

"I'm wrong, it was only seven boys that you'd promised me. And given that you're not fresh out of the schoolroom, I suppose that we'd best get started on that right away."

Stepping closer, Edwina pasted on a smile. "We'd also agreed not until after we're married, *my dear*."

"Oh the trials of marrying an upstanding lady." He grinned. "I need to request that special license right away."

"You're unconscionable, you know that, don't you?"

He pressed his hand to his heart. "Oh, how you flatter me, my lady."

Fanny was watching them, a curious look in her eye.

Setting aside his glass, Prescott offered his arm to Edwina. "Shall we go, my dear? It's time for the world to meet Prescott Devane's fiancée."

Edwina tossed back the last of her cognac. "Heaven help us."

Chapter 13

As the carriage slowed to a crawl, the clatter of the horses' hooves and the grind of the turning wheels quieted. The muffled street sounds echoed inside Edwina's coach.

"We must be getting close to the Vaughns' house," Edwina murmured with a nervous glance out the partially covered window. The lamp outside cast a shadow across her pale face, making her seem even more ethereal than before.

"We have a few moments, yet," Prescott reassured, peering out the window and identifying the scenery. "We're only at Argent Street. The line is quite long this time of night."

She swallowed and exhaled slowly, her hands clutching her fan before her as if it were an anchor and she an unsteady ship. "I must confess, I'm not looking forward to being announced. Or making our way down that long staircase..."

"Oh, I have a plan for dealing with that..."

She raised a brow. "You have a plan?"

"You're not the only one who can hatch a scheme, my lady," he teased.

"Yes." Her tone was sober. "But will mine succeed?"

"You've had no word from the blackmailer, I presume?"

"Nay. I would have told you. Yet, I can't help but feel that he's out in Society, watching and waiting for his next opportunity to cause harm."

"Let us hope he is, so we can spy his François Millicent shoes."

Again, Prescott wondered at the secret the blackmailer was holding over her head. Suddenly an image of Cat rose up in his mind. It still stung that she didn't love him enough to confide in him and share her terrible plight. Yet, sitting across from him in the carriage sat Edwina, a woman who'd sought him out in facing her troubles. What did Edwina Ross see in him that Cat hadn't?

Pushing aside the useless musings, Prescott forced himself to focus on his distraction, the intriguing Edwina Ross. He'd wanted an opportunity to see if the mystery of Edwina's kiss was real. What was he waiting for, a written invitation?

"It's funny, actually," Edwina murmured.

"What?"

"Ever since my husband died I've sworn never to remarry, and yet here I am, about to don the nuptial yoke once more." Suddenly realizing how that might sound,

Edwina felt the need to add, "I just meant to the outside world. I *know* it's not real."

Edwina pressed her lips together, praying she wouldn't say anything else so stupid. Lord, she was nervous. And her nerves certainly weren't helped by being alone in a small space with Prescott for the last fifteen minutes. And she wished he'd stop shooting her those searing glances that made her belly flip in the most stirring manner.

"It's quite warm in here, isn't it?" she asked breathlessly.

"It feels good to me." His rumbling voice roused her heart to quicken.

Oh how the man practically oozed charm, and he'd hardly been trying. What would happen when he was acting the attentive fiancé? He would only be pretending, of course. But just the idea of clutching his well-muscled arm, moving about with him on the dance floor, thigh pressed to thigh...

"What's wrong?" Prescott asked.

"Ah, nothing. Why do you ask?"

"You whimpered as if something ailed you."

"I'm fine." She looked away. Thank heavens he couldn't read her thoughts. If he could...

She'd spent hours going over that kiss again and again, like a song that she couldn't get out of her head. The brush of his lips to hers, how she clung to his broad chest, his muscled thigh pressing between her legs...As her fiancé would he...?

There will be no kissing! Sir Geoffrey, think of Sir Geoffrey!

Prescott leaned forward. "You're frowning. Pray tell me, what's bothering you, Edwina?"

"I, ah, I was just..." Think, Edwina, think! "...musing on what a terrible actress I am and...wondering if you have any tips for me." She swallowed. "Do you, ah, have any advice as to how it is appropriate for me to act tonight?"

"Well, I suppose the best thing to do is to follow my lead and do as I say."

Edwina straightened. "Just because I'm a bit green at pretenses doesn't mean I'm about to hand over the reins, so to speak."

"I'm not being arrogant, Edwina. It's all about the plan."

Pressing her hands together before her, she pursed her lips. "How so?"

"You're supposed to be in love with me, right?"

"Yes. But that doesn't mean I become your lapdog."

"Look, Edwina. A woman in love typically behaves in one of three fashions." He raised three fingers, ticking them off. "Either she purposefully ignores her lover to keep the relationship secret or in an attempt to manipulate him. Or she publicly flouts her lover's wishes, again, in an attempt to manipulate him. Or she does everything in her power to please her lover, because his pleasure gratifies her, or again, she wishes to manipulate him."

"There's certainly a lot of manipulation going on," she muttered under her breath, as her irritation quieted. He wasn't trying to order her about, and there was a certain ring of truth to his depictions. She'd definitely seen enough of such tactics between her mother and father.

"Women can't help it; it's second nature." He shrugged one of those burly shoulders as if it was obvious.

"What? Manipulation? On that point, we must disagree. But I do see how ignoring you won't further the plan. And flouting you...well, I'm hardly a decent enough actress to behave in such a hotheaded manner. Aside from the fact that it goes against my very nature to be so foolish."

"Nay." His teeth flashed white in the darkness. "I don't see you as one for melodramatic episodes."

She nodded, gratified. "I should certainly hope not."

"You're more one for a ripping good tongue-lashing, I'd think. Straight across the bow."

"If you are intimating that I am straightforward, then I'll have to concur." Snapping open her fan, Edwina fluttered it about her face and assumed a good-humored censorious tone. "As for the proper tongue-lashing, you only get one if you deserve it."

"Promises, promises," he teased.

His smile across the coach felt like a warm blanket settling over her and she couldn't help but grin in return. Heavens, she couldn't believe she was flirting, *and enjoying it*!

The carriage swayed to a stop and Prescott turned to peer out the window. His handsome face was cast in silhouette. Edwina's heart skipped a beat; he was so lovely to behold, no wonder so many didn't notice his other attributes. It was difficult to see past that shiny auburn hair, the easy smile...those deliciously sensual lips...

Edwina's hand rose to her mouth, where the remembrance of his kiss still lingered.

No more thinking about that kiss! Sir Geoffrey! Sir Geoffrey! She dropped her hand and folded her fingers together in her lap. "Aside from following your lead, are there any particular…gestures, physical actions that a woman in love uses when she is with her… ahem…the man?"

Slowly his head bobbed. "That's a very astute point. I would say…looking at her lover frequently. Not in a terribly overt way. More like stolen glances and such."

"Stolen glances." She nodded. "I can do that. Anything else?"

"Nearness. Standing, sitting and the like, just a bit too close for what's appropriate. And leaning, of course."

"Leaning?"

"Here, let me show you." Rising from his seat, he set aside his cane and sat beside her, his nearness causing a delicious flutter in her middle. She forced herself not to move away.

Pretense, she reminded herself. *He's pretending for the plan.*

"Look up at me." Gently he lifted her chin with his finger.

She swallowed, meeting his gaze. Seeing the passion blazing within his eyes, her belly flipped. *He's an astoundingly good actor.*

"Now lean."

"Lean?" She hated the breathless quality to her voice, but knew she could hardly help it; the man was practically on top of her.

"Like this." Releasing her chin, he cupped her shoulders and gently drew her closer. "It's a slight tilt from the waist."

"But one wouldn't…" *Kiss.* "I mean this is so very public…" *To kiss.* "It would be scandalous…" *To steal a kiss.*

"Remember." His voice was deep, throaty. "There is always the promise between lovers."

"Of what?" Her voice was barely a whisper.

"A kiss." Prescott's head lowered, so close Edwina could almost taste his cognac-scented breath.

This wasn't happening, it couldn't be. Prescott couldn't want...

A memory of Sir Geoffrey reared in her mind. Her husband had pulled back from her, exclaiming, "Just stop it! Stop it, I say! This is unpleasant for the both of us, so why don't we just dispense with this nonsense?"

"Non...nonsense?" she'd asked, her lips still stinging from where his teeth had smashed.

"This business is unnecessary between man and wife."

"Business? You mean kissing?" Disappointment had shafted through her; kissing had been one of the activities she'd been dreaming about enjoying once she was married.

He'd turned away from her then. "Don't speak like a harlot."

She'd stiffened, defensive. "You're my husband, for heaven sakes. There's nothing wrong—"

"What's 'wrong' is how you do it," he'd interjected, his tone scathing. "You don't know what you're doing and it makes it, well, to be frank, *disgusting*. If you try to do it again, I fear I won't be able to look at you in that way ever again. Do you want that? Do you?"

"No," she'd whispered, tears of humiliation burning the backs of her eyes. To repulse him so, she had to be the most terrible kisser on the face of the planet.

The scent of cognac brought Edwina back to reality. Prescott's head lowered.

Edwina gasped, rearing back.

He released her. "Is my touch so abhorrent to you, my lady?"

"No...of course not."

"Then why do you jump as if I'm a leper?"

She swallowed, hating the hurt she heard in his voice. "It's not you. It's me."

Moving to sit on the opposite bench, he crossed his arms. "I've used that line and know how absurd it really is."

"It's just, I'm not like the other ladies of your acquaintance," she replied lamely. "I'm just not." *The other ladies didn't repulse the men they wanted to entice.*

"You said that already." His tone was derisive. "In the woods."

Her mind scrambled as her cheeks burned. "Ah... what I meant was, this is a nasty business and if we're to handle it well, then we need to treat it like a business."

"Like a business?" His contempt was palpable, filling the small carriage with its heat, making Edwina so uncomfortable she shifted in her seat.

"Yes. We're partners, so to speak, and need to maintain our business integrity. To keep us clearheaded. Keep our eyes on the target." Was she babbling? She never babbled. "Maintain our focus."

"This is what you want? For the two of us who are supposed to be engaged to behave like business partners?"

"Yes." She swallowed. "It's for the best."

"What utter rot. But if it's what you want, very well then." Adjusting his hat and slinging his cane under his arm, he leaned over and grabbed the door handle.

"What are you doing?" she cried as the carriage pitched forward.

"Getting out."

Panic overcame Edwina. "But we've not yet arrived!"

With the carriage still rolling, Prescott stood and opened the door. His anger was still perceptible, pulsing off him in waves.

"We've not even stopped!"

With the door partially opened, Prescott studied the passing street. "You didn't want to be announced. Or have to come down the main stairs. So we will go this way. It's part of my plan. Unless my *business partner* has a problem with it?"

He'd said "we." He wasn't deserting her. But he wanted her to leap from a moving carriage? Was this some sort of reprisal?

The coach slowed and gently rolled to a halt.

Turning, he held out his gloved hand. "My lady?"

Her heart was racing and her mouth dry from anxiety. He was the one taking liberties, so why did she feel so guilty? Because she'd hurt him and hadn't meant to. Oh, how she wished she'd handled things better! It was all such a bloody mess, making Edwina feel like a fish out of water. A feeling she despised.

"We don't have all night," he ground out.

Well, the carriage wasn't exactly moving, but it certainly could...And there were no footmen to set a stool or lend a hand. "But what of my driver and my footmen?"

"I'll have a word with them when we alight. They'll be happy to join their waiting comrades with the other coaches sooner rather than later." He waited, his gloved hand still extended. "Are you coming with me or not?"

Did she trust him? Was she willing to follow Prescott Devane?

Hesitantly she placed her hand in his.

Chapter 14

❦

Still holding Edwina's hand, Prescott bounded out the door in one fluid motion and down to the cobblestoned street. Then, without missing a beat, he reached for her, grasping her about the waist and lowering her to the ground as if she were lighter than cotton. He promptly released her, stepping over to speak with her driver.

"Oh." Edwina was so disoriented, it took her a moment to catch her breath. Never in her life had she exited a carriage in such a fashion.

Edwina could hardly overhear Prescott's exchange with her driver Joseph as she willed her erratic heartbeat to slow. Joseph nodded to Prescott, tipped his hat to her and then called to the horses. The carriage peeled away from the line of coaches heading toward the Vaughns' residence.

Prescott re-joined her and extended his arm. "Ready,

my lady?" His tone was tight with contained anger. Her guilt flared, and along with it, a whisper of disquiet at trusting herself to someone so cross with her.

She tried to ignore the flutter in her middle as she nodded. "Uh, yes, of course."

He guided her away up to the curb and together they walked along the line of coaches waiting to pull up at the Vaughns' house. Pools of light shined on the sidewalk from the windows above as they passed the houses lining the street. The odors of pine, horse, leather and manure permeated the evening air.

Prescott's silence was like a vise, causing Edwina's chest to ache with guilt and worry. Were her plans in disarray before they'd even begun? But word of the engagement had already spread and it was too late to stop now. Aside from the dowager's visit, Edwina had fielded two calls from disbelieving friends already. And Ginny needed them. But how to repair the damage with Prescott?

"Ah, I didn't mean to offend you, Prescott," Edwina murmured. "I just, well, the ruse of the engagement only needs to be employed when we're in public."

"Perhaps I thought you could use the practice." His tone was sardonic.

Reminded of the shame of Sir Geoffrey's rejection, she bristled. "How dare you? I'm a widow! I was married!" Her voice pitched with anger, far preferable to the guilt. "Just because your morals are looser than a courtesan's ties doesn't mean that the rest of the world suffers your lack of principles!"

By the light from the window, hurt flashed in his emerald gaze, quickly veiled. He stopped short. And then something indefinable changed within him.

He straightened. His shoulders squared. His face darkened. His jaw set into a determined line. Any sense of languor fell away, leaving a fierce, determined man to be reckoned with.

Releasing her, Prescott turned to face Edwina. The impression of a lion hit Edwina full force, but now, she finally realized, that this was not a beast to be caged or handled, and certainly not to be toyed with. She had to resist the urge to step back.

"I can be insulted by hundreds of others," he growled, towering over her. "I needn't suffer it from you." He moved to step past her.

"Wait!" she cried, placing a hand on his arm.

Shrugging her off, he headed in the opposite direction from the Vaughns' residence.

Grabbing her skirts, Edwina dashed in front of him, blocking his course. She pressed her hands to his chest and held firm. It was like pushing a stone balustrade.

He froze. Then, with frightening intensity, he glared down at her hands. "I thought you couldn't stand my touch."

"Please, just give me a moment to explain."

It seemed there was some semblance of benevolence left within him because, thank heavens, he didn't move. He stood, arms slightly raised by his sides, legs apart, body squared, reminding Edwina of a boxer ready for a brawl. Slowly, she stepped back as her mind scrambled for some way to repair the damage.

"I...I'm sorry," she murmured. "What I said...I didn't mean it and it was uncalled for."

Her apology was met by the sounds of carriage wheels and horses as they moved past.

She swallowed. "I didn't mean to offend you."

"How can a lowly orphan like me be offended? Aren't we made of gingerbread?" His tone was derisive, referencing the old children's tale.

The hollow pit of shame sank deeper in her belly. "You surprised me, that's all." She shook her head. "I know...I realize now...that you didn't mean to kiss me. Not for real. You were only helping with the ruse." She looked away. "And I probably actually do need the practice."

With her heart racing with anxiety, she waited for some semblance of a response. But nothing came. He stood there as if carved from stone.

Hesitantly, she looked up and met his gaze. Those emerald eyes were like firestorms, barely contained. It took every ounce of Edwina's self-control not to look away, she was so ashamed. "I implore you to look past my...utter stupidity and continue to help me."

"Why?"

She blinked. "Why what?"

"If my very presence is so offensive to you, why did you pick me to help you at all? And don't give me any of your nonsense about being perfect for the job. You knew this plan of yours would require us to pretend to be lovers. Yet you jump at my very touch."

"I suppose...I suppose I picked you because I *wouldn't* find your presence offensive."

A look of derision entered his stormy gaze.

"No, I mean it, Prescott. I respect you and know that I couldn't pretend otherwise with someone I didn't."

"I've never heard such bloody poppycock in all my life." He stepped around her and strode down the street.

"I do respect you!" She rushed to follow, dashing

alongside him. "I respect the fact that you come from humble beginnings but are not ashamed of your past. That you've developed a stronger character from the experience."

Maneuvering so that she didn't fall down an under-staircase, Edwina bustled alongside him. "I respect the fact that you are working to improve your life, that you make choices and make no excuses for them. You are who you are and make no apology for it."

Was it her imagination or were his steps beginning to slow?

"I'm impressed by your ability to deal with people, when I feel like I botch up so many of the relationships I care about."

She licked her lips. "It is because I respect you I feel I can go through this whole charade, plot, ruse, whatever you may call it... with some semblance of... respect for myself. With some sense that I am allied with some-one... reliable."

He stopped short, facing her, anger darkening his handsome features. "Is that how you see me? As reli-able?"

Pressing her hand to her chest, she tried catching her breath. "As much more than that... I feel like with you, I'm not so very much..." She swallowed. "On my own."

"On your own? You've a family, money, friends, hell, you have a whole bloody society."

"Yes, but this blackmail business, it's all up to me." Her shoulders sagged with the weight of her worry for Ginny and all that would befall her and Judith if the truth of Ginny's affair and Judith's parentage came to light. "If I fail, then... well, it's all up to me to ensure that it doesn't. I feel like a dam holding back an on-slaught of water. I'm not strong enough and need your support."

She pressed her hands together in entreaty. "I need you, Prescott. And yes, you are perfect for the job because you are the only man I can imagine even *pretending* to be engaged to."

"I suppose I should feel flattered," he scoffed.

"As far as your touch...well." She looked away. "I wasn't lying, I'm not like the other ladies of your acquaintance. I'm not built for...passion. I'm not good at it and don't know how to handle it." She winced. "Which is obvious from how poorly I acted in the carriage."

His brow furrowed. "Not built for passion? I've never heard of such a thing."

"Well, it's true. And frankly, I'm a bit embarrassed by it." She wanted to close her eyes to ward off the mortifying confession, but it was too late now, the truth was out there, bared for Prescott Devane to see.

His mouth opened and closed as if he was going to say something. Then instead, he reached for her, seizing her wrist and drawing her into an alcove eclipsed by darkness.

Gripping her waist, he pulled her close, up against his hard, virile form.

Her heart jumped, her mouth dried. "Ah...what are you doing?"

"Consider it an experiment."

Then his head lowered and his lips pressed down to hers.

Edwina stiffened, waiting for him to be repulsed.

"This is not a tooth extraction, Edwina." His lips

softened, teasing her mouth with gentle kisses. "Please try to relax and enjoy it."

Relax and enjoy it! How could she when she was about to expose herself to the ultimate humiliation?

His hand began to move in little swirls on her back, feeling really, really good. She liked the smell of him, the musk and man and a hint of cognac. His lips were so soft and did the most delicious things to her mouth. Those innocent kisses really were quite nice. She shivered.

Gently his lips urged her mouth open, moist, confident and . . . not so very innocent anymore.

Hesitantly she parted her lips, tasting cognac and, oddly, cinnamon. It was positively . . . decadent. A heady delight. Very, *very* nice.

His tongue touched hers. A lightning bolt of desire flashed through her so shockingly she gasped. Before she could think, he pulled her closer, deepening the kiss. His tongue entwined with hers, in a dance so seductively intimate, she groaned, closing her eyes.

His hands drifted to the arch in her back and she felt her body pitch against him. Heat unfurled in her middle and her skin flushed as if bathed in warm water.

His palms lowered to cup her derriere and desire flashed between her thighs, hot, fierce and demanding. Her insides were melting, her body aflame. She clutched him, gripping his shoulders as if never to let him go. Her soft breasts were crushed against his superfine coat and she felt the evidence of his desire pressing against her belly. Nothing had ever felt so fantastic in all her life.

He was like an elixir that melted her from within, molten heat transforming her mind to mush and her body into a puddle of fiery sensation.

Her world collapsed into itself, leaving only the darkness, his fervent embrace, the feel of his tongue gliding over hers, his lips teasing, sucking, flooding her mouth with pleasure as his hard body pressed against hers.

His hand kneaded her bottom, grinding her against him. Her muscles clenched with desire. Beneath her skirts, her legs parted, wanting him, needing him... everywhere.

His hand slid to her side, then glided up to cup her breast in his palm. She gasped for breath and her head fell against his shoulder as her heart raced and her body flamed.

Streams of pleasure coursed from that breast through her veins to every part of her body, making her blaze. Through the thin gown, he kneaded the soft flesh, gently drawing her hard nipple into his fingers and then massaging the tight nub. Her heart was hammering, her breath coming in half gasps, and a liquid heat burned within her as desire pulsed in her womanly core.

She shifted restlessly, wanting—no needing—more of him. Unabashedly, she reached for his face and drew his lips down to hers once more. His mouth was hot, wet, and inspired a hunger in Edwina she'd never known existed.

Suddenly he gripped her arms and pulled away, breathing hard.

"I didn't mean for it to go so far..." he gasped.

She blinked, her mind muddled, her heart racing and her body still thrumming with desire. "Far...?"

Their panting echoed loudly in the silent alcove.

"So you're not built for passion, eh?" he gasped as if having run a long race.

"Oh my heavens." She blinked. "What the blazes?"

He straightened. "I, my dear Edwina," he said, a self-satisfied ring to his voice, "just disproved your theory."

"Smashed it to bits, more like it," she murmured, dazed with wonderment.

Smiling, he grabbed her hand and pulled her back to the street. "*Now* we can go to the ball."

"Ball? I think I need to sit down." Either that or he could haul her back into his arms. . . .

Pulling her into the light, he faced her and fixed her cowl. "There. You look fine. None the worse for wear."

No worse for wear? Her world had just been spun on its axis.

Pressing a kiss to her forehead, he grinned like the cat who'd licked the cream. "Come along, Edwina. We have a blackmailer to catch."

Ginny. How could she forget?

As she trailed alongside him, Edwina could no longer doubt she was in over her head.

But it was too late now; they were headed into the lion's den.

Chapter 15

Drawing Edwina up alongside him, Prescott guided her toward the Vaughns' abode, where evidence of the ball going on inside escaped from the open windows. Light from what seemed like a thousand candles spilled out onto the street and the sounds of an animated crowd and the chords of a minuet competed with the clattering horses' hooves and raucous drivers and servants outside.

As Edwina fell in step beside him, she recognized that Prescott had shortened his stride to complement hers. It was likely a tactic he used with all of his lady companions. The thought rankled even though it shouldn't.

She knew getting into this that Prescott Devane was no saint. Moreover, it was probably his vast experience with women that had enabled him to ignite her heretofore unknown passion.

The kiss, although earth-shattering to her, had obviously meant little enough to him.

Edwina couldn't decide if she was relieved or upset by the thought.

Regardless, she needed to keep her mind on the plan, as he so gallingly did. The kiss that had rattled her senses had left him seemingly unfazed. She should be happy he wasn't easily distracted. Thankful that he could keep his mind sharp, his senses keen, and the blackmailer foremost in his mind. Unlike how she'd forgotten about... well, everything, in the heat of that passionate kiss.

And she'd especially forgotten that her kisses were supposed to be repulsive.

Her mind still whirled with the revelations that she might just be built for passion after all. That she might actually appeal to a man, and a man who knew quite a lot about desire. Heady, mind-boggling, knee-melting desire...

Oh, Lord, if she didn't stop lingering on that kiss, she'd likely go mad and not do Ginny a bit of good.

Purposefully, she pushed the whole matter from her mind, trying not to notice how her skirts kept brushing up against Prescott's muscled thigh.

Ginny. She'd think of Ginny.

Prescott guided Edwina toward the alley running beside the Vaughns' house. As servants walked to and fro carrying various supplies, a few shot curious glances their way.

As they penetrated the muck-scented lane, the sounds of the street diminished behind them and the music spilling from the windows above signaled that the orchestra had moved on to a Scottish reel.

"We're not taking the servants' entrance are we?" she asked, somewhat horrified. On the night of the ball it would be a veritable thoroughfare on market day and they would be the focus of hundreds of questioning eyes.

"No," he reassured. "It would be too busy. And too overt." He guided her into a recess with a closed door and banged on the wooden entry with his knuckles.

As they waited in the darkness, Edwina couldn't help but feel a strange excitement; jumping from a carriage, stolen kisses in an alcove, secret entrances, well, it all felt so...illicit.

Suddenly the sounds of the bolt sliding in the barrel could be heard. The door creaked slowly open and light streamed into the passage.

Edwina blinked in the sudden glare, then a giant hulking form filled the entryway, blocking out any light from inside. She moved to step back, but Prescott pressed a hand over hers and held her closely to his side.

A sudden irrational thought flashed in her mind: She was alone in a darkened alleyway with Prescott and a giant stranger. What was she getting herself into?

"Don't worry, my lady," Prescott leaned over and whispered. "He's a friend."

The reassuring tenor of his voice and the knowledge of everything she knew about Prescott eased her qualms. But only somewhat. She reminded herself that she, and only she, was responsible for her safety and resolved to maintain her guard.

"Hello, Tomlin," Prescott hailed.

The man stepped farther into the passage and the light spilled out of the doorway illuminating him in a dim halo.

Edwina had to crane her neck as the man had to be one of the largest specimens Edwina had ever seen. He stood at least two full heads taller than Prescott, but it was hard to tell the man's exact height because of the lofty puff of wiry jet-black hair piled on top of his enormous head. A jaunty white cap perched in the black hair reminded Edwina of how a bird might sit in a bristly nest. It matched his white uniform, whose only adornment was gold embroidery on the high, stiff collar and cuffs.

The man's tea-skinned face was broad, just like the rest of him and upon seeing Prescott, his wide lips split into a yellow-toothed grin. "Upon my 'onor! It's the famous Prescott Devane!" The man's booming voice was so deep it sounded as if it was tumbling from a mountain.

Tomlin slapped a beefy hand to Prescott's back and Prescott barely held back a wince. "When Val told me you was coming, I almost busted a seam in me fancy new uniform." He gestured to his gold-embroidered white coat. "Like it?"

"Sally must love washing the chocolate stains out of that," Prescott replied.

"His lordship has his laundress cleaning my uniforms. And Sally's thrilled to be done with it. Thinks it's Christmastide every day, she does."

Prescott pursed his lips and nodded, seemingly impressed. "That's a sure sign you're moving up, Tomlin."

The man's great shoulders lifted in a shrug. "Things are better 'n yesterday, but who's ta say—"

"Not as good as tomorrow," Prescott finished for him.

The men shared a smile.

Edwina realized that there was an easiness between them, one she hadn't witnessed when Prescott was with Dr. Winner or Fanny. She wondered how they knew each other.

Tomlin scowled. "But why didn't ya come to me party?"

"I was feeling a bit...under the weather."

Even though Prescott had an amazing excuse, an injury from saving a young girl's life, he didn't seem to make much of it. Interesting.

Tomlin pointed a sausagelike finger at Prescott. "Next year then. But no excuses, naw. We go too far back ta let things fade."

"I wouldn't miss it for the world."

To Edwina, the big man explained. "Prescott 'ere, 'e's the one who made me go back into the kitchen when all the other lads were calling me 'Tomlin the Tartlet' and 'Pastry Fingers' an' a lot of other things I can't say in yer fine company. 'E tol' me the same wretches that made fun o' me would soon be beggin' for a taste o' the crumbs from my plate."

"You're 'Little Tom,' the famous pastry cook!" Edwina suddenly realized.

"So you've heard of him?" Prescott asked.

Recalling what Janelle had said, she gushed, "My friend told me that your pastry temple ruins could rival Rome's and that they tasted positively decadent."

The great man beamed. "The Lewiston grand dinner last month. That was one of my better *Pièces Montrés.*"

"Not as good as the one you made for Headmaster Dunn's birthday, I'm sure." Prescott turned to Edwina, his handsome face animated in the dim light. "It was magnificent. An exact replica of Andersen Hall, gates, stables, dairy and all. I've never seen anything like it." Prescott shook his head, obviously amazed. "He made the staff of Andersen Hall out of marzipan. It was brilliant!"

Tomlin cackled. "Getting that sour expression on the miniature Mrs. Nagel was the toughest part!"

Prescott grinned. "I don't know how you got the broom in her hand..."

"Landing right on Timmy's head!" Tomlin chuckled and his great shoulders shook.

"Do you remember when Headmaster Dunn ate himself?" Prescott beamed so widely his face looked younger, freer. "The kids screamed with merriment!"

"It was a fine day." Tomlin nodded, smiling. Then his face fell and his brow furrowed. He sighed. "A fine... day."

Heavy silence draped over them like a shroud as Prescott's and Tomlin's gazes locked in soundless empathy.

Prescott was the first to look away as he coughed into his fist. "I'm around you for a few moments, Tomlin, you big oaf, and I completely forget my manners." Not meeting her eye, he gestured to Edwina. "Lady Ross, may I introduce Tomlin Burk, pastry cook extraordinaire."

Tomlin bowed. "At yer service, me lady."

Edwina nodded, feeling an ache in her chest for the loss these men shared. "I know it may sound trite, but anyone who knew Headmaster Dunn is now all the poorer for his loss."

Tomlin nodded. "'E was as good as they come, my

lady. As good as they come." He fixed a hard gaze on Prescott. "I heard about Catherine."

Edwina felt Prescott stiffen.

" 'Twas a shock ta be sure. But part o' me ain't surprised." Tomlin opened his hands wide. "How are you—"

"Thanks for letting us in this way, Tomlin," Prescott interrupted. "I didn't want to be announced. You know how I hate drawing attention to myself."

The big man nodded, seemingly accepting Prescott's rebuff. "Oh, I'm glad to see ya, Devane. Even though, as usual, y'er going where y'er not invited."

It was nice how Prescott took the blame for her not wanting to be announced. But more importantly, who was Catherine and why was Prescott so uncomfortable discussing her?

Tomlin smiled at his friend. "Look, I gotta get back. I've got soufflés in the oven. Sally's been askin' after ya. When can I tell her you'll be comin' by again?"

"Her birthday's in a few weeks. How about then?"

The big man wagged a meaty finger. "I'm holdin' ya to it, Prescott Devane."

Prescott's handsome face split into a smile, not as full as before but it carried great warmth. "I'll be there with bells on, Tomlin. So long as Sally does the cooking. I'll not be eating any of the rubbish you call food."

"Oh, don't ya worry. She don't let me in her kitchen. 'Ere I'm the king o' my domain. At home I'm lucky if I get ta wash a spoon!" the man complained, but looked pleased as pudding with the situation.

Raising a brow, Prescott gestured to the house with his cane. "Don't you have soufflés that need tending?"

Tomlin waved a meaty hand. "Oh, be off with ya. Follow this corridor, then make yer first left, up the stairs, then follow the music to get to the main ballroom." Turning to Edwina, Tomlin jerked his thumb at Prescott. "Watch yerself with this one, me lady. 'E has a way of gettin' ya into fixes"—he winked—"that y'er glad he dragged ya into!"

Grinning, he turned on his heel and lumbered back down the hallway, turned a corner and was gone.

Shaking his head, Prescott chuckled. "Big oaf."

Edwina was fascinated by this aspect of Prescott. Discovering the many aspects of his character was like peeling away at the layers of an onion, but without the tears or smelly hands. These intriguing glimpses into his life before, and his character now, only heightened her already voracious curiosity about this man. "You and Tomlin, you grew up together at Andersen Hall?"

"Sally, too. They're fine people."

"Is Catherine someone you grew up with as well?"

The arm beneath her hand flexed and his face seemed to harden. "She's of no consequence."

Although his tone brooked no opposition, she found herself probing further, like an itch that must be scratched. "Was she likewise at Headmaster Dunn's birthday celebration?"

He looked away. "If you must know, she works at Andersen Hall. She's on the staff there, just like Mrs. Nagel."

Edwina somehow doubted that Catherine was like Mrs. Nagel. His reaction stirred her already curious nature and a slight twinge of something unfamiliar stung like a poison in her heart. "Yet, you call her by her Christian name."

He was quiet a long moment, then sighed with a mock sense of being put out. "You, my lady, are very dogged. And just as astute. Mrs. Nagel will forever be the stern woman who smacked me over the head with a broom whenever I misbehaved. Which was quite often, I might add. Catherine grew up at Andersen Hall and now helps manage the place. So it is hard to think of her as . . . Mrs. Dunn."

Mrs. So she was married. The tightness inside Edwina's chest eased and she felt better somehow. Not that it really mattered, did it? "Dunn? Is she related to Headmaster Dunn?"

"Yes. She's married to his son." He motioned to the open door. "Now, stop stalling and let us go inside and have a merry old time. Shall we?"

Had she been stalling? Perhaps that was the reason for her strange reaction to Mrs. Catherine Dunn.

Edwina stared at the open doorway a moment, suddenly mindful of all that lay ahead. Self-consciously she adjusted her hair.

"Tomlin is the only ogre in the building, Edwina," Prescott gently teased. "Upon my honor." He rested his free hand across his heart. "No one will dare try to eat you while I'm on duty."

Despite her anxiety about the ball, she couldn't help her lips from lifting at the corners. "I suppose I'm unused to playing the damsel in distress . . . Prescott."

"Oh, but you must, for the escapade to begin. All the best tales have a lady in need of rescuing. It gives the hero something to do. Else he'd be sitting around dram-drinking and playing dice. Now where's the adventure in that?"

Earth-spinning kisses, jumping from carriages, secret

entrances and giant pastry cooks...He was right. Being with Prescott Devane was like an adventure. And if she treated the night as merely an exciting escapade, then perhaps it wouldn't be so awful after all. She certainly had a wonderful escort...

Nodding, Edwina moved toward the candlelit doorway and let him lead her inside.

Chapter 16

❧❧❧

"Ah, there you are, Edwina."

Lifting her hands from the stone balustrade overlooking the moonlit gardens, Edwina turned. "Ginny! So good to see you." She couldn't quite hide the relief from her voice.

Ginny's arthritic hip must have been bothering her; she leaned heavily on a cane for support as she crossed the veranda, her peach-colored skirts swooshing with every step.

Janelle followed close behind, waving her lacy fan about like a weapon. "We've been looking for you in every blasted corner of that ballroom and yet you choose to hide out in the darkness?"

There was plenty of light shining through the French doors and open windows to illuminate the stone terrace, but Edwina didn't say so. Ever since Prescott had made Edwina aware of Janelle's vulnerabilities, it had

158

been much easier to be forbearing. Probably because it came from her own wish to be so, and not simply to placate Ginny.

"I was hoping for a little quiet," Edwina explained.

Janelle shoved her purple turban back on her head. "What? Sipping champagne, nibbling on lobster tails and accepting everyone's congratulations is a bit too taxing for you?"

"Oh, ignore her." Ginny waved a white-gloved hand. "She's just upset; Baxter is here."

"Oh." Edwina winced. "And how is your son?"

Staring off in the garden, Janelle lifted her chin. "Fine, just ... fine."

With a sad look on her face, Ginny shook her head. "Do you want us to leave, Edwina? Give you some quiet?"

"No, of course not." Edwina grasped her friend's hand. "I'm so glad to see friendly faces."

"I warned you," Janelle chided. "No matter Mr. Devane's good qualities, everyone will see it as a *mésalliance,* an unsuitable alliance. He's an empty-pocketed commoner and you're the daughter of an earl, for heaven's sakes."

"Oh, how you flatter me."

At the sound of Prescott's deep, rumbling voice, Edwina's cheeks heated as did the rest of her skin.

With the heels of his black-buckled shoes clicking loudly on the stone veranda, Prescott approached, carrying two glasses of lemonade. Halting before them, he bowed, managing not to spill a drop, his manners as fine as any courtier's. "Good evening, Lady Ensley. Lady Blankett. You're both looking quite lovely."

Janelle brandished her fan toward the ballroom, where the sounds of a cotillion played. "I was speaking of them. *They* don't know any better."

"And you do?" Edwina asked quietly, unable to help herself.

Exhaling noisily, Janelle shifted her shoulders. "I know it's not *real*."

"Shh!" Ginny chided, looking over at the door. "Someone might overhear."

Edwina accepted the glass from Prescott and sipped the lukewarm liquid. It was a bit on the tart side.

"So it's going well, I assume?" Ginny whispered.

"I've checked at least fifty pairs of shoes by now and haven't yet seen our pair." Edwina pursed her lips. "I have to think of something more creative to do or people might start believing that I'm becoming ham-fisted. I've dropped either my handkerchief or my fan at least thirty times thus far."

Ginny raised a brow. "So your suitors are not hampering you?"

Edwina smiled. "My suitors are making themselves scarce. So in that regard, yes, the plan is working and we've established the fact that we're engaged."

"And how are you faring, Mr. Devane?" Janelle enquired. "Have you had your fill of abuse?"

"Oh, I think I've the stamina for a bit more."

Leaning forward, Ginny blinked. "Abuse?"

His shoulder lifted in a shrug. " 'Legacy hunter' and the like."

Edwina winced. "I'm sorry."

Prescott's handsome face was relaxed, his smile amused. "Don't be. I quite enjoy it, actually. My favorites are the people who don't know what to make of me, so they simply nod and race off in the opposite direction."

Pursing her lips, Edwina's eyes narrowed. "I'd lay good money you were a prankster as a child."

"And you'd win. I was a devil. And loved every minute of it." His smile met hers and something warm floated between them. Still, it didn't quite lessen the effect those flashing eyes stirred in her middle.

Frowning, Janelle stabbed her fan toward Edwina. "Although I know I shouldn't be surprised, you seem to be getting the hang of this acting thing."

Ginny pressed her hand to her forehead. "Am I going to have to stuff your mouth with linseed to keep you quiet?"

"What are you so upset about?" Janelle adjusted the melon-shaped sleeves of her gown. "No one can hear. And if they could, what of it? It's all too preposterous to be believed."

Ginny sighed. "Oh, for heaven's sake."

Prescott leaned toward Janelle, his tone conspiring. "It's quite fun, isn't it? Being the only ones who know the truth."

Janelle nodded. "It does give one a sense of superiority…"

"We wouldn't want to spoil the fun then, would we?"

Tilting her head, Janelle acquiesced. "I suppose not."

Then pray keep your mouth closed, Edwina thought, an improvement over the week before when she'd have shouted it to Janelle's face.

"Devil take it, there you are!" a male voice called.

All four sets of eyes looked toward the French doors.

"Henry!" Edwina cried.

Her cousin stalked over to them, his black coat matched by the dark scowl on his face. "Tell me it's not true! Tell me that you're not throwing your life away with this grasping fortune hunter!"

"Ah, I think a visit to the retiring room is in order," Ginny declared, grabbing Janelle's arm. "Come along, dear."

Janelle waved her fan dismissively. "You go on ahead. I'll wait for you right here."

"But I need your help." Leaning on her cane, Ginny tugged Janelle's arm. "I have difficulty maneuvering though the crowd with my leg being what it is."

Making a noise of disgust, Janelle allowed herself to be pulled away. "Just when it was getting interesting..."

Squaring her shoulders, Edwina tried to ignore the nervous quiver in her middle. It was one thing to lie to acquaintances, quite another to lie to her cousin Henry. But she dare not tell Henry the truth or even hint of it. Although she loved him dearly, he was hotheaded and, frankly, rather judgmental. Moreover, he tended to be a bit obtuse when it came to matters that required a modicum of diplomacy. Which was why Edwina was particularly worried about her Cambridge project. The man of affairs they'd typically used for their acquisitions had taken seriously ill and Henry had gone in his stead. But first things first.

Swallowing, Edwina motioned to Prescott. "Mr. Devane, may I present my cousin, Mr. Blanchard. Henry, this is Mr. Prescott Devane, my...fiancé."

Henry's face paled, then infused with color. "He's a bloody lothario, Edwina!"

Edwina gritted her teeth. "I know you're only speaking out of concern for my welfare, Henry, but pray do not insult my betrothed."

The man shook his head. "If only you'd taken my advice and accepted the marriage to Viscount Bellwood, you wouldn't be in this wretched mess!"

Edwina's eyes narrowed and that decidedly stubborn gleam that Prescott was beginning to favor entered her gaze. "As I told you a thousand times before, Henry, I have no wish to marry Viscount Bellwood, any more than I—"

"You don't know what you're getting yourself into!" Shaking his head, her cousin spat, "It's your inexperience with men of his sort that's left you defenseless to his manipulations, Edwina."

"Henry." Edwina's tone was firm as she laid a white-gloved hand on the man's arm. "I'm no green chit fresh out of the schoolroom. You, of all people, should recognize that I am smart enough to make my own decisions."

"But—"

"Enough, Henry." Her tone brooked no opposition. "If I've chosen Mr. Devane it's because I have assessed the match and determined it to be in my best interests. It also means that I've taken Mr. Devane's measure and not found him wanting. I appreciate your concern, but please give me a little more credit than you are."

Prescott was impressed; she'd said the one thing that made it clear that any insult to him was an affront to her sound judgment.

Henry's pallid cheeks tinged with color as his gloved hands clenched and unclenched by his sides. If it weren't for his strong English accent, one might have mistaken him for Germanic, with his cool blue eyes, white pale complexion and blond hair cut short in the Greek style. He had that Germanic formality to him as well. Not the tedious pomposity that most English gentlemen assumed.

After a moment, Henry tilted his head stiffly and nodded in assent. "As you wish."

Apparently, Henry had a healthy dose of respect for Edwina. Prescott had to give him credit for his good sense.

After sending Henry an appreciative glance that would warm any man's heart, Edwina turned. "Now, once more. Mr. Devane, may I present my cousin, Mr. Blanchard. Henry, this is Mr. Devane, my fiancé."

Prescott nodded curtly to Blanchard, preferring not to shake hands. The man was likely one to try to exhibit his superiority by squeezing as hard as he could, something that, at the moment, Prescott preferred not to endure. And since Edwina seemed fond of this cousin, Prescott would attempt to treat the man with consideration. Unless the man's actions warranted otherwise.

"How was Cambridge, Henry?" Edwina enquired, obviously attempting to change the topic. "Everything go as planned?"

"You're comfortable discussing this now?" Blanchard asked, prickly about it.

"I am not ashamed of our business ventures. Are you?"

The man stiffened even further, if possible. "Of course not."

"Well?" she asked, with obvious eagerness. "Did the deal close? Do we get the property?"

We. So Edwina and her cousin were in the land business together. Cousins, partners... did Blanchard hope for more? Not if he was recommending that she marry Bellwood, a tack that indicated he might respect Edwina but didn't understand her.

Henry's chest puffed out and then suddenly deflated, like one of those flying balloons collapsing. "It all fell through to rot. Simply to rot."

"Oh." She tried to hide her disappointment, but Prescott could see that she'd been hoping for another answer. "What happened?"

Crossing his arms, Blanchard lifted a shoulder. "While I was speaking the King's English, they seemed to be speaking another blasted language entirely. I couldn't seem to say one thing right. They were against me from the start."

Disappointment shimmered in her luminous dark eyes. "How can that be, after all of our correspondence? Matters seemed so close to conclusion."

Blanchard shook his head, seemingly disgusted. "That one fellow, Linear, had it in for me, I'm sure. When I first arrived, he asked me to join them at a tavern for a drink, and I know it was simply to get my nose out of joint."

"Oh, dear Lord, Henry." Edwina's tone was aggravated. "Please tell me you said 'yes' and joined them."

Blanchard stiffened and lifted his chin a notch. "Of course not. I was there to conduct business, not make merry with the lower classes." He shot Prescott a sullen glare. "At least I have some semblance of propriety."

"Watch yourself, Henry," Edwina warned.

"Well, I wasn't about to drink with them, and after

that, well, things didn't go well." At the disappointed look on Edwina's face, her cousin exclaimed, "Now don't try to tell me that these men wouldn't come to terms with me because I wouldn't imbibe with them! That's bloody nonsense."

Edwina sent Prescott a helpless glance.

Looking out at the moonlit garden, Prescott remarked, "I know many men who wouldn't sell you a barren, diseased, three-legged cow unless you were willing to share a drink with them." He looked up. "It's seen as a way of showing respect between the parties."

"Respect?" Blanchard snorted. "What does that have to do with a business deal?" He shook his finger in the air. "Either it's favorable for them financially or unfavorable for them and they move forward if it's favorable and don't if it's not. Respect has nothing to do with it."

"To some men, it can only be favorable if there is a sense of mutual regard between the parties."

Blanchard crossed his arms and looked away. "I've never heard such rubbish in all my life."

Blanchard was bright enough to understand the problem, but simply couldn't get past his pomposity to act differently. Why would Edwina trust such a man with a business a transaction that obviously meant a lot to her?

Edwina stepped forward. "Did you happen to find out if there were any other buyers, Henry?"

"Not a one. Which is what makes their actions all the more idiotic. The fools, they'll be sitting on that property for the next twenty years and not have another buyer with a better price than ours."

"Then perhaps all is not lost." Edwina bit her lip and

Prescott could almost see the wheels turning in her clever brain.

"I'm coming to the conclusion that we're better off without the property," Blanchard declared. "I know you worked very hard on the plans, Edwina, but it was a mighty investment—"

"With amazing returns, Henry," Edwina interjected, her tone resolute. "And it's good for the community as well. Cambridge is exploding and the need for housing is great. It's advantageous for all involved. Especially us." She turned away, obviously trying to keep her frustration in check. "Why don't we finish this conversation tomorrow? When we've both had time to think it over and assess our next steps."

She faced Blanchard again, a tight smile on her lips. "I'm sure when we put our heads together we can think of something to do to bring them back to the table."

Blanchard's pale cheeks reddened and he pointed a finger at Prescott. "I'd rather talk about how you came to be..." He couldn't seem to get the word out. "... with...*him*."

"Henry..." she warned.

Blanchard crossed his arms once more, obviously the man's favorite pose. "Well, he's certainly not one of your set. It's a reasonable question."

"I sought out Mr. Devane," Edwina explained with a hard tone that any remotely observant man would know to heed. "I decided that it was time to remarry. He is a good man, of fine character—"

"You prefer him to me?" Blanchard's tone was shocked. "If you wanted to marry that badly, I would have taken you."

Edwina's smile was colder than a snake's bottom. "How condescending of you, Henry."

"That didn't quite sound..." her cousin blustered, so mortified, Prescott actually felt sorry for the bugger. But not much.

"Be that as it may, I have chosen to be with Mr. Devane. There's more to him than fancy clothes and gilded charm. He's trustworthy and wields good judgment."

Prescott liked how she was defending him to her cousin. She wasn't talking about his charm or his graceful dancing, but about his character. For once it was nice to be described in such noble terms, even if it was a ruse.

"Moreover," Edwina continued, "Mr. Devane treats me well and I appreciate his consideration. He's a good sort. Which you will soon discover once you get to know him."

"Get to know him?" Blanchard looked like he was going to have an apoplectic fit.

"You and I well know the damage that vicious tongues can inflict. I pray you don't judge Mr. Devane by reputation alone, but give him the chance to show you what kind of man he truly is."

Damn, if Edwina didn't manage to sound sincere. A small part of him was actually beginning to believe she regarded him so kindly. It was a bit boggling, but gave him a warm feeling in his chest just the same.

"And what of your father?" Blanchard asked, crustily. "He's likely to burst a blood vessel when he hears about this. As it is, he's already up in arms about you and your society of bluestocking, fix-the-world females." Pressing his gloved hand to his head as if pained, Blanchard declared, "Not that he'll hear it from me—he'd likely shoot the messenger."

"I can handle my father."

"Have a care, Edwina." Blanchard wagged a finger. "It's easy enough to defy him when he's not around, but when the Earl of Wootton-Barrett wants to impose his will, you know how futile it is to resist."

"Thank you for your concern, cousin. But I don't believe that I have much to worry over." Yet the lady's anxious mien belied her words. Her brow was furrowed, her lips pinched, and an apprehensive gleam clouded her luminous gaze. The impression wasn't helped by the fact that she was clutching her fan so tightly her hand quivered.

"I will call upon you on the morrow, cousin," Blanchard declared. "We can discuss things further then." He glared at Prescott meaningfully.

After the sounds of Henry's heels clicking on the stone veranda could be heard no more, Edwina turned to Prescott. "I apologize for my cousin's behavior."

"Oh, no apology's necessary." He held out his arm and looked toward the French doors. "Suddenly I'm finding that I've had my fill of hearty congratulations."

"I see your mask is in place once more."

He blinked, surprised she'd noticed. "Yes, I suppose it is."

She sighed. "I can hardly blame you. On the one hand, I'm a little envious that you can veil your feelings so quickly. Yet it must be taxing, and more than a little lonely sometimes."

"One gets used to it," he lied.

"I don't know that I could be so forbearing."

He tilted his head. "It's not forbearance, but selfishness. I won't let just any person see the real me." For if they did, they might just forsake him, an event to which he could never quite grow accustomed.

Chapter 17

〰〰

Sir Lee sat on a park bench puffing on his West Indian cigar and enjoying the afternoon sun. His old bones needed more warmth than ever before and nothing quite compared to nature's own hearth.

Although he sensed the man's presence long before the crunch of stones on the path ceased behind him, Sir Lee did not turn. "Good day, Wheaton."

After a moment of silence, his former protégé, Tristram Wheaton, stepped around the bench, moved the folded newspaper aside and sat down beside him. "What's so bloody good about it?"

Sir Lee motioned with his cane. "The birds are singing, the sun is shining."

"Don't tell me you asked me here for a diatribe on the scenery."

"Of course not. But can't you find a moment in your life simply to appreciate the world around you?"

"You're becoming melancholic, Sir Lee." Wheaton's icy blue eyes narrowed. "Speaking of which, you're not looking particularly well these days. Is the blackmailer turning out to be a bit too much for you?"

"Of course not." Sir Lee frowned, knowing that in this instance, at least, Wheaton wasn't simply egging him on. He *was* tired. Feeling every moment of his seventy-plus age down to his aching joints. "It's these blasted balls, musicales and the like. The *ton* is up and about until dawn and then sleeps the day away. It's unnatural, I tell you. No matter when I lay my head upon my pillow I am up when the sun rises. This social calendar is getting...well, tiresome."

"Growing a bit crotchety in your old age, are you?"

"Crotchetiness is highly underrated. Besides, I'm past seventy and entitled."

"Still, Sir Lee." Wheaton waved his cane toward the building across the park. "No matter your mood, it cannot be helped by the view."

Wheaton was one of the few people in this world who knew that the whitewashed indigent hospital across the way was where Sir Lee's daughter had died, destitute, alone, and without a stitch of family in the world to support her.

"It's coming here that keeps me on track." Sir Lee exhaled. "It reminds me that my work is all I have left. I have no family, I have no heirs. It also reminds me not to be too proud. Pride is a very lonely bedfellow at the end of a long life."

"She chose to leave..."

"After I'd given her an ultimatum." Shaking his head, Sir Lee couldn't recall the incident without shame. "Pride ran thick in our veins, but, after me, no more."

"So now you're consumed with death, are you?"

"Nay, Wheaton, consumed with life. And how to live out the rest of my days in a manner that does me some semblance of credit."

Sir Lee turned to his former protégé. "It was coming here that gave me the idea for how to trap our friend, Mr. Quince. Sniffing after the fellow at balls and soirees and the like leaves him in control and us flailing." Holding up his hand he curled it into a tight fist. "We need to *contain* the bugger."

"Contain?" Wheaton's bushy white brows lifted.

"I'm going to arrange a country house party where a number of the people on your list of suspected victims and possible accomplices are invited as guests. I will be a late addition to that guest list, a doddering old gent who couldn't harm a fly."

Wheaton scratched his chin. "Fish in a barrel, eh?"

"It's the best way to see which ones stink."

"So you've learned nothing about those fish so far?"

"Oh, I've scratched up a thing or two about the people on your list. By the by, have you ever heard of The Society for the Enrichment and Learning of Females?"

"Nay. What is it?"

"Supposedly a place where ladies gather to study and do good works together. One of the ladies on your list is a member there."

"You believe it's connected to Quince?"

"I cannot say for certain until I learn more. What I do suspect is that it is fertile ground for subversive activities. What better place to gain information or plant the seeds of unrest than in the bedroom or breakfast room? Daughters of earls, wives of viscounts, mothers of barons can be members. It's a perfect place for subterfuge." Resting his chin on his hands, he leaned on his cane. "I will discover the truth of it."

Wheaton chuckled, reclining against the park bench. "You're just upset that you didn't think of it first."

Sir Lee lifted a shoulder. "That doesn't mean I can't fashion the society for my own ends."

"You were always very good at turning traitors into resources, I'll grant you that." Staring off in the distance, Wheaton's cool blue eyes narrowed. "Hmmm. If there are any seeds to be planted though, they'll be mine to sow, you know."

"Of course, Wheaton. I'm retired, which you hardly allow me to forget." He shrugged. "When the time comes, I'll hand everything over to you."

Wheaton nodded. "Very well then. But what of this house party? How do you intend to ensure that Quince takes the bait?"

"I sent letters to a select few on the blackmailer's list and have no doubt they will attend. And if Quince is as crafty as I believe he is, then he will probably ensure that a few more of his players are part of the party." He licked his lips. "But to make it work, I need your man there, more than anyone. It will be far too tempting for Quince to ignore."

"Absolutely not!" Wheaton made a cutting motion with his hand. "I told you to leave him out of it! I want him back in town working for me, not off in the country subject to Quince's designs."

"I have enough means and can set the stage well enough to have a reasonable certainty that Quince will take the bait, but if your man comes, then he'll be a hooked fish for sure."

"It's too risky—"

"At a country house party? Be serious, Wheaton. You want this ended quickly. This is the fastest way to ensure results."

"Look, Sir Lee, I know how meticulously you plan such things—"

"And my proven results."

"Those, too. But even if I was to support this plan, he wouldn't agree to do it."

"Your man wants this nasty business over, doesn't he?"

"Yes, but he's rusticating at his estate, mind you. Unless you've arranged for the Prince to host the damned thing himself, what possible reason could he have for simply showing up at a house party midseason?"

Smiling, Sir Lee picked up the newspaper from the bench beside him and handed it to Wheaton.

"What, the broadsheet?"

"Read it."

Pulling his quizzing glass out of his pocket, Wheaton held the paper out. "It's the bloomin' gossip column!"

"Just read it."

After a long moment, Wheaton lowered the newspaper, and looked off to stare in the distance. "It's good..."

"Good? It's bloody well perfect! It explains his presence at the house party flawlessly."

"Then why not simply come back to London? Why go there?"

"Because things will be moving too fast. It will be a very well-coordinated spring-of-the-moment affair. Bags will be packed, unloaded, and all off and running within this side of ten days."

"As these things go, that's very last moment."

Sir Lee smiled. "I know. Which is why I will control the whole affair, down to the last detail."

Scratching his chin, Wheaton nodded. "I make no promises..."

Sitting forward, a surge of excitement shot through Sir Lee. "But you'll ask him? And press him to cooperate...?"

"That I will. But I want your assurance that he will be protected above all else."

Smiling, Sir Lee leaned back. "Of that, you have my word. I have this very well planned. Everyone I want accepts the invitation and Quince takes the bait. Fish in a barrel."

Wheaton held up the newspaper. "Did you notice this bit here, by any chance?"

"I took it as a sign that my plan is headed in the right direction." Agents by nature were a suspicious lot, as they both well knew.

"So there's no connection?"

"Nay, he's an orphan. From Andersen Hall. I'll dig a little more, but think it's a waste of time."

Wheaton stood, towering over Sir Lee and blocking out the sun. "So you think you can have this whole mess wrapped up in a few weeks' time?"

"I'm confident of it." Leaning on his cane, he rose.

"Good luck to you then." With the crunch of pebbles under his bootheels, Wheaton strode off.

Closing his eyes and inhaling a pine-scented breath, Sir Lee took a moment to savor the accomplishment of step number one.

He opened his eyes, resolved, eager and ready for steps two, three and four. Like a ball rolling down a hill, a plan once started speeds up until its natural or unnatural conclusion.

Sir Lee spun on his heel, set his cane and strolled in the other direction, the crunch of the pebbles announcing his procession.

Nearing the corner of the park, he took one last glance at the hospital across the way, the familiar regret still burrowed deep in his heart.

He stopped and turned to face the building, and for the countless time since learning of his daughter's lonely demise, sent off a prayer asking for her forgiveness.

He would do what good he could in the last days of his life. He only hoped he had a few left with which to work.

Chapter 18

A few nights later, Edwina noticed the interested stares, the hard looks and the couched whispers as they passed, but Prescott's ripping chatter and the way he capably maneuvered them through the crowded ballroom kept her safe from any controversy.

"Heavens, it's warm in here," Edwina commented. "How High Society loves a good crush. For the life of me, I can't understand why."

"It's the stimulation, my lady. The excitement that can only be generated by a mob."

Or a well-muscled thigh brushing mine. So long as it's scented with a little musk.

To Edwina's ultimate disappointment, tonight Prescott was behaving the perfect gentleman. There hadn't been a hint of the possibility of a kiss the whole carriage ride from her house, but given that Janelle had ridden with them, Edwina supposed that was to be expected.

Edwina was obsessed by the kiss in the alcove, playing it over and over in her mind. The heat of his body, the press of his hands, the silky touch of his tongue dancing with hers, the fiery sensations surging through her when he'd rubbed her breast...

The memory alone made her body burn with need. She felt parched for another taste of his elixir, her every moment haunted by the specter of the possibility of another kiss.

Not that they'd had much of a chance for one. Prescott had spent the last couple of days at Andersen Hall with Dr. Winner and Evie, since the little girl had fallen ill with a fever. It was endearing how Prescott had only left Evie once he'd seen that she'd recovered. He'd reported as much to Edwina this afternoon, when she'd finally gotten to see him again. But their reunion was abruptly cut short when Janelle and Lucy had charged in, insisting that Prescott join them in the society to see their latest charitable project.

Thereafter, the ladies of the society had hogged his attentions all afternoon. Not even Edwina's pretense about needing some air had peeled him from their grasp. Ginny, Lucy and Janelle decided that a group walk in the park was in order. Part of Edwina was delighted that her friends welcomed him so, the other part was wondering what might just happen if she stole a moment alone with her supposed fiancé.

And now they were surrounded by hundreds of interested eyes.

No, she sighed, *a kiss is not bloody likely.* Inwardly she chastised herself for her foul tongue. Or was it her foul thoughts that should garner the indictment?

Somehow, what she'd done with Prescott hadn't felt indecent; it had felt quite...heavenly.

"Don't worry." Prescott leaned over, his breath teasing the fine hairs on her neck, making her shiver. "The night is young yet and we're bound to spot those shoes, if the wearer is here. I'm thinking that we might have better luck if we check the card room."

"Ah, yes," Edwina replied, feeling silly that she was ruminating on a kiss when they had an evil blackmailer to find. "While the gentlemen are sitting. Sounds like a good idea."

"Move to the left, Edwina, I want to avoid Mrs. Warren."

As he negotiated her through the throng, Edwina wondered aloud, "I can't imagine she doesn't know how rude she is with her thousand questions."

Prescott lifted a burly shoulder. "She's simply trying to sort out what a lovely lady like you is doing with a wolfish muckworm like me."

The flattery about her revamped appearance pleased her but..."Don't speak in such denigrating terms, Prescott. Even if it's to represent someone else's view."

His eyes scanned the crowd. "If the reputation fits..."

"About as well as Lady Cartridge's skintight gown," she muttered.

He looked down at her, his brow furrowed and the corner of his lush lip lifted as if surprised. "Did you just make a jest, my lady?"

Her lips quirked. "Astonishing isn't it?"

A deep chuckle escaped from his mouth, a sound so joyous, Edwina suddenly laughed in response, feeling at once witty, charming and almost pretty.

"Heads are turning," he murmured, as the crowd pushed them about like seashells pitched by the current. "Everyone wants to be included in the jest."

It felt good to laugh; her anxiety seemed to dissolve in the sheer fun of being with Prescott. When she was with him she didn't fret about her father or Ginny's fate or feel like she was fighting a mighty current in pursuit of her future happiness. She simply enjoyed the moment, a very special gift.

As a dour-faced lady with almost as many diamonds around her neck as freckles on her face craned her red head to overhear, Edwina leaned toward Prescott. "You have a gift for making people feel comfortable, Prescott."

He shrugged. "It's what I do."

Reminded of Tomlin's praise a few nights before, Edwina wondered at how Prescott seemed to dismiss appreciation as nothing noteworthy. Or was it that he didn't deem *himself* noteworthy?

"I'm not talking about your ability to charm the scales off a dragon," she countered. "It's...I don't know, an ability to make someone feel...accepted. You don't judge people overmuch, do you?"

"Only myself," he replied. "And often the assessment is wanting. Here, there's an opening, let us go through."

Purposefully guiding her away from the dour-faced lady, Prescott led her toward the supper room and the crowd thickened around them. The scents of lily, rose, carnation, lavender and French violet blended together in a stifling concoction that smelled nothing like fresh flowers.

Edwina suddenly realized that Prescott seemed to

maneuver her away from the ladies whenever possible. "Why do you move me closer to the gentlemen? Is it because they are less inquiring?"

"Some of the ladies use pins to secure parts of their ensemble." Pressed together in the crowd, he smiled down at her. "In a crush like this, they don't tickle."

"Oh." Edwina blinked, marveling at Prescott's ability to be empathetic. She was reminded of a tale her banker had once told her. Leaning up, she asked in his ear, "Have you ever heard the story about the Hebrew scholar, Hillel?"

He shook his head.

"A group of pagans told him that they would convert if he could recite the entirety of his religion's teachings while standing on one foot."

A glimmer of interest flickered in his emerald eyes and she felt encouraged to go on. "He stood on one foot and said, 'Do unto others as you would have done to you. The rest is commentary.'"

His handsome face lighted with a wide smile and she was so gratified to have been able to amuse him she felt an answering grin lifting her own lips.

"You do that," she murmured. "It's very...gentlemanly."

His smile remained fixed but she could see the light in his eyes dim. And even though they were wedged closer than cabbage leaves, she felt his withdrawal like a raw wind on a wintry day.

"Did I...did I say something wrong?"

"Of course not." He looked away, his eyes scanning the crowd. "I think we're almost through."

"Prescott?"

"What?"

"Please look at me."

Exhaling noisily as if pained, his gaze met hers. "Yes?"

"I apologize if I offended you in any way. Obviously it was unintentional."

"You didn't offend me." His tone was curt.

"Then why do I still feel the draft on my face where you slammed the proverbial door?"

He stared at her a long moment, his brow furrowed as if she were some sort of enigma. Then his gaze softened. "I'm not offended, my lady, I assure you. It was something that...well, a gentleman is the one distinction that I will never call my own. So..." Those broad shoulders lifted in a shrug. "I suppose the arrow hit a bit too close for comfort."

Raising her hand in pledge, she declared, "I swear on my honor never to insult you by calling you gentlemanly ever again."

To her great relief, his face relaxed and he chuckled, the very response she'd been hoping for. He shook his head. "I must confess, my lady, you're not exactly how I imagined you'd be."

"How so?" She held her breath, hating that she cared so much what he thought of her.

"Well, for one thing, you've got a nice sense of humor. When I first met you..."

"I looked as if I should be carrying a broom, ready to give a sound thrashing?"

He smiled. "Something like that. You seemed so, well...reserved."

"I was. I mean I am." Her cheeks heated. "What I mean to say is that when I'm with you I don't feel that way."

"I think it was just your hairstyle. Wearing your hair that tightly had to hurt; no wonder you were a bit of a crosspatch."

She felt her lips quirk. "Curls do wonders for a girl's disposition."

His handsome face transformed into a wide, white smile that she felt all the way down to her toes.

She pursed her lips. "But I will not allow you to distract me from my purpose, Prescott, no matter how you try. I will spit out this compliment, even if it kills me."

He playfully rolled his eyes. "If you must..."

"Oh, I must. Though I dare not say you are gentlemanly, I will declare that the ease which others feel in your presence is generated from your chivalrous deportment."

He pressed a hand to his heart. "Oh how you flatter me, my lady."

"If the reputation fits..."

His smile was warm, blanketing her like sunshine on a cloudless day. "You know, Edwina, you have a tendency to know exactly the right thing to say—"

"After the very wrong thing that I say," she interrupted.

"Everyone puts his foot in his mouth at some point or other. You simply have a knack for removing it with aplomb."

"Thank you, Prescott, I do try. I simply attempt to be honest and say what I know would make me feel better if the positions were reversed."

"So you try to be 'gentlemanly,' do you?"

"Be careful with those insults, or I might just have to call you out."

His easy smile met hers and the warmth in his gaze

made her feel as if she'd peeked behind the mask shielding his heart. A small swell of victory blossomed in her chest and she hugged the feeling close, knowing that he only let in very few, and rarely at that. She understood that it was a special moment that she would revisit again once all this was over.

"Lady Ross." A stout man dressed in a peacock blue coat stood before them barring their way. His white breeches that were of a style better suited to a much slimmer gentleman, and the sour look on his face flattered no one at all. "Mr. Devane."

Chatter around them screeched to a halt and all eyes turned to stare at the imposing Frederick Millsboro, Baron Oxley, and his latest quarry. The man was known as being one of the nosiest rumormongers in the *ton,* only to be rivaled by his older sister the Viscountess Langston. The brother and sister looked alike as well; both had spiky russet hair, matching bristly brows, brown, piercing eyes and long, horsey faces.

Craning his neck in what had to be an uncomfortably intricate cravat knot, Lord Oxley stomped his cane on the floor and glared at Edwina through his quizzing glass. "I've heard that congratulations are in order, my dear. But I must confess, I'm surprised by your choice of future husband. He's not exactly cut of posh cloth."

Any remaining conversation in the nearby crowd hushed, and a pocket of silence entombed them within the raucous throng.

"Nay, my lord," Prescott replied. "My cloth is used to far more washings a year."

A lady giggled behind him.

"That, Devane, is obvious," Oxley huffed, not quite understanding the play on words. Darting his eyes about the crowd, he puffed out his chest. "And as such, I wonder at the wisdom of such a selection when there are far superior fabrics to choose from." His smile was smug.

Prescott turned to Edwina. "The man's right, you know. Orphans don't exactly make the best husbands."

"See." Lord Oxley waved his cane. "Even the man knows the lay of the land."

Perhaps it was the reassuring feel of Prescott's strong arm beneath her hand or the security of knowing he was by her side to help her if she faltered. But with an amazing sense of confidence, Edwina went along with the play. "I am most concerned. Pray, explain to me the shortcomings of marrying an orphan, Mr. Devane. For it might cause me to reassess."

Prescott scratched his chin. "Well, I don't have any relations to come stay with us for months on end. The house will be quiet and all our own, I regret to say. Likewise, I've no aged aunts or uncles to support in their dotage."

"So we would miss out on such engaging conversation? That is a shame."

"And I'm without any nieces in need of a season or two, which is always so exciting."

"I suppose we could always host a ball or two on our own."

"Yes, but you won't have all of those wardrobes to acquire and I know how ladies love those shopping expeditions."

"Although husbands tend to shudder at the bills." Popping open her fan, Edwina waved it distractedly. "Are you certain you don't have a cousin or two hiding out in the wings who are desirous of purchasing a commission in the army? I do wish to support our efforts abroad."

Shaking his head, Prescott sighed. "I can contribute none of the typical advantages of family to our union, I'm afraid to say."

Lord Oxley blinked behind his quizzing glass as it suddenly registered that these might not be so undesirable at all.

"Hmmm." Edwina tapped her fan to her lips. "That does raise an interesting question. So on holidays, there would be no conflict about whose family we would join?"

"I'm afraid not. Which means we will be even further entrenched into the bosom of your family."

Brandishing her fan, Edwina turned to Lord Oxley. "As a father of four girls, is that a good or a bad state of affairs?"

The whispers began and Lord Oxley's eyes nervously flitted about. No doubt Lady Oxley would be interested in his very public response. He licked his lips, groping for what words to use. "Uh, good. Of course." Lord Oxley exposed pink gums with his wide false smile. "A daughter can't be too close to home, I always say."

Edwina looked up at Prescott. "Are there any other shortcomings I should know of?"

"Well, as we'd agreed, when I die everything goes either to our children or back to your kin."

"But isn't that a favorable outcome?"

"Yes. But there's no one to challenge the will. Where's the sport in that? Solicitors need to eat, too."

Edwina patted his arm. "Always thinking of others. Well, I'm sure the solicitors will find something to dispute and charge us an exorbitant fee for, isn't that right, Lord Oxley?"

"Um, ah, yes, those devils can always find something to argue about. Ah…" Lord Oxley cleared his throat. "By the by, you look lovely, my dear."

Edwina patted a curl. "A new coiffure and a sensible engagement will do wonders, don't you think?"

A sheen of sweat appeared on Lord Oxley's upper lip and Edwina found herself feeling slightly sorry for him. But only slightly, the man was an atrocious busybody. "Sensible…I…ah…must be off, my dear. I well, I give you my congratulations."

The flustered Lord Oxley swept through the crowd.

Edwina let out a thankful breath and smoothed her gown, feeling elated by the jest, but sad all the same for having to go through it. She couldn't quite understand how Prescott always managed to keep that mask so firmly in place. It had to be a very isolating experience.

"Psst. Ladies' retiring room," a voice muttered. Edwina looked up in time to catch a glimpse of Janelle's retreating back and the violet feather of her turban flopping through the crowd.

Edwina's stomach dropped, knowing this had to be about the blackmailer. "Ah, if you'll excuse me, Prescott?"

His eyes narrowed. "Yes of course."

She made her way to the retiring room, her nerves on edge.

"Psst!"

Edwina jumped.

Janelle stepped out from behind a fern.

Pressing her hand to her racing heart, Edwina

chided, "Why must you be so wretchedly...dramatic?" She restrained herself from using one of the other choice words that had come to mind. "Prescott is no fool! He had to have seen you, and you're acting more shiftily than a spying Polonius jumping behind a curtain!"

"Oh, piffle! And although I adore Shakespeare's *Hamlet,* don't you dare compare me to an actor."

Waving an ivory-gloved hand, Janelle motioned for Edwina to move with her behind the fern.

Edwina couldn't quite believe she was hiding behind a tree, but did as Janelle wanted, whispering, "Where's Ginny?"

"Are you drunk? I told you, in the retiring room."

"And?"

Janelle frowned. "And she's mightily upset. She received a note. She has no idea how it managed to get into her reticule, but when she went into the retiring room, there it was."

Gritting her teeth, Edwina once more sent off a prayer for forbearance. "And what did it say?"

"She's to be at the Kendrick house party in five days time and be prepared to get all of her letters back."

Edwina's eyes widened. "All of them?"

"Yes, for a payment in the amount of five hundred pounds."

Edwina hissed.

Heads swiveled her way and eyes glistened with a speculative gleam.

Pressing her hand to her mouth, Edwina whispered, "The knave!"

"Ginny's very upset."

"I'd be, as well!" She bit her lip. "But this is actually

good news. At the Kendrick estate, Prescott and I can search the guests' rooms, looking for those Françoise Millicent shoes or the letters." Being in love and stealing off to bed early was the perfect excuse. Fleetingly, Edwina pondered how nice it might be for that to be true.

"You need an invitation first—"

"Isn't your nephew Albert married to Lord Kendrick's niece?"

Rolling her eyes, Janelle scowled. "Yes, fine, twist my arm, I'll try to secure it. But I make no promises..."

"Thank you." Edwina frowned. "But how does the blackmailer know that Ginny will be invited to the house party?"

Janelle shrugged. "How did he manage to get the note into Ginny's purse?"

"Probably in the crush of the crowd." She shuddered, looking through the fern leaves. "The man's a bit too crafty for comfort. Which begs the question—why is he returning all of the letters? Why the sudden change in tactics? Does he somehow suspect that we're hunting him?"

Janelle waved a hand. "He knows nothing because nothing's happened. I'll bet he's greedy and simply wants the entire blunt in one lot."

Edwina bit her lip, knowing she wasn't grasping all of the nuances. "I'll discuss it with Prescott. I'll bet he has some ideas." It was surprising how much that thought soothed Edwina. "But first, we must see to Ginny."

"You go on." Janelle adjusted the violet sleeves of her gown. "I fear you're right about raising Mr. Devane's suspicions. I'll see to him now, so when you present the note as your own he won't deduce a conspiracy."

"I don't know, Janelle, the man's astoundingly astute..."

Janelle glowered. "Don't start in again about telling him the truth, Edwina."

"Prescott ought to know. I mean, he's in as deep as we are."

"We promised Ginny, remember?"

"But—"

"Enough, Edwina. Ginny likes him and would be upset if he learned the truth. Don't you think she has enough distressing her?"

Edwina's arguments died instantly.

Scratching her chin, Janelle pursed her lips. "But I must agree with you on one point, Mr. Devane is turning out to be a surprising young man."

Sighing, Edwina stepped out from behind the fern, muttering, "More than you could ever know."

Chapter 19

⟨∽◦⟩

The next day, the afternoon's golden haze hung over the path as Edwina and Prescott strolled along Rotten Row at Hyde Park. The air was still, with no discernible hint of breeze, and damp with the potent scent of the nearby Serpentine.

A choir of gray-and-brown birds sang in the trees, diving now and again to snap up the crumbles dropped by playful children. Groups of people mingled about, chatting, laughing and enjoying Lady Hinsdale's birthday celebration at a picnic nearby.

As they walked arm in arm away from Lady Hinsdale's gathering, as usual, Prescott shortened his long-limbed stride to match Edwina's.

"I want to thank you, Edwina, for your assistance at the docks," Prescott remarked. "The contracts were signed this morning."

"Excellent. I'm so glad for you. Were they able to secure all of the space you required?"

"Down to the last container."

"I think your new venture will be quite successful." She nodded. "Your reflective lanterns provide more light and burn on much less oil. Very economical. I can't see how people won't be lining up for them."

"I appreciate your confidence, but people are used to burning candles at home since many don't like the smell or smoke of the oil. No matter that this is a far superior design to lanterns in place today, people won't spare money on them until the lanterns are in circulation for a time."

"Your capacity to understand human nature is admirable."

He shrugged. "I wouldn't spend my hard-earned money on something unproven simply based on the claims of its seller. I would want to see it in action, hear from people who'd used it."

"So what will you do?"

His lips lifted at the corner. "So you think I have a plan, do you?"

She smiled, enjoying how he teased her. "Don't you always?"

"Hardly, but in this instance, I do, as a matter of fact. I'm working with a friend in the Bow Street Office who is introducing me to some of the men in charge of the patrol forces."

Her eyes widened. "Why, that's a brilliant idea. The patrols need good light yet cannot carry too much. Your lanterns are a perfect fit."

"I think so. Now I have to convince the fellows in

charge of the patrol forces. When we're back from the Kendricks' house party I'll be meeting with the heads of the Horse Patrol and the Foot Patrol. Then once the lanterns are in circulation for a while, people will see how well they function, and, with any luck, will buy their own. It should build from there."

Edwina bit her lip, unsettled. Prescott was already thinking of the time after their plan was completed. Well, he had only promised her four weeks. But she'd hoped that now that he knew her, he might extend that time period...to catch the blackmailer and finish the job, of course.

"You're awfully quiet, Edwina," Prescott noted. "You're not still worried about the invitation, are you? As I told you before, the blackmailer wouldn't have set the exchange at the Kendricks' without knowing you'd be invited."

Once more, guilt washed over Edwina about not telling Prescott the whole truth. But Janelle's arguments were persuasive enough for Edwina to keep her mouth closed. Ginny's relief at Edwina assuming the role of victim was obvious, especially since she'd grown fond of Prescott.

But what did Prescott think of Edwina being subject to a blackmailer's scheme? Did he believe that she'd had a lover? That she'd broken her marital vows? The thought displeased. But then again, it might mean that she'd be open to taking a lover now...

"I'm sure the invitation will be waiting for you when we return to your house," Prescott assured.

Edwina pushed aside all thoughts of lovers and Prescott and focused on the more important issue at hand, the blackmailer. "Ah, when we do receive the invitation, will you be prepared to leave promptly?"

"My bags are already packed."

"Good. The earlier we're there, the sooner we can get started searching rooms. This is quite a favorable development, knowing that the blackmailer is one of a limited pool of people."

"I agree. The gods seem to be shining favorably upon your plan. Another turn, my lady?"

"Yes, please."

"It helps with your nerves, doesn't it?"

"Ah, yes, actually." She smiled up at him. "And I do enjoy the benefits of exercise." The actual benefit she was enjoying was his company, not the exercise. That, and the feel of his hand pressed reassuringly on hers, the now-familiar musky male scent that was exclusively his and the nimble way he moved alongside her.

It was a rare treat to have Prescott all to herself, and Edwina savored the delicious heat that being near him stirred. He was so strikingly handsome and so exceedingly attentive that she could hardly blame herself for being infatuated with him.

She tripped.

Holding her up, he asked, "Are you all right?"

"Yes, I ah, my toe caught on the edge of my skirt." Dear heavens, she *was* infatuated with him! Her traitorous cheeks burned.

"They're calling you 'The Blushing Widow,' you know."

"'Blushing'?" She felt her cheeks flame. "Really?"

The twinkle in his eye was amused. "I can't imagine why."

She bumped him with her hip and his smile only widened. "Don't blame me, I didn't come up with it. If they'd asked me, I would have come up with something much more spectacular."

"Like what?" She bit her lip.

"Oh, I don't know, perhaps, 'London's Wicked Widow' or 'The White-hot Widow.'"

"Oh, you..." She moved to pull away from him.

He hugged her closer. "No you don't. You're not going anywhere." Squeezing her hand deeper into the crook of his arm, he leaned so close she could smell the lemon on his breath from the ices they'd been eating earlier. "I'm only teasing."

"I don't like being teased," she lied, fancying how he held her.

"I meant wicked in the good sense. And what's wrong with white-hot? Would you prefer stone-cold?"

"Of course not. It's just all so...ludicrous. My clothes may be different and my hair rearranged, but I'm still the same person inside." Yet, that wasn't quite true. When Edwina was with Prescott she *felt* different; she felt witty, pretty and, well, interesting. She didn't feel like he was with her because she was the Earl of Wootten-Barrett's daughter, or because she was well-heeled or because her father had pressed him into it. She felt like he actually enjoyed being with her. Though it had all begun as a ruse, the friendship was there, she could feel it.

"Why do the gossipmongers choose to call me a widow when, to them at least, I won't be a widow for long?"

"I think some still believe that you won't go through with the wedding."

She started. "Really?"

"Don't look so surprised. Crying off's been known

to happen a time or two." He leaned over conspiratorially. "And in our case, it's not so very far from the truth. It's good, actually, and will make it all the more believable once we do break it off."

Edwina's stomach sank; he said it so coolly, as if it didn't matter. She'd miss the blazes out of him. That smile, those teasing gibes, the way she felt while with him. The friendship was nice, lovely in fact. But she wanted to explore more about how he'd made her feel when he'd kissed her. She'd never felt anything like it before and doubted that she ever would.

But she had hardly any time left with him before he'd be gone. And then what? Would her whole acquaintance with passion have been boiled down to two startling kisses?

She wanted more before he was gone. Much more.

But how to do it?

Lots of widows took lovers, so why shouldn't she have a taste of not-so-forbidden fruit? Especially since she would never remarry. Where was the harm?

A nervous flutter tickled her middle. Could she dare? Would she be able to go through with it? She, the woman who a handful of days before had considered herself "not built" for passion, now wanted to take a lover? It seemed too fantastic to be true.

Prescott coughed into his gloved hand. "Lady Blankett—Janelle, as she insists I call her—is turning out to be quite the little spy. She's already ascertained five of the other invited guests to the Kendrick estate. No doubt by tomorrow's end she'll know them all."

Edwina was surprised at the little twinge of jealousy in her heart at Prescott's use of Janelle's Christian name. Her stomach twisted with the stark reminder that Prescott was only *pretending* that she was the most special woman in his life.

What had she been thinking when considering an affair? He didn't want her. He'd called that kiss in the alcove an "experiment"; it meant nothing to him! Inside, she burned with humiliation. No matter what she was "built" for, it wasn't going to happen with Prescott Devane. Or anyone else for that matter. She determined to act normal and keep up the conversation as if disappointment wasn't spearing her heart.

"You and Janelle seem to be getting along better," Prescott remarked.

"Yes, I want to thank you, Prescott, for smoothing things over between us. She still manages to challenge every idea I propose, but there isn't the rancor that there used to be. You have a gift for understanding what makes people tick." The first hint of breeze rustled the leaves in the trees and a young lad took off running as he attempted to fly a yellow-tailed kite on a lackluster wind. "One that I, lamentably, lack."

"It would be hard for anyone to see past that barbed tongue when it's flaying one's hide."

She chuckled at the vision he described. "I like the blunt way you put it."

"Janelle really does remind me of Mrs. Nagel and of something that Headmaster Dunn once told me. He said, 'The sharpest tongue often guards an injured heart.'"

Edwina was touched by the headmaster's insight and by the fact that Prescott was wise enough to learn from it.

"Pardon me," a soft voice murmured from behind them.

Stopping, she and Prescott turned. A lovely young

lady with freckled cheeks, sea blue eyes and bouncy blond curls sticking out from her peach-colored bonnet stood before them. She clutched her lacy white fan before her as if in supplication. "Lady Ross, my name is Miss Matilda Gelds, and I wanted to know...wanted to ask...Well, I want to join The Society for the Enrichment and Learning of Females."

Edwina's smile slowly disappeared as she realized that her connection to the society had somehow become public knowledge. Her father would not be pleased. "I'm flattered, Miss Gelds, but, if I may be so bold, are you certain that your parents would approve?"

"Your parents didn't, and it didn't stop you."

Edwina stiffened. Who let that cat out of the bag? "A parent's approval is not dismissed so lightly, Miss Gelds. Especially when one is still living under her parents' roof. I was a widow—"

"I want to do good works. Enrich my mind with engaging topics—"

Edwina raised a hand. "Miss Gelds—"

"I know you're the president and I tracked you down before my friends Cornelia or Edith. I took action and sought you out. That should count for something."

Edwina's eyes widened. There were others? What in heaven's name was going on?

"I suppose Miss Gelds will have to go through the typical membership application process?" Prescott hinted.

Slowly, Edwina nodded. "Everyone must. Even the president cannot supplant procedure." The society didn't actually have a formalized process, but perhaps it soon would.

The young lady stepped forward. "I want to become

a member and follow in your footsteps, Lady Ross. Pray tell me how do I go about making my application?"

"Do you know the location of the society?"

"Of course, 183A Girard Street, adjacent to your home. My friends are waiting for you there. I decided it would be more shrewd to seek you out before the others made their requests."

Others waiting...Edwina pasted on a smile. "If you leave your information with Mrs. Lucy Thomas at the society, then I will be certain that your application is duly considered."

"Will you put in a good word for me, Lady Ross?"

"I cannot make any promises, Miss Gelds. But you will have as good a chance as any." Edwina had no idea what the process might be, but undoubtedly it would be fair.

The young lady whirled, making the fringe of her peach cottage vest and the skirts of her white jaconet muslin walking dress swirl. "Thank you, Lady Ross! I will go make my application straightaway!" In a cloud of peach and white, the young lady raced off.

"Oh dear heavens." Edwina pressed her hand to her heart. "What prompted that?"

Prescott looked down at her. "For every nasty dowager out there, there are impressionable young girls taken to romantic fancy who probably delight in the notion of a lady of means marrying a man with nothing. All for love."

"But what has that to do with the society?"

"Our engagement draws attention to you, and as a consequence to your endeavors. The most notable being the society."

"I had no idea the society would become so publicly known." She groaned. "Oh, my parents are not going to be happy."

"You mean that the comment about your parents' not approving was true?"

"Not approve? A club for ladies? My parents are utterly mortified." She pressed her fingers to her temple as a sudden headache came upon her. "Oh, I'm never going to hear the end of it."

"I can see why a harpy like your mother-in-law might not be so enlightened. But why do your parents disapprove of the society?"

"Where do I begin? My father is dismayed that we collect clothes for the needy and actually *deliver* them ourselves. He's mortified that we help women in prison. Heaven forbid these women can support themselves as servants, seamstresses and the like when released. He doesn't like my 'bluestocking' friends, my opening up my home, holding meetings. The list is long." She sighed. "I don't understand it and doubt I ever will."

"Perhaps the true reason your father disapproves of your society is because he knows what goes on at his own club? The drinking, the gaming, the friends the members don't necessarily want their families to know about...Nothing terrible, but all preferably undisclosed. Thus, no one can question their behavior."

Still massaging her temple, she couldn't help the smile that teased the corners of her lips. "It sounds as if you've met my father."

"Nay. Just a few fathers now and again. The rules for them are far different than any rules might be for their daughters. And I hardly blame him. Although I won't ever have children, I daresay that if I had a daughter, I'd likely lock her in her room and never let a man within ten feet of her."

She blinked. "You won't ever have children? Not any?"

"If you hadn't noticed, Edwina, I'm not exactly the kind of man for marriage and I'll certainly not cause my children the undue hardship of being born out of wedlock."

"Not the kind of man for marriage?" She straightened. "You seem exactly that kind of man to me."

"Very amusing." His tone was irritated. "Just because I allow ladies to give me gifts does not mean that I'm for sale."

"I didn't mean it like that, Prescott—"

"That's neither here nor there, I suppose," he retorted, looking away. Staring off into the trees, his face was expressionless, his body taut.

"I'm being sincere, Prescott. But I am a bit shocked, I confess, by your utter rejection of the marital state. Is it because you feel that you haven't had the benefit of seeing your parents' marriage?"

His brow furrowed as if he couldn't quite believe she was pursuing the topic. Well, neither, exactly could she. But she couldn't stop; it was like a bruise she felt compelled to poke, even if it hurt.

"It's because I wouldn't be any good at it." His tone was gruff. "I'm just not that sort of man."

"I must respectfully disagree. You're a first-rate listener, a highly uncommon trait in the male species, I'm afraid. Moreover, you're good-humored and dependable. I consider those admirable virtues for any husband or father, for that matter."

"Was your husband any of those things?"

"No, actually...he was not."

"My point exactly. Women don't want good listeners. They want money, status, ambition or in the best of circumstances, all three. I have none." His tone grew heated. "Moreover, I'll never put up with all of the idiocy that goes along with being leg-shackled to a woman."

She straightened, shocked by the strength of his conviction. "I had no idea you had such a negative view of women."

"Oh, I love women. I enjoy them immensely. I'll just never count on one for anything, and certainly not for the rest of my life."

Heavy silence draped over them, only to be broken by the birds' chirping in the trees and the shouts of the children playing nearby.

Edwina shook her head, upset by his declaration. "I wonder, Prescott, who has wounded you to the point that you make such a sweeping condemnation of my kind?"

He turned away from her then, taking off his hat and running his gloved hand gently through his hair. Staring off through the trees at the Serpentine beyond, he did not answer. The afternoon sun glistened on his auburn mane, streaking copper in the brown.

"Was it Catherine Dunn?" she asked quietly.

"I learned a lot at Andersen Hall." Turning back to face her, he set his hat back upon his head. "She was only one of my instructors." His tone brooked no further inquiry, and Edwina bit her tongue, despite her raging curiosity about Prescott and Mrs. Catherine Dunn.

His eyes were cold as marble. "So you can rest assured, my lady, that I will not hold you to the engagement."

Somehow this comment hurt Edwina more than the dowager's slap to her face.

Extending his arm, he did not meet her eye. "I need to get back to Andersen Hall and check on Evie. It's been too long. And I'm sure Dr. Winner would like a word as well. Shall we?"

With a sadness she didn't quite comprehend, Edwina slipped her hand into the crook of his elbow and moved in step alongside him, the sun seemingly less bright and the day far more somber than just moments before.

Chapter 20

‸‸‸‸‸

Holding aside the drape, Edwina peered out the window, looking for any sign of Prescott. Their discussion during the promenade at Hyde Park yesterday had left her feeling unsettled, and she was hoping for an opportunity to restore matters between them. They hadn't exactly quarreled, but the silence in the carriage ride home had been unnerving, to say the least. She felt his detachment like a splinter stuck deep in her finger; whenever she explored it, it stung like the dickens.

It was her own fault, really, for being such a nosy-body. The man had suffered greatly in his life and his convictions obviously reflected that fact. Who was she to question his choices? Yet, deep in her heart she just *knew* that he would make a wonderful father. And husband for that matter. He was so astute and considerate and good-natured...She was certain that with just a little encouragement...

She straightened. *What was she thinking?* She certainly wasn't going to marry him and yet she became fairly jealous when he even spoke another woman's Christian name! She must be going daft from all of the Machiavellian musings about the blackmailer. That had to be it. Why else would she be tying herself up in knots?

It was her friendship with Prescott that mattered; it had become quite precious to her during their short acquaintance. Lord it felt like much more than mere handfuls of days. That probably resulted from the fact that before she'd even met him she'd spent days investigating his makeup. Yet her studies had hardly scratched the surface of the wonderfully complex character that was Prescott Devane.

He was certainly forbearing enough to forgive a little prying, wasn't he? All she needed to do was apologize for being such a nosy ninny and all would be sunshine and roses between them. It had to be, or else...or else...She bit her lip as a shadow of doubt slithered across her heart.

The door to the blue room opened and Ginny peered around the wooden entry. "Ah, there you are, my dear." As she approached, her lacy blond skirts swooshed with every limping step. "Hiding out from the applicants?"

"Uh, yes." Quickly Edwina turned away from the window and dropped the drapery. "Um, I had no idea there'd be so many."

"We offer something they cannot get anywhere else: a safe haven where they get the encouragement to explore topics otherwise barred from them. A few even seem interested in our good works."

"We're drawing too much attention to the society, Ginny. I fear we may end up suffering for it."

Ginny held open her hands. "How? You own the house, we are all here of our own volition. If someone chooses not to be a member, there's nothing to keep her from leaving."

Edwina shook her head, worried. "If people feel that we are influencing their daughters in negative ways, then our lives could become exceedingly difficult. Besides, I don't want to be the cause of pitting daughters and their fathers against each other."

"Don't you mean parents?" Ginny's smile was gentle.

"Of course." Edwina looked down at her hands. "Although when the issue arises, I can't help but bemoan the discord my father and I suffered. If there's a way to avoid it, then we should do our utmost."

Ginny grasped her hand. "And if you had to do it all over again, would you not have founded the society?"

"If I had it all to do again I would've managed things better. Especially with my father. The way I told him about what I was doing with the society, the arguments, the shouting, the crying..." Pressing her face into her hand, she groaned. "When it comes to him I often feel like a caged bird smacking against the bars. And I'm not exactly...rational."

"He's your father; it hurts that he doesn't understand you."

"But I push him. I wish that I knew some way to handle things more diplomatically." Sighing, Edwina wondered if things might be different since she now had the benefit of Prescott's friendship. Mayhap she could learn from his example how to deal with people?

"Somehow I doubt diplomacy would work very well with the Earl of Wootten-Barrett." Ginny rubbed Edwina's back. "Have you had any word from your father?"

"Nay." Edwina brought her mind back to reality. "I'm praying Lady Ross was making idle threats about writing to him."

"And when he does find out?"

Shrugging, Edwina looked up. "It will be long over and my father will be counting himself blessed that he avoided such a carriage wreck to his precious lineage."

Ginny's brow furrowed and her pale blue eyes looked troubled. "But what of you, Edwina? Will you be counting yourself blessed that it's ended with Mr. Devane? You seem much attached."

Edwina opened her mouth to protest, but Ginny held up a hand. "I see how you stare out the window when he's expected. And how you blush every time his name is even mentioned. But it's the way that you light up when he enters a room that makes me wonder if you're as detached as you claim."

Edwina's cheeks flamed; she was mortified that Ginny had noticed. Who else had observed her reactions?

"To everyone else it's a perfectly reasonable response for a woman in love, which suits our ruse just fine. But I know you, Edwina, and acting is not exactly your forte."

"So I'm a bit smitten." Edwina shrugged and gave Ginny a reassuring smile. "But it's a lighthearted flirtation, nothing more."

"You, lighthearted? That's like calling Janelle lovable."

Edwina forced a smile. "Prescott Devane can charm the paint off a fence, Ginny. It's hard *not* to like him. But that doesn't mean that my heart's engaged."

Grasping Edwina's hands in hers, Ginny shook her head. "Please understand that I have nothing against Mr. Devane. I simply worry about you. When you care about someone, you commit everything, Edwina. He's a man with the reputation for enjoying many different women's company. I just don't want to see you get hurt."

Dropping Ginny's hands, Edwina turned and stepped over to the window to stare down at the street once more. "Well, you need not fear, Ginny, for Prescott is already making plans for his future, and they don't include me. What we have is a short time together to clean up this nasty blackmail business and then he'll be gone." At the reminder, a pinch of anxiety pricked her chest. She'd better repair things between Prescott and herself as there was so little time! "We're just friends."

Ginny pursed her lips, her gaze thoughtful. "If you say so." Then she exhaled and her face cleared. "I told the ladies who wish to be considered for the society that we'll make all decisions within the month. I hope I didn't overstep my bounds on that one."

Forcing away all wistful thoughts, Edwina turned. "Of course not. That should be plenty of time for us to sort things out."

"Don't you mean sort them out?" Ginny raised a brow. "I worry that some of the applicants are not quite..."

"Earnest in their quest for improvement?"

"Exactly."

"I agree, it's a bit of a challenge to separate the

wheat from the chaff. On the one hand we don't want to turn away a woman who is truly interested in enrichment and learning. But then again, if we take in too many people, especially if their interest is superficial, then it might dilute our foundation, and I would hate to lose the sense of community we've developed."

"I couldn't agree with you more, Edwina. But how to manage the whole business? There's no handbook on such things, is there?"

"There seems to be one for just about everything else..." Edwina muttered. Then she shook her head, feeling at a loss. "I will think on it. This is a critical juncture in the history of our society, Ginny. I would hate to make a misstep."

"There you are!" Janelle called from the threshold. She waved an ivory card in her hand as she glided into the room, her teal muslin gown swooshing with every step. "We've got it!" Her greenish blue eyes were bright with excitement and a satisfied smile played over her lips. "Pack your bags, ladies, for you're going to the country!"

"Edwina's gotten the invitation to the Kendrick estate?" Ginny reached over and grasped Edwina's hands.

Janelle waved the ivory card in the air. "Yes, she has."

"I can't believe it!" Edwina threw her arms around Ginny and hugged her close, pressing her nose into Ginny's soft hair. The delicate scent of lavender her friend wore washed over her.

"That means we're all invited now," Janelle declared.

"We? But I thought you weren't coming?"

Janelle made a face. "I'm certainly not shipping you two off to face the lions alone!"

Ginny reached for her friend and pulled her into the circle with Edwina. Despite Edwina's face being crushed into Janelle's rose-scented shoulder, it felt wonderful.

"Oh, you know how I loathe sentimentality, Ginny." Janelle moved away and pulled a linen from the knitted reticule hanging from her wrist. Pressing it to the corner of her eye, she sniffed.

"Are you crying?" Edwina's eyes were wide with wonder.

"Of course not." Janelle stuffed the linen away. "It's simply a reaction to the dreadful perfume you're wearing."

Ginny caught Edwina's gaze and smiled. Edwina felt her heart warm in response. This vile scrape had brought them closer together than Edwina had ever thought possible. That, and Prescott Devane.

As if conjured up from her mind, Winnows stepped into the room announcing, "Mr. Devane has arrived. Shall I show him in?"

A thrill rocketed in Edwina's chest, but she tried to temper her reaction, saying quietly, "Please do." There was nothing, however, that she could do about her faithless cheeks.

"Oh, I can't wait to tell him." Janelle exhaled. "And show him the map of Kendrick manor."

"You got a map? From where?" Edwina asked, amazed.

"It was Prescott's idea to find out if any renovations had been made recently and to see if we could see a copy of the architectural diagrams. The Lynnwood

Architectural Society had copies of the most recent renovations to the great hall, done in 1801."

"Why that's ingenious! I wish I'd thought of that!"

Janelle wagged a raised finger. "And we were able to get some sketches of the gardens as well. Mr. Francis Butterfield designed the gardens just last year and published his sketches in a pattern book. They have a very picturesque feel and I look forward to exploring them myself. Perhaps you and I can take one of those invigorating walks you like so much, Edwina."

Would wonders never cease? "Of course," Edwina replied, blinking. "That would be lovely."

"Mr. Devane," Winnows announced.

Prescott strolled into the drawing room and Edwina's heart fluttered in her chest and her cheeks warmed, as did the rest of her body as if lit to flame. She had to contain herself from rushing forward to greet him and instead dipped slightly with a nod in greeting.

He looked notably handsome today in a bishop's blue morning coat with bright brass buttons leading down to his slim waist where the fronts sloped off, showing tight white breeches tucked into glossy Hessians.

Edwina was relieved to see that his handsome face was smooth and carefree; gone was the dark cloud that had permeated his mien yesterday.

"Hello, ladies," he drawled in that deep rumble that Edwina felt low in her belly.

Ginny and Janelle nodded in welcome.

Edwina smoothed her lemon yellow skirts, hoping that she hadn't wrinkled the delicate muslin. Then she looked up and caught the amused glint in his emerald gaze. Her belly flipped, but she managed to raise a brow.

"You look lovely, Edwina. That color becomes you."

Perhaps Prescott wanted things to be all well and good between them also. He certainly seemed more genial toward her than when they'd parted.

"Enough about Edwina's new gowns." Janelle waved the card. "I have the most wonderful news! We've secured the final invitations to the Kendrick manor. Now we're all going!"

"That is auspicious news, indeed." Striding toward them, Prescott reached into his coat pocket and pulled out a sheaf of foolscap. "And I've managed to procure the guest list."

Edwina clapped her hands. "How wonderful!"

Handing Prescott the invitation, Janelle moved to stand beside him. "The architectural plans are in the library, awaiting your review. Lucy should have the pattern book with the garden sketches later today."

"Excellent work." Prescott nodded. "I think you might have the makings of a Bow Street Runner, yet."

Tilting her head, Janelle practically preened. "Oh, it was nothing, really."

Ginny stepped forward, wringing her hands. "Is there anything else we can do to prepare? I feel like everything is such a rush, how can we have everything we need?"

"Don't fret for Edwina, Ginny," Prescott soothed. "Against the four of us, the blackmailer doesn't stand a chance."

Janelle shot the two women a warning glance not to

correct him, then moved toward the door. "I will call for tea and we can review the guest list."

Prescott handed her the foolscap. "You and Ginny go ahead. Edwina and I have an appointment."

Edwina straightened. "Really? With whom?"

With his emerald eyes twinkling, he offered her his arm. "It's a surprise."

Chapter 21

"I can't believe how much information Mr. Leonard has shared with us," Edwina marveled as she and Prescott strolled through Green Park.

The leaves danced on an evening breeze as the final rays of the sun faded into darkness. It was amazing how quickly the air cooled once the sun had dropped below the rooftops of the nearby town houses.

"Was it helpful?" Prescott asked, staring off into darkening landscape.

"Immensely. His experiences at White's and Boodles are invaluable to our current situation at the society. I must confess, I had no idea who he was when you first mentioned him, but now, I cannot thank you enough for the introduction."

"Few people know Leonard. Discretion is his byword. Moreover, since he's not the day-to-day manager but more of a 'behind the scenes' facilitator, even fewer know of his connections to the clubs. Most of the club members have no idea of the influence that he wields, and he likes it that way."

"That story he told about pretending to be a footman and serving those two gentlemen who were making application to the club was absolutely astonishing." Edwina raised a hand to her heart and the reticule hanging from her wrist banged against her hip. "The wretched things those men said about the club's members without a dollop of consideration that he might overhear! I know that many view servants as inconsequential, but such indiscretion is unpardonable."

"Which is part of the reason the gentleman found themselves rejected. Although they have no idea that Leonard was the cause. So you mustn't repeat the story."

"Upon my honor! I would never betray the trust he placed in us by sharing such knowledge."

"He liked you, Edwina. And was most impressed with all you've done with your society."

They'd reached the end of the path, where a gazebo sat in a pool of shadow from the canopy of trees overhead. It had gotten very dark very quickly and Edwina noted that few people were about. Her heart began to dance just at the thought of being alone with Prescott in such a romantic setting.

She reminded herself that soon their friendship would be but a memory. A very short, unfulfilled one. Although they might be friends at the end of this adventure, never again would they be pushed together in this ruse of being engaged. The intimacy would be lost, as would any sense of romance, however imagined.

Prescott motioned that they go inside the gazebo.

Climbing the stairs, Edwina aimed for nonchalance as she continued the conversation. "His advice is already giving me the seeds of a plan of what to do with the society's newfound popularity. Now if only I can convince the board of the wisdom of such a course."

"Oh, no." His tone was mocking. "Edwina has another plan!"

Good-naturedly pinching his arm beneath her hand, she blushed, "Things haven't gone so wretchedly wrong yet, have they?"

"As a matter of fact." Stopping inside the cool gazebo, he drew her to stand beside him. "They have. There's something we need to discuss, Edwina, and now is as good a time as any."

At the seriousness of his tone, her stomach sank. "Look, Prescott, I owe you an apology."

"For what?"

"For yesterday. I shouldn't have pried."

Turning away, he removed his hat and brushed his hand through his hair. "I shouldn't have been so prickly. For some reason, when I'm with you, I have a hard time keeping my feelings masked."

"But you shouldn't have to hide your feelings, especially when they're so justified. Who am I to question your choices? It's none of my business." Even though she ached for it to be.

"You spoke out of consideration, Edwina, I know that."

"Let us face facts, Prescott; I'm interfering, bossy and more than a little full of my own good opinion."

White teeth glistened in the dimness. "Are you certain you haven't traded places with Janelle?"

"I'm being serious, Prescott. I had no right."

Turning, he walked to the edge of the gazebo and stared out at the woods. The wind blew and the leaves rustled in the trees. "As my friend, you've earned the right."

Her heart swelled with gladness, but she tempered it. "I'm pleased you consider me a friend, as I do you. But—"

"On that first day we met you asked that I be honest with you in all things..." Prescott's broad shoulders lifted in a shrug. "Well, I haven't been. About something important. At least to me."

Edwina pressed her lips together, waiting for the axe to fall.

"Catherine Dunn, Cat, well she's much more to me than an instructor at Andersen Hall. And, much more than simply another charge that I grew up with at the orphanage. Cat..." His voice trailed off with emotion. "Cat's been my best friend for ages." He turned to face her, but his features were cloaked in shadow. "And I love her more than I've ever loved another person in my life, save my mother."

Edwina swallowed, feeling a little ill. She wanted to ask if he loved her like a sister or something more, but no words would come.

"But Cat kept secrets. Not just from me, but from the world. Completely justifiable, understandable, reasonable secrets for her to keep—"

"But it hurts," Edwina supplied softly, "that she didn't share them with you."

"Terribly."

Edwina swallowed, her heart aching for him. "You feel betrayed."

"Yes. And a bit...lost." His pain was so tangible, it

was as if the very air Edwina breathed was tinged with sorrow.

He swallowed. "It's like everything I've counted on, my bearings have all disappeared..." His voice cracked.

"Headmaster Dunn."

Mutely, he nodded.

Stepping forward, she grasped his hand and squeezed. "I'm so sorry, Prescott."

He nodded. "Thanks."

Releasing her hand, he moved away, and she felt helpless, wishing there was some way she could ease his pain.

He began to pace, his bootheels thumping on the wooden floor. "Then Cat married Marcus..."

Edwina held her breath.

"And I felt even more betrayed."

Edwina's heart sank and she exhaled, trying to quell the deep disappointment slashing through her. He loved her. Cat. The woman of his heart.

Spinning on his heel, Prescott turned and paced once more. "But I realize now that I was simply feeling excluded, discounted from all she was doing, all she was facing, all she was suffering. Hell, I was her best friend and I didn't even know her real name."

"That had to hurt," Edwina murmured.

"Oh, it did. It still does. But not as badly as it once did. Not recently, anyway."

Edwina looked up.

"You see, I've been a little distracted."

"The whole blackmail affair..."

"That, yes, but it's been a bit more than that. You see, I find you altogether too distracting."

Edwina blinked, trying to make sense of this. Was he trying to bow out of the plan for the Kendricks' house party? But, no, he'd just said that *she* was altogether too distracting. *She. Edwina.*

Her stomach lurched. Did he no longer wish to be in her company? With Janelle and Ginny there, mayhap Prescott didn't feel she was needed at Kendrick manor after all.

In a panic, she blurted, "I don't necessarily have a pride of authorship, so to speak, about the plan. Well, that's not entirely true." Was she blabbering, again? "But I think that I can really contribute to this effort and see my role as very important."

He halted. "What are you saying, Edwina? It's your secret the blackmailer is threatening to expose."

"Oh, yes, yes, of course." She bit her lip, wondering at that idiotic lapse. "What was I thinking?"

"I'm talking about my"—he pressed his hand to his chest and then toward her—"attraction to you."

"To...me?"

"Yes. It's been altogether too distracting, but in a good manner. And it made me realize that I couldn't have loved Cat, not in that way, if I could find myself drawn to you so quickly. Don't you see it?"

"Oh." Edwina's brow furrowed. "Yes, of course." *Not in the least.* But she didn't want him to stop talking and certainly not to stop talking about this attraction to her.

He opened his hands wide. "I simply needed to get over my hurt pride and recognize that Cat and I weren't ever meant to be together that way. It's been quite liberating to realize that I was wrong, and now Cat and I can be friends once more. The way we were always meant to be."

"That's wonderful." *But what about that attraction to me?*

"Isn't it?" He exhaled. "I'm really quite relieved."

"I'm glad." *But what about the attraction?*

"And I feel like I'm regaining my footing once more. I'm not quite there yet, but things are improving. My business venture is moving forward, I have a sense of where I'm going..."

"That's all so...wonderful." *Would he ever get around to talking about his attraction?*

He stepped close. "You already said that, Edwina."

"Oh, did I?"

"Yes, you did." Lifting her chin with his finger, he traced the back of his hand across her jaw, searing her skin with his touch. "But enough about me, I want to talk about us."

Her breath hitched. "We can talk more about you if you'd like..."

"Would you like that?"

"Or we could talk about the attraction you mentioned..."

"Ah, yes. The attraction. It's...distracting, making me exceedingly...prickly."

Ever since leaving Hyde Park, Prescott had been thinking about it and had come to one conclusion; Edwina's appeal combined with the fact that he'd been too long without a woman made him thin-skinned. His abstinence hadn't bothered him until he'd begun spending time with Edwina, so it had to be the combination of the two. Otherwise, why else would he become so angry when it came to talking about matrimony and fatherhood? Why else would he become so irritable when thinking about Edwina's husband?

"This distraction..." Her voice was a throaty whisper. "Is it a good or a bad thing?"

Prescott could feel the delicious heat of her body as his fingers smoothed the line underneath her lovely jaw, traveling down her sloped throat toward the luscious swell of breasts underneath.

Her body quivered and her mouth opened, as if seeking air.

"I think the distraction is very, very bad," he murmured, pressing his lips to her temple and inhaling her lily of the valley scent. "And it threatens to get much, much worse."

He felt her lashes graze his cheek as she closed her eyes. "So what...what do you wish to do about it?" Her clove-scented breath teased his ear.

His own breath was heavy and his heart hammering in that delicious staccato of need. "I'd like to sate it."

"Oh...?"

"But I worry, Edwina. You've never had an affair..."

She leaned back. "No, I've never..." Looking up at him, she licked her lips, drawing his gaze. Oh, how he'd like another taste of Edwina's sweet mouth. "Before that night at the Vaughns' ball...I'd never even considered myself a likely candidate."

He wondered at her marriage but wasn't about to ask. It might break the mood, especially after what Dr. Winner had said about Edwina's devotion. A twinge of jealousy pinched his chest over what Sir Geoffrey Ross had had. "And now, Edwina...?"

"Now, I want to...experiment some more."

The pinch in his chest dissolved. A small smile teased his lips at the corners. "So I tempt you, Edwina?"

"In ways...in ways I've never imagined I'd be..."

A small bubble of delight surged inside of him, but he tempered it. This was her first dalliance ever; perhaps the novelty of it enhanced her keen desire.

"I've never felt the kind of...temptation that you inspire," she continued breathlessly. "Not...ever."

That swell of delight burst full bloom and Prescott gloried in it. She wanted him as badly as he wanted her. Could this night get any better?

Still, Prescott resolved to make this as good as he could for Edwina, knowing that she was not a woman of easy virtue.

Gently coiling his fingers into the curls at the base of her neck, he tilted her head back. Her creamy skin shimmered luminous in the darkness. With her petal-soft skin and delicious lips she was any man's dream. But tonight she was his, only his. "I don't want you to have any regrets, Edwina."

"How can I have any regrets when we haven't done anything yet?"

"Cheeky. I like that." His lips were still quirked when they claimed hers, so pure, so soft, so Edwina.

Gently he urged her lips apart and he savored the honeyed sweetness that was so particularly *Edwina*. Her tongue explored with an artlessly passionate hunger that had his body thrumming to be inside of her.

She pressed closer to him, a small movement, yet his manhood responded by straining against his breeches. She wrapped her arms around his shoulders, her body melting against him like hot wax to a candle.

This was everything he'd felt in the alcove, and more.

His hands traversed the plane of her shoulders, dipping into the shallow arc of her back and lower to reach for the lush flesh that he'd been dreaming about for days. Kneading the soft derriere, he pulled her closer, letting her feel his desire.

Shifting against him, she groaned. Desire spiked through him and his shaft pitched with need. She felt so good, so amazingly right, he knew he had to have her. And soon.

He pulled away, a little more roughly than he intended. "Not here." His voice was a rasp.

"Hmmm...?" She swayed slightly on her feet and he held her close. Her head fell backwards, exposing a tempting arch of creamy flesh and suddenly his lips were tasting the salty skin, sucking, licking and exploring that willowy curve of neck.

As if of its own volition, his hand curved around her waist and under the soft sarcenet mantle she wore up to the bountiful swell of her breasts, gently kneading the soft flesh beneath. Through the thin muslin he felt her nipple pebble and press deeper into his hand.

She moaned, a low rumble that shook him to his boot tips.

Exploring her honeyed neck, he groaned. "I want you, Edwina."

Her hand traced his shoulder, down to his elbow, his forearm and then to the hand that covered her breast. Then, as if realizing, she quickly pulled away.

He grabbed her hand. "Don't be afraid, Edwina."

"I'm not afraid, Prescott. It's just... well, I just realized, we're in a public park..."

Prescott blinked, then chuckled, then, throwing his head back, he roared with laughter.

"Don't mock me!" she chided, making him howl even louder.

He caught her hand and kissed her palm. "I'm not mocking you. You're just so bloody practical. I love it. You're right. We need to find some place private." *And soon.* He couldn't recall the last time he'd been this aroused.

"Where can we go?" There was an urgency to her words that he gloried in and longed to satisfy.

"I can't have you at Andersen Hall..."

She bit that swollen lip. "And I have to consider the ladies at the society and my servants..."

No, of course she wouldn't want them to know...

"Oh, I have an idea." She moved to pull away from him, but he locked his arms.

Leaning up on her toes, she pressed a moist kiss to his lips. "I'm not going very far."

Reluctantly, he released her.

Reaching into the reticule hanging from her wrist, she pulled something out attached to a ribbon and pressed a piece of metal into his hand. "Take this key. It's to the rear door of my house. It's not used by anyone past nine, as almost all of my servants are in bed for the night."

As she dragged him down the stairs to exit the park, he couldn't keep the hunger from his voice. "It must already be past seven..."

"I know." Her teeth flashed bright in the moonlight.

She giggled, then laughed out loud, a deliciously musical sound that echoed off the trees.

Sprinting alongside her, Prescott laughed, too, a guffaw from deep in his belly that felt so good that he laughed again. He felt lighthearted, expectant and intoxicated by Edwina's charm. Chasing after her, he thanked the heavens for the gift of Edwina Ross.

Chapter 22

E dwina was so nervous her movements were jerky and her heart pounded in her chest as she replaced the less expensive tallow candles in her bedroom with wax ones.

She couldn't quite believe she'd been so brazen tonight. Kissing Prescott was one thing, but actually discussing having an affair? Then inviting him over, knowing perfectly well what she was proposing! She felt as if her body and her mind had been taken over by some foreign being, one with a daring bravado that Edwina utterly lacked.

After lighting the wicks, she tossed another log into the grate and turned. Her chamber was an utter mess.

Her wardrobe and drawers stood open with the garments inside askew. The beautiful embroidered coverlet on the bed was layered with discarded dresses, petticoats and stays. Even her silk damask bed hangings were twisted like ribbons snaking the mahogany bed-posts.

Her writing desk sat open with assorted sheets of paper, quills, ink blotters and bottles strewn about from her fruitless attempts at making a list to ready for Prescott's visit tonight. Three or four of the efforts lay crumpled around the legs of the standing mirror nearby. She tried not to think about the fact that the gilded mirror was a gift from her father.

What time was it anyway? Oh, dear. The water in her basin was likely cold by now.

Hurriedly she walked over to the washstand, un-dressed and bathed her body with the now cool lily-of-the-valley-scented water.

The chilly air from the partially open window raised bumps on her skin, and quickly she put aside her wash towel and pulled a silk chemise from the pile on the bed. Donning it, she turned to examine her reflection in the tall mirror.

The ivory garment hung straight to the knees, like an oblong pillowcase with her sickly-pale arms jutting out, resembling sticks.

Biting her lip, Edwina fingered the chemise's only ornamentation, the muslin frill edging on the square neck threaded with a silken drawstring.

"Can there by anything less enticing?" she groaned, almost ready to give up.

But Edwina Ross never gave up. Besides, Prescott was attracted to her, he'd said so himself.

Sighing, she stared at her reflection. "Now what? I'm putting on the clothing simply to have it taken off." Hopefully. "So what does one wear to a proper seduction?"

The chills on her bottom gave her the first clue.

Reaching for her pink knitted silk drawers, she stepped into the tubular legs gathered in a band below the knee and bordered with pretty ivory Brussels lace. Twisting around, she struggled to tie the laced waistband in the back.

She'd been so excited and nervous about her rendezvous with Prescott that she'd sent Penny, her maid, off to her sister's for the night, and had directed the rest of the servants to quit the upstairs. Edwina hadn't wanted any witnesses to her brazen affair. It wasn't that she was embarrassed, well, not completely, but it was more like she didn't want anyone or anything to stop her or make her feel uncomfortable about her choices.

Penny had raced off to see her new nephew without a backward glance, leaving Edwina, unwittingly, to make garment decisions based upon what she could manage herself. That excluded most of the new wardrobe Fanny had helped her to procure and made for some interesting challenges when it came to her stays.

Staring over at the petticoats and stays lying on the bed, frustration welled inside of her. She wasn't very good at thinking strategically about seduction. She was quite terrible at it, in fact.

And then there was the matter of arranging her hair.

Her excitement slowly dissolved, to be replaced by an anxiety so acute it splintered her skin and made her belly twist in knots.

Oh, what a dreadful corner she'd painted herself into! Why had she given Prescott her key?

"Oh my Lord, what have I done?" Slowly she sank onto the bed in a puddle of woe.

She'd invited a deliciously dazzling man to visit her

in her apartments for a dalliance, yet knew not one whit about how to go about it! And Prescott was used to worldly ladies who knew exactly what to do, how to act and certainly *what to wear* to a seduction!

Deep in her heart, she knew that the clothing wasn't so important, but she was suffering a dreadful case of nerves. But for whatever rational thought, the fear welling up inside of her was as real as the tears dripping down her cheeks. Dropping her head into her hands, she sobbed.

"There you are!" a deep voice called.

Horrified to be found in such a state, with her chamber a veritable disaster, Edwina panicked. Jumping up, she grabbed the nearest bed hanging, whipped the damask across her body and pressed her face into the cloth.

"What's the matter, Edwina?" His footsteps on the carpet stopped only a few feet away. "Tell me what ails you!"

His sweet concern twisted something deep in her heart, making her feel all the more miserable. She shook her head, unable to speak from her crying. Unable, even, to pull her face from the fabric and look him in the eye.

Stepping near, Prescott wrapped his brawny arm around her shaking shoulders and hugged her. The scent of musk teased.

It felt so very nice to be held as if she were cherished.

"I understand, Edwina. Don't worry, we don't have to do anything. I'm a scoundrel for even trying."

Peeking out from the drapery, she inhaled a shaky breath. "Don't...Don't say that."

"It's the truth. I'm an unfeeling blackguard not to have considered how hard this would be for you."

Understanding and strikingly handsome? They must have broken the mold after Prescott Devane was born.

Coming out from the damask a bit more, she sniffed. "Well, I just don't..." A small hiccup escaped from her mouth. "Don't know how to do this."

"Do what?"

How could she explain that not only was she ill prepared, poorly dressed and as attractive as a haystack, but her nose was probably as red as a drunkard's from crying? Misery overwhelmed her and her face crumpled, so she quickly dropped her head into her draped hands once more.

"Shhh," he soothed, trying to draw her into the circle of his arms, but the bed hanging hampered him.

Winding her out and into his arms, he tugged the fabric free. He pulled her close and she buried her face into his broad shoulder. Her nose was pressed deep into the soft twill of his worsted wool coat. Shuddering, she sighed, wallowing in his heat and that delightful male musk he wore.

"I understand, Edwina." His hand caressed her hair. "Don't fret. We're not going to do anything."

Disappointment overlapped her misery. He didn't desire her any longer. And who could blame him? She was a blubbering mess. If she was in his shoes, she wouldn't want her either.

She couldn't quite believe that she'd been so brazen, had boldly invited him over and given him her key and it had all come to naught. Another sob escaped.

"Why don't we sit here for a bit, until you've calmed down, and then I'll go home."

Go home? He was leaving her to her misery? An ache of sorrow twisted inside her heart, and a fresh set of tears welled in her eyes.

But being a creature unused to weeping, Edwina found that the new tears did not come. It was almost as if the well had run dry. Her stock of tears for the year had been exhausted, and now it was time to start behaving like the rational lady she usually was.

Exhaling a shaky breath, she swallowed and pulled herself together. Her natural fortitude began to re-emerge and logical thinking came to the fore once more. She realized that she had two choices: She could either throw herself at Prescott in an attempt to rekindle his passion or try to gather the frayed tatters of her dignity. Since she doubted that any discerning man would want a red-nosed, hay-haired, blubbering woman, she opted for dignity.

Slowly drawing away from him, she turned around so he couldn't see her blotchy face and walked over to the open window. Staring out, she wondered, *How is it possible to save my dignity after such a pathetic display?*

Then she spied her reflection in the window. She was only wearing a chemise and drawers! And the neck of her chemise was hanging open making her look like a doxy!

Could this night get any worse?

Dropping her head into her hands, she suppressed a groan.

Well, there was naught to be done for it. He'd had the full view. Moreover, after seeing it all, he certainly wasn't pouncing on her in heated passion.

But then again, she could hardly blame him. In fact, none of this was his fault in the least.

Wiping the remnants of her tears with the back of her hands, she coughed into her fist. "I'm sorry..." Her voice cracked.

"You've nothing to be sorry for." His footsteps on the carpet and the warmth of his body indicated that he stood immediately behind her. Yet, he did not touch her. Another shaft of gloom pierced her heart.

"I shouldn't have led you to believe... Well, I'm just... sorry, Prescott."

"You haven't done anything wrong, Edwina. I'm the one who's to be blamed. I shouldn't have pressed you when obviously you weren't ready."

"Ready?" A hysterical giggle burst from her lips. "I don't know if it's possible to be any *less* ready than I am."

He stepped closer and she could smell the musk scent he wore.

Garnering her courage, she swallowed, deciding that she might as well get it over with. Slowly she turned.

His face twisted with concern. "Oh, Edwina." Then he reached for her, pulling her into his arms and hugging her close.

"That bad, eh?" she attempted to make light. Lord this felt so very, very good. Pressing her ear to his chest, she listened to the strong beat of his heart, savoring this moment, for she knew that it would too soon dissolve into mist.

"I feel terrible for causing you such distress," he murmured. "Your devotion to your husband is admirable."

She blinked, her lashes grazing his woolen coat. "Wh-what?"

"I should never have endeavored to tempt you into

besmirching the memory of your beloved husband. Obviously your feelings are still strong. He was a... very fortunate man."

Pulling back, she stared up at his face. "You think that"—she waved a hand at her blotchy face—"this is because I'm sad about my late husband?"

"I know you loved him dearly, and obviously even thinking about being with me upsets you very much. You are a woman of deep sensibilities, Edwina, and I couldn't admire you more for it."

"Oh, dear." Now she *really* felt pathetic. But she couldn't hide behind the façade of grieving widow; it simply wasn't her style to be so insincere, even if it would salvage her dignity as nothing else could.

Disentangling from his embrace, she stepped over to the bed, pulled out an icy pink dressing gown from the pile and put it on. She tied the wrap around her waist a bit too tightly, but left it knotted anyway, as a penance of sorts, she supposed.

Clasping her hands before her, she faced him once more. "I'm not upset about my late husband, Prescott."

"You're not?"

She sighed. "I suppose... what it all boils down to... is that I'm a novice at this passion business." She motioned to the room. "I'm a mess. I don't know how to be... enticing. I'm no worldly widow and I hate... well..." Her cheeks flamed. "I hate feeling so incompetent, especially when you are used to dealing with ladies who are so much more... sophisticated than I."

He stepped forward. "So this has nothing to do with your deceased husband?"

"No."

"It would be perfectly natural to feel a sense of... disloyalty."

Pursing her lips, she shook her head. "None."

A hopeful gleam filled his emerald gaze. "That by being with me you might be tarnishing his memory?"

She shook her head. "No."

"That you couldn't help but compare...?"

"Well, I suppose that it's impossible to avoid making comparisons."

His face fell.

She hid her smile. "But you fare much better than Sir Geoffrey in that regard."

Looking up, his gaze was doubtful. "Really?"

"By far. I'll venture it's like comparing... burned toast to a hot scone with melted butter, fresh strawberry preserves and a sizzling piece of bacon on the side."

"I wouldn't happen to be the scone, by any chance?"

"Oh, yes." She smiled. "Steaming hot."

"Now, a worldlier widow might have mentioned sausage instead of bacon."

Still smiling, she smacked her hand to her head. "Yet another ineptitude!"

She was rewarded with one of his heart-melting smiles that made her feel as if she were bathed in warm radiance.

Stepping over, he grabbed her hands and wrapped them behind her back, making her arch up at him. "I'm here, Edwina, because I want you. These... ineptitudes as you call them, are trivial."

"You caught me crying into my bed hangings for heaven's sake. Not exactly the most effective means of seducing you."

"It's certainly unique..."

"And in my drawers no less! Certainly not what one wears for a seduction."

"On that count, I have to agree. But you remedied that lapse."

"By putting on my pink dressing gown?"

"No, silly. By putting on your fresh smile. It's the only attire needed for a proper seduction."

Then his lips pressed down to hers, telling her with actions instead of words that Prescott Devane didn't give a bloody damn about her attire, her messy room, her mussed hair, her blotchy face or even her bright red nose.

Chapter 23

After kicking off his shoes and ripping off his coat, waistcoat and shirt, Prescott kissed Edwina so thoroughly her head spun. Her hands explored the glorious planes of his back, and she sighed blissfully.

His kiss was so inspiring she felt as if she were elevated to a higher plane, until she realized that Prescott had lifted her off the floor and carried her over to the bed.

Hugging her close, he reached down and swept the clothing off the bed. Then he laid Edwina down, covering her body with his hard, lean form. He pressed himself deeply between her legs, claiming her neck with hot, wet, open-mouth kisses that left her panting.

"You smell so good," he murmured as he laved her neck.

His mouth moved lower, circling the heated flesh of

her chest with his tongue, then dipping down to the muslin frill edging of her chemise. Pushing down the thin fabric, his mouth enveloped her bare breast, claiming the nipple and sucking gently.

Edwina's back arched. "Oh, oh...God..."

"No, it's only me," he murmured, smiling up at her. Then he drew her into his mouth once more.

Her eyes closed as her body thrummed with an overpowering sense of need building inside of her. No one had ever touched her this way, as if drawing forth her passion with a conjurer's hand...and mouth...and hard, glorious body....

Her hips moved of their own volition, pressing against his broad chest, wanting him inside of her.

Reaching down to the leg of her drawers, Prescott's hand teasingly caressed her ankle, then inched higher, untying the ribbon of the loose garments. He thrust his hand inside the knitted silk, grazing her calf with his titillating touch, then moved higher.

Edwina held her breath as his hand traveled steadily up to her knee, then thigh, grazing the fine hairs so that they stood on end. Her womanhood convulsed with desire.

"I need to touch you," he said, his voice a guttural growl.

Pulling his hand out from under the fabric leg, he moved to the slit between her thighs and through the seam.

His fingers slipped between the moist folds of her womanhood, teasing her flesh with a touch that seared her to her core. Her eyes flew open, then slammed closed. Clutching the mattress, she was lost to the sensation of his fingers teasing, enticing, arousing her to a state where there was nothing but the feel of him touching her.

As his deft fingers rubbed the hard nub between her thighs, heat surged, her body thrummed and she was frantic with a need she'd never felt before. She wanted him to fill her. Now!

"Prescott..." She was panting, moving against him with an urgency she hadn't known was possible.

Stopping, he looked up, his smile wide, white and wicked. "Yes, darling?"

"Please!"

"Your wish is my command, my lady."

He reached beneath her back and nimbly undid the laced tie at her waist. Slipping the drawers down, he kissed her bare hip, her thigh, her calf and her ankle, then moved up to her inner thigh once more, planting a moist hot kiss.

"Wh-what...?" Alarm caused her to sit up.

"Relax, Edwina. Trust me."

After a moment, she lay back. Staring up at the white ceiling, she wondered what in heaven's name he was up to down there.

His tongue teased along her inner thigh, raising every hair on her body and causing a new wave of heat in her core. Her legs widened giving him freer access. Then his mouth was on her, claiming her, suckling her innermost place.

It felt so good she wanted to scream, but she had no air.

His tongue delved inside of her, exploring, teasing, sucking. Her back arched and she flamed, every inch of her being consumed in a passionate inferno. She had no air, her heart was racing wildly, it was...

"Too much..." she panted.

Her world exploded. Her womanhood convulsed, heat rushed and she saw stars behind her closed lids.

With her heart still racing, the world slowly spun back into place. Breath filled her lungs once more and she shuddered. She swallowed, still overcome. Then she opened her eyes.

Prescott lay beside her, resting prone on his elbow. His auburn hair was tousled, his lush lips smiling, his golden cheeks flushed and his emerald gaze simmering with dark passion. His chest was a creamy plane of undulating muscle she longed to explore.

She reached for him, wrapping her arms around his broad shoulders and pulling him toward her as she slid closer to him. Her breasts rubbed against his hard nipples causing such arousal, a deep moan escaped from her lips.

She kissed him, tasting her ardor mixed with his own delicious flavor, savoring him the way he had savored her.

He hesitated, keeping himself up on his elbow, but she hugged him close and pulled him down, demanding that his body lie prone along hers, so close that every part of her felt blanketed by his hard, lean form.

Her tongue delved into his mouth, exploring, teasing, sucking him.

Slowly, he relaxed, kissing her back, grinding his hips into hers so that through his breeches his stiff manhood pressed into the soft flesh between her thighs, reviving the incredible pleasure of just moments ago.

Edwina rocked beneath him, lost to the sensation of his hard member stroking her core, her legs wide-open, her eyes closed shut, his mouth and body arousing her, making her feel as if she'd been asleep her entire lifetime until this night.

"God, you're magnificent," he muttered, breathing hard.

She opened her eyes and met his dark gaze, bereft of words. She so desperately wanted him, wanted him to feel as good as he'd made her feel.

Prescott watched Edwina's face as he slid up, gliding his stiff manhood against her.

She closed her eyes and moaned, rolling her head to the side. "I want you inside of me..."

Thank heavens, because he didn't know if he could last much longer.

Prescott had been with many women, women who knew how to bring a man to the heights of pleasure. But nothing he'd ever experienced had prepared him for the fiery pitch of Edwina's desire. Each groan came from deep within her, shaking him to his core, making his shaft thicken and throb with yearning to plunge deep inside her. Each hitch of her breath signaled a new level of pleasure, a delightful new experience of learning all that her body was capable of. She had the most astonishing capacity for passion. And he was ready to explore it to the hilt.

Rolling over, Prescott unbuttoned his breeches and pulled off his smallclothes. Then he turned to face her once more.

She was glorious, with her wild ebony tresses, her onyx eyes shimmering dark with passion, her porcelain skin flushed pink and her cherry red lips swollen from his kisses. One lush pink breast still spilled out from the top of her chemise and from the waist down she was exposed for his full perusal. Her arched waist fanned out at the hips, giving a perfect frame to a triangle of dark, soft curls. Her curvaceous legs lay open, spread before him as if ready for the taking.

She lifted herself up on one elbow. Her gaze fixed on his shaft and her eyes widened with wonder.

"Have you never...?"

Slowly she shook her head. "The candles were always snuffed..." Her tongue slipped out of her mouth and licked the corner of her lip. His rod jumped.

Leaning forward, she rose up on bare knees. "May I touch you?"

He swallowed, wordlessly nodding.

Hesitantly, her hand reached out, her fingers gently grazing the head.

He gripped the coverlet, hanging on to his control, but just barely.

"It's so smooth..." Her fingers skimmed down his shaft, burning him with her touch. "And warm."

Not since he was fourteen had he precipitately spilled his seed, but he was coming damned close.

"Edwina," he gasped. "I can't wait much longer."

Her eyes widened some more. "Oh, sorry."

"Stop apologizing."

He grabbed her then, laying her back on the bed and settling between her legs.

She giggled, then laughed, throwing her arms around him and kissing him with a passion that tossed all thought from his mind, except for being inside of her.

Reaching down, he fingered her curls and she gasped, opening her legs wider.

God, she was wet.

Bracing himself, he plunged deep, burying himself to the hilt. Then he froze for fear of losing control.

"Are you all right?" Edwina whispered, afraid that he was hurt in some way. His face was contorted as if he were in terrible pain. She, on the other hand, felt full, stretched, but the sensation was growing on her by the second. In fact, it was becoming quite...fantastic. Biting her lip, she withheld a groan.

"I'm...fine," he bit out, his eyes still closed. Then he began to move, sliding his shaft out and then plunging back in, deeper each time. Riding her, carrying her...

"Oh...oh...my." She closed her eyes, lost.

The world became a dark, glorious place of stars and heat and joyous sensation. Edwina's body bucked as her womanhood gripped him inside her.

He pounded into her, faster, harder.

Prescott cried out, and her insides thrilled. Clutching him for dear life, Edwina screamed as her womanhood convulsed around him.

He collapsed on top of her, his breath coming hard and warming her neck. They were both out of breath, their bodies slick with sweat, their heartbeats clamoring against each other.

Realizing that she was still gripping him so tightly her fingers were curled into his skin, she quickly released him, exhaling a long, shuddering breath.

After what felt like an eternity, she opened her eyes.

His skin glowed golden in the candlelight as· she traced his round shoulder, relishing the velvety feel beneath her fingertips.

Prescott Devane was a man among men.

She supposed it would take such a man, a man of

great experience with women, to draw her passion so memorably. She tried not to think about the many, many, many women he'd probably bedded...

Stop it, Edwina. Don't ruin it. Have the grace to accept this wonderful moment for what it is: special.

To her, at least. And she would savor the memory forever.

Her hands traveled to his back and down, delighting in the sensation of touching him. His smooth skin, the hard curves of his muscle, the bone beneath.

"You feel so good." Sighing, she hugged him close.

After a moment, he leaned up on one elbow and looked down at her, his face relaxed, happy. "You're lovely, Edwina."

She bit her lip. "I hope... well, I hope I did everything to your, ah... satisfaction."

His brow furrowed, and slowly, he disengaged from her, sitting up and pulling the sheet about his waist. She felt bereft, and a bit embarrassed as she grabbed her pink wrapper from the floor, donned it and sat across from him.

The silence grew thick.

Running his hand through his coppery mane, Prescott exhaled. "We don't need to talk about it now, not if you don't want to..."

She shrugged, repeating what he'd said in the gazebo, "Now is as good a time as any, I suppose."

He scratched his chin. "Well, I'm just wondering. What the hell was wrong with your husband?"

She straightened. "Wh-what?"

"Was he ill?"

She shook her head.

"An invalid?"

She shook her head.

"Then how on earth could he have been married to you, for how long...?"

"Three years." Tears of joy burned the back of her eyes.

"For three years and make you think that you 'weren't built for passion'? It's boggling!"

Edwina smiled. Then she giggled. Then laughed so hard tears ran down her cheeks.

"Come here." He pulled her into the circle of his arms and hugged her close. Inhaling the heady scents of musk and their desire, she sighed, feeling so very, very wonderful.

"Did he..." Prescott's tone was tight. "Did he ever hurt you?"

"No. Sir Geoffrey was...a bit of a cold fish, I think. I didn't realize it at the time. I didn't know...well, anything about what went on between husband and wife. And well, I'd rather not talk about it, save to say, that it wasn't a particularly enjoyable experience, for either of us."

"So you weren't 'ardently devoted' to him?"

She looked up at him. "Of course I was devoted to him, he was my husband."

His brow knitted and then relaxed. "Your commitment is admirable. But I have to ask again, in all those years together, not once..."

"No. I never had an experience anything remotely like the one we just had."

A satisfied gleam lit his eyes and he grinned like the cat who'd licked the cream.

"You don't have to look so pleased with yourself, Prescott Devane!"

"For pleasuring you? What's wrong with that?"

She smiled. "Nothing, I suppose. Especially since it's in the name of science."

His grin widened. "Science."

"Your experiments..."

"Oh, yes. Hmmm. I think I'm feeling the need for a bit of experimentation right now..."

Chapter 24

The next morning Janelle huffed, "You've got that look on your face again, Edwina."

"Hmmm?" Edwina tried to pull her mind away from memories of toe-curling, wet kisses and the caress of Prescott's magical fingers, as she blindly watched the countryside sail by through the window of the coach.

"You look as if someone sprinkled fairy dust on your head and you're in an enchanted haze."

Turning away from the view, Edwina glanced across the carriage and was thankful to see that Prescott was still sound asleep in the seat beside Janelle. His head had fallen forward, his soft auburn hair listing over his forehead, and his face was relaxed, his lush lips slightly parted. With each bump in the road, his hair would quiver and his breath would catch as if he'd been slightly roused, then he would immediately fall back to sleep. The man managed to look adorable even in slumber.

Not that they'd done much sleeping last night. Other nocturnal activities had taken precedence, and Edwina didn't miss her rest in the least. In fact, she felt practically electrified.

"There you go again." Janelle waved a hand. "How are you to keep your wits about you at the Kendricks' if your head is in the clouds?"

Edwina forced her brow to furrow and her gaze to focus. "Why, you're being positively ridiculous, Janelle. I'm perfectly alert and the plan is foremost in all of my thoughts."

"Good, because we may have a bit of a wrinkle."

Now that got Edwina's full attention. "What kind of wrinkle?"

Janelle's blue-green eyes veered over to ensure that Prescott was still sleeping. "I didn't want to say anything in front of him. Just in case... well, in case he didn't agree with our tactics."

"What are you talking about, Janelle? We can trust Prescott."

"Of course we can trust him, Edwina." Janelle waved a hand as if Edwina was being ridiculous. "It's simply that I have it on good authority that Lady Pomfry was lately added to the guest list and—"

"Really?" Edwina straightened.

"Yes, and that same authority informed me that Lady Pomfry is intent on reclaiming a certain man's attentions." She motioned to Prescott. "You know who that might be."

Edwina swallowed, her mouth suddenly dry. "Do you believe...?" Looking at Prescott, she whispered, "You don't think he still has feelings for her, do you?"

"It's hard to tell with him. He keeps his cards

facedown, this one. What I do know is that he likes the ladies he chooses to escort in the first place. And they did have quite the affair." Janelle shrugged. "So I'm sure to some extent, he's fond of her."

A tightness suddenly constricted Edwina's chest and she wondered why her stays felt so snug.

"Which is why I wanted to decide the matter before we inform him of our intentions," Janelle continued. "If we decide, that is, to inform him in advance of how we're going to deal with her."

"Deal with her?"

"She might become a nuisance, but more importantly, Lady Pomfry might interfere with the plan."

Edwina scratched her chin. "To be fair, I'm not sure that she will have a negative effect on our efforts. In fact, her involvement adds a certain...drama to the events, possibly providing diversion to cover our true activities."

Janelle tilted her head. "Perhaps. But it also might bring a bit too much focus on you two, thereby making it all the more difficult to execute the plan. If Lady Pomfry is intent on Prescott, then the two of you might not be able to slip away unnoticed."

"Would you be willing to act as an intermediary? Deflect her away if she becomes too overbearing?"

"You know I'm far too nice to make such pretenses, Edwina. Besides, she's a shrewd woman, not so easily deterred."

"Well, we must ask Prescott to reject her soundly." Edwina liked that notion. Very much. "Give her the cold shoulder."

"Prescott told me that he already gave her a firm *congé,* but she, very obviously, didn't accept the rebuff."

"Do you have a better idea, then?"

"As a matter of fact, I do." Janelle lifted her kidskin reticule from the floor. Pulling out a small satchel, she held it in her gloved hand.

"What is that?"

"Cat hair."

"Cat hair? What do you propose to do with that?"

"Knock the fox out of the henhouse. I have it on good authority that if she's anywhere near a cat, she falls into a fit of sneezes, her eyes go big as plums and she can't stop itching."

Edwina chuckled, she couldn't help it. But at the look on Janelle's face, she sobered. "You're actually serious?"

"If we put some in Prescott's pockets, then she'll be unable to go near him. And think of how unattractive she'll be."

"I would not impose such suffering on anyone and, besides, don't you think it's a bit much?" Edwina raised her brows. "I mean, we're all adults here..."

Stuffing the satchel back into her reticule, Janelle sniffed. "Ginny said that you wouldn't do it, but I wanted to offer the option just in case things got difficult."

"Well, I thank you for your initiative but doubt that we will have any use for such tactics."

"There was someone else lately added to the guest list, Edwina, and I cannot decide if it's significant or not. I would have had it sooner, but Lord and Lady Kendrick only completed the guest list last night."

"Nothing like waiting until the last minute with an assemblage of guests heading toward your home."

"Lord Kendrick is the kind of man who enjoys a bit of chaos. He's bored unless there is something to become frantic about. Luckily for him, Lady Kendrick is the exact opposite. I often wonder how they manage, but by all accounts, they're quite content."

"Hmmm. Based upon the short notice, I would presume that this event is of Lord Kendrick's making. So who is this new guest?"

"Sir Lee Devane."

"Devane?"

"Yes, Devane."

"What...?" Prescott roused, lifting his head and inhaling deeply. Yawning into his hand, he blinked bleary eyes. "Yes, what now?"

Janelle shot her a quelling glance. "Edwina and I were just discussing the fact that Sir Lee Devane will be joining the group in Essex."

"Sir Lee? I'm not acquainted with the man. Who is he?" Edwina was relieved and a bit surprised to see that there was no hint of distress or emotion in Prescott's emerald gaze in response to the name.

Janelle scratched her chin. "I would think that as an orphan you would seek out every family that shared your surname."

"Janelle!" Edwina chided, her cheeks heating guiltily for thinking the same thing. "Don't be such a nosing ninny."

Prescott shrugged. "I don't mind, Edwina, it's a reasonable question given my background. But to answer you, Janelle, I might care about the name if I actually had an interest in finding my family. Which I don't." Straightening his coat, he looked out the window. "And besides, Devane was not my father's name."

Janelle leaned forward. "So you know who your father is?"

"Don't answer that if you don't wish to," Edwina interjected. For all of her curiosity, she didn't want to open old wounds that could pain him. "It's really none of our business..."

After adjusting the hat on his knee, Prescott shrugged. "I don't usually discuss such things, but here, now, well, I consider myself among friends."

"You are." Edwina smiled and her cheeks heated with warmth.

Janelle shot her a quizzical glance, then turned to Prescott. "Most assuredly you are among friends. I consider everything we say to be of the utmost confidence. Now tell me, who is your father?"

"His name was Ronald Ives."

"That can traditionally be a woodsman's name..." Janelle raised a brow questioningly.

"He was a gamekeeper, actually."

"And your mother?" Janelle demanded. "What of her?"

"A gentleman's daughter who was cast off by her family for marrying beneath her."

Janelle tapped her finger to her chin. "So you're not a bastard?"

"Only to those who annoy me." His smile didn't quite reach his eyes and Edwina could tell that he was making light to cover what had to be painful for him.

"Why don't you use the surname Ives?" Janelle inquired.

Edwina shifted in her seat. "Really, Janelle, your prying knows no bounds!"

Prescott stared out the window a long moment, his gaze lost in memory. "After my parents married, well,

Ives wasn't around for long. He would send money now and again, but never bothered to know me. After my mother died of typhus—"

"Oh, how dreadful." Edwina raised her hand to her mouth and Janelle shot her a quelling glare. "I'm so sorry."

Prescott tilted his head, not meeting her eyes. "Thank you, Edwina." He stared out the window. "After she died, I lived with a neighbor for a while, then when the money stopped coming, she left me at Andersen Hall. When Headmaster Dunn asked me my name, I simply picked the first one to pop into my head."

"Devane."

"Yes, it was scratched into a Bible my mother left me. A beat-up old edition that she'd said she found in a circulating library and had forgotten to return."

Edwina's heart pinched. "You must have been very angry with your father to spurn his name like that."

"He'd ruined my mother's life."

"And yours."

Prescott shrugged, brushing it off. "I hardly knew him enough to care. Besides, from all my mother told me, I'm better off having been without him."

"I'm so sorry," Edwina murmured.

His gaze was cool. "Don't be. I'm not. I was so much better off than most; I had Andersen Hall and Headmaster Dunn."

She didn't believe him and it took all of Edwina's self-control not to reach out to comfort him. For all of his offhand discourse, she knew that it could not have been easy for him. A flash of resentment shot through her, directed at his wretched family. How could they forsake a wonderful man such as him? Fools.

Pursing her lips, Janelle's eyes narrowed. "Who were your mother's people?"

"I don't know." Prescott exhaled. "Mother refused ever to speak of them, except to say that they cared more about pride and honor than their own flesh and blood."

"So all those stories floating around town about you are wrong?"

Prescott's smile was tight. "People like tall tales. I let them believe what they will and usually don't discuss the truth; it's far too tedious."

"It doesn't sound tedious to me," Edwina cried. "It sounds downright tragic. And unsupportable. How could your mother's family have tossed her out like that? Especially with a baby?"

"They probably didn't know about me." Prescott looked away. "I came long after the rift."

"They might have guessed there would be a child!" Edwina crossed her arms, not knowing where to put all of this anger. "To abandon you goes beyond all reproach."

"What Prescott's family did was not, regrettably, uncommon." Shaking her head, Janelle folded her hands in her lap like a cleric making a sermon. "I hate to say it, but Prescott isn't the only one with relations who put great stock in pride, honor and fear of embarrassment. You've already tested your father, Edwina; I don't believe that you've much of his indulgence left."

Edwina looked away, anger and distress warring inside of her. She *hoped* that her father would do right by his daughter and never forsake her. But knowing him, he might see cutting her off as the right approach under certain circumstances. It was a good thing the engagement with Prescott would be long over before she had to face her father.

Somehow the thought only added to Edwina's distress.

Janelle sniffed. "Which is why I believe that your little plan, Edwina, is going to smash egg right in your self-satisfied face."

Prescott gently laid a hand on Janelle's arm, as if to say, "enough". "So what do you know of Sir Lee, Janelle?"

"He worked in the Foreign Office." Janelle sniffed. "Keeping an eye on all foreigners' whereabouts and performing other activities my connection was unwilling to discuss. All he did say was that Sir Lee's activities were quite clandestine."

Edwina stiffened. "Could he be the blackmailer? He certainly would come across many sensitive things in that post." *He also might have had contact with Ginny's former lover Gérardin Valmont through his work at the Foreign Office.*

"It's entirely possible." Janelle scratched her chin. "I propose that I get to know Sir Lee and appraise his character."

Leaning forward, Edwina urged, "Prescott, if you would do the same? You're good at gauging temperament and I would very much like to know what you think."

"Of course. We can also make Sir Lee's rooms the first on the list to be searched. In his position in the Foreign Office he may have traveled to Paris, hence the François Millicent shoes. He'd surely bring them along to such a gathering."

Noises could be heard through the opened window

and Edwina peered out. "We're nearing Witham, our last stop to change horses before we reach our destination." A small flutter of nerves quivered in her middle and she leaned back in the seat.

Prescott's eyes met hers, filled with compassion and soothing. "The sooner the better, Edwina, to remove the sword of Damocles from over your head. All will be well. I promise you."

Guilt twisted inside her gut. "I have a confession to make, Prescott..."

"Edwina..." Janelle warned with a glare.

"Prescott, I'm not being blackmailed, but someone I love dearly is." She bit her lip. "I'm sorry I lied. I just couldn't allow you to say no and didn't, well, didn't feel that I could breach my friend's trust."

"Ginny?"

"How...?"

His eyes shifted to her, then Janelle. "I suspected as much when the two of you were so 'cloak and dagger' at the ball the other night. And Ginny's the one person who seems able to draw you two together and make you more protective than a pair of mother hens."

"You're not angry?"

He shook his head. "In your place I might have done the same." His smooth lips lifted at the corners. "Although I would have done a better job at pretending to have a salacious past."

Looking out the window, she pursed her lips to stop them from lifting. "I don't know whether to be relieved or insulted."

"I have to agree with you, Prescott." Janelle wagged her finger. "Edwina is not a very credible actress."

"I know. It's one of the things I like most about her."

One of the things? There are more? Pleased, Edwina looked up, her gaze meeting his, and that familiar excitement flashed within her. His emerald eyes were filled with merriment, tinged with affection. Had he only been teasing? Or was she not the only one whose feelings were engaged? If his were, too, if only a little...her heart swelled at the possibility. But no, she was reading too much into the innocent little comment. Or was she?

He smiled. "Edwina doesn't alter her mien when she engages different people. A duke gets the same kindness as a shopkeeper. And, whether she's alone with me or out in the bosom of the *haut ton,* she always treats me with the same consideration. A rarity, in my experience."

Janelle pounded her hand on her thigh. "But don't you want to know Ginny's secret, Prescott? She would want you to know, since you're placing your neck on the guillotine for her. She said as much to me the other day."

Prescott's face looked doubtful. "I don't think there's any benefit—"

"She had an affair with Gérardin Valmont."

His eyes widened. "The infamous anarchist who published that dreadful book about the royal family?"

"The very one." Janelle nodded.

"Even though the newspapers like to bring up his name every time a new voice cries out in dissension, he was barred from the country almost twenty years ago. Their affair must have been ages past and wouldn't *necessarily* taint her reputation..."

"He's the father of Ginny's daughter, Judith, born during Ginny's marriage to Lord Ensley. If Judith's fiancé's family learns of it, the wedding would be off, her daughter shunned and Ginny, well, she might as well become a hermit."

Grimacing, Edwina shook her head. "Judith would never forgive her mother and it would be a disaster from which Ginny might not ever recover. Not socially anyway, which would destroy her."

"It wouldn't be good for The Society for the Enrichment and Learning of Females, either," Janelle added with a sigh. "It'd be a disaster."

Prescott's emerald eyes blazed with determination. "Then we will ensure that no one learns of it."

"Edwina is right." Janelle beamed. "You are the stuff heroes are made of, Prescott Devane."

"Janelle!" Edwina's cheeks flamed.

"A hero, eh?" Prescott scratched his chin, smiling. "You said that?"

"I, ah, I was jesting...well not really, but..." Tossing up her hands, Edwina sighed. "At this rate your head's going to be as big as one of those flying balloons."

Grinning, Prescott leaned back and closed his eyes. "I can live with that." That silly smile remained on his lips the whole way to the Kendrick estate.

And Edwina didn't mind in the least.

Chapter 25

"**I** must confess, I expected the man to be taller,"
Janelle murmured under her breath as she and
Edwina strolled down the tiered steps leading to the
garden.

"And younger," Edwina added, holding her hand to
the brim of her hat to block the afternoon sun. "He has
to be almost seventy years of age."

The topic of their discourse, Sir Lee Devane, stood in
the garden below, leaning lightly on a gold-topped cane.
The gray-haired wizened chap wore a black coat, old-
fashioned dove gray knee breeches with white stockings
and black-buckled shoes. He was examining something
in his hand flashing in the sunlight.

"Well, even if he looks harmless, we must be wary."
Janelle stepped down the last step and onto the white-
graveled path. "Of all the guests, he seems the most
suspect."

"You mean besides Lady Pomfry?" Edwina muttered under her breath, joining her. She'd been trying not to think about how much the woman's attendance was upsetting her, but a nasty heavy feeling had been brewing in her middle ever since she'd heard that the lady's carriage had arrived only an hour before.

Edwina's only comfort was in knowing that Prescott was searching Sir Lee's rooms at that moment, so he couldn't possibly be with his former paramour.

Janelle inhaled a deep breath. "Come, Edwina. Let us ensure that he doesn't return to the house anytime soon."

Sir Lee turned, waving his cane excitedly. "This Claude glass is positively ingenious!" He held out a mirror about a hand's width wide that was slightly bowed. "You must have a try! Everything looks quite different from this perspective."

"I don't believe that we've had the pleasure of an introduction." Janelle gave quiet rebuke. "I am Lady Blankett. And this is my friend Lady Ross."

He tipped his hat. "Sir Lee Devane, at your service."

Just as Edwina rose from her curtsey, the man pressed the mirror into her gloved hand. "Now have a look."

The glass flashed in the light, blinding her for a moment, then she held it up, seeing the cloudless blue sky.

"No, not that way." Taking the mirror from her hand, he adjusted it, holding it up for her view. "Like this."

Green trees, pink roses, and emerald grass spread in a panorama before her with a canopy of blue above. It was so lovely Edwina's breath caught.

"You see it, don't you, my lady?" Sir Lee's lips split into a loose grin, exposing tobacco-stained teeth.

"It's enchanting."

"Isn't it?" The man's green eyes twinkled and Edwina couldn't help but feel swept away in his delight.

"An old comrade gave it to me for my birthday and this is my first attempt at using it. I must write to thank him."

"Comrade?" Pressing her hands together, Janelle stepped forward. "You were in government service, I heard. The Foreign Office, wasn't it?"

"Yes. But now this old gent has been put out to grass."

"Retired, are you?"

"Purposeless, in other words."

"Don't say that," Edwina charged, liking the man, despite herself.

"Truth is truth. These days I'm at a loss for what to do to fill my time." Lifting his hands, he shrugged. "Which is why I attend parties far afield from my dear London, hosted by a man who frets that the artificial ruins he paid a fortune for don't appear authentic enough."

Edwina hid her smile. Upon arriving at the house a few hours earlier she had found Lord Kendrick sending his servant back to London to procure his pattern book for the grounds for that very same reason. Edwina had been tempted to offer the copy she had in her luggage, but Janelle had warned her that it would have raised too many questions.

Sir Lee chuckled. "I told Lord Kendrick if he wanted authenticity, then he needed to have a real ruin packed up and shipped here piece by bloody piece."

"You didn't!" Edwina cried, suppressing a giggle.

"Of course I did. My only regret is that Kendrick's poor man of affairs almost fainted when he heard the news."

"Thank heavens for Lady Kendrick," Janelle remarked. "I don't know how she does it."

"With great fortitude. There's a lady who knows how to captain a ship."

Edwina raised a brow. "A fine commendation, indeed."

"And I am not one to banter about compliments easily. You will have to be much more than a pretty face to earn my regard, Lady Ross."

Edwina smiled, almost believing his flattery. "I consider myself up to the challenge, sir."

Janelle was eyeing them with disapproval, as if she did not like how congenially Edwina and Sir Lee were getting along. Edwina tempered her regard, reminding herself that this man could, indeed, be the blackmailer. But he seemed so sweet and harmless, she somehow doubted it could be true.

"Here, Janelle, have a look." Edwina held out the glass.

"I have no care for such things. They make me dizzy. But I would very much like a stroll. Sir Lee, if you would be so kind as to escort us. If it's not too much trouble, that is."

"The old leg can certainly use a bit of exercise, particularly when the company is so engaging. I would, indeed, be delighted."

They fell into a line, the wide white-graveled path providing ample room for them to stroll side by side. Honeysuckle filled the air from the vines creeping up the nearby row of trees and pebbles crunched under their shoes as they proceeded along in silence.

Nearing the lake, Edwina turned to him. "Do you fish, Sir Lee?"

"Avidly. There's nothing like starting with an empty hook and landing a fat catch to eat."

Janelle shot Edwina a glance. Did Sir Lee's comment seem to have an underlying meaning?

"My only problem," Sir Lee continued, "is that I tend to fall asleep, and miss the strike every time."

Edwina relaxed. He seemed an unlikely candidate for wicked blackmail. "My uncle always said that fishing was more for catching a snooze than anything to eat."

"I believe I would like this uncle of yours." Sir Lee nodded.

"There you are!" a familiar deep voice called from behind them.

Hiding her relief that Prescott was safe and the room search was over, Edwina turned. She did not bother to disguise her overwhelming delight at seeing him again. They were supposed to be engaged, for heaven's sake.

Prescott strode down the path, his limber gait gaining ground quickly to join them. His coppery brown mane shone bright in the afternoon sun and his skin glowed golden as if he had a hint of Roman blood in him. He wore an ivory cravat, sea-green coat with ivory enamel buttons over a navy Marcella waistcoat and tight ivory breeches

Edwina's heart skipped a beat, he was so handsome to behold.

Grinning like a puppyish fool, Edwina turned to the gentleman by her side. "Sir Lee Devane, may I introduce my fiancé, Mr. Prescott Devane. With a shared name you're sure to have double luck to win at the Newmarket races."

Prescott shot her an amused smile as he tipped his tall black hat and bowed. "The pleasure of your acquaintance is mine, Sir Lee."

Wondering why Sir Lee was so silent at her jest, Edwina tore her gaze from Prescott's.

Sir Lee's craggy face had washed of color and his mouth hung open as if he needed air. The man swayed slightly on his feet and his hat fell over backwards, baring his thinning gray mane.

Prescott straightened and stepped forward, grabbing the man's arm. "Are you unwell, sir? What ails you?"

Frantic for what to do, Edwina snapped open her fan and waved it before his face. "He needs air!"

"There's a bench over here, lay him down!" Janelle ordered.

Prescott half carried the man over to the gray stone bench and gently seated him, with Edwina following close behind. "Maybe if we untie his cravat?"

Prescott reached forward, but Sir Lee waved him off and pulled at his cravat, loosening the neckcloth. His breathing seemed to become normal and the color returned to his face. "That's...what an old man gets for trying to be fashionable."

No one laughed, but Edwina released the breath she'd been holding. Her eyes met Prescott's in silent communion that the crisis seemed to have passed.

"Death by fashion," Prescott joked. "That would be a first."

Edwina shook her head. "First? Corsets are a plague to womankind."

Taking a handkerchief from his pocket, Sir Lee pressed it to his forehead, then his lips. "I'm sorry if I frightened you. But I am perfectly fine, I assure you." He exhaled loudly and Edwina was relieved to see the pink color in his craggy cheeks. He looked up at Prescott and his cheeks tinged even pinker.

"There's no reason to be embarrassed." Edwina sat down beside him. "Everyone loses his breath now and then."

"Not me." The elderly gentleman shook his head, still shaken.

Noticing the man's lost hat, Prescott rose and retrieved it. Dusting it off, he held it out. "Here you are, sir. No harm done."

"Except to my pride." Pain seemed to flash in his eyes and they shone bright.

"Does anything ache?" Edwina asked gently.

Sir Lee took the hat and set it on his head. "I'm fine, truly I am. I just...remembered something." He looked up at her, his green eyes filled with sadness. "You ever have a memory so powerful it sucks the air right from your lungs?"

She shook her head, feeling sorry for him. "It must be a horrible memory."

"No." His smile was melancholic. "Quite the opposite."

The birds chirped in the trees and a cluster of bees buzzed as they enjoyed the creamy white blossoms of the nearby lime tree.

Exhaling noisily, Sir Lee set his cane and stood. Funny, he'd never dropped it, even when he'd almost fainted. He extended his hand. "Good to know you, Mr. Devane."

Prescott shook it. "You as well. I can't help but feel as if I've made a bad impression."

"Not possible, with a natty name such as yours." The man's gaze sharpened. "Are you by any chance related to the Cheshire Devanes?"

"No, sir. I am an orphan and Devane is a made-up name. Rest assured I am no relation..." His smile was teasing. "Unless of course you have a fortune in need of an heir."

Sir Lee smiled, but his eyes did not twinkle as before. "No such luck, I'm afraid. But I do have a few outstanding accounts that I'd gladly pass on."

"I have enough of those on my own, thank you."

Edwina sensed an undercurrent coming from Sir Lee, but then decided that it must simply have been the scare he'd received.

"Oh, no!" Raising her hands to her mouth, Edwina rushed over to The Claude glass. It lay in pieces in the white gravel. "I'm so sorry, Sir Lee. I must have dropped it."

"Don't pick it up!" The elderly man's voice was shrill. "It will cut you."

"I'm so sorry! You said it was a birthday gift—"

"It was my own fault, for falling into a silly faint." Stepping over, he flicked the glass into the nearby grass with his cane. "I've caused enough spilled blood in my lifetime; I don't need to add yours."

Prescott firmly grasped Edwina's arm and helped her rise, holding her close. "How, exactly, did you cause spilled blood, Sir Lee?"

"Secret, lies and mayhem, Mr. Devane. I've quite the talent for it."

Edwina's mouth dried to dust and she was bereft of

words. Had Sir Lee just confessed to being the black-mailer?

Sir Lee adjusted the gold head on his cane. "At the Foreign Office I was able to keep my skills sharp."

"Do you still employ those talents, Sir Lee?" Prescott enquired.

The man's eyes were locked with Prescott's, sharp green flashing in the light. "Nay. I'm just an old man with a lot of memories, Mr. Devane. Some good, some haunting, but enough to make me understand that those days are better left behind me."

"Still, it must be hard to leave all that...excitement."

"I confess, I do miss it at times. Very, very much. But the baton must be passed to a new generation, and I often feel as if I now need to put myself to good use elsewhere."

Edwina felt Prescott relax beside her. "That is admirable of you, sir."

"Mayhap..." The man tilted his head. "You didn't by any chance hail from Andersen Hall Orphanage, did you, Mr. Devane?"

"I did indeed, sir."

"I'd heard that the headmaster had been murdered. Is it true?"

With his eyes hooded, Prescott nodded. "Yes."

"Nasty business." Sir Lee almost spat. Then eyeing the ladies, shrugged in apology. "I hear orphanages are almost as bad as the gaols. Is it true, Mr. Devane?"

Prescott's body tensed to iron, but his mask was firmly in place. "I wouldn't know, sir, as I've never been in prison to be able to compare."

The old gent chuckled. "Touché."

Squeezing Prescott's arm, Edwina tilted her head. "I'm proud to say that I'm a benefactor to Andersen Hall Orphanage. As are many enlightened people who appreciate the standards that Headmaster Dunn maintained. You would do well to visit the place and judge for yourself, Sir Lee. No doubt you'll be *inspired* by the people who hail from there and become a supporter."

"Edwina..." Prescott cautioned, and she looked away, knowing that he would prefer that she not make an issue of it.

"The lady is right, I'm afraid, Mr. Devane," Sir Lee intoned. "I'm being an insensitive sod. My apologies." He sighed. "I suppose I was simply trying to distract attention from my embarrassing fainting spell." Sir Lee bowed. "I hope that you can forgive me for both the faint and the insufferable probing. I would be most appreciative if you would."

Prescott tilted his head. "Of course."

Sir Lee motioned to the residence. "Come, let us walk back to the house for some lemonade. I'm feeling a bit...unequal to things."

"You two go on." Prescott waved a hand. "I want a moment with my fiancée."

My fiancée. Even though it wasn't true, it sounded so sweet on his lips.

While Janelle and Sir Lee strolled off, Edwina laid her palm on Prescott's chest. "Are you all right?"

He grasped her arms, nodding. "Yes, fine. I found nothing in his rooms to indicate that he's the one."

"I'm talking about what he said about Andersen Hall."

Looking down at her, his face softened. "It is what it is, Edwina. It doesn't matter."

"It matters to me! People can be so bloody tactless, it makes me just want to shake them!"

He smiled. "I doubt Sir Lee will make the same mistake again, not after you ever so tactfully straightened him out. Headmaster Dunn would've been proud."

"Still..."

"Shh." He pressed a chaste kiss to her forehead. "I don't want to talk about it anymore. I want to ask a favor of you, Edwina."

"Certainly."

"I want you to...um, well, stay away from Daphne, uh, Lady Pomfry."

Daphne.

Jealousy snaked around her heart so piercingly she almost gasped. "Why?"

He wouldn't meet her gaze. "She's just...well...apt to cause trouble."

Edwina licked her suddenly dry lips. "She still wants to be with you." It was a statement; any sane woman would want to be with him.

"Nay. She just likes drama."

Liar.

His hand rubbed her shoulder in a very brotherly way. "And I've asked the same of her."

Edwina stiffened. "So you spoke with her?"

"Her rooms are down the hall from Sir Lee's. I ran into her on my way back."

A terrible pit formed in her belly. What else had they discussed?

At the look on her face, Prescott hugged her close.

"You've nothing to worry about with Daphne. She and I are finished. There's nothing there."

Edwina swallowed, wishing she could believe it. She trusted Prescott, knowing he wasn't the kind to double deal, but Edwina didn't trust Lady Pomfry, not by a hair.

"We should join the rest of the guests," he urged. "Make ourselves seen so that later we can sneak off and take a turn at Lord Cunningham's rooms. He's next on our list." He kissed her temple. "The sooner we get started, the sooner we can put a stop to Ginny's nightmare."

It took every ounce of willpower for Edwina to resist the desperate urge to pull him deeper into the garden and ravage him right then and there, claim him for her own. But Prescott was right, they were here for a reason, and Ginny was counting on them.

"I will stay away from Lady Pomfry," she murmured. "But I want your assurance that you won't do anything to encourage her or attract her attentions."

"Please, Edwina." His tone was affronted. "Give me a little more credit than that."

"I just mean, well, not that you'd encourage her, but she may get the wrong idea in her head..."

"Look, Edwina. The only person whose head you should be concerned with is mine. And all I can think about is you." Wrapping an arm around her shoulders, he led her toward the house. Her legs felt leaden as she stepped alongside him.

"Daphne probably didn't even know I was going to be here when she accepted the invitation. I'm possibly the farthest thought from her mind."

Edwina doubted that was true. At this very moment Lady Pomfry was probably scheming and contriving a way to land herself back in Prescott's bed. For if the roles were reversed, Edwina would be doing exactly the same.

Chapter 26

~~~~~<❀>~~~~~

Edwina eyed Lady Pomfry as a mongoose eyes a
viper, knowing that they were natural enemies
and that with one wrong move she would be struck
dead.

It wasn't that Lady Pomfry had said anything particularly antagonistic. It was the way she looked at Edwina; with such vehement animosity that Edwina's hair
stood on end. Trying to keep in mind Prescott's words,
Edwina wondered if she wasn't being a bit melodramatic.

Mayhap her ill will stemmed from the fact that Lady
Pomfry stood in a circle of astoundingly fashionable
gentlemen and ladies, and Edwina felt like a straggly
weed standing next to the wine service all by herself.
And, she had to admit, from the fact that the lady was
lovely enough to cause even the most devoted man's
head to turn.

Tonight the blue-eyed, flaxen-haired matron wore a semitransparent ivory silk tiffany gown, showing off, in intimate detail, her voluptuous curves. The gown was cut low and her stays strung tight, causing her breasts to rise so high they looked like fleshy globes, bouncing with every movement.

The poor gentlemen gathering in the candlelit blue-and-gold salon seemed hardly able to look her in the eye, their gazes instinctively straying downward whenever she stopped to speak with one of them. Try as they might, their gazes seemed to flit back to those bouncing breasts, then quickly veer away once more, as if the spectacle was an undeniable magnet. Edwina was more than a bit fascinated and simultaneously disgusted by the display.

"Good evening, Lady Ross." Nodding to Edwina, Lord Elliott moved to stand before the wine service. "Two, please," he asked the servant.

As the white-gloved servant poured the claret, Edwina asked, "Perhaps you could assist me with something, my lord."

He faced her. "Yes, my lady?"

"You're an excellent dancer and I'm having trouble remembering the second turn in the *Rubingé*. Would you indulge me a moment and show it to me?"

The man scratched his balding head. "Here?"

"If you would, it's been plaguing me..."

"Very well." Positioning one foot across the other, he did the fanciful turn, exposing the entire soul of his black-bottomed shoe.

It had been a long shot, but it was worth a try. And it took her mind off of Lady Pomfry's bouncing bosom.

Edwina gave him a winning smile. "Ah, now I recall it. Thank you, my lord. I am most appreciative."

"You are very welcome." Accepting the two glasses of claret from the white-gloved servant, he nodded his farewell and trotted off.

"The man must think me daft," Edwina muttered under her breath as she moved to stand by the open French doors leading to the empty terrace. She'd be known as daft, clumsy, left at the altar...

Her pride pricked, but thinking of how Prescott didn't worry overmuch about how the world viewed him settled Edwina's ruffled pride. Perhaps she wasn't completely like her father after all.

The cool evening breeze pressed pleasantly against her back, and the fresh scent of the garden was preferable to the heavy aroma of wax from the many candelabra in the chamber. She sipped her claret and enjoyed the moment.

Leaning heavily on her cane, Ginny joined Edwina. Upon noticing Lady Pomfry across the room, Ginny glowered. "Her stays must be cut down. I've seen it done before, the better to expose her breasts for every licentious eye."

"I don't think she intends it for *every* eye." Janelle approached them. "Where is Prescott anyway?"

Trying to hide her discomfiture about Lady Pomfry, Edwina sipped her drink. "Since we knew that Lady Kendrick likes to gather for a time before moving in to dinner, we took a quick turn at Lord Cunningham's room after he'd gone."

"You went into a gentleman's bedchamber?" Janelle interrupted.

"Pray give me a little more credit than that." Edwina

scowled. "I stood guard. There's a perfect alcove for observing Lord Cunningham's rooms..." And for hot, toe-curling kisses once the searching was over...Those kisses did more for Edwina's confidence than any protestations that it was all over with Lady Pomfry.

"Are you feeling ill?" Janelle's gaze was sharp. "Your face is flushed."

Lifting the stemmed glass to her lips, Edwina swallowed the red wine. "I'm fine. It was just a bit... rushed."

"Well, did you find anything? Those frog shoes?"

Edwina shook her head. "No, but today is only the first day and we've already canceled two men off our list, Sir Lee and Lord Cunningham. That's good progress, for sure. And Lord Elliot is not wearing the shoes tonight."

Ginny's eyes flitted about the chamber. "I know I need to be patient, but...to know he's here...pretending to be one of us..."

Edwina grasped Ginny's hand, soothing. "Soon, Ginny. And we've hired two Bow Street Runners to wait for word at the local inn. Discreetly, of course. When the time is right, the knave will be gone faster than a flea can hop."

"So where's Prescott now?" Janelle eyed the crowd.

"He wanted to have a quiet word with the boot boy, to see if anyone has noticed a pair of the red-marked shoes we're looking for."

"I should have given him that cat hair," Janelle commented, eyeing Lady Pomfry as she threw her head back and a tinkling laugh filled the chamber. "From the looks of it, we're going to need it."

Edwina's gaze suddenly caught Lady Pomfry's. The

lady smiled and raised her glass, her eyes glaring with challenge, as if to say, I'm more beautiful, wittier and more fashionable than you'll ever be.

Pasting on a smile, Edwina lifted her glass and drank. The fine claret suddenly tasted like vinegar.

"You're not going to let her win," Ginny muttered.

"It's not a competition," Edwina lied.

Turning to look out the French doors, Janelle smiled. "Meow."

"You're despicable."

Sighing, as if greatly put out, Janelle sipped her claret and gazed about the crowded chamber. "So whose room's next on the list? I think it should be Lord Woodard or Mr. Gingrich. Or possibly that fat fellow, Lord Sloan. He seemed very interested in gossiping about the other guests when we spoke to him this afternoon."

"Which of us isn't?" Edwina huffed. "Prescott has a short list with Mr. Todd, Lord Unterberg, Mr. Gingrich and Lord Sloan. After dinner we will search Lord Unterberg's rooms. We understand that he likes to linger over his port, which should give us plenty of time if we make an early exit. Then Mr. Todd's."

"You actually think Mr. Todd could be the one?" Ginny turned to stare at the subject of their discourse, her eyes wide with apprehension. "He looks, well, too gentlemanly for such nastiness."

Mr. Todd stood speaking with Lord Kendrick, and the two men could not have appeared more different. The agitated Lord Kendrick was stout, with wiry blond hair and generous, bulbous features and skin colored by a constant flush. By contrast, the calm Mr. Todd was dark-haired and lanky with a handsome, moon-pale face. Where Lord Kendrick fluttered about in a persistent state of agitation, Mr. Todd stood at ease, his only movement in the dark eyes, which veered frequently to Lady Pomfry's bosom.

"He is a fine-looking man, I'll grant you that." Janelle tapped her chin. "And has a decent enough reputation. Is recently from Nottingham or thereabouts, where he owns quite a handsome property, I've heard. He's known to be good at cards and pays his debts with alacrity." She sniffed. "Lord Unterberg also seems unlikely. He has a respectable portion from an uncle who's a landowner in Wales and is generally well regarded. No gambling problem that I could uncover. No scandal between the sheets."

"You've quite the talent for this espionage business," Edwina marveled. "Your mind is like glue."

Janelle beamed. "Why, that's the nicest thing you've ever said to me, Edwina."

"Uh-oh," Ginny murmured. "Cat on the prowl."

Lady Pomfry approached Mr. Todd, her hips rolling to great effect. His eyes flew to her chest, and her half grin let him know she knew full well he was staring at her bosom. He said something, and the lady's laugh rang throughout the chamber, as if she wanted everyone to grasp how entertaining she was.

Edwina turned away. "One of us must try to get a peek at his shoes. Perhaps at dinner. Prescott says we must consider every male guest a possibility..."

"Prescott's been so astoundingly sweet." Pressing her hand to her chest, Ginny's eyes were bright. "And he's thrown his heart into this matter with such conviction. I am so blessed to have such dear friends."

Edwina stepped close and gave her small shoulders a hug, inhaling the familiar rosewater scent. "We all are."

Ginny's smile was shaky. "Prescott is such an excellent judge of character. We're so lucky to have him with us."

"I've been thinking that...when all is said and done here..." Edwina's cheeks heated as she looked down at the rim of her glass. "Perhaps Prescott can assist me and my cousin Henry with our Cambridge development. Calm the muddied waters, so to speak, and help me repair the transaction. It's not that far to Cambridge from here..." And it would give them more time together without having to say good-bye.

Just the thought of parting from Prescott felt like an iron shroud draped on her shoulders. He did seem fond of her. Mayhap not as infatuated as she was, but possibly fond enough to continue with the affair.

"I think that's a wonderful idea." Ginny smiled. "I know how disappointed you were with the failed negotiations."

"Yes, well, I will have to persuade him. He only promised us a short time..."

Gently hugging Edwina's waist, Ginny teased, "Somehow I don't believe that it will take much convincing." Her confidence soothed.

Another tinkling laugh rang in the chamber, along with some sounds of distress.

Edwina turned. Mr. Greene was flurrying about Lady Pomfry in a fit of agitation as he practically ogled her breasts while poor Mrs. Greene's face was beet red, her bosom heaving with obvious distress and her face crumpled as if she was on the brink of tears.

"What happened?"

Janelle scowled. "Mr. Greene dropped his quizzing glass into Lady Pomfry's wine glass."

"Oh dear," Ginny raised her hand to her mouth. "Poor Mrs. Greene."

Ever the perfect hostess, Lady Kendrick took the distressed Mrs. Greene by the arm and led her out of the room.

Lady Pomfry, on the other hand, had no notion of being anywhere but at the center of the attention. Her face was rosy, her smile wide and her eyes bright as they scanned the room with a self-satisfied gleam.

"I'll bet she's only disappointed Prescott wasn't here to see it." Janelle swirled the claret in her glass as she glared at Lady Pomfry. "No doubt she'll ensure that he hears of it, while she weaves it into the most comically entertaining story of the century. It will be practice for recounting the tale to the rest of society, a thousand times over back in town."

Edwina shook her head, disgusted. "Mrs. Greene will never live it down."

"I never thought I'd be the one to say it," Ginny intoned, "but I think I might hate that woman."

"Get in queue," Janelle muttered.

Lady Pomfry suddenly stilled, her bosom lifting, her glance ablaze as she turned to face the threshold.

Prescott stood in the doorway, resplendent in his black-and-white formal attire. His hair was slicked back with pomade, making his face seem sharper, more angular and his lips all the more sensual for the contrast.

Edwina's heart skipped a beat as she held her breath.

Lady Pomfry glided over to Prescott, a warm smile on her peach-colored lips. Edwina wasn't near enough to overhear, but she could just imagine what the matron was saying.

Prescott's eyes fixed on Lady Pomfry, his attention set.

Edwina's heart sank.

Then Prescott bowed and stepped around the sputtering Lady Pomfry as his gaze traveled the room. His eyes met Edwina's and he smiled.

Something lightened inside Edwina's chest and she breathed once more. Smiling shyly at him, she realized that it wasn't just her cheeks that warmed when he was near. Since knowing him, her body seemed to smolder in a constant heat, then blaze instantly when Prescott touched her. He was the flint, and she the wood, just waiting to be ignited. Oh, dear, she really was head-over-heels infatuated.

"Ladies." He accepted Janelle's extended hand and bowed, his swept-back hair glistening dark in the candlelight.

"You are looking very handsome tonight." Ginny beamed as he bowed in turn to her.

"I am but a pale shadow to the three muses standing before me." Reaching for Edwina's white-gloved hand, he raised it to his lips. "Especially, my fiancée, the muse of chaos."

The slow burn began at Edwina's fingertips then up her arm to every patch of skin. "Chaos?" Her voice was breathless.

"My mind seems to muddle when you are near, leaving only one thought."

"What's that?" Her heart began to dance and her skin flame.

"How long it will be until we are alone again," he said, his tone a husky burr. He lingered over her hand, his warm breath caressing her through the silk, a clear indication of what he would do to her once they truly were alone.

With his fingers caressing the underside of her wrist, the blood rushed through her veins so powerfully that she felt light-headed. If he weren't still holding her hand, she might just melt into the floor.

"That practicing seems to really be working," Janelle commented with a wry twist of her lips. "You're getting much better at this, Edwina. Even I'm half-convinced you're in love with him."

Edwina blinked. Then her cheeks heated. She removed her hand.

Prescott released her, yet the promise of what was to come flashed in his emerald gaze so powerfully, she felt as if they still touched.

"Prescott, darling." Lady Pomfry glided up and slipped her white-gloved hand into the crook of his arm. "You'd run off."

Edwina's heart sank as she saw Prescott's gaze drop to the woman's exposed bosom. Her heart dipped even lower when Prescott didn't break his arm away from the lady.

He tilted his head. "My lady."

"My lady? Oh, you're being so silly, darling. After how close you and I have been you know you can only call me Daphne."

"Yes, well, you know my friends, Lady Blankett, Lady Genevieve—"

"Yes, yes." Lady Pomfry waved her hand. "We're all acquainted."

"Good." Prescott extricated himself from her arm

and moved to step beside Edwina. "Then you also know that Lady Ross is my betrothed."

Edwina wanted to sing, but instead pasted a cool look of disdain on her face. She knew he was doing it for the ruse, but still, it was as cold a shoulder as he could give his former paramour.

Snapping open her fan, Lady Pomfry waved it about her face as her hand trailed her exposed shoulder, reminding Edwina of one of Fanny's maneuvers. "I can hardly believe..."

"Believe it." Prescott's tone was cool. "For it's true."

Lady Pomfry's eyes flashed blue fire. "A man makes mistakes, and upon realizing them, if he begs forgiveness, he may be welcomed back—"

"Daphne," Prescott warned.

"It's inconceivable that you'd choose this ugly, beak-nosed—"

"Didn't you feel the door slam on your derriere?" Janelle snapped. "The man sent you packing. Have the good grace to know when you're no longer wanted."

Lady Pomfry's eyes widened and then narrowed. "I suppose I shouldn't be surprised by your bitterness..." Stabbing her fan in Janelle's direction, she turned up her nose. "I'm sure the loss of your husband's affections must be very hard on you..."

Janelle's face drained of color.

"And if my son was such a public disgrace, a slobbering drunkard who—Ahh!" Lady Pomfry's gauzy ivory dress was suddenly coated in burgundy liquid.

Edwina looked down to find her wineglass empty. Discovering an ogre inside her glass wouldn't have shocked her more.

Lady Pomfry was shaking with fury, her mouth opening, then closing and then opening again, like a bug's.

The room fell silent, only broken by Lady Pomfry's gasping. Her breasts heaved and her eyes flashed with hatred.

"Bitch." Lady Pomfry tossed her entire glass at Edwina.

Prescott caught the glass, miraculously, but not before it splattered both of them with claret.

"I think you've caused enough trouble for one night, young lady." Sir Lee grabbed Lady Pomfry's arm. She struggled to pull away, but his grip was too tight. "Enough!"

"You're hurting me!" she hissed.

"It's time for you to retire to your rooms." Sir Lee's tone was hard.

"I'll go when I'm damn well ready and no sooner!"

"You'll go now," came a voice from near the door. Lady Kendrick's lower lip quivered and her eyes were bright. "I think we've had enough of your brand of entertainment, Lady Pomfry. I believe I'm ready for some of mine."

Edwina's heart twisted with guilt over her contribution to this debacle; their hostess had worked too hard to see her party crumble in a social mêlée.

Lord Kendrick moved to stand by his wife, for once calm as he offered his arm. "If you would lead the way, darling. I, for one, am ready for dinner." They turned and left the room, arm in arm, heads held high.

Lady Pomfry eyed the remaining guests as a cornered fox eyes the hounds. She lifted a shoulder, pretending to be *comme il faut*. "I've always said that country life is boring. I was just trying to liven things up."

Slowly, each member of the party drifted to follow Lord and Lady Kendrick, leaving only Lady Pomfry standing in a pool of candlelight, alone with her stained tiffany silk and her bitterness.

Chapter 27

～～✦✦～～

Later that evening, Prescott and Edwina stood next to an ivory column in the candlelit conservatory. By mutual consent they'd lingered with the other guests and not slipped out to search Lord Unterberg's rooms as originally planned. Their efforts to unmask the blackmailer were put aside, for the moment, as they tried not to draw more attention to themselves and to be the kind of guests that Lady Kendrick deserved.

All of the other guests had apparently felt the same, as they relaxed on or around the spindly Chippendale furniture near the French doors leading into the house. Janelle and Ginny stood with Sir Lee nearby, next to a lovely fountain with a statute of Gaia, Mother Earth, pouring water from a stone pitcher.

Sir Lee had been particularly attentive to Janelle since the incident with Lady Pomfry, and Prescott made a mental note to thank the man for it later. Sir

Lee seemed to be a good sort and a natural addition to their small circle.

The air was warm and heavily scented with the wild strawberries hanging in baskets around the conservatory.

With her eyes fixed on Lord Kendrick as he carried a cup of tea to his wife, Edwina murmured, "For all of his fluttering about and worrying over trifles, when it comes to the important things, he's very solid." Her brow furrowed and her dark gaze seemed sad.

Prescott stepped closer and rested a hand on her shoulder. "And this upsets you?"

She shook her head, looking down. "It makes me happy and yet sad all at once. I don't know why."

"Being dependable is important to you, isn't it, Edwina?"

Edwina let out a little breath. "It's the bedrock of every relationship. Take my mother and father, for example. For all of my father's indiscretions, bellowing bouts, and domineering tendencies, if my mother needs anything truly important, he's there for her."

"Was your husband reliable?" Prescott couldn't help but ask, an annoying trickle of jealousy snaking around his heart.

She stared off in the distance a long moment. "Yes. I do believe that he was."

Prescott reminded himself that the man was long dead, and that he was the one keeping Edwina warm at night. "How, ah, did your husband die, Edwina? If you don't mind my asking."

"He fell from a rooftop while instructing one of his tenants on the correct way to perform a repair. His injuries were extensive, and though he hung on for a time, he didn't survive."

Prescott's lips dipped. "I'm sorry, Edwina."

She tilted her head in acknowledgment.

"I must say," he felt the need to add, "I'm impressed. Most aristocrats wouldn't deign to assist with such a menial chore."

"Oh, Sir Geoffrey wasn't doing the work, he was directing it."

"Still, for him to take such an interest..."

Watching the guests' coming and goings, she waved a hand. "Sir Geoffrey took interest in an inordinate number of things."

"Like what?"

Facing him, her brow furrowed. "You really wish to know?"

"Actually, I do."

"Very well. He taught me the proper way to instruct servants, since there is a very specific manner to handle certain household duties. How to gut a pig, to clean a floor, to polish silver, the suitable way a woman should wear her hair—"

Prescott blinked, thinking of the tight chignon Edwina was wearing the first day he'd met her. "He told you how to wear your hair? Something so personal to you?"

"Well, ah, he liked it pulled back." Her lips pursed. "I suppose because that's how his mother wore it."

"Did he direct anything else pertaining to your person?"

"To my person...ah, well, the proper way to clean my teeth and, oh, yes, how to bathe—"

Prescott straightened. "Proper way? There is no 'proper way' to take a bath."

Sipping her port, Edwina's shoulder lifted in a shrug. "To Sir Geoffrey there was."

"And you put up with this...this...dictatorship? Even Mrs. Nagel never directed me in such an officious manner."

Edwina's eyes didn't meet his. "It doesn't matter. Why are we even discussing this?" Her cheeks were flushed pink and he could tell that she was discomfited, but he wanted to know, nay, he *needed* to understand who her husband had been and how he'd influenced the woman Edwina was today.

"What would your former husband think of your current coiffure?"

Her hand lifted to her hair. "Sir Geoffrey think of my coiffure?"

"And why do you refer to him as Sir Geoffrey? He was your husband for heaven's sake!"

"Lower your voice, Prescott," she chided. "Heads are turning."

He crossed his arms, leaning toward her and whispering, "No wonder you were so upset that you didn't have the 'proper' attire the other night, or always worry that you're doing something the 'wrong' way. I'll bet your mother-in-law was even worse than her overbearing son. I'll warrant they used to go at you, two on one, with the very *proper* manner to do this or that."

Her cheeks reddened and from the look on her face, he could tell he'd struck a nerve.

"They did, didn't they?" he demanded. "Directing you, correcting you, chastising you. They probably had you hopping about so that you hardly knew which way to turn."

"All right, Prescott, I understand your point. They weren't as agreeable as they could have been and I wasn't as self-possessed as I should have been."

"Self-possessed? You were a fresh young lady of barely seventeen hoping to be accepted into the bosom of your new family. Of course you would try to please them."

Looking away, she straightened. "I know I should've stood up for myself more often, but to be frank, when I did bother to, it was most...unpleasant, and not exactly worth the tension it caused. So it was easier simply to do it their way. Like referring to my husband by his title. He preferred it and it didn't matter much to me." But by the irked look in her eye, obviously it *had* mattered.

"Oh, Edwina." He grasped her hand. "No wonder you don't wish ever to marry again. For you, it's the equivalent of purgatory."

She looked up, her brow furrowed and her mouth open as if she was going to argue, then she shook her head, her eyes wide with wonder. "I never...never considered the connection. I just knew I never, ever wanted to feel that way again."

"And why should you? A strong spirit like yours shouldn't be oppressed with such trifles. You have much better things to do with your amazing energy, more important considerations on your mind. In twenty years will anyone care that you put both stockings on before either shoe? Or is it a stocking, then a shoe and then your attention shifts to the opposite foot?"

"You're right. It really doesn't matter." Exhaling as if relieved, she stared up at the night sky. "It's astonishing to me that I didn't see the connection. To me, marriage means submitting myself to someone else's dictates for the rest of my life. It's really, quite...liberating to understand why I've felt so strongly about not wanting to marry. I mean, *feel* about it. I don't wish to marry. Ever."

"You said that already," he bit out, irritated and not knowing why.

"I know, I just..." She beamed. "This is really quite amazing." Then her brow furrowed. "But this still won't make a lick of difference to my father."

"Our engagement is going to end his matchmaking days, though, Edwina. Isn't that the plan?"

"Yes, but that doesn't mean that we won't have a stunningly awful row over it." She frowned. "I just wish..."

"What?"

"I just wish that I knew how to handle things better. Like before, with Lady Pomfry..."

Guilt washed over him. "That wasn't your fault, Edwina. Daphne isn't half the woman you are."

She raised a brow. "Yet somehow you chose to be with her, without the benefit of a blatant lie."

He felt like kicking himself, the fool that he'd been to have resisted Edwina so. But he hadn't known her. Hadn't known how wonderful and sensual and exciting she truly was. But arguing the point would get him nowhere. She wanted to talk about Daphne. The same way he'd wanted to talk about Sir Geoffrey. Fair was fair, even if he didn't like it.

He exhaled, looking away. "I had no idea she could be so...ugly. I mean, she wasn't like that when I was with her." But he'd known. He'd always had the sense that she was the kind of woman who turned on people. Not caring if she attacked him, Prescott had selfishly never worried about anyone else she'd go after. Sleep with a viper and eventually someone close to you will get bitten. And Prescott *did* mind that.

Edwina tilted her head. "What was she like? When you were with her, I mean."

He shrugged. "Amusing. Good fun. There wasn't a whole lot more to it than that." Prescott realized that there hadn't been much more to any of his encounters. Until now.

"Is that why you became a *cicisbeo*? For the fun of it?"

"Yes, and because, well, it was easy."

"Easy?"

Exhaling, he ran his hand through his hair, awkward talking about that chapter of his life, which he so desperately wanted to close. "Six or so years ago a young widow came to Andersen Hall to meet with Headmaster Dunn about becoming a patron. She'd heard good things about the orphanage and wanted to learn more." He shrugged. "At the time I was living with a friend in town and trying to scratch up a living. I'd come back to visit with Cat and ran into the lady."

"So you were about twenty-one years of age?"

"Yes. Well, the lady was impressed with my elocution and manners and, to be frank, was lonely—"

"So she bought your clothing, set you up and in return expected...?"

"She didn't want anything more than some companionship, a listening ear, an arm to hold on to at balls and the like. It was perfectly innocent."

"Perfectly innocent? You're stunning, Prescott. I can't quite believe that she didn't want—"

"Thank you for the compliment, Edwina. But no, she didn't." He shook his head, remembering. "She was a good woman who'd married an older cousin hoping to sire an heir and keep the property in the family. She'd miscarried several times, and when her husband died without issue, she blamed herself. She wanted an undemanding companion, nothing more."

He tilted his head. "She had a tight circle of friends who soon came to call on me as an escort as well. I sort of fell into it and after a while, it just seemed to be one long ride that I had trouble getting off."

"Until Headmaster Dunn's death."

"Yes."

"And Lady Pomfry? Was it all innocent with her?"

Prescott pursed his lips, knowing that this answer was very important to Edwina and he didn't want to make a mess of it. He exhaled. "No."

Her face tightened. "I suppose I can understand. She's a beautiful woman, on the outside, at least."

"Not half as beautiful as you—"

"Please stop."

"But—"

"Enough, Prescott." She held up her hand. "I know my nose is large. It is what it is, I cannot change that. I'm not upset about what she said. Well, not much, anyway."

"Then what's bothering you?"

"Mostly, that people can be so awful to each other." Unwinding her arms, her hand clenched and unclenched at her side. "That I'm capable of such spite."

"Lady Pomfry is the spiteful one—"

"I tossed a glass of claret on her dress, Prescott. For shame."

"You didn't plan it. She was abusing Janelle. You can hardly blame yourself."

She shook her head. "There are better ways to deal with nastiness than sinking so low as to assault someone."

"But it was very effective, you'll have to admit," he tried to joke.

"No it wasn't." Her tone was serious; she didn't want to be amused, she wanted to be heard.

He sobered. "You're right, but—"

"My conduct escalated the entire affair. She tossed a glass at me. Someone could have really been hurt."

"It's not your fault she threw it."

"I should have stopped the confrontation, not worsened it."

Reaching down, he grasped her hand, unfurling her tight fingers.

Looking to ensure that none of the guests were paying them any mind, he pulled Edwina into a shadowed pocket deeper into the conservatory and then behind a pair of huge buddleia bushes. "It's admirable that you are taking this matter to heart. But you're being very hard on yourself, Edwina. You've already apologized to Lord and Lady Kendrick and they hardly blamed you. How can you blame yourself?'"

"Don't patronize me, Prescott. I'm trying to learn from my mistakes, not placate my guilt. If I am to deal with the Lady Pomfrys of this world, I had better figure out a better way to handle myself."

"The Lady Pomfrys?"

She shrugged, looking away. "The women you've bedded."

"Oh." Prescott ran his hand through his hair, not wanting to touch that one with a fifty-foot pole. Still, Edwina had a point. He lifted a shoulder, uncomfortable. "In all my time out and about in Society, it rarely ended in such a way that a lady should give you a difficult time."

"I know."

He looked up. "You know?"

"I studied you, remember? I spoke to some of your lady friends under the guise that I was considering an escort to an event."

"And...?"

"And most spoke highly of you. The biggest complaint was that you were too independent. 'Yank on his strings and he walks' one lady had said."

"Ah, that must have been Lady Tyler. She was always razor-sharp."

"But it's not just those ladies, but all difficult people that I'm concerned with, Prescott. You understood Janelle when I was oblivious. I was ready to kick her out of the society. For shame." Her lovely face was troubled. "I want to do better. I need to do better and not always leave a confrontation feeling like I've failed. Can you help me?"

Chapter 28

❦

Looking into her dark, shimmering gaze, Prescott realized, not for the first time, that Edwina Ross was a very complex woman. The fact that she shouldered some of the blame for the confrontation was a credit to her strong character. That she was examining her own actions in the hopes of improving how she dealt with others was downright inspiring.

"Whom are you preparing yourself to deal with, Edwina?" Prescott felt an unfamiliar sense of protectiveness. "Your father?"

She sighed, looking away. "Well, yes."

"Is your father a spiteful man? Has he ever…" His gut tightened. "Hit you?"

"He hasn't laid a hand on me since I was ten. And I certainly couldn't blame him then, I'd just shorn my sister's hair."

"Really?" he asked, relieved. "Girlhood antics?"

"Nay. I was bemoaning my own dark locks and she very sweetly offered me a few of hers. I cut her hair and then glued it onto my own."

"What were you thinking?"

"It seemed like a wonderful plan at the time. But in execution…" Her smile was tense. "Let us hope that my plans have improved over time." She shook her head. "But getting back to Lady Pomfry…well, if I'm truly being honest with myself, she brings out the green-eyed monster in me and I handled it—"

"You've nothing to be jealous of, Edwina. What you and I have goes far beyond anything she's even capable of." He wrapped his arms around her, enjoying how she leaned into him. "My feelings for her never held a candle to the way I feel about you."

She sighed and her body relaxed. They fit quite agreeably together, like two pieces of a puzzle. "Well, that's certainly nice to know."

"And how, my fair lady, do you feel about me?" He was holding his breath and he knew it, and was unable to do a bloody thing about it.

Leaning her head back, she toyed with his cravat, pressing the linen. "You're trying to change the topic, Prescott Devane…"

"True, but that doesn't mean I don't wish to know how you feel about me."

She sighed, pretending to be greatly put out. "Well, if you must know…" She smiled shyly. "I'm really quite…fond of you. Quite…very much…a lot. A very lot."

He chuckled, feeling inordinately relieved. "That's quite a jumble of the King's English…"

"I can take it back if you insist…"

He hugged her tighter. "Don't you dare."

She bit her lip. "Prescott?"

"Yes?"

"I was thinking that, perhaps when all is said and done here, that mayhap you might consider staying on with me for a bit."

He blinked, his heart skipping a beat. "What are you asking me, Edwina?"

Busying herself with his cravat, she shrugged. "Well, you see...that transaction my cousin and I were trying to close in Cambridge. Well, I was thinking that you are so good with people and all, that you might help repair the damage."

Prescott felt the disappointment like a musket ball stuck in his chest. What had he expected? She wanted his help in a business transaction in the same way she wanted his help in combating the blackmailer. She might be fond of him, but it was his *usefulness* that mattered. "We'll see," was all he could think to say.

"Well, it's just that, I was thinking, that if you and I stay together, which I hope...I would very much like...well, then, at some point, well, I am going to have to face my father about it. Which brings me back to the topic that I seem to be mucking up so badly...

"What I've been trying to articulate, very poorly I might add, is that the run-in with Lady Pomfry..." She motioned toward the house. "It reminded me of how I often feel when I'm facing my father. All anger and no positive effect. So I want your guidance. Well, when it comes to you...us, I want to be clear, I want to be understood."

"Why?"

"Because it's important to me that it go as well as possible with my father."

"Why?" He knew he sounded like a nine-year-old lad asking "why?" every other sentence, but he couldn't help it. His heart hurt and he wanted to know "why" it ached so excruciatingly and how to make it stop.

She didn't meet his eyes. "Because I want it, us, to be about you and me without a whole lot of everyone else butting in. I want us to . . . last."

Licking his dry lips, he swallowed. "You wish to be together for a long time? Even after you no longer have a need for me?"

Her brow furrowed. "A need for you? I know that we started out as partners in an effort to the stop the blackmailer, but I would hope that our relationship, what we have now, isn't as mercenary as that."

Suddenly that musket ball in his chest didn't feel quite so excruciating. "So you want to be with me, simply to be with me?"

"Of course. I care for you. Don't you want to stay together?" She peered up at him, her eyes anxious. "Even after we're finished with everything . . . ?"

A knot deep inside his heart slowly unwound. "That would be . . . most acceptable to me."

"*Most acceptable* . . ." Narrowing her eyes, she swatted at him. "You're torturing me now, aren't you? For giving you grief over Lady Pomfry."

"No, just for the fun of it." He smiled.

He kissed her temple, feeling giddy with relief. She wanted him just because she cared. Not for his usefulness or for convenience. Because she cared. She truly cared.

Inhaling her sweet lily of the valley scent, his heart

swelled with a heretofore unknown joy. But part of him still didn't fully trust it. Joy was the underside of grief and despair, as he well knew. But he wasn't willing to let this wonderful feeling go, not just yet, and he savored the moment, holding Edwina tightly in his arms.

"Hmmm." Laying her head on his shoulder, she leaned into him, sighing. "You feel so good."

Caressing her silky soft shoulder, he closed his eyes, relishing the feel of her soft body molded into his.

The earthy scents of vegetation, roses, hydrangeas, oranges and lemons filled the dark space and the moist air clung to Prescott's skin. The air was thick tonight, charged with moisture as if a storm would soon be upon them.

Edwina shivered, her skin warming beneath his caressing fingers. "Hmmm." She shifted against him, her skirts swirling about his legs.

Desire spiked through him, fierce, powerful and predicated on a need much deeper than simple passion. He wanted Edwina and needed her, more than he'd ever wanted another woman in his life.

"Do you think we might say our good-nights?" At the sensual cadence of her voice, his blood quickened even more. "People in the country keep country hours..."

Grabbing her hand, Prescott pulled her deeper into the shadows of the conservatory, the sounds of his shoes and her slippers echoing on the stone-flagged floors.

"Don't we have to say—"

"To hell with good-nights," he growled.

A blaze of light flashed in the distant sky.

Moments later thunder boomed in the night, the conservatory seemed to shudder, then all was quiet.

Halting, Edwina pulled on his hand and looked up at the glass ceiling. "That sounded close."

He stopped. "Nay, it's miles away."

Lightning flashed once more in the distance.

"See?"

"Yes," she breathed. "I do." Wrapping her arms around his shoulders, she pulled his head down to hers.

Cloaked in shadow, they clung to each other, seeking, needing and giving to the other all that they longed for themselves. While in the distance, nature played her orchestra, with flashes of light illuminating the darkness.

Digging his hands into her soft hair, Prescott kissed her until he was breathless with need, his heart pounding, his body thrumming, his shaft thick and insistent, straining against his breeches.

Prescott's arms snaked around her bottom, lifting her, showing her how much she affected him, how desperately he wanted her. Her legs parted, wrapping around his hips so enticingly his shaft thrummed.

Her kisses deepened, her tongue mating with his. Her hips bucked against him, urging him to take her. He pressed himself deep into her, feeling her moist heat through the thin muslin of her gown.

There was only her soft body molding to his, the heat flaming between them, the heady scent of her desire overpowering all else, and the thunder playing on in the distance.

A small voice in his mind called out warnings that this was too feral, she was too much of a lady...

Catching his breath, he muttered. "God, if only the rooms were closer..."

"What's wrong with here?" The invitation in her voice was unmistakable. But still...he couldn't quite imagine taking her on the floor. Actually he could, and the picture wasn't displeasing...

She licked her lips. "I heard once about a man and a woman, well...standing..."

He needed no further urging. Grasping the firm globes of her bottom, he lifted her higher and carried her over to one of the thick columns, pressing her back up against the smooth marble.

Pulling at his cravat and unbuttoning the top of his waistcoat, she pressed her soft lips to his neck, suckling.

As rain spattered on the glass ceiling above them, Edwina hitched herself higher on him, enclosing his shaft in such excruciating pleasure that his knees almost collapsed underneath him.

"Edwina," he groaned.

She clung to him, her skin flaming, her mouth working on him until all thoughts escaped save for getting inside of her.

"Now, Prescott," she breathed. "Please..."

His last shreds of control unraveled; he was mindless with need, driven to a passion that had to be sated.

Holding her aloft, he tugged at his breeches, all the while being urged onward by Edwina's panting breaths and honeyed kisses.

Reaching beneath her gown, he found her drawers, seeking the ties behind.

"Just tear it open, Prescott," she moaned. "Fill me."

The rip screeched in the darkness, the very act making his body pulse with anticipation.

She groaned, clinging to him, parting her legs and wrapping them around his waist so that his member pressed against the moist heat of her inner thigh.

Groaning, she shifted, urging him inside. He locked his legs, his body quaking, his shaft pulsing and his heart beating so wildly he thought he might just die. She bucked, ramming him deep into her wetness. Moaning, Edwina squirmed, pulling his mouth down to hers.

He was consumed by the darkness, her heady-scented desire, her mouth on his, her tongue loving him, thrusting inside of him just as he rammed his shaft deep into her hot core. She took him, encased him, molded herself around him and ground him so deep inside of her he wanted to scream.

A cry filled the night, quickly muffled against his shoulder. Edwina clasped him so hard as he thrust into her again and again, spilling his seed.

Panting, they clung to each other in a sweaty, passion-scented muslin cloud, waiting for the world to stop spinning. Waiting for reality to breach the fantasy.

But when Prescott opened his eyes and looked down, Edwina was still there, still sweetly beautiful in the flashes of lightning. And still his. For the moment, at least, not all dreams faded into mist.

Chapter 29

The next afternoon Prescott strolled down the carpeted hallway toward Edwina's rooms, his mind filled with the memory of leaving her just a few short hours before.

As he'd slid out of the bed, trying not to wake her, she'd reached for him, her eyes closed, her breath heavy as she was obviously still under slumber's spell. Her unconscious appeal had caused such a warm feeling in his heart that even after he'd slowly disentangled his arm, he'd been reluctant to leave her.

As he'd stood over her, watching her sweet sleep, he'd realized that when he was with her he felt connected to her and content in a way he hadn't ever known. It wasn't just the undeniable attraction between them. It was more than the head-spinning kisses and earthshaking passion. More than the sense of affinity that seemed to bind them. His feelings went deeper, to a powerful sense of regard that Prescott had never felt for a woman, other than Cat.

Yet, somehow this was totally different from anything he'd ever had with Cat. His feelings for Cat had been an adolescent fascination. What he felt for Edwina wasn't confused, up and down or immature in the least. It was fully developed, yet still ripe with promise. Whole, but as-of-yet undiscovered. It didn't make much sense, but undeniably, it felt *right*. As if destiny had led him to Edwina.

He'd been so shaken by these unfamiliar thoughts, so foreign to his sense of who he was and how he fit into the world, that he'd quickly dressed and fled her room.

He didn't believe in destiny, any more than he believed in Father Christmas.

Any more than he believed in true love.

The problem was, he seemed to be falling into the very thing he didn't believe in.

"Oh, pardon, sir." A maid exited Edwina's chambers, her arms loaded with a tray. Quickly, the stout, black-haired girl dipped into a curtsey.

Prescott promptly stepped back, knowing enough maids to understand that finding herself alone with a male guest might not be an auspicious situation. "Good afternoon. By chance, do you know where Lady Ross might be?"

Eyeing him warily, the maid held the tray before her like a shield. On the platter were the remnants of a meager breakfast: half a piece of toast, saucer of jam and a white mug stained with evidence of cocoa. A similar brown coating adorned the young maid's upper lip.

Delicately, Prescott raised his finger to his mouth, indicating that she should clean it.

Her dark brows knitted and her lips twisted. "'Ave you got an itch, sir?"

"Cocoa."

Her dark eyes narrowed and then widened, and then she hastily swept her sleeve across her mouth and looked to him for confirmation.

"All clean. Now I don't want to keep you any longer from your duties..." Prescott tried to keep the eagerness from his voice. He told himself that he simply wanted to share his interesting news with Edwina, that any person in his situation would feel the same. "Do you know where might I find Lady Ross?"

"I heard the butler mention battledore, an' the mistress 'ad the lads set up nets on the west lawn."

"Very well. Then to the west lawn I shall proceed. Thank you."

A short time later, Prescott spotted Edwina in the distance. She was standing beneath an old oak tree with battledores and shuttlecocks scattered about the ground. The rackets lay in assorted piles with a play-piece beside each, as if group play might be in the offing.

A few of the guests huddled near her and Prescott would have to pass them to get to Edwina. He approached, wondering how long it would be before he could politely get a moment alone with Edwina. To tell her his news, of course.

"Just so long as I'm not on Lady Pomfry's team." Janelle tossed the shuttlecock in the air and swung the battledore, whipping the play-piece aloft. A young liveried servant raced to fetch the piece and bring it back.

Mrs. Greene adjusted the ribbon of her straw beehive bonnet and then picked a leaf from her fawn cloak. "There's not enough money in all of England to place me on her team."

"That woman's a menace," Ginny agreed, nodding.

"Then whose team will she play on?" Mr. Todd shielded his eyes with his hand as he watched Lady Kendrick directing the servants in securing another net. The hostess was like a battle commander, ordering everyone to and fro.

"We cannot cut her out," Mr. Greene declared, his neck flushing slightly pink. At the stormy look on his wife's face, he argued, "What will Lady Kendrick say?"

"Of course we can cut her out." Sir Lee smiled, drumming his fingers on his gold-topped cane. "Since she's already gone."

"What?"

The group turned to stare at the old gent, just as Prescott stepped close to join them. "Lady Pomfry's gone?" he asked, careful to use her surname.

Sir Lee swung his cane, an impish look on his weathered face. Obviously he liked being in the know as much as the next person, if not more. "She left a short time ago. It seems the woman somehow couldn't manage to stop sneezing, and her nose itched her so that she rubbed it bright red and her eyes swelled so tightly she could hardly see." His gaze traveled the group. "Lady Kendrick swears that she doesn't have any cats in the house, yet Lady Pomfry insists upon contradicting her. Did any of you happen to bring a favored pet along?"

"A cat to a house party?" Mr. Todd scoffed. "I think not."

Negative responses went all around, yet Ginny was eyeing Janelle with a very speculative gleam and the storklike matron was studying her battledore as if divining the world's secrets.

What had Janelle done?

When Ginny noticed Prescott watching her, she quickly turned to Edwina, asking, "You're awfully quiet today, dear."

Prescott turned to face Edwina. "Yes, my dear, how are you this morning?" To his alarm, Edwina's complexion was ash white and she leaned heavily on the tree with one arm while holding the other to her middle. "Are you all right?"

She closed her eyes and swayed.

Fear twisted in his gut as he reached for her. "Edwina!"

"Don't touch my stomach!" she cried, her voice panicked, her eyes flying open.

"What's wrong?"

"I feel..." She was panting, her cheeks were now flushed bright red and sweat lined her brow. "...ill."

"Sit, darling, sit down." Prescott gently eased her to the ground, being careful to hold only her arms. "Tell me what ails you."

"Back away!" Janelle waved for the others to disperse.

Lady Kendrick came bustling up in a burgundy muslin storm. The hostess's long oval face was filled with concern. "Step back! Give Lady Ross some air!"

"I'm so queasy..." Edwina groaned, closing her eyes.

"Might she be in the family way?" Mr. Todd muttered under his breath.

Prescott glared daggers at the man, and if he hadn't been holding Edwina, he would have trounced the bastard.

Nevertheless, a whisper of a hope threaded through his heart.

"I was once sick as a dog when I ate some bad mutton," Sir Lee countered, then turned quickly to Lady Kendrick. "Not that I am blaming it on your wonderful cuisine, my lady. All I'm saying is that before rumors get started, let us get the lady some help!"

Prescott could have kissed the old gent.

Gently mopping Edwina's brow, he urged, "How does it feel? What exactly are your symptoms?"

"Pain," she panted, motioning to her middle. "Here."

"Sharp?"

Her face suddenly turned green as chard. "Oh, my Lord, I feel like I'm going to . . ." Pushing him away, she jumped up and raced around to the back of the tree.

Mr. Greene's lip curled. "Someone should get Lady Ross back to the house."

"If you're so disgusted, you go to the house!" Ginny glared. "The lady's sick, for heaven's sake!"

Prescott found Edwina leaning back against the tree, her face frighteningly pale. She was panting, sweat had broken out all over her face and neck.

Fear sliced through him, and a terrible sense of impotency. He knew as well as any that fatal illnesses gave no warning, that they did not distinguish between their victims. But his fear would not help Edwina; what she needed was his comfort.

Pulling his handkerchief from his pocket, he gently

swabbed her forehead and mouth, then folded the cloth and set it aside. "I'm going to carry you back to the house, Edwina. Lady Kendrick," he called out. "Will you please send for a doctor?"

"Call for a doctor?" Mrs. Greene cried. "A weak stomach does not necessitate such an extravagance."

"I'll pay for it," Prescott ground out.

"No, I'll pay for it." Ginny crouched down beside him, concern marring her face with lines of worry. "How is she?"

"Not good."

All of the color had washed from Edwina's face and she was deathly pale.

Sir Lee circumnavigated the tree and leaned over to examine the splattered brown evidence of Edwina's illness. "This looks like it was only recently digested."

"Sir Lee!" Prescott could not contain the disgust from his voice.

Edwina groaned, pressing her forehead into Prescott's arm. "Oh, can everyone please just leave me alone to die in shame?"

Prescott felt his heart contract. "Don't say that!"

"I'm sick as a dog in front of a crowd! It's . . . ooooh . . . appalling."

The old gent looked up. "Did you happen to ingest anything with garlic this morning, Lady Ross?"

"Garlic for breakfast?" Lady Kendrick peered from around the tree, made a face and then her head disappeared. "I think not!"

Edwina shook her head, looking so sickly green that Prescott's chest constricted with anxiety. "Just toast . . . oooh, I can't even think about food . . . oooh . . ."

Sir Lee quickly stepped away, just as Edwina leaned over once more.

Prescott did what he could to keep her hair from her face and to hold her steady while she did her business. He felt so bloody impotent, so damned useless, it killed him just to see her suffering so.

When she was done, Ginny used her handkerchief to help Edwina clean herself up while Prescott held her close, being careful of her sensitive middle.

Sir Lee stepped near once more. "Did you, by any chance, take any antimony salts today, Lady Ross? You know, the kind for digestive ailments. One must be very careful to take the correct dosage, very little, in fact, since too much can be exceedingly harmful."

Edwina leaned so heavily on Prescott's arms he worried that the retching was weakening her. And no wonder, the fits were violent and he feared that she couldn't take many more of them. But she was strong, she just had to be.

Edwina shook her head. "No salts. Nothing. I have..." she corrected herself, "I had no digestive ailment before now."

Exhaling noisily, Sir Lee scowled. "Then I do believe that you, my lady, have been poisoned."

"Poisoned?" Mr. Todd cried from the other side of the tree. "A deed most foul!"

"My dearest!" Mr. Greene exclaimed, then there was a rush of movement.

"Someone bring my smelling salts for Mrs. Greene!" Lady Kendrick commanded. "Straightaway!"

"What makes you say that it's poison, Sir Lee?" Prescott demanded, hugging Edwina close.

"I smell garlic, indicating antimony salts. Antimony

salts are used primarily for digestive issues, purging and the like. But they can also be a dangerous poison if administered improperly. They cause nausea, vomiting and abdominal pain, which fit Lady Ross's symptoms. Indications usually start within thirty minutes to two hours from ingestion. The vomit…" He waved his gold-topped cane toward the ground. "Is dark brown, signifying cocoa, which would have been consumed at breakfast and would have hidden the flavor."

"The cocoa did taste a little odd," Edwina muttered. "Oooh…"

Setting his cane down and leaning on it with both hands, Sir Lee nodded. "Which bolsters my conclusion that Lady Ross has been poisoned. In her cocoa, this morning. *Intentionally*."

Prescott blinked as his brain scrambled to make sense of this. Had the blackmailer discovered their plans? But Edwina hadn't done anything. And the only people whose rooms that they'd searched had been Lord Cunningham's and Sir Lee's…

"If you're behind this!" Prescott growled at the old man.

"Don't be ridiculous!" Sir Lee waved him off. "Why would I tell you that I believe she'd been poisoned if I'd done it? Besides, I bear no ill will toward Lady Ross. Someone else, however, obviously does."

Prescott couldn't dispute the logic of Sir Lee's argument, all he knew was that he wanted to hurt someone, and badly.

"Who would want to harm Edwina?" Ginny clutched her fist to her mouth. "If I'm somehow—"

His gaze caught Ginny's and Prescott reached over and squeezed her hand. "We don't know that any such thing has happened. Or why. So let us not jump to conclusions too quickly. Or lay blame." *It's certainly not your fault,* he hoped his eyes conveyed.

"I have to disagree with Sir Lee," Lady Kendrick stepped around the tree to join the old gent. "I cannot see it as poison. It's just too far-fetched. Too impossible to believe."

Sir Lee dipped his head. "I am confident in my conclusion."

"She might have simply caught something, and stomach ailments are most foul."

"Call for the doctor, Lady Kendrick," Ginny begged. "We must do all we can for Edwina."

Lady Kendrick moved toward the house. "I will do so at once."

"Wait!" Prescott cried. "There was a maid in Edwina's rooms! I think she drank some of Edwina's cocoa. If she's sick, then we'll know!"

"Good thinking, my boy!" Sir Lee nodded approvingly. "If the maid is ill and they both drank from the same cocoa, then we will know with a considerable amount of certainty if poisoned cocoa was the cause. Let us hurry to the house and find out if I'm right."

"You go ahead, I'm staying with Edwina." Prescott reached beneath her and gently lifted her in his arms. She felt like a rag doll, she was so limp, and his heart fluttered with concern. Leaning forward, he whispered in her ear, "Just let me know whenever you need to stop, darling."

Her eyes welled up with tears. "What if I don't tell you early enough? What if I—"

"I don't care, Edwina. We'll just do the best we can."

Slowly, she nodded, laying her head on his shoulder. "Thank you, Prescott."

"It's nothing. I'm only taking a stroll, you're the one who's doing all the work."

Then Prescott took the longest walk of his life.

Chapter 30

"**I**'m going to kill that conniving, vicious, oh, she doesn't deserve to be called *lady*, Pomfry," Janelle ground out, as she leaned over Edwina's still body on the bed. "Pull every hair from her head, grind her eyes out, make her eat dirt..."

Standing next to Janelle, Ginny raised a sodden handkerchief to her eyes. "I still can't believe Lady Pomfry actually poisoned Edwina. What kind of hateful person does such a thing? And to employ servants to do her dirty deeds..."

Janelle nodded. "That footman she bribed to poison Edwina's cocoa ought to be hanged. Thank the heavens, Sir Lee, you were here to interrogate the man, so we could learn the truth of it."

Ginny turned to Sir Lee standing by the window. "Do you believe, as the man claims, that he didn't know what was in the draught?"

"What difference does it make?" Prescott growled as he paced alongside Edwina's bed, fairly plowing a rut in the carpet with each turn. "It was wrong and he could have killed her!"

Ginny wrung her hands. "We must count our blessings that Edwina didn't drink the entire mug. And that poor maid...Lady Kendrick says she's sick as a dog."

"Serves her right for sneaking from Edwina's cocoa," Janelle declared.

Leaning on his gold-topped cane, Sir Lee tilted his head. "If it weren't for her, we wouldn't have known for certain that it was poison. And that the trail led right to Lady Pomfry."

For the thousandth time Prescott hovered over Edwina, seeking some semblance of reassurance that she was all right. This past hour had been the longest hour of his life, as he'd watched Edwina gag and choke so that his heart wrenched with agony for her suffering. Now, spent and exhausted, Edwina lay still in the bed, deathly pale, her closed eyes hosting a halo of red spots from all of the retching.

"She's sleeping, finally," Ginny murmured. "I think the worst of it has passed."

Whipping his coat off of the chair where he'd laid it an hour before, Prescott declared, "I'm going after Daphne. She can't have gotten far."

"Why go after her?" Sir Lee demanded. "What good will it do, now?"

"What if it's not antimony pills? What if it's something else? What if Daphne has an antidote? With a fast horse I can overtake her. Get whatever we need from her."

Sir Lee's eyes narrowed. "If I can have a word with you outside, Mr. Devane."

"You'll not stop me!" Prescott moved to step around the man, but Sir Lee was swifter than he looked.

The old gent laid his hand on Prescott's arm. "I'll have that word, if you please!"

"Fine." Prescott shook the man off under the guise of adjusting his coat sleeves. "But only a moment. Then I'm going after her!"

Out in the hallway, Sir Lee wheeled to face him, standing close. "You'll stay here, Mr. Devane, where your lady needs you."

"There's nothing I can do here! There, at least, I can be of some help!"

"There is no antidote, other than time."

"Daphne must know something! She can confirm that it was the salts! She can...she can..."

"Pay?"

Prescott wrapped his anger around him like a welcome mantle. Anything was better than the impotent torment of watching Edwina suffer. "Why not? She should. Anyone who would hurt Edwina..."

"Do you really believe that you could harm Lady Pomfry? Teach her the error of her ways?"

"I certainly want to."

"But can you? Can you raise a hand to a lady, one you obviously, at some point in time, were fond of?"

Prescott wanted to say "yes," but the word was stuck in his throat. He wanted to exact righteous vengeance on the person who harmed the woman of his heart, but he had to be honest with himself.

Curling his fists, Prescott gritted his teeth. "I don't...

know. Probably not. But I know I must confront her. I cannot let things lie—"

"Better to leave her to the authorities—"

"Oh, they'll have her, I'll ensure! She's not getting away with this!" He squared his shoulders, his resolve fixed once more. He might not be capable of violence against Daphne, but she didn't know that, and a good scare certainly wouldn't hurt. At least he'd find out what she used to poison Edwina. "Now your minute is up, sir, and I will be on my way."

"I cannot let you go, Mr. Devane. I cannot watch you make a grave mistake. You see, poisons can be fatal. I am hopeful that Lady Ross expelled the salts in time, but one cannot know until the victim either recovers or dies."

The anxiety constricting Prescott's chest tightened so that he could hardly breathe. "How can you speak so calmly about Edwina's demise?"

"I am all too familiar with death, I'm afraid."

"And poisons? Are you familiar with those as well?"

"What I do know is how poisons work and, regrettably, their consequences."

"So you know why I have to go. Why I have to find out if there's any hope...any antidote..."

"What I know, Mr. Devane, is that there are others who can hunt down Lady Pomfry. Others who can make her pay for her crime. But there is no one else who can comfort Lady Ross like you can."

"But..."

"Look, Mr. Devane, I know that you and Lady Ross are not really engaged."

"What...?"

"Janelle, Lady Blankett, confided in me about your fake engagement to Lady Ross and the reason for it."

His shock must have shown on his face, for Sir Lee rushed on, "I tend to inspire confidences, so don't blame her, and she simply needed someone to talk to about her concerns. She felt that I could be trusted, which, of course, I can. I shall not say a word. But that aside, although you and Lady Ross aren't truly betrothed, I can see how much you care for one another. No one else's presence will ease Lady Ross's suffering like yours. And no one else would regret it more than you if she dies without you being by her side."

The old gent's eyes glistened with unshed tears and he swallowed. Sadness filled his green gaze and his craggy face drooped like a deflated balloon. "I have more than my share of regrets, Mr. Devane, but that, by far, is the worst. I shall not see you suffer it if there's anything I can do to stop it."

Unbidden, the memory of Headmaster Dunn swept over Prescott, and grief pierced his heart. The larger-than-life headmaster could have been standing before him, for his sentiments would have been the same as Sir Lee's. He would have given the identical counsel, would have spoken with similar concern for Prescott's well-being.

The ache of his recent loss dissolved Prescott's anger, leaving only the fear that ate at him like a parasite. "I can't lose her," he whispered as his vision swam with tears. "I only just found her..." Being with Edwina had alleviated his grief, made him not feel so wretchedly alone. Losing her would just be too much...

Dropping his face into his hands, sorrow and anxiety

and pain sliced through him. "I don't want to be...I just can't..."

Sir Lee draped his arm across Prescott's shoulders. "I know you can't lose her, son. You love her."

Love her? Prescott looked up, about to argue, but the words would not come. *Do I? Does what I feel for Edwina amount to love?*

He certainly admired her, immensely. She had an amazing ability to inspire him and move him. And her influence did motivate him to be a better man, to be a more considerate person. And when he was with her, he didn't feel like "the great pretender," but was accepted for himself. He didn't have to mask his feelings, but felt free from judgment. Could that be...was that love?

She made him feel as if he had a dear advocate who cared for him and his well-being. As if he had a partner on his side. Someone who knew who he was and was all right with that. That, because of her, he wasn't so terribly alone. But was that love?

Indeed, she garnered an astonishing feeling of *rightness* within him. When they kissed, touched, he felt *connected,* whole.

And he definitely looked forward to seeing her, couldn't wait to share things with her, wanted to be with her as much as possible, and enjoyed every moment they were together...

With Edwina, for the first time in his life, he didn't feel like a rudderless ship, adrift in an inconsistent current without a harbor to claim. He felt like he was wanted, like he had a *home.*

The truth smacked him in the head so hard, he saw stars.

"I...I do love Edwina. I really do."

"So go to her. Leave everything else to me. I will contact the authorities. I will ensure that this terrible deed does not go unpunished. You be where you're needed most, by Lady Ross's side."

Prescott nodded, wiped his eyes with the back of his hands. "If love means falling to pieces, then I don't know that I can endure it."

"You can if you have a good woman by your side." Sir Lee stepped away. "It makes everything more supportable."

Prescott straightened, struck by a horrible fear, very different from Edwina dying, but equally as terrifying. "What if she doesn't love me back? What if my feelings aren't reciprocated? I have nothing to offer a fine lady like Edwina. No purse, no title...I don't even have my own name!"

Sir Lee shook his fist. "You fight for her, son. Devanes are fighters and given name or no, you are now a Devane. You will fight until you are damned and bloodied if you must, but you must fight for her! Or you're not the man that I believe you to be."

"Fight for her? What does that mean?"

"Declare your intentions. Make your feelings known. Let her appreciate all that you are willing to do for her, for your future. Make what was a pretense something real."

"Are you...speaking of marriage?"

"Of course! To what else would I be referring?"

A hodgepodge of emotions swept through Prescott. Hope, fear, an uneasiness about the man he'd always considered himself to be and who he felt like at this moment. "I...I don't know...I've never thought that I would marry..."

"Not marry? Why in the blazes not?"

"I don't exactly have encouraging feelings about the parson's mousetrap, sir. My parents' experience was less than pleasant."

"But you don't have to repeat their mistakes."

The irony was not lost on him: marrying Edwina would be an *exact* repetition of his parents' mistakes. It had all of the makings of a play, a tragedy, of course; fine lady of noble family marries beneath her and comes to regret it. For undoubtedly her family would disapprove, hence a host of familial censure and heartache. In the second act the heroine shuns her unworthy husband and then dramatically dies from disappointment. Well, disappointment mixed with typhus. In the final installment, the child of that ill-fated marriage repeats the same mistakes all over again. The curtain falls and the theatre house is dark.

Prescott's mind reared away from the disturbing memories, as suddenly a glimmer of hope sparked inside of him. Perhaps it could be different if they simply didn't marry. If they remained lovers and only that? Then her family might not object so terribly. People had been known to have wonderful, caring, happy relationships for years without the blessing of a cleric. Perhaps they could, too.

The lines around Sir Lee's mouth deepened into a scowl, as his canny eyes fixed on Prescott. "And you must marry if you are to bring children into this world. You must give them your name."

Children. With Edwina. His heart skipped a beat. It was a dream beyond all expectation. To have such a joyous connection with Edwina. An amazing bond between them, and the wonder of bringing a child up together. To give a child the love and caring and support...

The door slammed closed on Prescott's dreams so hard, he could almost feel its jarring boom. He had little enough to offer Edwina, he would not condemn a child to a life of "less thans." The disapproval and rejection by all family. The censure by society. The nightmare of watching the separation between the parents as the pressures of life bore down upon them.

"No." He shook his head. "No children."

"You would be a good father, Mr. Devane," Sir Lee urged. "I have seen how you deal with others, your caring and consideration for Lady Ross. And Lady Ross would be a wonderful—"

"Of course she would," Prescott interrupted. "That's not the point! Hell, I don't even have a home to call my own. I certainly can't have a child. It would be irresponsible. And I will not condemn a child to a life of heartache."

"Like you had?" Sir Lee offered softly.

"I would not have a child suffer it, not for all the gold in Cairo."

Ginny poked her head out into the hallway. "Oh, I'm so glad you haven't left yet! She's calling for you, Prescott. Edwina wants you."

She wanted him. Needed him. And he would go to her. Stay with her as long as possible. Love her as long as she was willing to let him.

He would give her everything, including saving her from sharing his unworthy name.

Resolve settled upon him and he turned to Sir Lee. "Thank you for your wise counsel, sir. I am in your debt."

"But—"

"I must go."

Shaking his head, Sir Lee waved him off. "Of course, go to her, she needs you. But please bear witness that one day I may call in that debt."

"As is your right," Prescott called over his shoulder as he strode into Edwina's chambers.

"Nay," the old gent whispered to the now-empty hallway. "It is my duty."

Chapter 31

❦

The next afternoon, Edwina and Prescott sat in the large armchairs in the salon in her chambers.

"Ugh." Edwina wrinkled her nose at the musty-smelling liquid in the mug Prescott held out to her. "I don't like barley water."

"Stop complaining and drink." Prescott pressed the cup into her hands and then reclined in the chair across from her.

Today he wore a hunter green coat that made his eyes appear more jade than emerald. Every time the sun shining in through the open window flickered in his gaze, her breath caught. He was so handsome and so astoundingly attentive. When she began this ruse she never would have imagined how dear he would become to her.

His hair was loose, without pomade and uncovered, the way she liked it, and she had to wrap her hands around the mug to keep from reaching out to brush them through his coppery brown mane.

But she kept her hands to herself, worried that Prescott might not be interested in her that way any longer. The specter of Sir Geoffrey's disgust hovered over her like a foul vapor, along with something that her cousin Henry had once told her. Henry had said that husbands were kept out of their wife's birthing chambers because a man wouldn't be able to touch his wife ever again after seeing her in such a wretched state. Edwina feared that the same concept might apply to her ghastly bout with antimony salts and Prescott.

The concept was so disheartening, she had to push it out of her mind for fear of breaking down and weeping. Just when she'd discovered her passion, to have it whisked away so abruptly, and by a devious witch like Lady Pomfry...

Well it was all too unjust to consider. So she simply wouldn't.

Instead, she would focus on what a saint Prescott had been. Catering to her every need, bringing her a hundred different drinks until he found something that she could hold down, reading to her, taking her outside for some fresh air while the maids cleaned her rooms.

He'd insisted that the bed chamber be scrubbed and the sheets changed, thankfully eliminating the horrible odors associated with her malady. He'd said that he knew from past experience that smell alone could exacerbate her nausea. His ability to put himself into her shoes was astonishing.

And yet through it all, he hadn't kissed or touched her in any way different than he would a sister. She hungered for his lips, longed for his musky male scent, and yearned for the feel of his hard body pressing against hers.

And deplorably, he seemed completely oblivious to her as a woman. She was a patient in need of caring, a friend in need of company, but not a woman in need of her man. She was being utterly selfish, she knew, but she couldn't help it. She wanted him to desire her, madly, hungrily and with the deep abiding passion that she felt for him.

But she wasn't about to press the issue. It would be like asking a man why he didn't send flowers. Once the criticism was out there, then any gesture he made would be seen as insincere. Where was the good in that? The only thing Edwina could do was be grateful for Prescott's kindness. How utterly demoralizing.

"Come now, drink it," Prescott urged, pulling Edwina from her gloomy woolgathering. "Or I will have Janelle force you to take it, and you know what a martinet she can be."

"My, aren't you bossy." She raised a brow, pretending that her heart wasn't breaking. "One would think you might be a little bit sweeter to a poisoning victim." She forced a smile to let him know that she was only teasing.

"I really appreciate all you've done for me, Prescott. These last few hours have been, well, better off forgotten. But I'll never forget your thoughtfulness. I want you to know how much I appreciate your kindness."

He shrugged. "You would have done the same for me."

"Of course. But that doesn't diminish the significance of your thoughtfulness." She sipped from the lukewarm drink. It was dreadful, but settled her stomach as nothing else would. "I just hope that you're still not blaming yourself for what happened."

"You seem determined not to let me." He smiled, but there was a sadness in his gaze that pinched at her heart.

She couldn't help herself, reaching across the small table, she squeezed his hand. "Please don't. It's hard enough feeling wretched without being guilt-ridden for somehow being responsible for making you feel to blame."

"That makes me feel even guiltier!" His face was stern but his tone was joking.

"If I agree to discard my guilt, then will you as well?"

"Deal." Smiling, he stood and leaned over, kissing her parted lips so sweetly, she almost swooned.

Relief whipped through her along with an exhilarating thrill.

He still desires me!

The smells and sights of the last few hours might have cowed a lesser man. But Prescott Devane was no ordinary man! Thank the heavens.

Raking his hand through her loose curls, he murmured, "Oh, how I've missed your delicious lips." He swallowed. "I know the doctor said no exertion, but I don't think a little kissing would hurt, do you?"

The dear man had been anxious about overexerting her! And all the while she had worried that he no longer desired her. An overwhelming, head-over-heels rush of affection surged through her for this wonderful man.

Reaching up and caressing his smooth, square jaw, Edwina murmured, "I'm feeling much better...and the doctor said that I do need to stay in bed..."

He nibbled her mouth, gently sucking the soft flesh between his lips. "I think I can figure a few ways to keep you lying down, perhaps not quite resting..."

"Ahem." Someone coughed behind Prescott. "Ahem." The lady coughed again.

Reluctantly, Prescott pulled away, his blazing eyes meeting hers. "Later," he whispered, his breath drifting across her ear, causing a shiver.

"Promise?"

"Definitely." Straightening, he moved aside.

Lady Kendrick stood in the threshold, a businesslike smile on her long oval face. The stout woman was like a ship's captain, forever in charge and at work, executing her tasks with gusto. Clasping her hands together before her, she declared, "It warms my heart to see the color back in your cheeks, Lady Ross."

Edwina felt her cheeks burn. "Your gracious hospitality and the thoughtful efficiency of your servants have ensured that my every need has been met. Thank you for everything, my lady."

"Yes, well, we'd all be better off if the whole mess hadn't started in the first instance." The lady scowled. "I don't know what I was thinking including that dreadful Lady Pomfry in the party."

Prescott shot Edwina an endearing glance, "As a wise woman once told me, assuming blame only continues the round of guilt and we'd all prefer a round of something much more palatable."

"Yes, well." She grimaced. "My gathering would have been a social success had I not invited that woman. And as it stands, well..."

Prescott scratched his chin. "I hate to say it, my lady,

but you will likely come out of this misadventure with a reputation for throwing memorable parties."

The matron's face lit up. "I hadn't thought of it that way!"

"Moreover, not only will everyone hear about what happened to Edwina, but they will also learn of your gracious hospitality."

"You do have a talent for looking at the brighter side of things, Mr. Devane!"

A liveried servant entered, bowed to the guests and then whispered something in Lady Kendrick's ear. The matron nodded to the man and then looked up at them. "If you will excuse me for a moment?"

After she was gone, Edwina grabbed Prescott's hand, whispering, "I'm starting to feel bad that we're using this house party to catch the blackmailer, Prescott. I feel like we're imposing on Lady Kendrick's gracious hospitality."

"We didn't set this stage, if you recall, Edwina. The blackmailer did. And we are doing what we can to keep Lady Kendrick from ever knowing." He leaned close, keeping a keen eye on the empty doorway. "And since Ginny hasn't heard from the knave, we have no choice but to continue with our efforts."

"I wonder why he hasn't made his demands yet."

Prescott shrugged. "My guess is he likes to make people squirm. Or mayhap the escapade with Daphne threw off everyone's schedule, including his?"

"I can't help but wonder if mayhap Ginny isn't the only guest who's here for purposes other than country entertainment. Can there be other blackmail victims amongst the guests?"

"Gather your victims and collect payment much more easily? You may be right. And perhaps that's why she hasn't heard from the blackguard. Mayhap she's lower on the list of targets."

"All the more reason we must stop this villain. We will have to search more than one room a night—"

Squeezing her hand, his eyes widened. "In all of the chaos, I forgot to tell you!"

"What?"

"First, Sir Lee knows all and is more than willing to help."

"How wonderful. I like him exceedingly and he certainly brings some valuable skills to the hunt."

"I like him, too. But there's something else. Yesterday, before you were poisoned, remember I didn't leave your room until almost dawn?"

"Oh, I remember," she breathed, the memory causing her blood to stir.

"Well, during the night someone searched my room."

"What? Did he take anything?"

"No. That's the strange part. It was as if he was simply looking around. Nothing was missing."

"Do you think it might have been Lady Pomfry?" Even saying her name caused a vicious twist in Edwina's middle and she pressed a hand to her tortured belly.

Prescott shook his head. "Daphne would have ravaged my room, not tried to put everything back in its place."

"Are you sure someone searched? It wasn't simply the maids?"

"Yes, I'm very particular about the page placement in my Bible. The special bookmark Headmaster Dunn had given me had been moved."

"A Bible-reading burglar?"

He shrugged with a smile. "Odder things have been known to happen."

"So what do you think the searcher was looking— Lady Kendrick!"

Prescott straightened, still grasping Edwina's hand.

The matron's smile was apologetic. "Pardon my absence, but I just learned we have a new arrival. One who I'd been hoping would have arrived sooner. But he's here now, so all is well."

"Who is it?"

Lady Kendrick beamed. "The Earl of Wootton-Barrett. Your father."

Edwina felt her stomach lurch, and it wasn't the antimony salts.

"I must go make preparations. He waits in the parlor off the garden. If you will excuse me." Turning, the matron strode from the room, her steps purposeful.

"Are you all right, Edwina?" Prescott crouched before her. "You look pale. Do you feel ill?"

"Yes. But no. It's not the salts." She shook her head, bewildered. "It's just, well, I knew I'd have to face my father at some point. It was part of the plan. But I didn't expect him to race halfway across the country to do it." She bit her lip. "I thought I'd have more time..."

"He must be very upset," Prescott muttered, adjusting his cravat as if it was too tight. His handsome face was marred with unease and his eyes were clouded with disquiet. "Are you going to tell him that it's over?"

"No." Shaking her head, she clutched his hand tighter. "No, I meant what I said, I want us to stay together. Do...you?"

"Yes, of course, but breaking off the engagement was the plan. Then your father would be so relieved that you and I didn't marry that he'd leave you alone."

Rising, Edwina released his hand and moved to stand before the window. Staring out, she crossed her arms, hugging herself. "I think, well, I think that my plan was a bit...infantile. If I want to stand up to my father, then I need to do it and not hide behind a sham engagement or make up things that will detract from what I'm truly trying to do, namely stake my claim for independence. I'm a grown woman, for heaven's sake. I need to start behaving like one."

"But if you don't break off the engagement, then your father will be furious."

"I'll not submit to his intimidation. His wants should not influence how I live my life. Mine should. And I'm not willing to let you go."

"But at what cost?"

She looked up. "What do you mean?"

"He's your father. You should keep peace between you."

"Not at the risk of losing my sense of self." She shook her head. "This isn't about you, Prescott, it's about me and my father. You're simply the reason that brought me and my father face-to-face, but this stand is long overdue."

"But can't you see his side of it? He believes what he wants is best for you. That you should marry well, have a solid future..."

"Those are the very reasons why I married Sir Geoffrey, and I was miserable. Granted, our temperaments weren't well suited, which bears witness to the fact that my father doesn't understand me, not one whit. Else he never would have chosen Sir Geoffrey for me." Sighing, she rubbed her hand down her arm, to comfort herself. "But I suppose it's to be expected. My father has never understood me, or what makes me happy. He's always seen me as a bit of an oddity, someone to be 'managed' because of my 'abnormal tendencies.'"

"He said that?" Shock shimmered in his emerald gaze, quickly replaced by anger. "'Abnormal tendencies'?"

"Oh, yes and much more. Which is why I usually wind up crying and behaving in a somewhat immature fashion when he begins one of his diatribes. I feel like I'm eleven years old once more and he's scolding me for liking to sit and talk with Nana, the woman who ran the dairy."

"You're not going to face him without me."

She looked up. "Thank you, Prescott. But I can't stand up for myself with you standing up for me. Does that make any sense?"

Stepping forward, Prescott clasped her hands. "I want to be your knight and protector, Edwina. For you I would slay dragons, including irascible earls."

She smiled, touched by his gallantry and knowing that he meant every word. "This is one battle I must fight on my own, Prescott. It's been mostly my fault for not facing my father sooner. It was easier to skirt around the conflict and not clash with him. I suppose in the same way that I went along with everything Sir Geoffrey and the dowager wanted. I let them either walk over me or influence my every step. It's time for me to start walking on my own."

Drawing her close, he wrapped his arms around her. "But you *have* been walking on your own. You established The Society for the Enrichment and Learning of Females—"

"But it's not the same. I did it without my parents knowing about it until after it had been established. I hid it, Prescott. I hid what I was doing from them, for fear that they might try to stop me, and succeed." Hugging him close, she inhaled his familiar musky scent and took comfort from his support.

"But you didn't kowtow to them once you'd succeeded. And what of your business ventures?"

"My parents don't know about what I'm doing with Henry. It's all on the sly. It's time that I stopped hiding, Prescott. It's time for me to start living the life I want to live without cowering in fear. Or hiding behind a lie. I want to be more like you, Prescott, making no excuses for being who I am."

He tensed. "But what if the consequences are too much for you to bear, Edwina? What if your father cuts you off? Not financially, but well, everything..."

"Like your grandfather did to your mother?" she asked gently.

"Yes. I'm not worth losing your family over, Edwina. Family is everything." He swallowed. "If you lost them because of me, if you were cut off, well, I would never forgive myself."

She sighed. "I can't live my life by 'what-ifs,' Prescott. I need to find out what I'm truly made of. And how much my father loves me. And there's only one way to do that: face the Earl of Wootton-Barrett."

Chapter 32

~~~⌒⌒⌒~~~

Standing in the shadow of a large oak tree, Prescott raked his hand through his hair and stared at the closed French doors to the parlor.

Blast! He couldn't see a thing with the sun reflecting off the glass doors and Edwina and her father having moved to the other side of the room.

"So you're a Peeping Tom, now, eh?"

Prescott jumped. "Oh, Sir Lee. You startled me."

With his gold-topped cane, Sir Lee strolled down the garden lane to where Prescott stood in the shade. "I presume Lady Ross is in there with her father."

Prescott nodded. "She . . . well, she said that she wanted to face the firing squad on her own."

"Firing squad, eh?" The old gent's gray brows lifted as he tucked his thin cigar into his mouth and puffed. Smoke billowed around him in a pungent cloud. "Wootton-Barrett does like to ride roughshod over people."

"I should be in there..."

"Then why aren't you? You're not feeling toothless, are you?"

"I want to respect her wishes..."

Sir Lee snorted. "Now I know you're in love." Pulling a thin cigar from his coat pocket, he held it out, offering his own as a light. "Smoke?"

"No thanks. It would be a waste of a fine cigar." *What is going on in there?* Reaching down, he grabbed his watch fob and clicked open the gold timepiece for the tenth time. *It's been seven minutes already, yet it feels like three hours.*

"As you please." The old gent stuffed the cigar back into his pocket. Leaning on his cane, he jerked his chin toward the French doors. "So you think the Earl of Wootton-Barrett is a mite upset about your engagement to Lady Ross?"

"Why else would he race across the country on horseback?"

Pursing his lips around the cigar, Sir Lee puffed. "Why else indeed."

"I bet he hardly even stopped to water his horse, unable to wait to rake Edwina over the coals for cavorting with the likes of me. Can't sully the bloodlines, can we?"

"Is she telling him that the engagement is off?"

"No. She wants to make a stand...that this isn't about me. But she *should* be telling him that it's over, for at some point or another, she'll come to regret this whole affair. She'll come to regret...choosing me." Prescott moved toward the doors. "I won't let her destroy her life..."

Sir Lee grabbed his arm. "Isn't that her choice to make?"

He shook his head. "I love her too much to watch her come to despise me. And she will, for staying with me will cost her everything. And that I cannot bear."

Shrugging off the old man, Prescott stormed the French doors and burst into the parlor.

Edwina's back was to him as she faced her father. A lesser woman would have been cowering in the corner when confronting the burly black-haired bellowing giant that was Wootton-Barrett. With his high black hat, pea green coat and darkened features he loomed over Edwina like a Goliath.

Edwina turned, her eyes red-rimmed and her lower lip quivering, yet she hadn't shed a tear. *You show him your mettle!*

The earl looked up and his eyes, black as coals on a broad craggy face, widened, then narrowed as they fixed on Prescott. "You must be the devil's spawn I've been hearing about!"

Even from across the room, Prescott could smell horse, sweat, and a hint of Jockey Club cologne; the man must not have even refreshed himself before accosting his daughter. Prescott's resolve hardened.

The earl shook his fist. "Get your grasping arse out of here! This is none of your damned business!"

"Actually, your lordship, it is. You see I want to settle your concerns, by informing you that I have no intention of marrying your daughter."

"Bloody well right you won't!"

Edwina's face looked stricken.

Prescott stepped deeper into the room. "I'm sorry,

Edwina. But I have no title, no money, hell, I don't even have my own name. I have nothing to offer you."

Wootton-Barrett's bristly brows knitted. "What are you about, Devane? Is this about a payoff? For if it is, I'll not give you a blasted shilling."

"I don't want anything from you, your lordship. Least of all your daughter."

Edwina seemed to sway on her feet and Prescott was immediately by her side, holding her arm. "Are you all right? Do you feel weak? Sick?"

She shook her head. "I'm fine, I was just taken aback by your declaration. I know how you feel about marriage, but..." She blinked as her eyes glistened with unshed tears. "I suppose I didn't expect it to hurt so much hearing you say it like that."

"The last thing in the world I would ever want to do is hurt you, Edwina. But the cost is too high and you know it would never have worked out between us."

"I know nothing of the sort—"

"What do you mean the cost is too high?" Wootton-Barrett demanded. "She's not paying you, is she?"

Ignoring the bellowing earl, Prescott whispered in her ear, "I can't have you throw away your life for me, Edwina. I'm not worth it."

"But this isn't about you—"

"It is. Establishing the society, living life on your own terms, those your father can handle, but staying with me? That's something he won't abide."

"But if I have to choose—"

Prescott shook his head. "I'm not worth losing your family over. Family is everything, I should know, I have none. And if you lost them, if you were cut off, well, I would never forgive myself."

"You're damn right you're not worth it!" the earl bellowed.

Pushing herself out of Prescott's arms, Edwina squared her shoulders and rounded on her father. "Don't you speak to him like that! Prescott Devane is kind and considerate and as honorable a man as I've ever met!"

Prescott's heart swelled at the way she was defending him.

"If I decide never to marry," she continued, "then it's for my own reasons, not for any lack on his part."

A pit formed in Prescott's middle. She'd decided *never* to marry? He knew this, Edwina had told him, and although it was completely illogical to be hurt by this intelligence, he was.

"You will marry!" the earl bellowed. "And not to a scurrilous dog like him!"

Edwina's eyes flashed with fury. "Don't you dare insult Prescott." Her voice was low, angry. "You may criticize my actions, but don't you dare defame a hair on his head."

"Why you ingrate!" Wooton-Barrett shook his meaty fist. "To take up sides with a lecherous knave instead of your own father! You should be kissing my boot tips with gratitude for all I've done for you!"

"I am grateful, Father," Edwina bit out. "But I'm a grown woman now—"

"Who doesn't have an ounce of sense in her dippy head!"

"Now see here!" Prescott stepped forward, trying desperately to keep a rein on his temper.

The earl stabbed his finger. "Don't speak until spoken to!" He turned on his daughter. "You're an odd one, always were. But it's high time I stopped indulging your foolish fantasies that you can do as you please. You will marry Viscount Bellwood—"

Edwina's face was awash in hurt and disbelief. "Haven't you heard a word I've said?"

"And what it cost me to keep Bellwood still interested after all of your shenanigans!" the earl plowed forward as if Edwina hadn't spoken. "The arrangements have all been made, the special license secured. You're fortunate that I'm convincing enough to have him still take you!"

"Still take her?" Prescott screeched. "The man is the luckiest sod on the face of the earth!"

"I told you to keep your mouth shut! She's my daughter and I know her worth down to the last bloody pound!"

Clenching his fists, Prescott closed the gap between them. "You obviously don't know a thing about Edwina!"

"I know she's better off without the likes of you! I know she's cost me more headaches and far too many pounds to unload—"

"Unload? You speak as if she's a bag of oats! She's your daughter, for heaven sakes!"

"And I know what's best for her! And it's not you! She'll be married to Bellwood by the end of the week."

"The hell she's marrying Bellwood!" *Or anybody else!*

Besides me.

The idea was in his head before he could stop it; heady, enticing and ripe with the promise of happiness.

The earl brandished his fist. "You have no say in my

daughter's affairs, you...*greedy guts!* If you try going near my daughter, there'll be hell to pay! And you'll be praying you'd never laid eyes on her!"

Edwina's face blanched white. "Enough, Father! You cannot threaten him with harm! You push too far!"

Wootton-Barrett's lip curled. "Bellwood'll teach you to behave like a proper English lady. I don't care if he has to beat the obedience into you! He'll have my blessing to do it!"

Something deep inside Prescott went cold. Without thought, he slammed his fist into Wootton-Barrett's arrogant nose.

The earl staggered backwards and fell onto the chintz sofa, blood spurting out his nose and all over his shocked face.

"Father!" Edwina's eyes widened, then she rushed toward the toppled earl.

"See what an animal he is? See what you've caused?" Pulling a handkerchief from his coat, Wootton-Barrett held it to his face. "He's a brute!"

Watching Edwina tend to her father, Prescott's heart fell to somewhere beneath his knees and he might have staggered, if he weren't so rigid with shock. He'd just cuffed Edwina's father! There was no coming back from that. His misty hopes burned to ash.

Edwina shot him a glance. "Prescott should not have punched you, Father."

His heart dropped even lower, if that was possible, as shame overcame him.

Edwina faced her father. "But you were egging him on, insulting him, threatening him and me—"

She was defending him? He looked up as a wisp of hope skated across his heart.

"One cannot insult a scrounger! This is the man you called 'A gentleman in action if not by birth!' As if there is such a thing!"

A gentleman? Edwina had said that? Hope budded within him. Still, he'd just corked her father...

"Threatening to have me beaten? Abusing a man who's done you no harm?" A familiar fury flashed in Edwina's gaze as she stood, glorious and proud. "Rules of conduct are very different when they apply to you!"

"I'm not the one who resorted to fisticuffs!"

"No, just threats and bullying!"

Wootton-Barrett's face turned a nasty shade of red. "Why you impertinent—"

"That'll be enough!" a voice called sharply. "Enough I say!"

Three sets of eyes turned toward the open French doors.

Leaning easily on his gold-topped cane as if seeing a bloodied earl was a common happenstance, Sir Lee nodded. "Wootton-Barrett."

"Have this man arrested, Sir Lee!" Pushing himself up from the sofa, Wootton-Barrett waved the blood-spattered linen at Prescott. "He accosted me!" Turning to Prescott, he threatened, "I'll see you hanged for this."

"Hanged?" Edwina gasped, stepping over and gripping Prescott's arm. Her face was drained of color.

Prescott's mouth suddenly went dry; he knew that many men had been hanged for less.

Wooton-Barrett sneered. "He'll swing for sure for striking me!"

Shaking his head, Sir Lee stepped forward. "As if you didn't deserve it, Wootton-Barrett."

"Wh-what?"

"I know what's going on here." The old gent's eyes glistened and his craggy mouth pinched with sorrow. "All too well, I'm afraid."

The earl's eyes narrowed. "What the blazes are you talking about?"

"I sat in your place, thirty years ago, making the same pigheaded declarations, berating my headstrong daughter and abusing the man she loved."

Prescott's heart skipped a beat as the shadow of a notion slithered across his brain.

Sir Lee shook his head, his eyes watering. "Barbara was always a headstrong lass. Had pride a mile high, just like her father's."

"Barbara," Prescott staggered. "My...mother..."

Swallowing, Sir Lee looked up, pain and grief evident in his green gaze. "I wanted to break her damned obstinacy." Shaking his fist before him, tears dripped out of his eyes and trailed down his weathered cheeks. "But I only broke my family. And my heart."

"What the blazes does this have to do with the fact that his man struck me?" Wootton-Barrett demanded. "I want him arrested, now!"

Edwina signaled her father. "Be quiet."

Wootton-Barrett blinked, then blustered, "Don't you speak—"

"Enough, Father! For once think about someone besides yourself!" Turning her back to the earl, she grasped Prescott's arm even tighter and he was grateful for her support.

He was reeling...But it couldn't be. It was too much of a coincidence, too much a dream...

Swallowing, Prescott held his hand out to Sir Lee. "What are you...what are you saying?"

Sir Lee brushed aside his tears. "I'm saying that thirty years ago I told my daughter that if she married the man she loved, then I would cut her out of my life. Had I known then what I know now, Prescott..."

"You searched my rooms..."

"Yes. I saw the Bible. I gave it to Barbara when she was a girl. The family name Devane was still inscribed inside the front cover."

Prescott felt as if the world were spinning on its head. Dropping onto the settee, he pressed his hand over his eyes. "I don't believe this." He looked up. "You're my...grandfather?"

The earl stood. "I don't give a damn if he's the Prince Regent's only heir! He hit me!"

"Didn't you hear me, Wootton-Barrett? He's my grandson! And I've missed his whole life. I've suffered, more than you could know. I lost my daughter, lost my grandson, lost everything because *I—was— an—ass.*"

Sir Lee pointed his cane at the earl's chest. "Can you be a bigger man than I, Wootton-Barrett? Can you be wise enough to know that nothing will stop these two because they are truly in love? That your inflexibility will damn you to a hell no father should have to endure?"

Edwina crouched beside Prescott, concern marring her lovely features. "Are you all right?"

Slowly, he shook his head. "It's a bit too much to grasp..."

Hugging Prescott close, she murmured in his ear, "I'm here for you. Whatever you need. I'm here with you." Her support was probably the only thing keeping him sane at this moment. Everything he'd known about himself was a lie. Well, part of one. His name was really Devane...

"Can't you see how much they care for each other?" Sir Lee demanded.

"I don't give a fig. Grandson or not, I'll see him hang!" Turning, her father stormed from the room.

Edwina hugged Prescott even tighter, hoping to impart all of her love and caring in that connection, knowing he must be going through hell.

Sir Lee's steps were hesitant. "Can you ever forgive me, son?"

Edwina held her breath.

Prescott was silent for a long moment, then he slowly pulled away from her. Reluctantly she released him and stepped aside, keeping a hand on his shoulder. Her heart wept for his pain.

With his brow furrowed, Prescott shook his head. "You knew. You knew all along, didn't you?"

"No, not until I came here. Not until I saw you." With his eyes glistening with tears, Sir Lee's brow rutted with grief. "You're the spitting image of her..." He nodded, fresh tears spilling down his weathered cheeks like rivers of sorrow. "When I saw you I knew. But before then...I didn't know about you, I swear..."

The old gent dropped onto the ottoman as if his knees couldn't hold him any longer. His shoulders were hunched, his head dropped to his chin; he looked almost crushed by the weight of his sorrow. "My daughter died hating me. Hating me so much, she didn't tell me I'd had a grandson. I can't blame her. For any man who was heartless enough to cut off his own flesh and blood could hardly be trusted with such a precious gift..." He choked, overcome, pulling a linen from his coat and covering his eyes. "She never knew how sorry I was. How much I regretted..."

Edwina's heart ached for the man, for the tragedy he'd caused, endured, and suffered still.

Looking up, Sir Lee sniffed. "I didn't even know she was dead until weeks after she'd gone." He laughed, but it was a cheerless sound. "Me, the commander of a hundred intelligence officers, master of a thousand secrets, and I didn't even know my daughter lay dying... I didn't know that my grandson, my only flesh and blood was being left in the care of strangers. I was a fool. A stupid, headstrong fool."

Sobbing openly, the man hung his head, his bony shoulders shaking with sorrow. "I'm so sorry, Prescott, so terribly sorry..."

Funereal silence draped over them, the pain and heartache of a thousand regrets choking the air.

Shrugging off Edwina's hand, Prescott moved toward his grandfather.

She stepped aside, her hands clasped before her, prayerful, hoping beyond all hope that this ordeal might turn out well.

"I've fantasized about this moment a million times in my head." Prescott's tone was flat, emotionless. "The moment when I would tell the man who destroyed my mother's dreams, left us to die in poverty... that I didn't need him, that I came out just fine. That he could take his lousy family and bugger off."

Sir Lee's tear-stained face was bleak and filled with shame. "I don't blame you, son..."

"But I can't."

Sir Lee looked up, hope in his green gaze.

Blinking as if surprised, Prescott shook his head.

"You're a shrewd sod, I'll hand you that. You let me know you, like you even. I've had the chance to hear your words, to hearken to your advice, to understand you..."

Sir Lee wiped his eyes and sat a little straighter.

"I know you enough now," Prescott continued, "that I can't ignore your sorrow. I can't dismiss your remorse. I can't doubt...that you truly regret it all."

Sir Lee rose. "I would give my life ten times over to have done it differently...To have saved you from all you've suffered...I know that I'm too late, offering too little..." Swallowing, Sir Lee extended a shaky hand. "But can you ever forgive me?"

Prescott brushed aside his grandfather's outstretched hand and threw his arms around him.

Sir Lee burst into tears, holding Prescott so closely, shaking, crying and hugging Prescott so tight as if to never let him go.

Edwina's vision swam with tears.

"There's been too much overindulged pride." Prescott's voice was thick with emotion. "Too much heartache."

Hugging his grandfather, Prescott looked over his shoulder, his gaze meeting Edwina's with such intensity her breath caught. "I'm ready for a family to call my own."

Chapter 33

A few hours later, Edwina stood by the open window in her chambers, staring out at the moonlit sky. A multitude of stars sprinkled the horizon and Edwina wondered if she wished upon them, might her dreams come true.

She couldn't quite erase the blazing intent in Prescott's eyes or the ferocity in his voice when he'd said, "I'm ready for a family to call my own."

The memory alone caused her stomach to jolt and her heart to flutter. Could he have meant with her? Dare she hope to dream?

She knew that it wasn't matrimony that didn't suit her, but marriage to Sir Geoffrey. Or anyone who tried to "manage" or control her.

But Prescott wasn't like that. He understood her, accepted her and wouldn't ever try to rule her. She knew it deep in her heart. In fact, he supported her and the things that were important to her. He didn't disdain The Society for the Enrichment and Learning of Females. Instead, he understood the issues she was facing and helped provide her with tools so that she could manage well enough for herself. Like when he'd introduced her to Mr. Leonard to help with the new applicants. His support was remarkable, actually. As was he.

When she was with him, she felt herself, she felt free, she felt respected and cared for, and so blessedly happy she might as well be one of those stars shooting through the midnight sky.

The idea of being married to him, of being with him forever, caused a sweet reverberation deep in her soul. It felt right. It felt better than any hope she could have wished for.

Still, he hadn't asked. And, come to think of it, he'd been prepared to end everything. Granted he'd intended it to prevent strife with her family. But still, he'd been very willing to make the sacrifice.

She frowned. A little too willing, perhaps? Prescott hadn't wanted her to marry Viscount Bellwood, but that didn't mean that he was willing to pop the question himself.

Mayhap she was hearing wedding bells when there were merely chirping crickets? Seeing nuptial bands where there were only the rings of smoke from one of Sir Lee's cigars? She knew that he cared for her, admired her even, but that might be sufficient for an affair, not necessarily matrimony. Could that be enough? She wondered.

Then there was the matter of her father. Her stomach sank. Her raging bull of a father was calling for Prescott to be hauled before the magistrate. Drawn and quartered, hanged, whipped until he collapsed.

Edwina rubbed her temple as a sudden piercing headache came upon her. She'd better think about keeping her lover's head out of a noose, not daydream about shackling his leg in matrimony. Where was her usual good sense? A plan. She needed a plan. Mayhap a list would help.

Stepping over to the secretary, she pulled out a scrap of foolscap, and her writing instruments. She sat, readied, and...nothing came. Not a blessed word entered her mind. Like the foolscap before her, her mind was wretchedly blank. The only thing she could think of was how desperately she loved Prescott and one couldn't make a list for that.

"Nay." She shook her head, trying to clear it. She needed a list of...what? Things she loved about him? Admired him for? If she wrote it would her father read it and change his mind? She snorted, feeling desperate. Her father *never* changed his mind. The only thing that might help was if she threw herself on her father's mercy, offered to end the affair to save Prescott's neck...

The very thought of never seeing Prescott again, of never hearing his deep rumbling voice, never again enjoying his dry wit, never smelling his rich, musky scent...There would be no more watching him laugh with her dearest friends, no more touching his velvety skin or kissing his smooth lips or loving him. Never again to enjoy his charming company or feel that amazing sense of confidence that she experienced whenever he was near. Never to have that beautiful sensation of harmony when they touched, when they said the same thing at once or when they communicated without the need for words...

The thought of missing all that, of never again being with Prescott caused such heartache she didn't know if she could breathe.

But to save his life...? To rescue him from the hangman's noose? The whip...?

She shuddered. It was a devil's bargain for sure, but she would do it, to spare the man she loved.

Grimacing, she slowly dipped her quill and wrote, *Matrimony.* Then she crossed it out with a thick "x." *Affair.* Then she crossed it out with a thick "x." *Nothing.*

She stared at the page a long, miserable moment, wondering if she'd be able to endure it. Her heart felt leaden, her eyes burned with unshed tears.

A knock resounded on the door.

Instinctively, Edwina crumpled up the foolscap and shoved it into a drawer. "Come."

"Edwina!" Ginny swept into the room, panting as if she'd run all the way from her rooms. She clutched a leather reticule to her chest, an odd thing to be carrying about the Kendrick manor.

Closing the door behind her, Ginny practically skipped across the carpet, her arthritic hip giving her a bit of a hop. "Oh, Edwina! I must tell you the most wonderful news!" The matron's rosy-cheeked face was brimming with excitement. "I can hardly believe it!"

"So you've heard?"

"Heard what?"

"About Sir Lee being Prescott's grandfather."

Ginny's pale blue eyes widened. "Why that's wonderful!"

"If you hadn't heard then...?"

Holding up the satchel, Ginny cried, "You'll not believe what I found on my bed just moments ago!"

"Your reticule?"

"Don't be silly!" Reaching into the bag, Ginny pulled out a packet of letters wrapped with a long, fox-colored ribbon. "My letters! To Gérardin!"

"But how...?"

Ginny shook her head with wonder. "I've no earthly idea. They were simply lying there with a note saying that I would no longer be bothered by that wretched blackmailer again. I didn't receive any demands or make that five-hundred-pound payment! I don't even know who left them!" Her eyes brimmed with tears. "It's a miracle. My Judith is saved."

Edwina wrapped her arms around her dear friend, hugging her close. "I'm so happy for you."

"It's all been such a terrible nightmare." Pulling away, Ginny shook her head, wiping her eyes. "I almost can't believe it's over."

"You need to burn those letters, Ginny, you know that."

"I do." Ginny stared at the packet of letters, her face wistful. "But I would very much like to read them once more..."

"I understand they mean a lot to you, but we have a chance now, before anyone else could possibly see them..."

Ginny grasped Edwina's hand. "May I read them here? Will you stay with me? Then we will burn them together. Tonight. And hopefully Janelle and Prescott will join us. It would only be fitting."

Edwina hesitated. Her father couldn't do anything

within the next half hour, could he? It was unlikely, especially since Lady Kendrick had promised to work upon him. She'd told Edwina that she would do her best to calm him down and dissuade him from acting in anger. Edwina didn't have much confidence that Lady Kendrick could sway her father completely, but mayhap she could persuade him to not press charges? Then there wouldn't be any devil's bargain! She wouldn't have to offer to give up Prescott.

Yes, Lady Kendrick needed time to convince Edwina's father to settle down and consider his actions. There was no point in pressing the matter before then.

Edwina squeezed Ginny's hand. "Of course I will stay while you read them."

Ginny stepped over to the armchair, dropped her reticule and sat. Untying the fox-colored ribbon, she slowly unfolded the first letter and began to read. Her gaze grew dreamy, a secret smile on her lips.

Feeling like a voyeur, Edwina turned away and stared out the window, wondering what it must be like to have loved so deeply and yet to have been forced apart. Ginny seemed to have survived it. If Lady Kendrick failed, perhaps so could she? Would she and Prescott exchange letters? Reminisce over their time spent together?

Edwina's heart skipped a beat. One of the reasons Ginny had begun her correspondence with Gérardin was to tell him about their child. Was it possible that she and Prescott...in their time together...?

A child would change everything.

Thank God she hadn't gone to see her father yet!

If she was indeed with child, she couldn't ever deny the babe its wonderful father. Any more than she could keep the news from Prescott, knowing deep in her heart that he would want to be the father he'd never had.

Oh, dear Lord... What am I to do?

A knock resounded on the door and Edwina's eyes flew to Ginny's. Ginny quickly stuffed the letters beneath her hip and only when they were all out of sight did Edwina call, "Come."

Prescott opened the door and strode into the room, looking more relaxed, happier even, than Edwina had ever seen him. His broad forehead was smooth, his eyes bright and his lips lifted in a half smile.

Her heart skipped a beat and danced with that special joy whenever he was near.

She rushed over to him. "Are you all right?" He and Sir Lee had gone off to become reacquainted, now as grandfather and grandson.

Wrapping his arms around her, Prescott hugged her close. "Astoundingly, I'm doing well. Better than I ever thought I would under the circumstances."

"I can't believe how remarkably you're handing this. If it were me, I'd be needing smelling salts every three minutes."

"Rubbish." He kissed her temple. "You're hardier than you look. Don't forget, I saw you standing up to the great Earl of Wootton-Barrett." His brawny arms squeezed her tighter. "You were magnificent, defending me... it was inspiring."

Pressing her nose into his shoulder, she murmured, "I was shaking in my shoes."

"Still, you weren't cowed."

Pulling back, she met his eyes. "I'm so sorry how abominable he was to you."

"Regardless, I shouldn't have corked him."

"You struck the Earl of Wootton-Barrett?" Ginny cried, standing.

"Ginny!" Prescott released Edwina, but then snaked his arm around her waist hugging her close. "My apologies, I didn't see you there."

"I was reading." Holding up a packet tied with a fox-colored ribbon, she beamed. "My correspondence with Gérardin. Every last letter. Some beneficent soul left them on my bed with a note saying that I would be bothered no more."

"Hmmm." Prescott scratched his chin as an odd thought suddenly struck him. Sir Lee hadn't known about Prescott, not until seeing him at the house party. So why had Sir Lee ventured to this house party when he'd been telling Prescott how much he hated leaving London? London was where the action was, he'd said. Unless the "action" had moved to the country for Sir Lee?

When Sir Lee had searched Prescott's rooms, he'd done so with admirable expertise. If it hadn't been for the bookmark in Prescott's Bible, Prescott might never have known about the inspection. And now, knowing how affected Sir Lee had been by the discovery, Prescott had no doubt that in other circumstances he never would have been able to detect Sir Lee's search. Sir Lee wasn't quite as harmless as he'd like everyone to think...

Prescott pursed his lips, his ideas coalescing. Since the confrontation with Wootton-Barrett in the salon, Prescott and Sir Lee had sat in the garden trying to bridge an almost thirty-year gap. Then, about forty-five minutes ago the old gent had begged off, saying that he'd had too much excitement for the day and needed to rest. Prescott had remained behind to gather his thoughts.

"When were the letters returned, Ginny?" Prescott asked.

Ginny's brow furrowed. "Um, it couldn't have been more than thirty minutes ago. The maid was called downstairs and then sent to come get me. So whoever left them had the room to himself for a few moments."

It seemed too much of a coincidence. Sir Lee hadn't seemed taken aback in the least when mentioning the blackmail scheme. He'd said that he'd wanted to put himself "to good use" in his old age. Be on the side of good so he could sleep better at night. Edwina had wondered if anyone else at the house party was a victim of the blackmailer. They'd never considered that they might not be the only ones *hunting* the blackmailer.

Edwina looked up at him, her eyes concerned. "Is something bothering you, Prescott?"

"There you are!" Janelle rushed into the room looking frazzled. "Have you heard the news? Two Bow Street Runners just hauled off Mr. Todd, but they kept calling him Mr. Quince!"

"Mr. Todd?" Ginny gasped. "But I thought he was from Nottingham?"

Panting, Janelle fanned her face. "He was newly to London and no one checked in Nottingham to know for certain."

"He moves in the very circles we were focusing on." Edwina nodded. "And he was on our list."

Janelle motioned for Edwina to stop talking. "But the officers kept calling him Mr. Quince! They said that Todd was an alias for Quince! A secret identity! But even more intriguing, these officers weren't the Bow Street Runners we'd hired! They were two entirely different men!"

Ginny bit her thumbnail. "So you think these Bow Street Runners are the ones who returned my letters? How did they learn of the blackmail?"

"You have your letters back?" Janelle cried. "Even better!"

"Mayhap our supposition that there were other victims was true and they retained the police officers?" Edwina offered. But she shook her head, her gaze doubtful. "It makes sense, but if the letters are evidence, why would they return them?"

Prescott definitely wanted to have a word with his grandfather. Sir Lee was just the sort to "tidy up" on behalf of his friends, thank the heavens. Hugging Edwina's waist, he nodded. "I'm sure all will be known in due time." *Once I speak with Sir Lee.* "For now, let us celebrate the return of Ginny's letters and Mr. Todd's arrest."

"We do have much to celebrate!" Janelle added, with a twinkle in her eye. "I'm so very glad for you about your grandfather. I always liked Sir Lee. A very agreeable man."

Prescott tilted his head. "Not always, it seemed."

"Have you forgiven him?" Edwina's eyes searched his, the concern reflected therein warming his heart.

"I think so. I'm still upset, all is not forgotten, yet... I can't seem to be angry with him. He's suffered so much..." He shrugged. "I haven't worked it all out yet. But I know, all will be well...eventually. I only wish..." A lump formed in his throat. "I only wish that

Headmaster Dunn was alive to see it. He'd have been so very pleased…"

Janelle threw her arms in the air. "In all of the excitement, I almost forgot! I came to warn you!"

"Of what?"

"The Earl of Wootton-Barrett is heading this way! And he looks mad as hops!"

Chapter 34

Prescott tensed. He'd known this confrontation was inevitable, but he'd been hoping to spare Edwina.

Janelle waved her hands, agitated. "The earl's nose is as big as a cantaloupe!"

Edwina gripped Prescott's arm, her lovely face filled with anxiety. "I won't let them arrest you. We'll find a way to stop it...I'll think of something..."

"I punched an earl, Edwina. He's not exactly the kind of man to let that pass." And certainly not one to let Prescott marry his daughter. Still..."Devanes are fighters," he muttered under his breath.

"A bit too much of them." Janelle wrung her hands. "What are we to do?"

Stuffing her letters into the reticule and snapping it shut, Ginny straightened. "Do you think Sir Lee might help us?"

We. Us. A warm feeling blossomed in Prescott's chest and he suddenly smiled. "You ladies certainly know how to make a man feel part of your group."

"Group?" Janelle cried. "You're family!"

"We adore you, Prescott," Ginny declared.

Edwina hugged him close. "We do."

His heart skipped a beat. "Do you, Edwina? Truly?"

She looked up, her onyx eyes shimmering with tenderness. "I love you, Prescott. With all my heart."

Joy shot through him. Could the gods have truly decided to shine so favorably upon him? "Really?"

"Yes. I've never loved anyone like I love you." Pulling away to look up at him, Edwina swallowed, vulnerability and determination blazing in her lovely gaze. "We needn't marry. We can stay just as we are. I want to be with you on whatever terms you're willing to have me."

"I might have something to say about that, child." The door swung open wider and the Earl of Wootton-Barrett stood in the threshold. His flushed red face was marred by a nose swollen to twice its normal size.

He'd changed into a burgundy velvet coat, eggshell Marcella waistcoat, white L'Orientale neckcloth and ivory breeches. A red watch fob hung from his waist and he fiddled with it as he eyed the four of them, each in turn. His eyes were like fiery coals, filled with challenge, as if daring any of them to cross him.

Prescott tensed, pulling Edwina close. No matter her courage, she loved her father and feared losing him, as evidenced by the taut muscles beneath the palm of his hands.

She loves me! She truly loves me! He tempered his

joy, knowing that this was a precarious moment, for Edwina, for their future, and possibly for his hide.

"What a pleasant surprise, your lordship." Janelle dropped a quick curtsey, then stepped over to stand beside Prescott. "I didn't know you were going to be joining our country party."

Ginny moved beside Edwina and dipped, stating coolly, "Your lordship."

Prescott peered behind the big man, wondering where the earl's minions might be. Where were the police officers or at least a burly servant or two to haul him off?

The earl's lips formed an ugly scowl and a long moment passed. Then another. The tension in the room was so thick, Prescott felt like he was breathing it like a vapor.

Wootton-Barrett's hand clenched and unclenched. "If you would unhand my daughter, Mr. Devane. I would speak to her. Alone."

His grip tightened. "No. I'm not leaving her."

Edwina pulled away from him. "Let me go, Prescott. I want to speak with my father."

Reluctantly, he complied. "But I'm not leaving."

"Please don't." Shooting Prescott a comforting glance, Edwina then turned to face Wootton-Barrett. Her shoulders were squared, her lovely face resolute, and her chin lifted. "It's one thing to try to control my life, Father, but I will not permit you to hurt Prescott."

Stepping forward, Edwina shook her head. "I don't wish to cross you, but I will do everything in my power to fight you, tooth and nail, if you so much as harm a hair on his head."

The earl's eyes narrowed and he flinched as if pained.

"You would renounce your family...everything...for him?"

"Renounce...?" Her voice caught. "I don't want to, no, but..."

This was the moment where Prescott was supposed to step forward, declare his intention to give up Edwina to save her place in her family, help her avoid the tragic mistakes of his mother.

But he couldn't.

There was no breath in his lungs for such a declaration, no selfless sacrifice pumping in his veins. *He loved her.* And, remarkably, *she loved him. She truly loved him.* He couldn't give that up, not in a million years.

Raising her head, Edwina motioned to Prescott. "Here is a man who has cared for me when I lay ill, has championed me and my friends, has shown me how to forgive the unpardonable...He has taught me how to be the woman I want to be..."

Inhaling a deep breath, Edwina squared her shoulders. "I cannot stop you from rejecting him, or disowning me, but I will not forsake him. Not for you, not for anyone."

Prescott's heart swelled. Edwina was gloriously defiant, bold, beautiful and if he wasn't already head over heels in love with her, he would be now.

The earl exhaled, his nose making a terrible whistling sound. "I'm sorry to hear that. You give me no choice then."

Prescott's heart began to pound as charged silence hung over the room. He knew, without doubt, that if they tried to hang him, Sir Lee would step in and try to use his influence to help. So odds of execution would be slim. What was it to be, then? The whip? He could survive that. Just so long as he had Edwina waiting for him, he could survive just about anything.

"I have no choice"—The Earl of Wootton-Barrett jutted out his chin and tugged at his neckcloth as if it was too tight—"but to stand aside. Remove all objections to him, and to your association."

Prescott blinked, wondering if he'd heard right.

"What did you say?" Janelle barked, much too loudly.

Coughing into his hand, Wootton-Barrett looked pained. "I said, I withdraw all objections to her association with Mr. Devane."

"Oh, Father!" Edwina rushed to him, throwing her arms around his burly chest. "Thank you, Father! Thank you!"

"Ahh...that's not necessary..." The earl awkwardly raised his arms, not knowing quite what to do with his impassioned daughter. "Really...Edwina...get ahold of yourself..." Something slipped from his coat and fluttered to the floor.

Prescott quickly stepped over and scooped it up, coiling it into his palm. Rising, he grasped the earl's hand in his, the fox-colored ribbon, one just like Ginny's, pressed between their palms.

Wootton-Barrett stiffened and when his eyes met Prescott's, fear and defiance flashed within them. So the Earl of Wooten-Barrett had been one of the blackmailer's victims as well. That added a new shade of color to his visit to the Kendrick manor. And gave Prescott a fresh understanding of the earl's abrupt change of heart.

If Sir Lee was, as Prescott strongly suspected, the

man who'd nailed the blackmailer and recovered any incriminating evidence, then he'd be sure to use his "influence" to guarantee that the earl didn't harm Prescott. Moreover, Sir Lee would do his utmost to ensure that the earl didn't make the same mistakes Sir Lee had made with his own daughter's marriage. His grandfather was turning out to be quite the puppeteer. Prescott didn't mind, so long as the man didn't let it go to his head.

Prescott squeezed the earl's hand, pressing the ribbon into the earl's palm. "Just so we understand each other, your lordship. I want none of your money, don't need your connections and don't want a damn thing from you other than your daughter. She's the *only* thing that matters to me."

Wootton-Barrett's bushy brows lifted.

"And since her happiness is paramount to my own, I will do everything in my power to ensure that she is not distressed by anyone or anything." Carefully, Prescott removed his hand, leaving the earl with the fox-colored ribbon. "That includes you...and any affront to her good name and that *of her family's*."

Wootton-Barrett's face relaxed. "I see. That's very... reassuring to know." Disengaging from his daughter, the earl slipped the ribbon into his coat pocket. "But it brings us to the crux of the problem then."

"What problem?" Edwina was breathless, her face exultant as she stepped into Prescott's embrace. "If you make no issue of our association, then what problem could there be?"

"There's the problem of your good name."

"Sir Lee has pledged to recognize Prescott," Janelle argued.

Ginny crossed her arms. "He's a nobleman's grandson—"

Wootton-Barrett shook his head, adamant. "But still, there is a matter of Edwina's reputation—"

"But Father!"

Janelle wagged a finger. "Of all the outdated, ridiculous—"

"How can you say that?" Ginny huffed. "There's nothing wrong—"

"Stop!" Prescott cried, holding up his hand. "Lord Wootton-Barrett is right!"

The three ladies started, shocked as their heads all turned to him. "What?"

"Edwina's father is correct." Lowering his hand, Prescott faced Edwina. "Your name is too good to be coiled in an affair with me."

Edwina blinked, looking crestfallen. "But...but..."

"I love you, Edwina, too much to see you entangled in a casual dalliance. You deserve, much, much more."

Dropping down onto one knee, Prescott grasped her hand and held it to his heart. "I don't have a lot to offer you, Edwina. But I finally have a name—"

"You have much more to offer than that, son." Sir Lee swaggered into the room, swinging his gold-topped cane. "You have my money. Every last shilling of it."

Prescott's eyes widened, overwhelmed. "That's very generous of you, sir—"

"And don't worry." Sir Lee waved a hand. "No matter what I said before, I'm quite well-off. I wasn't about to advertise my fortune when I wasn't sure who you were or what you were about. But what's mine is now yours."

"Thank you, sir."

"There's no need to thank me." Sir Lee beamed. "There's no one else I'd rather see have it. Besides, I'm simply protecting my interests."

"Interests?" Janelle raised a brow.

"Those of my grandson, and of my great-grandchildren, of course." Sir Lee motioned to the earl with his cane. "Wootton-Barrett's grandchildren."

Prescott's heart thrilled. Children. With Edwina.

Clearing his throat, the earl shifted restlessly, his face flushed a familiar shade of cherry. "Yes, ah... which brings me to the matter of a dowry."

Edwina's eyes met Prescott's and the stupefaction in hers could only be matched by the utter shock reflected in his.

"Dowry?"

"Well, I'm certainly not having my grandchildren rely on the meager earnings of an employee from the Foreign Office."

Instead of being affronted, Sir Lee's smile only widened.

Wootton-Barrett waved a hand. "So I've decided to settle a substantial dowry on my daughter to ensure that she and her children, my grandchildren, are well taken care of."

"How wonderful!" Ginny beamed, clapping her hands.

Janelle nodded approvingly. "That's quite magnanimous of you, your lordship."

"I am most appreciative of all of your support,"

Prescott declared, still kneeling on the floor. "But I'm trying to propose here!"

"Well, you're certainly taking your time about it," the earl complained. "There's not much to it. Just ask and be done with it."

"There *were* certain matters to be clarified." Sir Lee raised his bushy gray brows meaningfully at Wootton-Barrett.

Prescott's eyes narrowed; he was definitely going to have to have a little chat with his grandfather.

"And you only just got to the subject of the dowry," Janelle interjected.

"Oh, how I love a happy ending!" Ginny wiped a tear from the corner of her eye. "So much celebrating, so much joy!"

Edwina smiled down at Prescott, her face radiant, her eyes bright with happiness. "Family. Do you think we'll be able to endure it?"

"Oh, I think we'll survive. I know just how to handle them."

Rising, Prescott approached Ginny and Janelle. "Ladies, if you will please inform our hostess that we will have something to celebrate over dinner?"

"Dinner!" Wootton-Barrett started. "I promised Lady Kendrick I'd escort her!" Motioning to Sir Lee, he remarked, "We'll talk more later." Then he rushed from the room.

"Ladies." Sir Lee offered Janelle one arm and then Ginny the other. "I believe our presence is no longer required."

"I know when I'm not wanted," Janelle huffed, but her eyes were twinkling as she accepted his arm.

Ginny leaned forward whispering, "Pray, don't be too long, Prescott. I want to toast to your happiness. You will let me, of course?"

"Of course. And we'll need yours and Janelle's assistance with the wedding arrangements."

"I get to help plan another wedding? Glorious!"

"I envision doves," Janelle pronounced as the three of them headed out of the chamber. "And we must have that famous pastry cook, 'Little Tom,' make the cakes. He's simply the best."

Prescott slammed the door closed behind them, then turned to face the most beautiful woman he'd ever known, the woman of his heart. "Where were we?"

Licking her lips, Edwina motioned to the floor.

"Oh, yes. The proposal." Striding toward her, Prescott swept Edwina into his arms and kissed her soundly. "I love you, Edwina. With every inch of my being. I want to marry you. As soon as possible. Will you have me?"

"Yes! A thousand times yes!"

He hugged her close. "I don't know what I've ever done to deserve you—"

"Shhh." Edwina pressed her finger to his lips. "Let me show you what you deserve, Prescott Devane."

Epilogue

～✦～

Edwina and Prescott were married in the chapel at Andersen Hall Orphanage later that month. It was an unconventional affair, being in an orphanage, with the Earl of Wootton-Barrett giving away the bride, Dr. Winner serving as best man and Janelle, Ginny and Sir Lee standing up as witnesses.

From her seat, Fanny Figbottom waved proudly to her fiancé as he executed his duties as best man, and she winked when, not caring that anyone saw, he blew her a kiss from the pulpit.

Sitting next to her, Mrs. Nagel commented to Miss Figbottom that there had been an awkward moment when Lady Ross had first been introduced to Catherine Dunn, but that the two ladies had soon been comparing notes about their nuptials and were now dear friends.

Only one guest, Lord Kendrick, was heard to remark on the irregularity of having a scarred child be part of the bridal party. But Mrs. Nagel gave him a resounding thwack on his knuckles with her fan as Little Evie happily tossed rose petals down the aisle for the procession, and the man never said another word.

Catherine had insisted that she and her husband Marcus host a banquet in the garden in the bride and groom's honor, and all gave thanks that the gods shined favorably upon them, providing the loveliest day they'd had in weeks.

The only people missing from the excitement were Lady Daphne Pomfry who was at that moment trying to charm Warden John Newman into letting her have a second maid in her quarters at Newgate Prison while awaiting trial, and Mr. Todd, also known as Mr. Quince, the man who'd started the whole drama.

At Sir Lee's urging, Mr. Quince had confessed all, and the only thing that had saved his hide from hanging had been that he hadn't killed "those two blokes" from the Foreign Office, having instead granted each an expenses paid holiday in the country. Mr. Poppet and Mr. Wiggins hadn't even been aware that they'd been missed.

Mr. Tristram Wheaton, Sir Lee's former protégé at the Foreign Office, also interrogated Mr. Quince, and thereafter decided that he had a use for the man on distant shores. So the choice was given: prison or government service under Tristram Wheaton.

Never having been one for cramped places, Mr. Quince was now on his way to Australia, courtesy of the British government. Sick as a dog, he hung over the side of the *Mary IV,* bemoaning his sins. All he had left for his troubles were a hole-ridden pair of François Millicent shoes.

Author's Note

I hope you enjoyed Edwina and Prescott's story. I
always knew that *What to Wear to a Seduction*
would be about Prescott Devane. First introduced in
More Than a Scandal as Catherine's best friend, he
developed into a man tortured by his parents' mistakes
and in need of the right woman to unlock his heart.

I don't recall the instant that his story came to me;
there was no "aha" moment. It was more of a natural
evolution, originating with one of my favorite charac-
ters, Sir Lee Devane.

First presented in *All Men Are Rogues,* Sir Lee was
inspired by my cousin Lee. Sir Lee is nothing like my
cousin, in temperament, age, physical stature or in his
panache for manipulation. My Sir Lee is an old gent
burdened with regrets of mistakes past and trying to
do better in his sunset years. Nothing remotely like my
cousin Lee. But Sir Lee has that bit of prankster, of

good-humored sensibility, that had its origins in his namesake. Inspiration is in the eye of the writer, I suppose.

So thank you, Lee, for the seed of a concept that blossomed into Prescott's story. Edwina and I are both grateful.

Avon Romantic Treasures

Unforgettable, enthralling love stories, sparkling with passion and adventure from Romance's bestselling authors

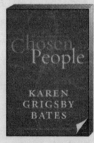